THE
RANGER
OF
MARZANNA

"Tell your elder I'm sorry about the mess. But at least you get to keep all your food this year, right?"

She patted Vadim on the head, then sauntered over to her beautiful gray-and-black stallion, who waited patiently nearby. She tied her horse to the wagon, then climbed onto the seat and started back the way the soldiers had come.

Vadim watched until he could no longer see the Ranger's wagon. Then he looked at all the dead men who lay at his feet. Now he knew there were worse things than imperial soldiers. Though he didn't understand the reason, his whole body trembled, and he began to cry.

When he finally returned home, his eyes raw from tears, he told his mother what had happened. She said he had been blessed, but he did not feel blessed. Instead he felt as though he had been given a brief glimpse into the true nature of the world, and it was more frightening than he had ever imagined.

For the rest of his short life, Vadim would have nightmares of that Ranger of Marzanna.

The Goddess War

The Ranger of Marzanna

The Queen of Izmoroz

The Wizard of Eventide

The Empire of Storms

Hope and Red

Bane and Shadow

Blood and Tempest

THE
RANGER
OF
MARZANNA

THE GODDESS WAR: BOOK ONE

JON SKOVRON

orbit

www.orbitbooks.net

ORBIT

First published in Great Britain in 2020 by Orbit

1 3 5 7 9 10 8 6 4 2

Copyright © 2020 by Jon Skovron

Map by Tim Paul

Excerpt from *We Ride the Storm* by Devin Madson
Copyright © 2018 by Devin Madson

The moral right of the author has been asserted.

A CIP catalogue record for this book
is available from the British Library.

ISBN 978-0-356-51485-7

Printed and bound in Great Britain by Clays Ltd, Elcograf S.p.A

Papers used by Orbit are from well-managed forests
and other responsible sources.

MIX
Paper from
responsible sources
FSC
www.fsc.org   FSC® C104740

Orbit
An imprint of
Little, Brown Book Group
Carmelite House
50 Victoria Embankment
London EC4Y 0DZ

An Hachette UK Company
www.hachette.co.uk

www.orbitbooks.net

For Ryan, a brother not in blood, but in heart

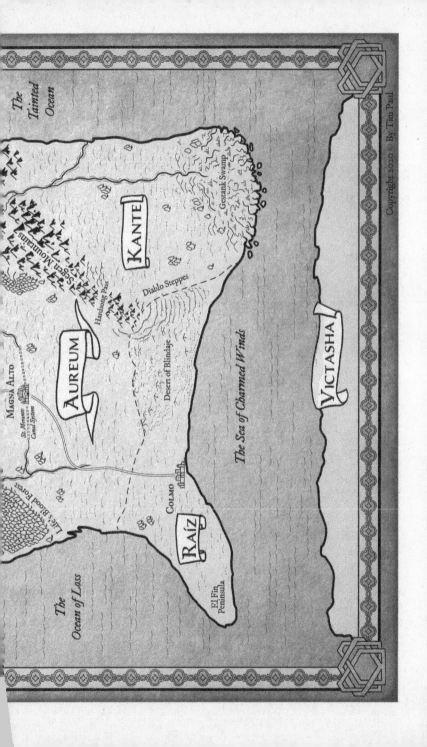

The Tainted Ocean

KANTE

Gestank Swamp

Sægen Mountains

Hardsong Pass

Diablo Steppes

AUREUM

Desert of Blindaje

MAGNA ALTO

St. Monate Canal System

Lic's Blood Forest

COLMO

RAÍZ

El Fin Peninsula

The Ocean of Loss

The Sea of Charmed Winds

VICTASHA

Copyright 2020 © By Tim Paul

PART ONE

THE RANGER OF MARZANNA

"Of all the enemies I have faced during my many years of loyal service to the empire, none have equaled the Rangers of Marzanna in sheer unflinching savagery. It was said they had sacrificed their very humanity in exchange for power, and that they worshipped Death itself."

—General Matteo Fontanelli,
Memoirs of a Humble Servant to the Empire, Vol. 8

Part One

I

Istoki was not the smallest, poorest, or most remote village in Izmoroz, but it was close. The land was owned by the noble Ovstrovsky family, and the peasants who lived and worked there paid an annual tithe in crops every year at harvest time. The Ovstrovskys were not known for their diligence, and the older folk in Istoki remembered a time when they would even forget to request their tithe. That was before the war. Before the empire.

But now imperial soldiers arrived each year to collect their own tithe, as well as the Ovstrovsky family's. And they never forgot.

Little Vadim, age eight and a half, sat on a snow-covered log at the eastern edge of the village and played with his rag doll, which was fashioned into the likeness of a rabbit. He saw the imperial soldiers coming on horseback along the dirt road. Their steel helmets and breastplates gleamed in the winter sun as their horses rode in two neat, orderly lines. Behind them trundled a wagon already half-full with the tithes of other villages in the area.

They came to a halt before Vadim with a great deal of clanking, their faces grim. Each one seemed to bristle with sharp metal and quiet animosity. Their leader, a man dressed not in armor but in a bright green wool uniform with a funny cylindrical hat, looked down at Vadim.

"You there. Boy." The man in green had black hair, olive skin, and a disdainful expression.

Vadim hugged his doll tightly and said nothing. His mother had told him it was best not to talk to imperial soldiers because you never knew when you might say the wrong thing to them.

"Run along and tell your elder we're here to collect the annual tithe. And tell him to bring it all here. I'd rather not go slogging through this frozen mudhole just to get it."

He knew he should obey the soldier, but when he looked at the men and horses looming above him, his whole body stiffened. He had never seen real swords before. They were buckled to the soldiers' waists with blades laid bare so he could see their keen edges. He stared at them, clutched the doll to his chest, and did not move.

The man in green sighed heavily. "Dear God in Heaven, they're all inbred imbeciles out here. Boy! I'm speaking to you! Are you deaf?"

Slowly, with great effort, Vadim shook his head.

"Wonderful," said the man. "Now run along and do as I say."

He tried to move. He really did. But his legs wouldn't work. They were frozen, fixed in place as if already pierced by the glittering swords.

The man muttered to himself as he leaned over and reached into one of his saddlebags. *"This* is why I'm counting the days until my transfer back to Aureum. If I have to see one more—"

An arrow pierced one side of the man's throat and exited the other side. Blood sprayed from the severed artery, spattering Vadim's face and hair. He gaped as the man clutched his gushing throat. The man's eyes were wide with surprise and he made faint gargling noises as he slowly slid from his saddle.

"We're under attack!" shouted one of the other soldiers.

"Which direction?" shouted another.

A third one lifted his hand and pointed out into one of the snowy fields. "There! It's—"

Then an arrow embedded itself in his eye and he toppled over.

Vadim turned his head in the direction the soldier had been pointing and saw a lone rider galloping across the field, the horse kicking up a cloud of white. The rider wore a thick leather coat with a hood lined in white fur. Vadim had never seen a Ranger of Marzanna before because they were supposed to all be dead now. But he had been raised on stories of the *Strannik*, told by his mother in hushed tones late at night, so Vadim knew that was what he saw.

"Get into formation!" shouted a soldier. "Archers, return fire!"

But the Ranger was closing fast. Vadim had never seen a horse run so swiftly. It seemed little more than a blur of gray and black across the white landscape. Vadim's mother had said that a Ranger of Marzanna did not need to guide their horse. That the two were so perfectly connected, they knew each other's thoughts and desires.

The Ranger loosed arrow after arrow, each one finding a vulnerable spot in a soldier's armor. The soldiers cursed as they fumbled for their own bows and let fly with arrows that overshot their rapidly approaching target. Their faces were no longer proud or grim, but tense with fear.

As the Ranger drew near, Vadim saw that it was a woman. Her blue eyes were bright and eager, and there was a strange, almost feral grin on her lips. She shouldered her bow and stood on her saddle even as her horse continued to sprint toward the now panicking soldiers. Then she drew a long knife from her belt and leapt toward the soldiers. Her horse veered to the side as she crashed headlong into the mass of armed men. The Ranger's blade flickered here and there, drawing arcs of red as she hopped from one mounted soldier to the next. She stabbed some and slit the throats of others. Some were only wounded and fell from their horses to be trampled under the hooves of the frightened animals. The air was thick with blood and the screams of men in pain. Vadim squeezed his doll as hard as he could and kept his eyes shut tight, but he could not block out the piteous sounds of terrified agony.

And then everything went silent.

"Hey, *mal'chik*," came a cheerful female voice. "You okay?"

Vadim cautiously opened his eyes to see the Ranger grinning down at him.

"You hurt?" asked the Ranger.

Vadim shook his head with an uneven twitch.

"Great." The Ranger crouched down beside him and reached out her hand.

Vadim flinched back. His mother had said that *Strannik* were fearsome beings who had been granted astonishing abilities by the dread Lady Marzanna, Goddess of Winter.

"I'm not going to hurt you." She gently wiped the blood off his face with her gloved hand. "Looks like I got you a little messy. Sorry about that."

Vadim stared at her. In all the stories he had ever heard, none of them had described a Ranger as *nice*. Was this a trick of some kind? An attempt to set Vadim at ease before doing something cruel? But the Ranger only stood back up and looked at the wagon, which was still attached to a pair of frightened, wild-eyed horses. The other horses had all scattered.

The Ranger gestured to the wagon filled with the tithes of other villages. "Anyway, I better get this stuff back where it came from."

She looked down at the pile of bloody, uniformed bodies in the snow for a moment. "Tell your elder I'm sorry about the mess. But at least you get to keep all your food this year, right?"

She patted Vadim on the head, then sauntered over to her beautiful gray-and-black stallion, who waited patiently nearby. She tied her horse to the wagon, then climbed onto the seat and started back the way the soldiers had come.

Vadim watched until he could no longer see the Ranger's wagon. Then he looked at all the dead men who lay at his feet. Now he knew there were worse things than imperial soldiers. Though he didn't understand the reason, his whole body trembled, and he began to cry.

When he finally returned home, his eyes raw from tears, he told his mother what had happened. She said he had been blessed, but he did not feel blessed. Instead he felt as though he had been given a brief glimpse into the true nature of the world, and it was more frightening than he had ever imagined.

For the rest of his short life, Vadim would have nightmares of that Ranger of Marzanna.

2

Sebastian Turgenev Portinari sat on the floor of his bedroom and stared at the bowl of water in front of him. He took one of the rusty bolts from the small pile beside him and gripped it tightly in one hand. He stared at the water in the bowl, focusing his intent on the metal in his hand. After a moment, he felt a surge—the bolt crumbled to rusty flecks, and the water spiraled up into a delicate point of ice.

"Oh, that's lovely, Sebastian. You're getting quite good at controlling it."

Sebastian turned to see his mother, Irina Turgenev Portinari, standing in the doorway. Her pale face was framed by her long white silky hair as she smiled down at him.

"Thank you, Mother," he said. "But I would *prefer* to practice at the lake, where I could really let loose."

"Your father said you must not be so ostentatious right now."

"But why, Mother?"

She sighed. "Why don't you come down and ask him yourself. Dinner is ready."

"Fine…"

Sebastian followed his mother downstairs to the small dining room in their farmhouse. His father, Giovanni Portinari, was already seated at the head of the table. He was a solidly built, clean-shaven man with the olive-tinged complexion of an Aureumian, close-cropped gray hair, and thick bushy eyebrows.

"Sebastian," he said by way of greeting.

Sebastian nodded. "Father." He noticed that a fourth place had been set at the table. "Is Sonya coming home?"

"She usually makes an appearance after the first snowfall," said his father. "If not today, then perhaps tomorrow."

Sebastian wasn't entirely sure what his older sister did for months at a time out in the wilderness. Hunting, camping, becoming one with nature, he supposed. Or as best as she could without the gift of elemental magic. Whatever it was, she'd been doing it for a couple years now, only stopping in now and then, and more often than not getting into an argument with their father when she did. She always upset the normal routine of the house whenever she appeared, and these days Sebastian found that he somewhat dreaded her visits because of that.

He sat down at the table as his mother brought in a platter of sour bread and boiled potatoes.

"Really, Mother?" he asked. "Potatoes again?"

"Now that it's winter, we need to be conservative with our stores," she said.

"No, we don't," he said. "I could go out there right now, thaw that field, and have a whole new crop growing in weeks."

"No, you can't," said his father. "It draws too much attention."

"From *whom*?" asked Sebastian. "I'm tired of keeping my magic a secret."

"Tough." His father sliced a potato as he spoke with the calm authority of a retired general. "You are only sixteen and as long as you live under my roof, you will do as I command."

Sebastian glared at his father as he gnawed on a chunk of bread, but his father seemed not to notice. It really wasn't fair. Ever since Sebastian had discovered he could perform elemental magic, his parents had constantly pushed him to hone his abilities. But what was the point if he was never allowed to show anyone what he could do? His sister was only two years older than him, yet she could go off and do whatever she wanted, while he was stuck here, practically a prisoner in his own home.

Then Sebastian heard an odd noise outside the house. Something he couldn't place. The clank of steel, perhaps? His parents paused in their eating.

"Is that Sonya?" asked Sebastian.

His father's thick eyebrows curled down into a scowl. "No."

Suddenly the sound of breaking glass and splintering wood filled the house. Imperial soldiers charged into the dining room, their sabers drawn.

Sebastian froze, partly in terror and partly in awe of the absolute precision that these men displayed. But his father was a hardened veteran of the war. Without hesitation, he flipped the table, sending bread and steaming potatoes into the air, then grabbed Sebastian and his mother and hauled them in the only direction available: the staircase that led to the bedrooms.

Sebastian stumbled up the steps as his father yanked him roughly by the arm. Once they were inside his parents' bedroom, Sebastian's father slammed the door shut and shoved the wardrobe in front of it.

"Why are soldiers here?" Sebastian asked in a shaking voice. "What do they want?"

"Sebastian, you must listen to me!" Giovanni pulled his own imperial-issued saber down from the wall, his face set. "I will hold them at bay for as long as I can. You jump out the window and run to Olga Slanikova's farm down the road. Hide in her cellar until..." He paused. "Until the soldiers are gone."

Sebastian gaped at his father. Even in the fog of his panic he could see that those instructions made little sense. How would Sebastian know when the soldiers were gone if he was hiding in a cellar? And even more importantly, what would he do after?

"Father, do you want me to try..." He looked meaningfully down at the sword in his father's hand. Steel would work even better as a conduit for his magic than iron bolts. It would destroy the sword, of course, but he was certain he could finish off the whole group of soldiers with one fiery explosion.

"Absolutely not!" his father said. "I forbid you to use magic. That would be playing right into their hands."

Before his father could explain further, the soldiers knocked the door off its hinges and the wardrobe fell forward with a loud crash.

His father squeezed his shoulder. "I have told you what to do, Sebastian! Go now!" Then he placed himself between Sebastian and the soldiers, his sword held at the ready.

"Mother..." Sebastian turned to where she was huddled on the bed.

"Listen to your father," she said in a pinched voice, her eyes glistening with tears behind a curtain of long, snow-white hair. "Go!"

He gritted his teeth, feeling the hot shame of helplessness fill his throat as he yanked open the window and climbed out onto the ledge. The clang of steel on steel rang behind him as he half slid, half fell down the side of the house and into a snowdrift. Since he was only dressed in a shirt and trousers, the harsh, biting chill of winter suffused him immediately. He stumbled to his feet, shook the snow from his clothes, then turned in the direction of Olga Slanikova's farm.

Except his father had underestimated the imperial soldiers. Sebastian only took two steps before the tip of a sword appeared inches from his throat.

"The commander said to take you alive, unless you resisted," growled the soldier with the sword. He was flanked on either side by several more soldiers, all with swords drawn. "Are you going to resist?"

Above, the sounds of combat from the bedroom window ceased. Then he heard his mother scream out his father's name, followed by her heartbroken sob.

Sebastian closed his eyes and took a deep breath. "If you give your word not to harm my mother, I will come without a fight."

The soldier nodded approvingly. "That's a good boy."

Sebastian almost lashed out at him for that. People were forever calling him a "good boy," or worse, a mama's boy, and it was never a compliment. But it was precisely to protect his mother that he kept himself in check.

The soldier whistled shrilly. "Bring the old lady out unharmed!"

Sebastian stood shivering silently in the cold with his captors as two soldiers emerged from the house holding his mother between them. Her long hair was disheveled, but she walked with her usual quiet dignity toward Sebastian. She had never been one to show weakness.

The lead soldier looked to see if there were any more soldiers coming, then grunted. "Did we lose the rest?"

One of the men escorting Sebastian's mother nodded tersely.

The soldier looked impressed. "Pretty good for an old guy. I'd heard stories about Giovanni the Wolf but figured they were mostly exaggeration." He shrugged, as if he found the loss of life of little import. "Let's move out. The commander is expecting us back at the garrison by morning."

The soldiers placed Sebastian and his mother in the back of a carriage with bars on the windows and a door that locked from the outside. But it was surprisingly comfortable inside. Sebastian and his mother sat across from each other on benches padded with soft quilting, and there were several thick wool blankets to keep them warm during the journey.

Sebastian immediately pulled one of the blankets over his shoulders, but he noticed that his mother merely sat there, shivering as she stared blankly into a corner of the carriage. Sebastian leaned forward and draped a blanket across her back.

She gave him a sad but grateful smile as she took the edges of the blanket in her hands. "Thank you, dear."

"Are you okay, Mother?" he asked. "Are you hurt?"

"My Giovanni is dead," she said quietly. "His loss feels like a limb has been severed from my body."

"I'm sorry, Mother."

Even as he said the words, Sebastian realized with an odd shock that he wasn't as grieved by his father's loss as he was by the pain it caused her. It was true that he had never been close with his father. For all their arguing, his sister had always been much closer to the man. Even so, surely Sebastian should feel more than fleeting grief for the death of a man who had sacrificed everything, including his life, for him.

His mother reached out her hand, her skin so pale he could see the blue veins beneath. He took it in his own hands and tried to warm it.

"Don't worry about me, my son," she said. "Your father is dead, and now you must be your own man and make your own choices."

"Yes, Mother."

Her red-rimmed hazel eyes held his. "Do what *you* think is right. Understand?"

"Y-yes, Mother."

She smiled and tucked a lock of his blond hair behind his ear. "Good."

He didn't really understand, but his confirmation seemed to comfort her, and that was all he could do at present. He had already looked around the carriage and found neither metal nor crystal within reach. Even the bars on the windows were made of wood. These soldiers clearly understood the limits of his ability and had taken no chances.

As their carriage rattled down the road, the snowfields slipped past the barred windows, gleaming luminous in the moonlight. Mounted imperial soldiers surrounded the carriage, riding in perfect formation. Again Sebastian could not help feeling awe at their precision. His father had often spoken of the ruthless efficiency of imperial soldiers, but had neglected to mention their almost serene discipline. Every one of them seemed to know exactly what to do at all times. Sebastian envied them that surety.

3

Sonya Turgenev Portinari reached her parents' farm just as the dawn was breaking across the horizon, staining the snowy fields a cozy pink. But the warm nostalgia she felt at seeing her childhood home was cut short when she saw the barn door wide open. It was not an oversight she could imagine her father or Mikhail allowing. Then she saw a cow wander through the courtyard, and she knew that something terrible had happened.

She had a strong urge to rush in, but she didn't give in to it. Instead she pushed back her fur-lined hood and shook out her long dark hair. Now she would be able to hear the potential sounds of ambush better. She guided her black-and-gray stallion, Peppercorn, slowly down the path from the trade road to the farm, her hand resting on the pommel of the long knife belted at her waist.

The cow stopped along the side of the barn and began half-heartedly pushing the snow aside to see if there was any brown grass beneath it she might nibble on. Beyond the barn, Sonya saw some of the sheep milling about in the field. They were unattended, despite the fact that winter sometimes brought wolves that were hungry and desperate enough to brave human settlements.

The main house, a simple, two-story wooden structure painted a pale blue, was quiet and motionless, except for the curtains, which blew in and out of broken windows. The door to the house was also open.

"Shit."

Sonya closed her eyes and inhaled deeply. Underneath the powerful smells of manure and hay that always accompanied the farm, she caught the smell of fresh blood, bright and coppery. After a few moments, she heard someone cough wetly inside the barn. She dismounted Peppercorn and tied his reins to the hitching post. Then she drew her knife and made her way silently into the barn.

Only a feeble amount of sunlight made its way between the cracks in the wooden planks, but it was enough for her to see. Her boots made no sound as she passed the empty sheep and cow pens and crept toward the pig pens where the smell of blood was strongest.

"Mikhail," she said quietly.

Mikhail Popov Lukyanenko turned at the sound of his name. He was an older man, with shaggy white hair and stringy muscles. She was accustomed to seeing him full of spirit, rich humor, and quiet courage. But now he lay in a trough of pig slop, clutching pointlessly at the huge gash in his belly as he slowly bled to death. He had served Sonya's family since before she was born, but to her, the old man was far more than a servant.

"*Uchitel*," she whispered as she crouched next to him. It meant *teacher* in the language of the Izmorozian ancestors.

"Ah, Sofyushka." His weathered face was creased with pain. "I am rewarded...for my stubbornness...to see your face...one last time."

"What happened?"

"Imperials." His mouth sounded dry, even though his throat gurgled with blood. "They came..." He tried to swallow but couldn't, so Sonya carefully poured a small amount of water from her skin into his mouth. After some effort, he continued. "They took your brother."

"Father would never allow that," she said.

"I saw them...put Sebastian and your mother into a small carriage...with bars on the windows..."

His mouth worked open and closed a few times, as if he was trying to form more words. She held up the skin of water, but he shook his head.

"It's okay, *Uchitel*." She tied the skin back to her belt. "I'll figure out the rest, just as you taught me."

"I want to tell you..." He lifted his blood-soaked fist from the wound in his stomach so that it began to flow freely. "I tried to stop them."

She took his sticky red fist in her gloved hands and forced a smile. "Old man, you shouldn't have done that."

He grinned up at her, his mouth now full of blood. "A *Strannik* is free..." Blood ran down the side of his mouth. "Free to do as they choose."

Sonya's attempt at stoic resolve failed. Sorrow welled up in her chest and tears coursed down her cheeks before she'd even realized they'd left her eyes. She wiped fiercely at them as she took in a shuddering breath.

"Sofyushka." Mikhail's eyes locked on to hers. "I return."

And then the life left him, and the man known as Mikhail Popov Lukyanenko was nothing more than food for the earth.

"*Uchitel*." She gently closed his eyes, then intoned the prayer Rangers spoke when a soul went to the cold embrace of Lady Marzanna. "One day I will return as you now return. Until then, I will travel light."

She stood and gazed down at the man who had taught her so much. Who had believed in her when no one else had. As a Ranger of Marzanna, she knew that death was not loss. It was a blessing to return to the Lady. But Sonya could not help feeling a yawning emptiness in her gut, as if his departure had left a gap in her soul.

When she emerged from the barn, she stopped for a moment to stroke Peppercorn's velvety nose. He nickered and swished his black tail.

"It's okay, *Perchinka*," she murmured, her voice quavering more than she would have liked. "I'll be okay."

She forced herself to focus on what was before her. Her childhood home, seemingly broken and abandoned. She had not been wrong before when she'd said that her father would never allow the imperials to take her brother. The only explanations were that he was incapacitated, or dead. And imperial soldiers were not generally inclined to spare someone. Not even a decorated war hero like her father, Commander Giovanni Portinari, known to comrades and enemies alike during the Winter War as Giovanni the Wolf.

Her father had been born to a wealthy merchant family in Aureum, the country that lay to the south and was the seat of the Aureumian Empire. He had enlisted in the imperial army as an officer and quickly distinguished himself by both his intelligence and ferocity. When the empire came to conquer Izmoroz, he was made general in the army, and later promoted to commander. He distinguished himself in the war to such a degree that once he achieved victory, the empress granted him a title and property in the newly annexed land. After such a violent, blood-drenched youth, he was content to marry a beautiful young Izmorozian noblewoman and settle down on his farm to raise his family in rural domesticity.

As Sonya stepped through the door and into the kitchen, she observed the overturned table and shattered remains of the door. The violence and bloodshed her father tried to walk away from all those years ago had finally caught up with him.

She made her way through the house, and the gentle memories of her childhood clashed strangely with the evidence of chaos that was now all around her. Furniture lay askew, and all the windows had been broken inward, suggesting that the soldiers had surrounded the house and attacked simultaneously from all sides. Some might have seen that as excessive in dealing with an elderly couple and their sixteen-year-old son, but only those who didn't know her father. Even at his age, and retired from making war for over twenty years, he remained fearsome in his skill with the sword. Throughout her life she had seen him practice every day in the yard. So many of those days Sonya had begged him to teach her what he knew, but...

Sonya stopped and closed her eyes. The past was a ghost that sought to strangle the present. Mikhail had taught her that. Now that he was dead, she was more determined than ever to honor his Ranger teachings. It didn't matter that her father had refused to teach her the sword. She had found her own way—a *better* way, as a Ranger of Marzanna.

When Sonya entered her parents' bedroom, she saw that the great war hero Commander Giovanni Portinari had done an admirable job of fending off the soldiers. Five of them lay dead, their leather and steel uniforms crusted with dry blood as they formed a loose semi-circle around her father's body. Her father was slumped forward on his knees, the tip of a sword protruding from his back.

She knelt down next to him and felt for his pulse, though judging by the smell and discoloration of the skin, she already knew she wouldn't find it. After a moment, she carefully leaned him back and pulled the sword from his chest. His face was relaxed in a way it never had been in life. Typically his mouth had a hard, thin set to it. But in death, it was open and soft.

"One day I will return as you now return," she whispered. "Until then, I will..."

Would she travel light where her father was concerned? *Could* she? Even now, so many conflicting emotions boiled within her. They'd had many arguments, particularly during these last few years after she'd been accepted by the Lady Marzanna as a Ranger. But despite all their disagreements, he had been her father, her hero, and the most magnificent man she'd ever known.

"Daddy..." Her voice warbled as tears once more coursed down her face. "I wish..."

If wishes were fishes, I'd never be hungry. That's what Mikhail used to say, usually in a mocking tone when Sonya had been complaining about something. It angered her now as it had always angered her then, but that anger brought focus, as it was meant to do. There were more pressing concerns than her regrets, such as finding her mother and brother.

"The dead are with the Lady," she admonished herself. "I must look to the living."

She emerged from the house with a cold, burning intensity in her heart.

It wasn't difficult to locate the wagon tracks and the cluster of indentations from iron-shod horse hooves. The tracks led east, most likely toward the imperial garrison at Gogoleth. She could tell by the depth of the depressions that some of the horses had been riderless for the return trip, no doubt thanks to her father thinning their ranks. She saw no sign of her brother fighting back. Perhaps her father had forbidden him to use magic. He could be stubborn like that. Or perhaps Sebastian had merely been too frightened to use it. He could be cowardly like that.

Regardless, Sonya's best hope of rescuing her surviving family was to catch up to them before they reached Gogoleth. Weary as the soldiers no doubt were, and with their ranks depleted, she was fairly certain she could take them. And if she could slip a bit of metal to Sebastian, he might even pluck up the courage to assist her.

She returned to Peppercorn, who snorted and stamped his hoof eagerly as she unhitched him from the post. She stroked his warm neck for a moment.

"Yes, *Perchinka*. It's time to run."

She untied her bow and quiver from her saddle and slung them across her back. Then she vaulted into her saddle with a pointless flourish that had always made Mikhail roll his eyes. Thinking of him, she turned and gazed back at the open barn door for a moment.

"*Spasibo*," she said, which meant *thank you*. It was inadequate, but the only other way she could hope to show her gratitude for all he had done was to live without fear and serve the Lady Marzanna, as all Rangers must. Then she touched her heels to Peppercorn's sides and they began their pursuit.

4

As further testament to the orderly efficiency of the imperial cavalry, the carriage that carried Sebastian and his mother reached Gogoleth early the next day, just as the captain said they would. Sebastian hadn't been to the capital in years. He remembered as a child being simultaneously frightened and delighted by its frenetic pace and boisterous inhabitants, so different from the placid farm life to which he was accustomed. But at this hour, the streets were nearly empty. Without all the distractions, he was able to fully appreciate the buildings themselves, a fascinating mixture of grand old Izmorozian black stone structures beside bright new wood buildings built by the Aureumian Empire in the aftermath of the war. *The best of both worlds,* he thought.

They swiftly crossed the city and passed through the eastern gate to the imperial garrison, which comprised four buildings spread across the short stretch of land between the city's outer wall and the Sestra River.

A man stood in front of the large central building and watched them draw near. His bearing was proud, and he wore the bright green jacket with white stripes and gold buttons that marked him as an officer. His tall green hat was held under one arm, and his other hand was placed on the pommel of his sheathed saber. Like all soldiers, his cheeks and chin were clean-shaven, but unlike the others, he had a thick mustache that had been meticulously waxed into points and curled up on the sides. Sebastian had never seen facial hair on an imperial soldier before and wondered if it was a privilege only given to the officer class.

Once the carriage came to a stop, the soldier leading the escort hurried over to the officer and spoke briefly with him. The officer nodded, then walked with firm, unhurried strides to the carriage. He unlocked the door and bowed to Sebastian and his mother.

"Lady Irina and Sebastian Turgenev Portinari. I am Commander Franko Vittorio, and I will be overseeing your accommodations here in Gogoleth."

"You mean our imprisonment?" Sebastian asked bitterly.

"Good heavens, no," said Vittorio. "Let me first apologize for any brusqueness you may have received from my soldiers during your journey here. They are but simple men, I'm afraid, with little experience in the niceties of more civilized company. I can assure you that from this point, I will personally ensure that you are accorded the courtesy and dignity you so rightfully expect."

Sebastian had no idea how to respond to such a bizarrely formal speech. His mother seemed equally baffled.

"Lady Portinari," continued Vittorio. "May I also offer my most sincere condolences on the loss of your husband? Although I realize it is scant comfort, I have been informed that he comported himself valiantly right up to the end, as befitted the great war hero he was."

"You offer sympathy even though it was your men who killed him?" asked Sebastian incredulously.

Vittorio nodded gravely. "Had he surrendered peacefully, his life might have been spared. But he chose to fight, and his death was the inevitable fate of any who stand against the might of the empire."

"But why did you order your men to attack in the first place?"

"All who break the law must face the consequences of their actions, regardless of who they are or how well respected they might be," said Vittorio. "Anything less would breed disorder and, ultimately, the most profound injustice."

"And just what law did my father break?" demanded Sebastian.

The commander looked surprised. "Why, refusing the command of a duly appointed representative of Empress Morante, of course."

His eyebrows and mustache curled into a frown. "Oh dear. Had he not shared that knowledge with you? No wonder you are so perturbed. This must all be such a terrible shock to you, then."

"*I* was aware of it, Commander," said Sebastian's mother curtly. "He made his choice and believed it to be the correct one with all his heart."

Vittorio seemed untroubled by her coldness. "I have always heard your husband to be a man of conviction, with a deep sense of personal justice. I certainly respect that, but freedom to choose is not freedom from consequence."

The commander let that statement hang in ominous silence for a moment, then in a more brisk and businesslike tone, said, "Now, if I may speak of your lodgings, I fear our humble barracks would not be suitable for a lady of refinement such as yourself, so I have taken the liberty of securing more appropriate accommodations within the city. If you will allow it, I would very much like to ride with you in the carriage to our destination." He turned back to Sebastian, his hazel eyes thoughtful. "However, if you wish me to ride separately so that you can acclimate to the series of surprises you have just received before we speak again, I will honor that request."

Sebastian struggled to keep his expression neutral. This man was like his father in so many ways. Overbearing, stiff, arrogant. And yet there was a perceptive thoughtfulness to how he conducted himself— a *sensitivity*, really—that Sebastian could have only dreamed his father might exhibit.

"I would appreciate having some time to speak with my mother privately on the matter," he said after careful consideration, trying to match the commander's formal tone.

Vittorio nodded. "Very well. We will meet again at Roskosh Manor."

Sebastian saw his mother's eyebrows rise at the mention of that name, but she remained silent.

The commander stepped away from the carriage and closed the door, but did not lock it. He placed his tall cylindrical green hat on his head, then nodded to the soldier at the head of the formation. A few moments later, the carriage began to move.

"Roskosh Manor is one of the finest residences in Gogoleth, and home to Lord and Lady Prozorova," said his mother. "I'm not certain why, after everything that's happened, the commander would take us there."

"Mother, what did he mean about Father disobeying a command from the empress?" asked Sebastian.

His mother sighed. "Your father did not want you to enlist in the imperial army as he had done."

As a child, Sebastian had often fantasized about joining the mighty imperial army. The crisp uniforms, the orderly formations of infantry and cavalry, the gallant officers leading the charge. It all seemed so... *important*. He'd assumed that his father, as a veteran of the last war, would be overjoyed. But when he'd shared his dreams, his father had told him to put such foolish thoughts out of his mind and would speak no more of it.

"Yes," Sebastian said now, his voice bitter. "Father made that perfectly clear, although he never said why."

"My sweet boy..." Sebastian's mother pressed her cool hand to his cheek. "He did not want you to experience the same horrors of war that he had. And he was afraid that if the empire were to learn of your gifts in elemental magic, they would exploit you."

"That was why he wanted me to keep my magic a secret?"

"There has not been forced conscription since the war. But the empress may command that a person of exceptional ability present themselves for consideration to be included into the officer class of the imperial army. Your father tried to keep your abilities hidden for as long as he could, but eventually word got out. And when it did, the empire naturally saw great potential in including a gifted elemental magic user in their ranks. So you were commanded to present yourself at the garrison in Gogoleth."

"And Father didn't tell me?"

She nodded wearily, as if this was an argument she and his father had had many times. "I told him it wouldn't work. That they would come for you eventually. But you know how your father could be."

"I do." His father had been a hard man. An unrelenting, uncompromising man who stuck to his principles no matter what. It had probably made him an excellent commander, but it had also made him a difficult father.

Sebastian's mother briskly patted his knee. "Wipe that scowl away, my son. We are in a tenuous position and must be careful to present ourselves in a positive light. This Commander Vittorio seems willing to act the gracious host, and we would do well to encourage that and be as cordial and pleasant as possible."

Sebastian's eyes widened. "After he killed Father? That hardly seems right."

She took both his hands in hers. Her expression was gentle, but her voice was hard. "Moral judgment is a luxury we cannot currently afford, my son. There are few options open to us. Do you think your father would have preferred that you nobly stand up against this commander in honor of his memory, even though it might mean your own death?"

"M-my death?" The fear that had begun to fade during the long carriage ride returned immediately to the surface.

"Disobeying an imperial command is punishable by execution, and we have no proof that the knowledge of that order was kept from you. If the commander chose, he could press the issue and see you hanged by sunset. When you next speak with him, you would do well to keep that in mind."

"Y-yes, Mother."

Then a smile rose to her lips. "I don't mean to frighten you, Sebastian. You should also keep in mind that he has *not* pressed that case, and instead seems intent on making peace. If he considered us prisoners, he would not be taking us to Roskosh Manor."

"But what does he want, Mother?"

"I cannot say for certain, but my guess is that his desire to have you in the ranks of the imperial army outweighs his desire to punish you for your father's crimes. He will reveal his intent in time. For now, we must be patient and pleasant."

When they arrived at Roskosh Manor, Sebastian decided he had never seen so fine an estate. It was more than four times the size of his family's farmhouse, with walls of polished stone instead of wood, and two towers that jutted proudly up from the roof, each topped with a swirling blue-and-white striped dome. The building was set up on a higher plane than everything else around it, and a wide marble staircase swept clean of snow led up to the lavishly carved front doors.

When the carriage halted in front of the steps, Sebastian was uncertain what to do. After all, Commander Vittorio had left the door unlocked and there was no one blocking the door. But if they were to attempt an escape, where would they go? And if they were caught, he was certain that whatever cordiality Vittorio had shown him would vanish. His mother seemed content to sit and wait, so he did the same.

A few moments later, Commander Vittorio reappeared with another respectful bow. He opened the door and held out his white-gloved hand to Sebastian's mother.

"If you will allow me, Lady Portinari."

With surprising confidence, Sebastian's mother took his hand and let him help her out of the carriage and up the steps toward the great front doors. Not sure what else to do, Sebastian followed.

Upon crossing the threshold, Sebastian found himself in a wide foyer at the foot of a sweeping staircase. The inside of the manor was strangely familiar. It took Sebastian a moment to realize that while it was far more opulent than his own home, with gorgeous oil paintings hanging from every wall, lush carpets cushioning the polished stone floors, and ornately shaped brass oil lamps mounted on the walls, the overall aesthetic was very similar to the one his mother had given their own home. Of course, he realized, this was the sort of environment she'd grown up in, so naturally she had tried to replicate it as best she could with the limited resources available to her.

"Ah, there you are at last!"

A short, plump lady of perhaps middle years stood at the top of the stairs. She wore a pale blue gown that left her round shoulders bare and showed perhaps a bit more cleavage than Sebastian was accustomed to seeing.

"Lady Inessa Odoyevtseva Prozorova." The commander removed his hat and bowed deeply to her. "May I present to you Lady Irina Turgenev Portinari and her son, Sebastian Turgenev Portinari."

"Pishposh, you silly walrus," said Lady Prozorova. "It might be twenty years since I've seen her, but I'd recognize the grace and beauty of Lady Irina Turgenev anywhere."

"Ah, so you are acquainted," said Commander Vittorio without a trace of surprise. "How wonderful."

"Darling Irina, it's been ages!" Lady Prozorova stretched out her hands as she moved grandly down the staircase. "I don't mind telling you, I've been beside myself with worry!"

To Sebastian's amazement, his mother's face suddenly lit up as brightly as Lady Prozorova's. "My darling Inessa, it's so lovely to see you again!"

She stepped forward to meet Lady Prozorova at the bottom of the steps, where they clasped their hands together and kissed each other's cheeks.

"I must confess, dearest Inessa, it has been a difficult time for my son and I," said the woman who Sebastian was still fairly certain was his mother. He had never seen her behave like this. She had always been a calm, quiet presence in his life, but now she acted as bright and gay as a noblewoman from a romance novel. Was it an act for Lady Prozorova's benefit? For Commander Vittorio? Or had she been hiding this side of herself for his entire life?

"Ah yes, your son!" Lady Prozorova nodded toward Sebastian with as much gravity as she seemed able to muster, which wasn't a great deal. "I hear he's an astonishing prodigy."

"Oh yes, I'm quite proud, of course," said Sebastian's mother without a trace of the humility she had shown throughout his life.

"Dear ladies," said Vittorio. "While you two get reacquainted, perhaps I might have a word in private with young Sebastian." He inclined his head to Sebastian's mother. "With your permission, of course, Lady Portinari."

There was a flicker of doubt in Sebastian's mother's eye, and she hesitated.

"Please, Mother, may I?" asked Sebastian, somewhat surprising himself. He wasn't quite sure why he was asking. Perhaps he was so disturbed by his mother's abrupt change in demeanor that he needed time away from her to process it. But he also felt somehow he must face whatever the commander had in store for him with courage.

Sebastian's mother seemed as surprised by his request as he had been to give it, but quickly recovered. "Naturally I consent. Commander, you've been such a kind host thus far. I trust you will remain that way."

"You have my word, Lady Portinari," he said with intense sincerity.

Lady Prozorova clasped his mother's hand again. "Dearest Irinushka, shall we wake my tailor and have him fashion you a splendid new gown?"

"Please lead on, dearest Ina. It has been too long since I've worn something so grand."

Sebastian and Vittorio watched the two women ascend the stairs. Then the commander turned to him.

"Perhaps you would follow me to the study, where we might converse more comfortably?"

Sebastian reminded himself of his mother's advice to remain cordial and pleasant to this man who had ordered his father's death. "Please, uh, Commander, lead on."

He followed Vittorio down a hallway into a small, cozy room with walls lined in bookshelves and a few mounted animal heads. There were two leather chairs set beside a hearth that had already been lit. It occurred to Sebastian that perhaps the commander had thought through and planned much of this. Although the idea was a little unnerving, Sebastian was still without a coat, and therefore very grateful for the warmth as he sat down beside the fire.

Vittorio sat across from him, placing his hat on his knee as he looked earnestly at Sebastian.

"I hope that perhaps you and I may speak openly, man to man."

Sebastian couldn't help feeling a tingle of pleasure at the sentiment of camaraderie. Whatever else Commander Vittorio might be, he was a picture of masculine virility. The perfect soldier, just the sort Sebastian had fantasized about becoming when he was a boy.

"Er, yes." Sebastian straightened in his chair, and tried to match the commander's bearing. "That is why I asked my mother to allow us this privacy."

Vittorio nodded approvingly. "I trust that she has now acquainted you with at least the general nature of my interest in you."

Just as Sebastian's mother had suspected. "You want a magic user in your army?"

"Ah!" Vittorio raised a finger and smiled. "Not *merely* a magic user. A magic user with profound natural talent, and one who is both Izmorozian and Aureumian and can therefore represent the interests of both peoples. Although the empire began in Aureum, the empress, in her benevolence, believes it should represent *all* its subjects, not just those from Aureum. That includes the people of Izmoroz as well."

"That's not what my sister said." The words leapt from Sebastian's mouth before he could stop them. It was true that Sonya often railed against the empire, believing it to be a threat to the "true" Izmorozian way of life. But she was the last person he wanted to talk about.

"Yes, your sister." Vittorio tapped his mustachioed upper lip thoughtfully. "When was the last time you spoke to her?"

He shrugged. "Half a year at least. She lives for long periods of time out in the wilderness communing with foxes, or whatever it is she does out there. Why?"

Vittorio waved his hand dismissively. "It is of little import at present. What I'm far more interested in is whether you will heed the summons of Empress Morante and serve the Aureumian Empire."

Sebastian struggled with how to respond. He had never truly relinquished those childhood dreams of military gallantry. Had he known about the summons, he would have begged his father to allow him to enlist. But his father had sacrificed his own life to prevent it, and surely there had to be an important reason he had done so.

Vittorio held up his hand. "I am perhaps overeager. Forgive me. Might I share something from imperial history that I think would interest you?"

Again the commander's solicitousness struck Sebastian. It was so unlike his father, or really any man he'd ever known in Izmoroz. "Of course, Commander."

"It's doubtful that you would remember this, since you were only an infant at the time, but about fifteen years ago, a terrible pox spread across the entire continent, killing countless citizens all over the empire. Can you imagine? The mighty army of Aureum felled by an invisible foe? It was a nightmare, and everywhere was grief and fear, because none knew how to end it.

"But then, a gifted apothecary named Stephano Defilippo—a singular young man much like yourself—came to Empress Morante with a bold solution. By purposefully exposing subjects to a weakened version of the pox by means of a tiny incision in the arm, Defilippo had discovered that the subject was not only able to fight off the infection, but develop an immunity to it. Many thought he was mad, and that he would doom the empire with such a dangerous plan, but he presented his evidence to the empress so convincingly that, in her wisdom, she commanded him to treat herself and her family with this procedure, which he called inoculation. Once she found it was safe, she ordered that the entire empire be inoculated. So while other lands, including our hated enemy, the barbarous Uaine Empire to the west, suffered countless waves of death during the decade that followed, the Aureumian Empire held strong, granting us the opportunity to solidify and expand our influence to become the most powerful force in the world."

Vittorio was quiet for a moment, and only the hiss and crackle of the hearth fire filled the silence.

"Do you know why I tell you this story, young Sebastian?"

Sebastian felt it might be a failure of some kind, but he shook his head.

"It is a fine thing to be a genius. But if you want more—if you want to *change the world* as Stephano Defilippo did, you must have powerful allies who will provide the resources and support you need to achieve the true greatness we both know you are capable of."

"I—I see..." Sebastian's voice was not as firm as he would have liked.

The true greatness we both know you are capable of? It was difficult to hear such words of praise from the man who had ordered his father's death. Words he had often longed for his father to utter. His father had always affirmed his abilities and encouraged him to develop them, but only as a means of controlling them, never for greatness or glory. Sebastian didn't want to keep his gift a secret. He didn't want to pretend he was just like everyone else. In his fondest daydreams, he longed for greatness. And he wanted someone who saw that greatness within him and encouraged it.

"Your father didn't want you to enlist in the army," Vittorio said quietly.

Sebastian's stomach twisted as the conflict grew within him. "M-my father didn't want me to experience the horrors of war."

Vittorio nodded. "A noble goal. Every father longs to save their child from the suffering they themselves endured. And I won't lie and tell you there won't be suffering somewhere along this path. But there is *always* suffering. On *any* path. That is an unavoidable part of life, regardless of what you choose to do with it. Suffering is what makes us who we are. And so, Sebastian Turgenev Portinari, when I ask you if you wish to enlist as an officer in the imperial army and serve the Aureumian Empire, what I am really asking is whether you wish to passively wait for the suffering that life will inevitably visit you, or whether you wish to choose the nature and fruit of that suffering for yourself. With the empire, you could use that suffering, along with discipline and sacrifice, as a means to achieve *glory*."

Sebastian found that his hands were clutching the soft leather of his armrests. Everything the commander said made it seem as though he could see into Sebastian's heart—like he knew the truest expression of his dreams, perhaps even better than Sebastian. And yet, it had been his father's dying wish that he escape the military. Had he done so with good reason? Or had the great war hero Giovanni Portinari merely been an overprotective and overbearing parent so set in his ways that he preferred to die rather than admit when he was wrong?

"If...I joined the imperial army, would I be doing good in this world?" Sebastian asked plaintively.

Vittorio thought carefully, as if respecting the tumult in Sebastian's heart. At last he said, "I am unable to tell you the particulars unless you enlist, but I will say that the empire as we know it is in grave danger, and the empress believes that it is promising young people like you who will see us safely through this terrible time. I do not exaggerate when I say that, should you heed the empress's call, you might save millions of lives. Will you help her and all the citizens of the empire in their time of most desperate need?"

When put like that, Sebastian found there was only one answer within him. Even his father would have agreed that helping those in need was a man's most paramount responsibility.

"Yes, Commander." His voice was firm and unwavering now. "I would be honored."

5

Jorge Elhuyar decided that Izmoroz was by far the coldest, most unforgiving place he had ever been.

When he'd set off that morning from Gogoleth to pick foxtail for his master, he'd had a somewhat different opinion. In fact, as he'd hiked along the side of the trade road with the sun gleaming across the snowy fields, he'd been rather taken by its rugged beauty. The barren tree branches were encased in ice so that they glittered like crystal, and solemn black stone peaks jutted majestically above the powdery white landscape in the distance.

The odd hodgepodge of wool, leather, and fur clothing that the locals favored had seemed to be sufficient protection at the outset of his journey. But now the sun was sinking back toward the horizon, taking its meager warmth with it, and he was chilled to the bone. Even worse, a snowstorm had suddenly descended. The snowflakes that had once seemed a peace-inducing blanket upon the world now swirled around him like a cloud of angry stinging insects that found their way into every exposed crevice in his clothing—clothing that now seemed barely able to protect him from the cold, despite being uncomfortably bulky.

As Jorge trudged through the narrow valley between two craggy rock formations known as Bear Shoulder Pass, he wondered, not for the first time, how the Izmorozian people thrived in such low temperatures. But of course one of the reasons he had journeyed the long distance north was to answer that very question. Was it simply conditioning from a lifetime of living in this frozen tundra? Or was there something inborn in the Izmorozian people that allowed them to more easily tolerate the cold? In either case, could the trait be replicated in other people, at least temporarily, with a potion or tincture? Furthermore, if such a thing *could* be replicated, could the opposite effect be achieved? Could a potion or tincture be created that would allow someone to tolerate the heat as readily as the people in Jorge's homeland of Raíz? This had been the line of inquiry he presented in his application to the Imperial College of Apothecary in Gogoleth, and combined with the evidence he provided to support his theory, it had been met with such enthusiasm that he had not only been accepted into the college (the first Raízian to be given such an honor) but he had also landed an apprenticeship with one of the most renowned potion masters in the Aureumian Empire, Anton Semenovich Velikhov.

This morning, Master Velikhov had needed fresh-picked foxtail for his work, and so it had been Jorge's duty, as the apprentice, to find those ingredients for his master. But now, as he stumbled through Bear Shoulder Pass in a blinding flurry of white, he worried that not only might he fail in delivering the foxtail, he might fail to return at all.

The bag of foxtails was much heavier than he'd expected. Jorge was not a hardy person, so his arms ached from the weight of the sack, and his legs ached from the weight of his snow-caked fur boots. He began to wonder in an abstract sort of way how long it would take someone to discover his frozen corpse. Probably not until spring thaw. After all, he'd hardly seen anyone along the road that day. He was utterly alone out here in this frozen and cruelly indifferent land.

"Stop right there," came a gruff voice somewhere high up on the rocky slope to his right.

Jorge's heart rose. He wasn't alone after all and might not have to freeze to death.

"Hello?" he called, squinting his eyes against the snow as he tried to pinpoint where the voice came from.

"Well, you're a friendly one," came the voice. "And since you're being so friendly, why don't you save us some trouble and drop all your valuables so we don't have to fill you full of arrows and strip them from your corpse."

Jorge's heart sank as he dutifully dropped the sack of foxtail on the road and raised his wool mittens in surrender. Maybe being alone hadn't been so bad after all.

"My friends." He strove to keep his voice amiable. "I am sorry to disappoint you, but I have no valuables. I am only a humble apothecary apprentice who is out gathering ingredients that you could easily find yourselves not an hour's walk from here."

"Apothecary student, huh?" asked the voice. "Like a potion maker?"

"Yes, that's it exactly, my friend!" said Jorge.

"What's that accent of his?" came a second voice up on the left side of the pass. "And he's got brown skin. Find out where he's from."

"Where you from, potion maker?" asked the first voice.

By then Jorge was able to at least make out a silhouette of the man. Broad shoulders and what seemed likely to be a drawn bow aimed at him.

"I am from Raíz, my friend, which is located in the southernmost region of our great and bounteous empire. My name is Jorge Elhuyar, and I have come to the nearby city of Gogoleth to learn at the feet of the finest apothecaries in the world."

"Huh," said the bandit. "You got any potions on you?"

"I'm afraid not, my friend. I was only out to gather foxtails for my master to make his potions. You are of course welcome to search me if you like." He smiled as he squinted up at the silhouette, still clinging to the hope that they might let him go without further incident.

"You know, Nikolai...," said a third voice that was near the first. "We could use ourselves a potion maker."

"I was thinking the same thing," mused the first voice, who Jorge presumed was Nikolai. "Hey, Alexi, you still got that itchy foot problem?"

"Damn right!" said the voice on the left. "Smells terrible, too!"

"And, Vasily, ain't you having trouble taking a shit?" asked Nikolai.

"It's been a week since I dropped a load!" called a fourth voice from much higher up the slope. "I'm ready to burst!"

"You hear that, potion maker?" asked Nikolai. "I sure hope you can fix these problems for us."

"Well, I—"

"Because if you can't, we might as well just kill you."

Jorge could not keep the anxious fear from creeping into his voice. "Ah yes... Then, I would, eh, be happy to assist. In whatever way I can."

"That's the spirit," Nikolai said cheerfully. "Pytor, go bring up our new potion maker."

A few moments later, a large, hairy man suddenly appeared next to Jorge in the snowy haze. The Raízians were a worldly and open-minded people, but there had always been stories... more like tall tales, really, of the savage, hairy barbarians, more ogre than man, who ranged lawless and half-wild across the icy tundras of Izmoroz. The man who now stood before Jorge looked and smelled very much like the subject of those tales. He had no need of hat or scarf, since his lion's mane of yellow hair and beard provided more than enough warmth. He reached out with a thick hand encased in a glove of what smelled like imperfectly cured hide and took hold of Jorge's shoulder.

"Lord of Heaven, you're as thin as a bird," said Pytor as he shoved Jorge over to a narrow, steep path that led up the side of the rocky cliff.

"Don't break 'im, then!" called Vasily. "I expect to be having the best shit of my life by sunrise!"

Jorge focused on keeping his half-numb feet from slipping on the icy path as he made his way up the side of the cliff. He tried to imagine how his situation could be made worse. Usually, this was a thought exercise that made him feel somewhat better regarding his current predicament, whatever it might be. But in this particular case, the only thing worse would have been death, and even that wouldn't have been worse by much. After all, once he had cured these bandits of their various ailments, what was to stop them from killing him anyway?

The path opened to a ledge that was sheltered by an outcropping of rock. He could see another bandit waiting for him, similarly large and threatening, with bright red hair and beard. This was probably Nikolai. Farther up the cliff was a third bandit, presumably Vasily the constipated, who was positioned as a lookout. Jorge could also just make out Alexi on the opposite side of the pass. There was far less snow flying around this high up, and they were somewhat sheltered from the harsh glare of the late-afternoon sun, both elements that contributed to making it so difficult to see anything down below. It was, Jorge had to admit, a well-chosen spot to waylay travelers on the road.

"So, potion maker," said Nikolai as he clasped Jorge's upper arm in an alarmingly possessive way. "Is it true that there are potions that can make me an even better shot with my bow?"

"W-well, there are tinctures that can temporarily increase visual acuity and steady one's hand," admitted Jorge.

"Temporarily?" asked Nikolai. "Meaning it only works for a little while?"

"Yes, that's right."

Nikolai gave Jorge's arm a painful squeeze. "Luck's upon you then. Sounds like we'll have to keep you alive for a good long while."

"Our very own potion maker," said Pytor. "Reckon we're moving up in the world."

"Told you, Pytor!" said Nikolai. "We put our heads together, the world's ours. Just got to think *long-term*."

It was about then that Jorge began to wonder if death might be preferable to a lifetime of servitude to a group of bandits.

"Rider coming from the east!" Vasily called down from his perch.

"Everyone back into position," called Nikolai. "Wait for my signal."

He pushed Jorge down onto the frozen ground and crouched next to him so they could peek over the edge to view the road below.

"You just watch and marvel at our skill, potion maker," Nikolai advised. "Don't get any ideas about warning them off, or I reckon Alexi will just have to suffer with his itchy feet awhile longer, if you catch my meaning."

Jorge nodded, and tried not to show the sudden surge of hope he felt at the prospect of being rescued. Perhaps it was a battalion of soldiers. Or a formidable band of mercenary warriors...

But a few moments later, any hope of rescue vanished. It was a lone rider on a black-and-gray stallion riding slowly against the snow and wind that funneled through the pass. The rider wore a coat of thick leather lined in white fur, their face hidden in a deep hood. Whoever they were, they were not particularly large. Not much bigger than a child, in fact. They were armed, but only with a simple longbow and a small quiver of arrows that would be all but useless while so blinded by the swirling, gleaming snow. Jorge could expect no aid from this poor, lone traveler.

But then he heard Nikolai draw in a sudden gasp.

"Is that... a Ranger of Marzanna?"

"Couldn't be," Pytor whispered back as they stared down at the slowly approaching rider. "They were all killed in the war." He glanced worriedly at Nikolai. "Weren't they?"

"Of course they were." Nikolai's voice firmed somewhat. "None left. The empire made damn sure of it. This has to be someone dressed up like a Ranger to scare off men more gullible than us."

"Yeah." Pytor sounded like he wanted to believe it. "Whoever it is probably pulled that coat off a corpse on a battlefield all them years ago."

"Right," said Nikolai.

They watched the rider draw closer.

"Even if it *is* a Ranger that *somehow* survived the war, it's only one," said Nikolai. "We've got the advantage of surprise, position, size, and numbers."

Pytor stared down at the rider. After a moment, he said, "You know... We *could* let 'em pass. Just in case."

Nikolai chewed on his lower lip, then nodded. "It doesn't hurt to be cautious."

Jorge had never heard of these Rangers of Marzanna. It surprised him that knowledge of what was apparently an infamous organization had never reached Raíz. But the rider proceeded along the pass, and despite having all the advantages, it appeared that Nikolai and his bandits were going to let them through unmolested.

But then the rider stopped directly below their perch. They pushed back their deep, fur-lined hood to reveal the face of a young woman no more than twenty years old with the pale skin of an Izmorozian but the wavy dark hair of someone from Aureum.

She looked directly up at where Nikolai, Pytor, and Jorge were crouched, as if she could somehow see them through the snow that swirled all around her. Then she smiled.

"Hey! I don't suppose you boys saw an imperial cavalry detachment pass through here in the last day or so? Probably pulling a small jail wagon?"

Nikolai spat. "Nearly scared off by a fucking girl playing dress-up." His voice was flat and angry. "We're going to teach this little bitch a lesson."

6

Peppercorn was a swift horse, so they reached the beginning of Bear Shoulder Pass in only a few hours. There the road cut through a narrow valley between a pair of small, jagged mountains that were full of nooks and crannies perfect for bandits to hide.

Sonya reined Peppercorn in to a walk. They probably could have been through the valley before the sluggish bandits had time to spring their trap, but she was hoping she could get some information on the soldiers who held her mother and brother captive. It was a Ranger's responsibility to slay any bandits that plagued the honest people of Izmoroz. But if this group proved useful, she might even let them go. For now, anyway. Once her family was safe, she could hunt them down at her leisure.

The reason Bear Shoulder Pass was so beloved by bandits, besides all the convenient nooks and crannies, had to do with the shape of the narrow valley, which focused the wind at a downward angle. During a storm like this, it kicked up so much snow that travelers were forced to make their way through the pass nearly blind.

Although, thought Sonya as she nudged Peppercorn into the swirling mass of white, *they certainly reveal their presence with that smell.* It was the same rank stench of unwashed bodies and poorly cured hide that always seemed to permeate bandits. In this case, there was also an insistent strain of foxtail mixed in with the rest of the scents. Curious, but not particularly worrisome.

She reached the center of the pass where the swirling snow was thickest. She could hardly make out the rocky slopes on either side. This was typically where bandits made themselves known. But it appeared these bandits had no intention of trying to rob her. Normally, it would have pleased her to know that the garb of a Ranger of Marzanna still held some sway. But today it was inconvenient.

She pushed back her hood and gave a nice big smile to show the timid bandits that she was not scary looking.

"Hey!" she called up to where the smell was strongest. "I don't suppose you boys saw an imperial cavalry detachment pass through here in the last day or so? Probably pulling a small jail wagon?"

There was a long pause, and some angry muttering. Then she dimly saw the silhouette of one of the bandits rise up, and heard the creak of his bow as he drew it taut. A moment later, another one appeared next to him, then one higher up, and a fourth on the other side of the pass.

"You stupid bitch," said the first bandit. "I don't know why the hell you're wearing those clothes, but they won't save you. Throw down your weapons before I have to put an arrow in one of your pretty little eyes."

Sonya had hoped to do this peacefully, but they doubted that she was a real *Strannik*. With Mikhail's death so fresh in her memory, she could not let such an insult pass. Her lip curled, her eyes narrowed, and she felt the hot rush of bloodlust surge through her veins.

"I wear these clothes because I earned them."

She unslung her bow and drew an arrow in a single fluid motion, then used the sound of the bandit's voice to hone in on his exact location and shoot him in the throat. She listened with satisfaction as he choked on his own blood, then toppled over.

His fellow bandits stupidly cursed in anger, or made some other pointless noise that gave away their location in the swirling snow as well. Without thinking, she instinctively released three more arrows, and three more bandits fell.

She sat there for a moment, smiling with satisfaction as the scent of blood drifted down to her. Then, when her wrath cooled and the bloodlust had dissipated, she realized that once again she'd been too impulsive. She should have left one alive so she could question him about the soldiers. Mikhail would have been disappointed in her lack of restraint.

"Don't shoot!" came another voice from above. "Please! I was only a prisoner of these men!"

She still couldn't see much through the snow, but the man sounded genuinely terrified and had a foreign accent, neither of which suggested a bandit.

"Foxtail?" she asked.

"Sorry?"

"You reek of foxtail. A little strange for bandits."

"Ah! Yes!" He sounded relieved. "I was out gathering them when I was captured."

"Why were you gathering foxtail? Not exactly good eating."

"It acts as a wonderful binding agent in potion-making."

"Oh, you're an apothecary! All right, I believe you. Come on down, I promise not to shoot." She made a show of tying up her bow and quiver on her saddle.

She heard him half stumble, half slide down the side of the cliff. Then he emerged cautiously from behind the cloud of flurries. Even beneath his thick coat, she could tell he was a scrawny fellow, with brown skin and long black hair twisted into braids that hung down beneath his comically large fur cap.

"You're from Raíz, huh?" she asked. "Long way from home."

"I am studying at the College of Apothecary," he said proudly. Then his face took on a wary, almost crafty expression. "I saw an imperial detachment as I was leaving this morning, just as you describe. If you promise to give me safe passage to Gogoleth, I will tell you where they are."

"Except you just told me. You saw them this morning as you were leaving your home in Gogoleth. Obviously they'll be at the garrison by now." She watched his face fall, then grinned. "I'm just messing with you. Since we're both going to the same place, I might as well give you a ride."

"R-really?"

"We aren't all bandits out here in the wilds of Izmoroz."

"Of course. I'm sorry if I offended. I had begun to lose hope that there was any courtesy to be found in these lands."

He was such an earnest person, Sonya couldn't help liking the guy. She held out her hand and pulled him up behind her. "I'm Sonya Turgenev Portinari."

"Jorge Elhuyar."

"Well, Jorge Elhuyar, you don't seem all that comfortable on horseback, so you better hold tight. Peppercorn is about as fast a horse as you'll ever find."

"Oh, uh . . ." He held up his mitten-covered hands. "Where should I . . ."

She drew his hands around her waist. "Just like this. But go too low or too high, and you'll lose those hands. Just a friendly warning."

"Y-yes, Sonya Turgenev."

"I don't go in for all that formal stuff. You can just call me Sonya."

"Oh, well, in that case, please call me Jorge."

"You got it, Jorge."

She tapped Peppercorn's sides with her heels and soon they were headed down the road toward the great city of Gogoleth, which held the largest imperial garrison in Izmoroz. And apparently, the surviving members of Sonya's family.

"May I ask why you are pursuing a detachment of imperial soldiers?" Jorge had to shout over the thunder of Peppercorn's hooves to be heard as he clung to Sonya's waist.

"Because they abducted my mother and little brother," she said over her shoulder.

He was silent for a moment, then said, "Why would imperial soldiers want to abduct a woman and a boy?"

"My brother's an elemental magic user."

"Really? So few are born in Raíz that I've never actually seen one."

"It's rare everywhere," she said. Then added, "Thankfully. Could you imagine the chaos if there were a bunch of people running around with that kind of power?"

"Still, why would imperial soldiers wish to abduct him because of that?"

"So they can turn him into a weapon for the empire."

"That sounds like a worthy cause, doesn't it?" asked Jorge tentatively. "Defense of the Aureumian Empire?"

"Defense." She let out a snort. "More like subjugation of yet another group of people to add to the empire's strength."

"Surely that is an...oversimplification?" She couldn't see his expression, but he didn't sound particularly sure. "Regardless, I take it your brother does not wish to lend his abilities to the empire."

"My father forbade it, actually."

"He is a pacifist, perhaps?"

"He was a highly decorated veteran of the Aureumian Army who served in the Winter War. You know, the war that forced Izmoroz to join the empire."

"Surely a war hero would want his son to follow in his footsteps, then."

"I take it you've never talked to a veteran of that war," she said.

"I have not," he admitted.

"Every night of his postwar life, my father woke up screaming from the nightmares that he'd either witnessed or perpetrated. He loved my mother very much, but that didn't stop him from almost choking her to death several times in his sleep. Personally, I would have started sleeping in a different bed after the first time. Instead, she broke his thumb."

After a pause, Jorge said, "I take it from the way you speak of your father that he is dead."

"He was killed last night by the same group of soldiers I'm pursuing."

"Perhaps you also seek revenge, then?"

"Of course not. A Ranger of Marzanna doesn't believe in vengeance. It's rotten meat. It may fill you up, but it's foul and poisonous, and I will have no part of it."

"I see..." He didn't sound convinced.

"Anyway, death is a natural part of life. If anything, we should rejoice that our loved ones have returned to Lady Marzanna's embrace." Did she sound defensive? She worried she might, and stopped talking. It wasn't that she didn't believe what she was saying, but...sometimes it was still hard for her to reconcile her beliefs with her emotions.

After a long silence, Jorge said, "I confess I'd never heard of these Rangers before today."

"They are the guardians of Izmoroz. They protect the innocent and keep the natural balance."

"Those bandits seemed to think they had all died in the war."

"When Izmoroz was invaded, it was the Rangers who rallied the people against the invaders. So naturally when the empire won, the first thing they did was exterminate every Ranger they could find."

They rode in silence for a while again, passing an ice-covered lake where children skated in circles. On the other side of the road was one of the many small farmsteads that dotted the land in this area. A few cows stood in the white fields, thin and miserable looking. Winter had only just begun, and it was already shaping up to be a cruel one.

Jorge cleared his throat. "So...you are the last Ranger of Marzanna, then?"

"I don't know," she admitted. "I...hope not. But I've been searching the forests for a long time and haven't found any others."

"It must be lonely." It sounded like he was pitying her, which was ridiculous, of course.

"Are you kidding? A Ranger thrives in the solitude of nature."

"Oh, I see" was all he said.

7

Well, Irina, my dear, it's not perfect but I suppose it will have to do until your new gown is ready."

The Lady Inessa Odoyevtseva Prozorova stood in the center of her dressing room and gazed critically at the gown that hung from the dress form. Irina stood beside her, wincing as Inessa's servant cinched up her corset. Irina hadn't worn a corset since before Sonya's birth, and she was remembering all over again why she loathed them so much.

"The gown looks lovely," Irina assured her host.

"It's from before Vanya's birth so it's several years out of fashion," said Inessa. "See these puffy shoulder caps? No one wears those anymore."

"I like—" Irina was momentarily cut off as the servant girl yanked on the corset ties. "The color."

Inessa nodded. "It is a lovely shade of red. I think it'll set off your hair nicely. And it should fit you reasonably well. But just you wait. When my tailor is finished with your *real* gown, you won't give this one a second thought."

"I look forward to it," said Irina.

"Are you quite finished there, Alena?" Inessa asked sharply. "Goodness, girl, how long does it take to put on a corset?"

"Apologies, my lady. I've just finished."

"Well then, let's try it on."

Irina was quite capable of dressing herself, and over these last two decades had grown accustomed to it. But she knew that, at least in Inessa's presence, she must act the part of a pampered noblewoman. So she allowed Alena to dress her while Inessa continued in an endless torrent of words on whatever topic happened into her soft little skull.

"I should think you're terribly pleased that Sebastian has chosen to accept the commander's invitation to enlist in the officer class of the military."

"I'm overjoyed," said Irina. Relieved was more accurate. She would never dictate her son's life choices as her husband had tried to do, but she had strongly hinted to him what the proper course of action should be, and she was grateful he'd had the sense to see it. Had he rebuffed Vittorio, she suspected neither he nor she would still be alive.

"Unfortunate that it happened right after that business with Giovanni," continued Inessa. "But I'm glad the commander didn't hold that against Sebastian. After all, it's not your son's fault his father wouldn't listen to reason."

Irina kept her voice and expression neutral. "Indeed."

"And I'm certain he'll do well in the military," said Inessa. "He has his father's gallant visage, but none of his arrogance."

"Quite so."

Inessa paused and looked at Irina in concern. "Oh, dearest, I'm sorry. I should not speak ill of your departed husband."

Irina shook her head. "I know you meant nothing by it, dearest Ina. You have only ever spoken from your heart." *And hardly ever with your brain*, she thought. "And how is *your* husband, my darling? I have not seen him yet."

Inessa's ever-present smile tightened until it looked slightly painful. "I'm afraid some urgent business has taken Sergey out of town for a few days."

"I understand completely, dearest Ina."

That is to say, Irina understood that Inessa had most likely sent her husband out of town for the next few days so he would not be anywhere near Irina. Long ago, when they had both been around Sebastian's age, Sergey had courted her. If Giovanni hadn't swept her away with his dashing soldierly charms, burning brown eyes, and unexpectedly gentle touch, Irina would have probably married Sergey. Apparently, Inessa feared that a flame for Irina might still burn in Sergey's heart, and that Irina might feel the same, especially now that Giovanni was dead.

Of course, the last thing Irina wanted at present was a husband, but she knew she'd never be able to convince someone like Inessa of that. Still, she wished she could have spoken to Sergey, even briefly. It would have eased her worries slightly if she'd been able to get some assurance that he would not allow her to be cast into the streets the moment Commander Vittorio no longer found her necessary.

Once the gown was on, Irina examined herself carefully in the mirror. She had to admit, it was nice to dress in civilized attire again.

"Now, dearest Irinushka," said Inessa, "why don't I show you all the things I've done to the manor since you moved out to the country."

"That would be delightful."

In fact, Irina hadn't slept since her husband's death the previous night, so what she wanted more than anything was to fall into bed and let exhaustion and grief sweep her into unconsciousness. But admitting such weakness would have put her at a disadvantage during this precarious time. So she would have to force herself to continue on at least until the end of the day.

She allowed Inessa to take her through every room in the largest home in Gogoleth. She gave the appropriate responses to everything Inessa pointed out to her, from the new painting commissioned from one of the most renowned Raízian artists currently living (according to Inessa), to a bizarre table imported from Kante made entirely of a shiny metal alloy that was surprisingly lightweight. Like many noble-women who lacked any real sense of culture, Inessa relied on others to tell her what sort of decorations she should have in her house, which resulted in an odd hodgepodge of aesthetics and moods throughout the house. It was a far cry from the cohesive harmony that Sergey's mother had carefully cultivated for Roskosh Manor all those years ago, but Irina acted suitably impressed, and that seemed to please Inessa greatly.

Eventually a servant came and told them supper was ready. It was a lavish feast, despite the fact that the only people eating were Irina, Inessa, and Inessa's sixteen-year-old daughter, Galina. Inessa's son, Ivan, was only three and therefore too young to eat at the supper table.

Irina hadn't had such rich, heavy food in a long time. In fact, she'd eaten nothing but her own barely serviceable cooking for the last twenty years. She feared her bowels would punish her for such decadence later, but her effusive compliments to the chef were entirely genuine.

After supper, they retired to a drawing room. Galina sat curled up in a chair reading a book, while Inessa filled Irina in on all the latest dreary courtly gossip. Irina did her best to appear interested until at long last, the setting sun through the window indicated that she could retire for the night without appearing rude.

"Oh, how thoughtless of me, my dear Irinushka," said Inessa after Irina begged her leave. "Why of course you must be beside yourself with exhaustion."

Irina smiled, making sure not to actually show any weariness. "I admit it has been a trying couple of days, dearest Ina."

"Well then, allow me to show you where you'll be staying."

"I would be grateful," Irina said sincerely.

Inessa took her up to the bedroom where she would be sleeping. It was sizable, and exceptionally lavish, but Irina was certain that was true of all the bedrooms in Roskosh Manor. The bed looked extremely inviting, and all Irina wanted to do was strip off her corset and fall into its embrace. But Inessa stood in the doorway, caught up in some tangent about the many mistresses Lord Levenchik, their mutual childhood acquaintance, had collected during the five years since he'd been married, so Irina was forced to stand there and smile awhile longer. As she watched Inessa prattle on, her hands tensed up and she suddenly felt the urge to reach over and strangle that soft, bejeweled neck. Instead, she stood and waited out the torrent of words as if weathering a storm.

At last, Inessa took her leave, and Irina was alone. She took off her gown with unhurried care and hung it up properly, then released the clasps on her corset and hung it up as well.

She stood in her underclothes and stared down at the bed, which suddenly looked much too large. Much too . . . empty.

She took off the simple silver chain necklace that Giovanni had given her when he'd begun courting her. She coiled it up on her palm and stared as it caught the dim light from the oil lamp beside the bed. When she'd first received the necklace, she'd been mildly insulted. She had been one of the most sought-after young ladies of the Izmorozian court, after all, recognized for her intelligence, poise, pragmatism, and of course her beauty. Other suitors had showered her with gold, jewels, and priceless fabrics from faraway lands. If she hadn't been so charmed by Giovanni's demeanor, she would have dismissed his suit right then.

But the more she'd examined the chain, the more she'd realized that while it was not ostentatious, it was exquisitely crafted. Each link was perfectly shaped. There wasn't a single flaw in it. And that was entirely appropriate for Giovanni. He hadn't been perfect, of course. No man was. But each choice he'd made was careful and deliberate, filled with his own awe-inspiring mixture of firmness and compassion. Except the last one.

For of course, while the necklace was perfect, there had been one weak link in Giovanni. His absurd refusal to allow his son to enlist in the military. There had been no conceivable way for him to stand against it, and yet he had done so. It was tempting to put the blame for his death solely on Commander Vittorio, but the truth was, Giovanni, that infuriatingly obstinate man, had deliberately put himself in harm's way. He had knowingly been complicit in his own death. Even as she watched him bleed out on the floor of the bedroom where they'd shared so many happy moments, he had not apologized to her. In fact, the bastard had *smiled*.

"God damn you, Giovanni, for forcing me to continue on alone," she whispered as she gripped the necklace so hard the chain links bit into her palm.

Irina was no stranger to loss. She had lost her parents and her sisters during the war. She had more or less lost her daughter to that peasant-pandering, quasi-mystical death cult. And now she had lost her husband to his own stubborn, foolish pride . . .

Her eyes were wide, glistening with unshed tears. She wrapped her arms around her torso and held in the sobs that threatened to break free. She would not let them. She would not be weak. She would guide and protect Sebastian, no matter the cost. Nothing else mattered. Certainly not her own pathetic grief for an idealistic Aureumian cretin of a husband.

But despite her resolve, the convulsions pounded against the inside of her chest like impatient and unruly children. She knew that she could not hold them back forever.

"Fine, Irina Turgenev, you weak, simpering dolt." Her voice was little more than a growl in her throat. "You get one night to grieve. But when the sun rises, you will leave it all behind. For your son's sake, you will steel your heart and look only to the future."

With that vow, she collapsed onto the bed, covered her face with pillows so as to muffle the sound, and let out one anguished howl after another until her throat burned and her abdomen was sore from heaving. Only then did she finally sleep.

8

The sun had set by the time Sonya, Peppercorn, and Jorge reached the ancient city of Gogoleth, making the skyline appear as a dark looming mass in the purple, star-speckled sky. The outer wall was constructed of the same black rock as the nearby mountains. It was sixty feet high, ten feet thick, and stretched over two miles to encircle the city. On the whole, Sonya preferred the open wilderness to cities, but even she had to concede that Gogoleth was something special. It was older than the empire, certainly, and possibly older even than Izmoroz. It had always been there, the history of its founding and initial construction lost to time.

When they neared the front gates, Sonya reined in Peppercorn. "Need to change my coat. Last I heard, imperial soldiers still have orders to shoot Rangers on sight."

"Oh, I see..." Jorge was clearly nervous about such danger, but he attempted to cover it with a smile, which Sonya thought was sweet.

She took off her fur-lined leather coat and folded it carefully before placing it into one of her saddlebags. She shivered for a moment, enjoying the bite of the winter night air through her thin tunic, then pulled out her patchwork wool hooded cloak. She had constructed it from old clothing scraps discarded by her parents, brother, and Mikhail and it was no less beloved than her Ranger coat, partly because she had worn it all through her training and initiation, including the day she slew a polar bear with nothing but her knife and her wits.

Once Sonya had fastened the patchwork cloak around her shoulders, she looked back at Jorge. "It would be a good idea not to tell anybody I'm a Ranger while we're in Gogoleth."

He nodded gravely. "You may rely on my discretion."

She gave him a smile. "Good. Because they'd probably kill you, too." Then she nudged Peppercorn toward the gate.

"State your business in Gogoleth," said one of the soldiers in a bored voice.

"I—I am a student at the college, just returning from gathering ingredients," said Jorge. "This is my . . . guide."

It wasn't the smoothest response, but the guards were clearly not in an inquisitive mood. The one who had spoken nodded and motioned for them to proceed.

It had been years since Sonya had been inside Gogoleth. She had forgotten, or perhaps in her youth and ignorance hadn't noticed before, what an odd mixture of old and new it was. Many of the original buildings had been destroyed during the war. Nestled in beside ancient black stone edifices chiseled with the faces of snarling wolves or fierce hawks were newer, garishly painted wooden buildings in the Aureumian style. It was a city at conflict with itself.

But that was just the architecture. Everything else was quiet. Strangely quiet, in fact. Granted, it was after sunset, but the last time Sonya had been in Gogoleth, the main streets had thrummed with boisterous, often drunken voices from taverns and inns.

"Where is everyone?" she asked as Peppercorn's hooves echoed loudly on the cobblestones.

"Oh, well, what with the curfew, I expect most people are at home," said Jorge.

"Curfew? How long has that been in effect?"

"The last year or so, I think? Ever since that new commander took charge of the garrison. The one with the big mustache, I can't remember his name. He said it was for the safety of the public."

"Of course he did," Sonya muttered.

Jorge looked nervously around. "In fact, perhaps we should hurry to the college before we get stopped by a patrol. If they search your saddlebags and find your coat . . ."

Sonya nodded and nudged Peppercorn into a trot. She didn't want to make trouble for Jorge.

When they finally arrived at the iron gates of the College of Apothecary, she found herself unexpectedly awed. Judging by the weathering of its black stone, it might very well have been the oldest building in the city, which made it very old indeed. It was several stories high, with a spacious courtyard between the front gate and main doors.

"I guess this is where we part, Jorge," she said. "Good luck with the potion-making."

"Please, my friend." He dismounted and held out his hand. "I beg of you, stay the night. You must be famished and exhausted. After your timely rescue, the least I can do is provide a night of room and board."

"Well..."

The truth was, she hadn't eaten since the night before, and hadn't slept in almost two days. She was most certainly not at her best, and although she was reluctant to keep her family waiting on her rescue any longer than necessary, she knew her limits.

"Okay, I'll stay the night," she said. "But remember, nobody can know what I am. Not even your teacher."

"May I use your name?"

She thought about it as she dismounted. It was possible someone might still recognize the name Portinari from the war. And of course, her mother was originally from Gogoleth, so she probably shouldn't use Turgenev, either. "Call me Sonya Lukyanenko."

"As you wish, Sonya Lukyanenko. Let us get your horse boarded for the night in the stables, and then I will introduce you to Master Velikhov."

Sonya led Peppercorn across the courtyard to a small stable set into the side of the building, where a sleepy stable boy took charge of him. Then they entered the main building and walked down a long, dark hallway. The doors along the way were closed, but she could smell all sorts of unusual scents emanating from within, some floral, some foul, some unlike anything she had encountered in nature. Sonya supposed it wasn't terribly surprising that the College of Apothecary would have such a bizarre bouquet of smells.

Finally Jorge stopped at a door that looked like all the other doors and smelled just as strange. When he opened it, they were met by a blast of warm, stuffy air. The odors that had been faint before were now so dizzyingly strong to Sonya's sensitive nose that she felt half-dazed as she followed Jorge into the cozy space. It was lined with worn rugs and faded tapestries that no doubt contributed to both the warmth and the stuffiness, and off to one side was an equally worn sofa and pair of chairs. The bulk of the room, however, was taken up by a cluster of tables filled with all manner of vials, tubes, jars, burners, and small instruments.

"That's the potion lab, I take it?" she asked.

He smiled proudly. "Yes. When I first arrived, you wouldn't believe what a state it was in. I have no idea how Master Velikhov managed to get anything done. It was simply—"

"Jorge? Is that you?" came a quavering voice from another room.

A moment later, an old man with a long gray beard appeared in a doorway at the back of the room. He was dressed in robes that had probably been red once, but had long ago faded to a gentle pink.

"Oh, good," he said when his rheumy blue eyes found Jorge. "I was beginning to worry." Then he saw Sonya, and he smiled, showing oddly orange teeth. "And who is this lovely young creature with you?"

"Master Velikhov," Jorge said in a formal tone. "I thank you for your concern for my well-being. I fear it was warranted, since I was waylaid on my return trip by bandits. It was only thanks to Sonya Lukyanenko's timely rescue that I am alive."

"Oh dear," said the old man. "My thanks, Sonya Lukyanenko, for the safe return of my apprentice."

"No problem." Sonya dropped her saddlebags next to the door. "And just call me Sonya."

Jorge cleared his throat nervously. "Since she is traveling through the region, I was hoping we could provide her with room and board for the night as a way of repaying her gallantry and kindness."

"Splendid idea!" said the old man, clasping his hands in an oddly childish gesture. "I'll begin making supper at once."

Jorge looked panicked. "Actually, Master. It is my debt to pay, so perhaps *I* should do the cooking?"

The man tugged thoughtfully at his beard. "Quite right, Jorge. I suppose then it is up to me to entertain our lovely guest while we wait."

Jorge gave a relieved smile. "You are most kind, Master."

"Think nothing of it." The old man shuffled over to one of the chairs and eased himself slowly into it. "Please." He gestured to her. "Sit."

"I will return soon with a hot meal, Sonya." Jorge's eyes begged her to indulge the old man. "Please make yourself comfortable."

Sonya nodded, then sauntered over and flopped down on the sofa.

"Lukyanenko...," mused Velikhov. "It sounds Izmorozian, but you don't *look* quite Izmorozian."

"I'm half," she said.

He seemed thrilled by that idea, his cloudy eyes growing wide. "Mixed ancestry? How thoroughly modern! Tell me, do you prefer one over the other? Or do you find both cultures equally agreeable? Or perhaps equally *disagreeable*?"

She considered that a moment. "I suppose there are aspects of each that I like and don't like. But I've only lived in Izmoroz, so I lean toward that."

"Fascinating," said the old man with as earnest an expression as any she'd seen on Jorge. Clearly, the two were well matched. "So you are traveling somewhere?"

"I've been traveling awhile," she said. "So I thought I might go home."

"And where is that?" he asked.

"Wherever I decide it is."

He laughed at that, clapping his hands again in delight. He was a bit daffy, but Sonya decided she liked him. He had an innocent wonder about him, as if even after all these years, he was still in love with the world. Or at least, the world as he knew it. She suspected he didn't often leave these comfortable chambers.

The rest of their conversation centered mostly around aspects of apothecary that Sonya pretended she understood, until finally Jorge returned with steaming bowls of a surprisingly spicy vegetable and rice mixture.

"Flavor! Wonderful!" exclaimed Velikhov after he'd had a spoonful. "I thought my poor abused tongue had lost the ability to taste anything long ago. But then I took in Jorge as my apprentice and his native Raízian cuisine has proved me wrong!"

"Thank you, Master." Jorge settled into the empty chair with his own bowl as he explained to Sonya, "Potion-making is hard on one's senses of smell and taste. Often by the time one becomes a master, both are quite insensible to anything but the most powerfully seasoned meals."

By then Sonya had already tasted it for herself. And while it was certainly delicious, her keen senses were crying out in pain, and she couldn't stop her eyes from watering.

"So...this...is a Raízian dish?" she wheezed.

"A modified version," he said. "Some of the stronger spices cannot be easily acquired outside the hot climate of my homeland."

"The *stronger* ones?"

She could already feel her tongue going into shock and wondered just how it was possible something could be spicier. But she was hungry, and it was tasty, so she continued to eat until the bowl was empty and her face was slick with sweat.

After supper, Velikhov bid them good night and retired to his own chambers in the back room.

Jorge brought a blanket over to her. "I'm afraid we don't have a spare bed, so you'll have to sleep on the sofa."

"I'm not sure I need a blanket after that bonfire you built in my stomach," she said. "But don't worry about me. I'm used to sleeping on the ground." She bounced up and down on the sofa a few times. "In fact, this might be a little too soft."

She slid down onto an open portion of the rug and stretched out. After a moment, she sighed. "Yeah, this is much better."

"Whatever is comfortable for you." He knelt down on the rug next to her. "I...hope you will indulge me by sticking around long enough tomorrow morning for me to feed you breakfast."

She narrowed her eyes. "Is it going to be as spicy as supper? Not sure I could handle that so early in the morning."

He laughed. "I will endeavor to make my mildest dish." He glanced toward the back rooms. "Trust me, you would not want Master Velikhov to cook for you."

She nodded. Someone with almost no sense of taste probably made a lousy cook. Then she thought of something.

"Are your teeth going to turn orange like his someday?"

"They might," he conceded. "Or perhaps a grayish blue. Unfortunately, teeth discoloration of some kind is almost inevitable for someone who must regularly sample ingredients and imbibe their own potions to test their efficacy."

"But you love it, huh?" she asked. "Potion-making?"

He nodded. "The art of apothecary is my chiefest joy."

"Hold on to that," she advised. "Not everybody has one of those."

He considered that a moment, then nodded. "I am very glad to have met you, Sonya."

"Me too, Jorge."

He stood up. "Good night, then. I'll see you in the morning."

"Sure."

He walked over to the lab tables and blew out the series of candles that flickered and danced there, then retired to the back rooms.

Sonya lay on the rug in the darkness. She was grateful for a full belly and a warm place to sleep, but when she closed her eyes, her mind returned to the images of her father and Mikhail, both now gone from this world. In one night, her family had been cut in half. If she'd only stayed home more often...

No. She was doing the work she had vowed to do as a Ranger, protecting the people of Izmoroz and undermining the empire that had outlawed the worship of the great Lady Marzanna. And once she had rescued her mother and brother, she would return to that work. Maybe now, after they had experienced the harshness of the empire for themselves, they would be more supportive of her efforts. Maybe her brother would stop being such a selfish brat and even use his power to aid her cause.

She smiled as she drifted off to sleep, imagining what mayhem the two of them together could unleash upon the empire.

9

Of course Sonya didn't stay for breakfast. Jorge seemed very nice, and she was already growing fond of him, but she'd indulged them both quite enough. She awoke before dawn as she always did, grabbed her saddlebags, and slipped out of the college.

She had to rouse the stable boy from his loft again. Peppercorn nickered happily when he saw her. She'd snagged an apple from a bowl on her way out, and now she fed it to him.

"Will that be all, miss?" asked the stable boy, his eyes still only half-open.

"Yes, thanks." She was unsure if he was waiting for some kind of payment, which would be a problem, since she didn't have any money. But he just nodded sleepily and headed back to his loft. People at the college certainly were fond of sleep. Perhaps it was caused by all the fumes they inhaled during the course of their work.

Sonya refastened her saddlebags, then climbed onto Peppercorn's saddle and nudged him into a walk. As she made her way through the streets of Gogoleth, she noticed that it wasn't just the people at the college who loved their beds. Most of the city was still asleep, even though the first pink blush of predawn light was already creeping up above the building tops. That might not be a bad thing in her current circumstances, however. With luck, she could sneak into the garrison while everyone was still asleep. She certainly didn't want to wait another day until nightfall. She had no idea what sort of terrible conditions her mother and brother were being subjected to, so the sooner she rescued them, the better.

The imperial garrison was located just outside the city proper, protected by the city's eastern wall on one side, and by the mighty Sestra River on the other. The river was too cold and swift at this time of year, and the two sides of the garrison without a barrier would be heavily guarded at all times. That left entry by way of the sixty-foot wall the garrison shared with the city. No problem for a Ranger of Marzanna.

Sonya led Peppercorn to the inside of the eastern wall, where she found a place to tie him up.

"You behave yourself, *Perchinka*," she told him, and he shook his mane in reply. She wasn't particularly worried about him being stolen, but just in case, she gave a swatch of soft mink fur to an old woman who sat on a nearby stoop in exchange for keeping an eye on him. Sonya might not have money, but she was not without valuable items to leverage when necessary.

She took out a length of rope, secured her knife on her belt, and slung her bow and quiver onto her back. Then she walked along the bottom of the wall until she found an adjacent building that she deemed tall enough, if just barely.

From where she stood on the ground, she could see a guard's head peeping over the top of the wall. She waited as he walked slowly along the battlements. When he turned his back, she scampered up the side of the adjacent building.

Once she reached the roof, she flattened herself out in the thick snow and waited until the guard made another pass. Then she pulled the harpoon arrow out of her quiver. It had a heavy pronged tip and the back had a small iron ring behind the fletching. She tied one end of the rope to the ring, then scanned the battlements. She could see a few large crates through the crenels that were too large to fit between the merlons. As long as they maintained their structural integrity, one of those crates could be used as an anchor for the rope.

She waited until the guard made another pass, then fired the arrow into one of the crates and gave it a few tugs to make sure it was secure.

Then, holding the rope in her teeth, she cleared some of the snow off the roof and pried up one of the thick, cedar shingles to expose the wooden frame beneath. She tied the end of her rope to the frame so that it was taut.

She tested her makeshift rope bridge with her foot and did not like the vibration she was feeling. The wooden crate at the far end might not be as sturdy as she'd hoped. The safer option would have been to cross hand over hand, but that would take more time than she suspected the crate would provide. So instead, she took a deep breath, fixed her eyes on the crate, and sprinted along the rope.

She was only halfway across when the crate began to splinter.

She was three-quarters of the way when she felt the rope begin to give beneath her feet.

She lunged forward, grabbed the rope with both hands, and yanked as hard as she could. That shattered the crate and destroyed her anchor, but also gave her enough forward momentum to catch the edge of the battlements with one hand.

She hung there for a moment, forcing her breath to slow. She heard the guard making his return trip toward her and she knew she'd have to hang there until he turned back. All she could do was hope he didn't notice the gloved fingers of her left hand gripping the cold stone edge of the battlements.

She listened to the doltish tread of his boots as he drew near. He reeked of cabbage and cheese.

"What the hell?" he muttered.

For a moment she thought he'd spotted her. But then she heard him sifting through the broken remains of the crate. Her fingers burned with fatigue, but since he was just on the other side of the battlements now, she was afraid even switching hands would draw his attention. When she felt like her hand was about to give out, she forced herself to look down at the sixty feet of empty air between her dangling boots and the unforgiving cobblestones beneath. The resulting surge of terror was enough to keep her hand in place until she heard the guard say, "Strange...," and then make his way back in the other direction.

She quickly switched hands, but then waited until she could no longer smell him before hauling herself up onto the battlements.

She allowed herself a moment to regain feeling in her hands, then rolled onto the other side of the battlements, where she crouched among the remaining crates. Such meager concealment wouldn't be enough to hide her from the guard on his return trip. She would have to figure out her next move quickly.

She scanned the layout of the garrison below. Four buildings in total, all made of wood in the imperial style, although not painted brightly like the buildings inside the city. One building seemed to be a barracks, judging by the soldiers who were beginning to emerge. Local boys for the most part, still shirtless in the cold morning air as they smoked a pipe or splashed some water on their faces from the well. It was strange to see Izmorozian men without beards, but imperial soldiers were required to be clean-shaven.

The second building was likely the mess hall, judging by the chimney that already belched out thick clouds of smoke as the cooks made what was no doubt the massive amount of food required to keep so many soldiers alive.

She guessed the third building to be storage, or perhaps an armory, because of the lack of windows. That left the fourth and largest building. She saw a few officers enter and leave, so she suspected it might serve as officers' quarters, and perhaps a strategy center for the garrison. But it was also large enough that it could serve other purposes, such as a brig or place to keep valued prisoners. She would check that building first.

A wooden scaffolding with stairs had been lashed to the outside of the eastern wall, no doubt to allow the patrol guards to reach the top more easily. The sides were covered in sheets of leather canvas to keep the snow from building up, but they also allowed Sonya to reach the ground without being spotted. From there, it was a simple matter of slipping between buildings and avoiding the early risers in an army that was only now beginning to wake up around her.

Once she reached the building, she used her knife to pry open a window, then slipped into what appeared to be an officer's living quarters. It was fairly unadorned, with a wardrobe, a writing desk, and a bed that still had a middle-aged Aureumian man asleep on it. The man's mouth was open in a snore, and Sonya was tempted to stick something up his nose or draw a silly mustache on his face with a piece of charcoal before she moved on. But she resisted the impulse, feeling certain Mikhail would have called that a sign of maturity.

She crept silently past the sleeping officer and out into the hallway. After checking several other rooms, she determined that the whole wing was probably dedicated to officers' quarters. She was just about to try her luck in a different part of the building when she glanced into one of the open doors and saw a familiar blond head.

Her brother was not trapped in some horrifying torture chamber or prison, but in a comfortable officer's quarters without even a locked door. He sat at the desk with his back to the door, examining a piece of parchment.

Why was he just *sitting* there? Maybe the imperial soldiers had stashed their mother away somewhere to ensure he wouldn't try to escape. Even so, as she watched her brother carefully examine his parchment, he seemed surprisingly calm. She wondered if he knew their father was dead. If not, she didn't relish being the one to tell him. He was such a crybaby...

But first things first. Before she told him the bad news and reduced him to a puddle of sobbing goo, she had to get him out of there.

"Don't worry, I'm here, little brother," she announced briskly as she entered the room. "Let's find Mom and get out."

"*Yasha?*" He turned in his chair to gape stupidly at her. "Wh-what are you doing here?"

"I'm breaking you out, Bastuchka. *Obviously.*" She said it in that nonchalant way she knew would irritate him.

"But I'm not leaving," he said.

"Of course you are." She peeked out the window. Sebastian was neither swift nor stealthy, but at the moment they had a clear shot back to the staircase up the side of the wall. "Do you know where they're keeping Mom? I'm going to get you out, then come back for her. I'm pretty sure that's what she'd want."

"No . . ." He shook his head, looking flustered. "I—I won't go."

"Don't be stupid. Whatever they told you, I'm sure I can find Mom before they do something to her." She snatched the parchment he was holding—a map of some kind—and tossed it aside. "So *come on*. Let's get you out of here while we have the chance."

She grabbed his wrist and pulled him up out of his chair.

"You don't understand." He yanked his arm from her grip. "I don't *want* to leave. Father was wrong. This is where I *belong*. In fact, I've already enlisted in the imperial army."

She stared at him for a moment as the succession of crazy statements he'd just uttered slowly bored into her brain.

"Hold on a moment . . ." She noticed that while he was only wearing a thin cotton undershirt, his trousers were the bright green of an imperial officer and they were tucked into tall, black, brightly polished boots. Hot anger seeped into her gut as she began to comprehend the full enormity of it. "You did *what* now?"

"Please, Yasha." He held up his hands placatingly. "Calm down."

"How can I possibly be calm?" She grabbed his shirt and pulled him close. "Are they threatening Mom? Is that why you're doing this?"

"Mother is perfectly safe and content." He carefully pried her hand loose from his shirt. "If you don't believe me, go ask her yourself. She's staying as Lady Prozorova's guest at Roskosh Manor."

"I just . . ." She took a step back from him. "How could you do this? *Why* would you do this?"

"Because it's the right thing to do." He picked up the map she'd knocked out of his hand and showed it to her. "Have you ever heard of the Uaine Empire?"

"That place with the blue-skinned demons on the other side of the tundra?"

"Yes, the ones who can *raise an army of the dead*? Well, they're massing their forces, and Commander Vittorio believes there's a good chance they will try to cross the tundra during the next thaw. If they succeed, they will sweep in and decimate all of Izmoroz. But the commander believes I can stop them. *I* can save us all!"

"Save the empire, you mean," she said. "While wiping away the last traces of the true Izmoroz culture."

"God, you sound just like Mikhail when you say things like that."

"You mean Mikhail who gave his life trying to stop you from being abducted by the empire?"

"He did?"

"You didn't even notice?" She shook her head in disgust. "Of course you didn't, little genius. You were too busy getting your ego stroked by these imperial snake charmers. I can't believe you would betray everything Father sacrificed just so you could feel important."

He drew himself up and glared at her in a way she'd never seen before, like he was trying out a new posture. "I didn't ask Father to sacrifice anything for me. I didn't even *know* he was doing most of it, and if I had known, I probably would have begged him to stop. So why should I be bound by it? Look, I'm sorry he's dead. But he broke the law, and if we're going to reap the benefits of living in the empire, we need to follow its laws, or pay the consequences."

"My God," she said quietly. "You've already become one of them, haven't you?"

"Maybe I was all along, and just didn't know it," he retorted.

"Maybe you were," she said.

He took a deep breath, as if to calm himself. "I know that you don't agree with me, but can't you at least try to understand?"

She could only stare at him and think of how ashamed their father would have been.

"Please," he whispered. "Yasha..."

She shook her head when he spoke the nickname he'd given her when they'd been little. "No. You don't ever get to call me that again. Got it?"

He nodded sadly. "You should go, Sonya. Civilians aren't allowed in the garrison without permission, and I don't know if I could stop them from arresting you."

"Or if you would even try." She yanked open the window and climbed through.

As she hurried back toward the wall, Sonya felt a wrath unlike any she'd ever known. Even when she'd watched Mikhail die in front of her, even when she'd had to pull the sword from her father's chest, she had felt more sadness than rage. Neither emotion was particularly becoming of a Ranger of Marzanna, but just as the feeling of loss had been undeniable before, the fury she now felt at her brother's betrayal was all consuming. It clouded her head so profoundly that when she reached the top of the wall, she didn't even check to see where the patrol guard was.

"Hey! You there! St—"

"Fuck you!" she snarled as she shot him in the throat.

He fell onto the battlements, spurting blood and flailing wildly. Even worse, the spear he'd been holding dropped over the side and into the garrison below with an audible clang. Mikhail would not have been pleased with this clumsy, emotional behavior. It was very un-Ranger-like.

She would beat herself up about it later. Right then, she needed a quick escape. Except that was another problem. She felt her lack of experience in urban settings keenly as she realized she hadn't quite gotten around to working out how she was going to get back down the other side of the wall now that her rope was gone. Even if she had managed to convince her brother to come with her, how had she expected to get them both out? It would have been terribly embarrassing...

She angrily pushed those thoughts aside. It didn't matter, because he hadn't come. So all she had to worry about was herself.

She sprinted along the wall, scanning for anything on the far side that might assist her. The rooftops were too far away to reach without the aid of a rope, and the battlements she stood on had nothing that could help.

Then, far below on the street, she saw a horse drawing a wagon filled with straw. Would it be enough to cushion a fall from sixty feet?

She heard a bell begin to clang down in the garrison, and the patrol guards on the other sections of the wall converged toward her. Time was up.

She jumped.

The wagon rushed toward her as she twisted around, trying to find the least-worst position to land.

Then there was darkness.

IO

"Miss? You okay?"

Sonya stared up at a concerned-looking old man. Everything hurt. Her head. Her body. And especially her arm. Apparently one could survive a jump from sixty feet into a wagon filled with straw, but not without great cost.

"Hrgh," she said.

"How did you even get back here?" asked the old man.

"The worst way possible." She sat up, noting that her arm was mostly unresponsive. She looked down and saw that it was not at a natural angle.

"Oh my, that doesn't look good at all," said the old man.

She smiled at him through the pain. "Thanks for the use of your wagon, *dedushka*. I'm hoping you can help me out with one more thing."

She got slowly out of the wagon, her insides protesting in any number of alarming ways. She looked around and saw with relief that she was about ten blocks from the wall, and there were no soldiers rushing through the streets toward her. At least she'd escaped.

Her bow, like her arm, had broken when she hit the wagon. She discarded the splintered limbs and handed the bowstring to the old man. Then she gave him a few arrows.

"I'm going to set it, and then you use these to splint it," she told him. "Understand?"

"How are you going to set your own arm?"

"You just wait, *dedushka*. I'll show you how it's done." She'd never actually done it, of course, but understood the principle, and she had seen Mikhail do it to himself when she'd been much younger. She just hoped she didn't pass out before she finished, because if she didn't set the broken bones properly before splinting them, they would heal crooked.

She walked over to the side of the wagon. She removed her belt and strapped the hand of her broken arm to one of the wooden slats in the wagon.

"Okay, you ready? I'm going to need you to reach in here and do it quick when I tell you. I doubt I can hold it for long."

He nodded, his eyes wide.

She set both feet against the side of the wagon, then pushed as hard as she could with her legs so that her arm was being pulled in opposite directions. She thought she'd been in pain before, but that had only been a prelude to this new wave of suffering. Her vision swam from the wrenching agony, and she tasted blood from biting down on her lip.

"Now?" asked the old man.

"Not…yet…," she grunted as tears rolled down her face.

The pain stretched out like an ocean in all directions. She barely knew what she was doing anymore, or why. She only knew that she must do it.

Finally, the broken bones shifted and realigned.

"Now!" she shouted.

The old man hurriedly placed a few arrows along her arm and bound them all together with the bow cord, coiling it tightly from upper arm to wrist.

"Finished," he said.

Sonya dropped back to the ground, her face drenched in sweat. She tried to stand, but the world spun, and blackness once again swallowed her up.

"Miss? Miss?"

It seemed to Sonya like she'd only been unconscious for a moment, but when she looked around, she found that she'd already been untethered from the wagon, and was now lying on the ground, her upper body cradled in the old man's arms.

"I just want you to know...," she said groggily as she looked up into his worried, bearded face. "I don't normally pass out this often."

"You must be in a great deal of pain. Is there somewhere I can take you?"

"Yeah," she said. "Roskosh Manor."

He helped her up to the bench at the front of the wagon next to him. Then he shook the reins and his horse began its slow, very bumpy way forward.

"I wish I had something to give you," she said. "To thank you for helping me out."

He shook his head. "I have a granddaughter around your age. I hope someone would help her out in her time of need."

She nodded and pulled her patchwork wool cloak tight around her with her only functional hand. She felt rude not talking to him further, but she needed to focus on not passing out again. The pain was like a constant hum that made it difficult to concentrate. It wasn't just her arm, either. Her entire body seemed to object to every movement she made and every jolt of the carriage.

After some time, they pulled up in front of a large mansion set above all the buildings around it.

"This Roskosh Manor?" she asked.

"You haven't been here before?"

"No, but it'll be okay." She hoped it would be okay.

"If you say so."

"Thanks again...what's your name?"

"Olin."

"Here." The final test to become a Ranger of Marzanna was to kill a polar bear with nothing but a knife. After, they would use the bear's white pelt to line their jacket. A Ranger also kept the claws of the bear with them at all times. Sonya had hers in a small pouch on her belt. She fished one out and placed it into Olin's hand. "In case you ever need help with something."

He looked down at it, and his eyes widened. "*Strannik?*"

She gave him a weary smile and held a finger to her lips.

He returned her smile and nodded, then quickly hid the claw.

It was a code of sorts. Having a claw meant that the Rangers of Marzanna were in his debt, and if he ever needed help, he could present the claw, and any of the Lady's followers would be honor bound to assist him. Of course, since she was probably the only Ranger left, he would have to find *her*. But still, it was all she had, and she reasoned it was better than nothing.

She climbed down from the wagon and watched the old man drive away.

Once he was out of sight, she leaned over and vomited a sizable amount of blood onto the sidewalk. As she watched the dark red liquid spread across the cobblestones, she thought maybe she'd been a bit premature to assert that she'd survived that fall.

She turned and slowly climbed the steps to Roskosh Manor. She opened the front door without knocking and stepped into the warm glow of a world at once alien and familiar. It reminded her vaguely of her parents' home, but bigger, finer, and much more opulent. If she hadn't already been too exhausted and pain-ridden to care, it would have made her uneasy. As it was, she just snorted in disgust.

"Can I help you..." A woman in the black-and-white uniform of a maid stood before her looking rather uneasy, or perhaps disgusted. "Miss?"

Normally, Sonya would be inclined to turn on the folksy charm at this point, but she was too far gone for that. "I'm looking for my mother. Irina Turgenev Portinari. Is she here?"

"Ah. Lady Portinari. And you are her...daughter, you said?"

"Disappointing, I know. Where is she?"

"Please allow me to take you to her."

Sonya followed the maid through one heavily decorated, unoccupied, and probably useless chamber after another. At least her brother hadn't been lying about their mother being here. And this did not seem a likely place to keep someone prisoner, so perhaps he'd been truthful about her being here willingly as well. Sonya wasn't sure what to make of that at all.

They finally reached a large room with a piano and several pieces of finely upholstered furniture. Her mother sat on one of the sofas, sipping tea as she looked out through a window onto a small central garden.

"Lady Portinari," said the maid. "This girl claims to be your daughter."

Claims. It sounded about as unsure as Sonya felt when she gazed at the woman in front of her. A woman who had the face of her mother, but little else. Irina Turgenev Portinari wore a fine red gown and her long white hair was piled up in some sort of intricate weave on top of her head. She was even wearing makeup. How had everyone changed so drastically since Sonya had last seen them? Had Father's death brought this all about? Or had her mother and brother been changing gradually over time? How long had Sonya been gone, anyway? She didn't always bother to keep track of the days when she was out in the wilderness, but it couldn't have been *that* long, could it? Certainly less than a year. Although she had to admit that even when she'd last visited, she hadn't stayed long.

"Thank you, Masha," her mother said to the maid in a strangely haughty voice. "That will be all."

The maid bowed and hurried out.

Her mother regarded her for a moment. "Sonya, my darling. You look frightful."

Sonya had a sudden, intense urge to run bawling into her mother's arms. To seek comfort for the pain, loss, and betrayal she had endured over the course of the last day or so. But the person before her spoke and acted in a way so unfamiliar, she saw no possibility of comfort in those arms. So she held her ground and did not buckle.

Her mother gave a little sigh, then said in a warmer, more familiar voice, "Dear heavens, Sofyushka. Come sit down before you fall down."

Sonya moved cautiously across the room and sat on the edge of the squishy chair next to her mother. It smelled of stale lilacs, and her mother smelled unfamiliarly of hibiscus.

"I suppose you know everything that's happened," said her mother. "That your father is dead."

"Yeah."

"*Yeah*," her mother said critically. "Why must you insist on speaking like a peasant? I know I taught you better than that."

"Really, Mother?" Sonya's voice grated in her throat. "Yesterday I pulled a sword out of my father's chest and you want to talk about *grammar*?"

Her mother closed her eyes and sighed again. "No, of course not. And presumably you've already learned that your brother has enlisted as an officer in the imperial army?"

"I spoke to him earlier this morning. Seems to be fitting right in."

"You don't approve."

"Don't *approve*? He betrayed our father's memory less than a day after he died."

"You're not a child any longer, so don't pretend it's as simple as that, Sofyushka. What do you think Commander Vittorio would have done if Sebastian had refused? Besides, your brother genuinely thinks he can do some good serving the empire. Is it really such a terrible idea?"

"Joining the empire is a betrayal of our people."

"Our people, you say? I know you're referring to Izmoroz, but aren't your *father's* people your people as well? You like to ignore this fact, but you are as much Aureumian as you are Izmorozian. Honestly, sometimes I regret allowing Mikhail to bring you into all that Ranger foolishness."

Sonya looked at her sharply. "They're not foolish. They protect the people. *I* protect the people."

Her mother shook her head. "The Rangers of Marzanna are a savage peasant cult. All they ever did was stir people up. I think the empire was right to purge them from Izmoroz."

"Well, if you hate them so much, why did you let Mikhail train me to become one of them?"

"I wasn't thrilled about it, but..." Sonya's mother sighed wearily. "Please understand, you were such a...difficult child. Especially after your brother started to show signs of being gifted. Even then, I was reluctant to let Mikhail teach you, but your father insisted that I allow it."

"They were friends," asserted Sonya.

Sonya's mother rolled her eyes. "They were *something*, anyway. I never understood your father's fondness for the man. But to be honest, you were a much better behaved child under his guidance. The longer it went on, the more reluctant I became to intervene, because it allowed me to focus on helping your brother learn to control his gifts."

There it was. Her mother had just confessed that she'd spent most of Sonya's childhood grateful that someone else was dealing with her willful daughter. The callousness of the admission hurt more than she expected. Her relationship with her mother had always been distant. As often as she'd argued with her father, she'd always been much closer to him.

"So I take it you're fine with Sebastian serving the people who conquered Izmoroz," said Sonya.

"I've never had much interest in politics, Sofyushka," said her mother. "If it makes him happy, then yes, I'm fine with it. That's all I've ever truly wanted for *either* of you. That you find happiness. So if it makes you happy to be a lone outlaw, then go with my blessings. I hope that you live as long as your mentor." She gave her a critical look. "Although you'd better not have too many days like this one if you plan to do so."

Sonya's lip curled up into a snarl. "I'm fine."

She wasn't fine, of course. Her arm throbbed with such pain that it was difficult to focus, her head still pounded from the aftermath of a concussion, and there were odd twinges in her gut that she didn't like at all. But she'd be damned if she was going to let even a little of that show in front of her mother.

She stood up as quickly as she could without wincing. "I'm glad you are safe, Mother. And I hope you are happy as well." She bowed even though it caused even more pain. "Goodbye."

"You are welcome to stay here," said her mother. "At least until your injuries heal. Or as long as you like."

"I would not like to stay here at all."

Her mother's eyes softened and it seemed there was just a tiny bit of…regret, perhaps? "My Sofyushka, why must you always be so difficult?"

"A Ranger does not choose the easy path."

Then she turned her back on her mother and made her way slowly through the mansion and out into the street.

She began the long walk through Gogoleth back to where she'd left Peppercorn. Once she had her beloved *Perchinka*, at least she wouldn't feel quite as alone as she did now. And they would go…she wasn't sure where. Away from Gogoleth. Maybe back into the forest for a while. Away from people and their messes. If she got bored, she could always harass some imperial outposts, or flush out some bandits who were preying on peasants. Those were things she was good at. She was not good at family. She never had been.

She didn't really know why she'd always been so difficult. It had been hard to compete with Sebastian the genius. Her parents had all but ignored her, which was why she'd begun spending so much time in the stables with Mikhail. It was why she'd been so eager to learn all the things he had to teach. She'd had some vague idea that she would use those skills to impress her parents. To show them that *she* was the child they should focus their attention on. But it never swayed them. So what if she could hit a bull's-eye while riding at top speed. Her brother could call forth a fireball or melt a field of ice in seconds. Who cared if she could kill a bear with nothing but a knife. Her brother could make crops grow in half their normal time, even in the coldest months of winter.

This was an old bone that she had chewed on for most of her life, and it held little flavor now. But as she stumbled through the streets, her mind kept circling back to it. Her vision was narrowing, and she could hear a strange rattle in her breath. She threw up blood a few more times. Far too much blood. It seemed likely she was dying after all. Not that she intended to give up. She would walk until she reached

Peppercorn, and then she would ride until she could no longer ride. Perhaps the destination didn't matter anymore.

When she finally reached Peppercorn, she was able to unhitch him and climb into the saddle before she collapsed. As she slumped forward to rest her cheek on Peppercorn's coarse mane, she sighed.

"Lady Marzanna, I return..."

Then darkness overtook her that day for the third and final time. At least she died in the saddle.

II

Perhaps Sebastian's sister was right. At least to some extent. While he did believe the menace of the Uaine Empire had to be stopped, his motives for enlisting in the imperial army had not been purely altruistic. She was wrong that it stemmed from ego, however. It was the promise of freedom. The freedom to stop hiding who and what he was. To proudly show what he could do, not just to his parents, but to the world. He decided, then, that the best way to silence his sister's accusations, which still rang in his ears hours after she had left, was to express that new freedom.

He stood in front of the mirror in his officer's quarters and put on his crisp new green jacket. It was made from a thick, stiff wool, and when he cinched the gold buttons up the front, it felt almost like armor. He examined his reflection and decided there was something reassuring about the smart, severe look of it. Admittedly, it was rather plain compared to Commander Vittorio's jacket. Sebastian touched the empty place at his breast where the commander had so many ribbons and medals. Someday, he would have the same.

Sebastian placed the round green cap of a junior officer carefully on his head, checked his appearance once more in the mirror, then made his way down the hall and out into the yard. A small group of infantrymen in blue uniforms were being drilled by their captain off to one side. The shield bearers, heavily armored in both chest and shoulders, dropped to one knee, their convex rectangular shields of ironbound wood planted in the cold mud. Behind them, the lightly armored spear bearers quickly thrust their steel points through the gaps between shields. At the command of their captain, the spears were rapidly retracted, the shields were lifted, both lines stepped forward, and the entire sequence was repeated. It was a near impenetrable wall of bristling steel that moved forward at a slow but unstoppable pace. Sebastian watched them for a moment, recalling how impressed he'd been with the precision of the cavalry even in that frightening moment when they'd invaded his home. The infantry appeared to be just as formidable. It was comforting to know that he was now on the side of such awe-inspiring discipline.

After admiring the soldiers for a few minutes, he made his way across the yard to the armory, a squat, windowless building near the outer wall of Gogoleth. The chief armorer, an Aureumian whom the commander had briefly introduced the day before as Sergeant Costa, sat on a stool in front of the door in his shirtsleeves, carefully sharpening a saber that lay across his lap.

"Good day, Sergeant." Sebastian saluted respectfully, pressing two fingers to his forehead, the elbow out to the side, as Vittorio had taught him.

Costa looked up from beneath his thick, gray eyebrows and nodded. "At ease, Lieutenant... Portinari, wasn't it? Commander Giovanni's boy?"

"Yes, sir."

"I served under Giovanni during the war. Hell of a man."

"Thank you, sir." It still baffled Sebastian how soldiers could express admiration for his father, untroubled by the fact that their fellow soldiers had killed him. Perhaps he would understand such things in time.

"Commander Vittorio told me you wouldn't require a saber," said Costa. "So I'm not sure what you need from me."

"Do you have any scrap metal, sir? Preferably small pieces that are no longer of any use to you?"

One of his eyebrows rose. "I suppose so. I take it I won't have to worry about disposing of them myself, then?"

"No, sir."

He nodded. "Saves me the trouble. All right, I'll see what I've got."

He carefully leaned the saber against the doorway and went inside. Sebastian waited at the door, listening to the sharp clang of metal bits knocking against each other. A few minutes later, Costa returned, lugging a small crate filled with irregular pieces of metal.

"Some of them are rusty. Not sure if that matters."

"It's not a problem, sir. Thank you."

When Sebastian took the crate from the old man, it nearly brought him to his knees. He tried not to show the strain that merely holding the crate put on him, but it was clear he wasn't fooling Costa.

The old sergeant gave a short laugh. "How far you going with that?"

"To...the...riverbank," puffed Sebastian.

"Maybe you'd like some help, then." He turned and called into the armory. "Rykov! Put that damn thing down and come out here."

A loud clank came from within the armory, then after a few moments, a tall, hugely muscled Izmorozian man in his early twenties with incurious eyes, bright red hair, and an almost square face emerged. He wore his blue uniform jacket unbuttoned, possibly because his chest was too broad for it to easily close.

"Sir?" he asked Costa.

"Carry this crate down to the river for Lieutenant Portinari here, then stay on to assist him in whatever he's doing until he dismisses you."

Rykov showed neither interest in nor irritation about this order, but only nodded, his square face impassive. "Yes, sir."

Then the large redheaded man reached out and easily plucked the crate from Sebastian's shaking arms. Sebastian strove not to show his relief, but feared that he again failed to maintain any semblance of stoicism.

"Lieutenant, this is Private Sasha Rykov," Costa told Sebastian. "You can borrow him for the day to do...whatever it is you're doing."

Sebastian saluted again. "Thank you, sir." Then he turned to Rykov. "It's a pleasure to meet you, Private Rykov."

Rykov merely nodded.

"He's not much for talking," said Costa, "but as you can see, he's got other qualities that recommend him."

Sebastian led the way across the yard and down to the banks of the Sestra River, with Rykov plodding slowly behind him. He was relieved to note that the other soldiers and officers in the yard were all preoccupied with their own tasks and took no notice of him or his lumbering assistant. As excited as Sebastian was to practice magic out in the open, he didn't exactly want an audience just yet.

Once they reached the edge of the river, Sebastian asked Rykov to put the crate down next to him, and Rykov wordlessly complied. Sebastian was fairly certain that Rykov was supposed to respond verbally, using a proper title, each time Sebastian ordered him to do something, but he suspected that Rykov was not a typical soldier. Perhaps like Sebastian was not a typical officer.

Sebastian leaned over and picked up a small piece of metal from the crate. "I suppose you're wondering what I intend to do with this."

Rykov merely looked at him, his face expressionless.

"I may not be as…robust as you, or as commanding as the other officers," said Sebastian. "But I, too, have other qualities that recommend me."

He gripped the metal tightly in his hand and looked down at the rushing water before him. The Sestra was the largest river in Izmoroz, stretching more than two thousand miles, all the way down into Aureum. At the point where Sebastian and Rykov stood, it was just over a mile wide, and since it flowed down from the Cherny Mountains directly north of Gogoleth, the current so was swift that even in winter, it never froze.

Not until today, Sebastian thought to himself.

He held out the piece of metal, and focused his intention on it as he visualized the river slowing down and hardening into ice. After a short buildup of concentrated energy, the metal flared with a bright light, then crumbled to a small pile of rusty flecks. Sebastian shook the dust from his hand, then looked down at the river.

The section directly in front of him was now a solid block of ice that reached all the way down to the riverbed.

Unfortunately, now that the way was completely blocked, the current from upriver began to flood the banks. In moments, Sebastian's shiny black boots were submerged in ice-cold mud.

He stumbled back, then realized he'd need another piece of metal to reverse the change. He splashed forward, accidentally drenching not just his boots, but his trousers as well. He shoved his hand into the crate, cursing as he nicked his palm on a jagged edge, then pulled out another piece of metal.

It was more difficult to concentrate this time, partly because of the brutally cold water that was already numbing his toes, and partly because of the knowledge that if he did not fix this quickly, the Sestra River would flood the garrison.

The water was well above his ankles by the time he found the focus, and the new piece of metal flashed and crumbled to rust. Instantly the block of ice dissipated in a puff of steam, and the river resumed its usual course.

Sebastian breathed a sigh of relief as he shook the rusty powder from his hand. Then he realized that Rykov had been watching him the whole time.

Sebastian straightened up, needlessly adjusted his jacket sleeves, and looked over his shoulder at the large redheaded man. *"Well?"*

Rykov nodded. "Pretty neat."

Sebastian couldn't decide if Rykov was generously overlooking his blunder, or merely indifferent to it. Perhaps it didn't matter.

"Yes." Sebastian picked up another piece of metal. "It's not a bad trick, is it? There were a few variables I hadn't considered, but I just need more practice."

So Sebastian continued to practice through most of the afternoon, with Rykov standing patiently by his side. Once he got used to the hulking, silent man's presence, he decided he rather liked it. He found it improved his concentration when he described what he intended to do out loud before he did it. And it was better to have someone else there, lest a passerby think he was merely a madman talking to himself.

"Good afternoon, Lieutenant." Commander Vittorio's deep baritone rang behind him. "I'm pleased to find you hard at work."

Sebastian turned to see the commander smiling fondly at him from beneath his tall officer's hat. Sebastian dropped the piece of metal he'd been holding into the crate and saluted sharply.

"Good afternoon, Commander."

"At ease," said Vittorio.

Sebastian dropped his salute. "Sergeant Costa was kind enough to provide some old scrap metal so I could get in some practice."

"It appears he also lent you Private Rykov as well." Vittorio looked speculatively at the large man. "Now that I see the two of you together, it occurs to me that your skill sets complement each other rather well. I could speak to Costa and see if he'd be willing to let Rykov become your official aide-de-camp. What do you say to that?"

"I would be overjoyed, sir. Private Rykov has already proved immensely useful."

"Wonderful." Vittorio glanced at Rykov, who did not seem to care either way, then back to Sebastian. "Now I'm afraid I must ask you a rather delicate, family-related question, Lieutenant. Do you wish to dismiss the private for a few minutes?"

Sebastian gave him a puzzled look. "Sir? I have nothing to hide, I can assure you."

Vittorio smiled. "Of course not. And I suppose one of Private Rykov's most valuable traits is his habitual silence. Very well. I have received a troubling report that a young woman was spotted fleeing the garrison this morning."

Sebastian nodded glumly. "My sister."

"I thought as much."

"She was under the mistaken impression that I was being held against my will and came to rescue me. I corrected her misapprehension, of course, and assured her that both my mother and I were well and free to do as we chose. One might have hoped this would please her, but she was...quite vexed."

"Indeed," Vittorio said gravely. "So much so that she killed one of the guards on duty as she fled."

"*Sonya* did? My sister?" Sebastian tried to imagine such a thing.

"She shot him in the throat with an arrow, no doubt to stop him from shouting out an alarm," said Vittorio. "You seem surprised that she would take such an action."

"Well, I know she's a hunter, and I'm sure she's killed more wild animals than she can count. But *murder*? I had no idea she was capable of such violence."

"I don't need to tell you, Lieutenant, that this is a serious crime. Do you know where she might have gone?"

"She would have gone to verify that our mother was indeed free, but after that..." He shook his head. "I'm sorry, sir, I have no idea. We haven't been close in years. I suppose she'd go back to the wilderness to hunt tigers or whatever it is she does out there."

"I see. How disappointing." Vittorio frowned so that the carefully groomed tips of his mustache sank. Then his expression suddenly brightened. "Oh my. With all this tumult, I nearly forgot to issue you your new weapon."

"A weapon, sir?" asked Sebastian. "Sergeant Costa made it clear that you did not think it fit for me to have a saber."

"Quite right. We have plenty of men who can wield such weapons. For you, I have something truly special."

He reached into his pocket and pulled out a diamond the size of a walnut dangling from a leather thong.

Sebastian could only stare at this unearthly treasure as the faint winter sunlight sparkled off its edges.

"I'm glad to see you so economically minded and using scrap metal during your practice," said Vittorio, "but after making some inquiries with colleagues at the imperial capital of Magna Alto, I learned that diamond is the ideal conduit for elemental magic. Not only will it not disintegrate under the strain like metal, but it has even been known to amplify the power of the magic user."

"Sir...I don't know what to say..."

"Say that you will use this weapon for the glory of Empress Morante and the Aureumian Empire."

"I will, sir! I most certainly will!"

Vittorio pressed the diamond into Sebastian's suddenly shaking hands. "I expect great things from you, Lieutenant."

"I swear I won't let you down, sir!"

"I'm happy to hear that. Now, I was planning to go to Roskosh Manor to see how your mother is settling in. Would you care to join me?"

"Oh, uh…" Sebastian stared down at the diamond in his hand. The weight of it, the feel of it. He could already imagine the incredible things he would do with this gem.

Vittorio laughed good-naturedly. "I suppose you're eager to try out your new weapon. Very well, I will convey your apologies to your mother and tell her you are in the middle of an important and delicate task and will call upon her another time."

Sebastian blushed. "Thank you, sir."

"Not at all. I was young once, too, and vividly recall the thrill of testing my abilities to their limits." Vittorio turned to Rykov. "Private, geniuses can often lose sight of obvious things such as hunger and exhaustion when working at their full potential. Make certain Lieutenant Portinari has eaten and gone to bed by midnight."

"Yes, sir."

"Now, if you'll excuse me, gentlemen."

Sebastian saluted sharply, unable to keep the ecstatic grin from his face.

Commander Vittorio chuckled again, and took his leave.

"Now we'll see what I'm *really* capable of, Rykov," said Sebastian as he held the diamond tightly in his grip.

"Okay," said Rykov.

12

I hear your daughter stopped by today."

Irina did not immediately react to Commander Vittorio's statement. Instead she continued to chew her food with deliberate calm. She should have known it wouldn't take long for him to get wind of Sonya's visit, however brief.

The commander had arrived at Roskosh Manor a half hour earlier to relay Sebastian's apologies that he was far too busy with work to join them for supper, and then Vittorio had humbly offered himself as "a poor replacement." Now he sat with his fork poised over his slab of gravy-drenched roast as he gazed across the table expectantly at Irina and she wondered if he had even conveyed the invitation to her son.

She gave him a practiced smile. "She did indeed visit, Commander. Most unexpectedly. Sonya's always been such a free spirit, I'm afraid I never know where or when she'll turn up."

"What a shame she didn't stay," said Inessa, who sat at the head of the table. "I would have loved to meet her."

"As would I," said Vittorio, then took up his knife and slowly cut into his roast.

Irina was fairly certain the commander's interest in Sonya was not as benevolent as it was toward Sebastian. That was, if any interest from him could truly be called benevolent at all.

"I believe she spends most of her time hunting in the forests," Irina told the commander. "So I'm afraid I don't know when she'll visit again."

"Oh? Do you know which forest?" Vittorio's tone was light, as if only mildly curious, but his eyes were back upon her, and they were as piercing as ever. "I rather enjoy a bit of hunting now and then myself, so perhaps I could join her sometime."

"An excellent idea, Commander, but I fear she rarely bothers to share such details with me." Irina quickly switched the focus to Inessa, giving her host a forlorn look. "Daughters take such little notice of their mothers when they grow up. You'll see soon enough, Ina my dear."

"I see it already!" Inessa took a large fortifying gulp of wine from her crystal goblet. "Only sixteen years old and already Galina can hardly be bothered with me."

"Mother . . ."

Galina, who sat to her mother's right, was pale and thin, with long blond hair and the most melancholy eyes Irina had ever seen. Unlike her more effusive mother, Galina never smiled. Instead, there was a keen, watchful intelligence behind her sad green eyes that reminded Irina far more of her father, Lord Sergey Prozorova, than her mother. Thus far, Irina had also never seen Galina without a book. Even at the supper table, a slim volume of poetry by Gregor Bortniansky lay closed but safely within reach. Irina suspected that such a well-read young woman found her gregarious but vapid mother frustrating, or at the very least mildly embarrassing.

Not that Irina cared much for Inessa, either, of course. But now she smiled fondly at her. "At least we have our sons, dear Ina, and they will never forget us."

"I do hope so." Inessa's carefully painted eyebrows puckered. "It would break my heart if my little Vanya were ever to ignore me."

Ivan Prozorova was eating with his governess as usual, but Irina had met him and found him to be a jolly, mild-mannered little boy more in keeping with Inessa's temperament than his older sister.

"I'm certain you have nothing to fear," Irina assured her.

"A good man will honor his mother not only for her entire life, but his own," said Vittorio. "Given young Ivan's privileged upbringing, fine stock, and the shining example of Lord Prozorova, I'm certain he will grow up to be such a man."

"Is *your* mother still alive, Commander?" Irina still knew far too little about the Aureumian commander who held so much power over her fate and the fate of her son.

"Alas, no. In fact, I no longer have any family at all." Vittorio gazed into his goblet with somber eyes for a moment. Then his expression brightened and he looked at each of them in turn, including Galina, as he said, "But that is one reason I am so well suited to this post, an appointment I cherish deeply."

Irina found it hard to believe Vittorio truly cherished his post. Giovanni had once told her that high-ranking Aureumian officers viewed any appointment to the cold, hard lands of Izmoroz as a punishment. Still, if this was all an act for the benefit of the Izmorozian nobility, it was a flawless one. So Vittorio was either a consummate performer, or merely an unusual officer. Perhaps the latter was more likely, but time would tell either way. Until then, Irina would respond to him as if she had no doubts regarding his earnestness. It was the safest option, given her tenuous position.

Once supper was finished, Inessa stood and curtsied to Vittorio. "Commander, you've been so kind to keep us company, especially during my husband's absence, but I'm sure you must have a great deal of work to attend to."

"Indeed I do." The commander rose and bowed.

"My dear Irinushka," continued Inessa. "What do you think of taking the carriage out for a ride?"

"That sounds wonderful," said Irina as she also rose from the table.

"Galina, go fetch your cloak and meet us at the stables."

Galina remained seated, her nose already buried in her book, and only said, "Mmm?"

"*Galina!*" Inessa said sharply.

"Yes, Mother." Galina reluctantly closed her book, lurched out of her seat, and hurried off.

"I can see myself out, Lady Prozorova," said Vittorio.

Inessa nodded as she allowed him to kiss her hand. "I look forward to seeing you again soon, Commander."

She left the room, heading toward the stables.

Commander Vittorio then turned to Irina and bowed. "Lady Portinari, a pleasure as always."

As she felt his curling whiskers press against the back of her hand, she realized that except for the servants who hurried to clear the supper table, they were completely alone for the first time.

"Commander...," she said as if it were an idle thought that had only just occurred to her. "Out of curiosity, what would have happened if my son had not agreed to enlist as an officer in the imperial army?"

He looked up from her hand, and for just a moment, she caught a flash of something dark and seething in his eyes. Then he smiled, and it was gone.

"Let us not speak of unpleasant things that might have been, Lady Portinari. Especially when we have so many years of fruitful cooperation to look forward to."

Irina forced a warm smile to her lips even as icy dread crept into her heart. "An excellent suggestion, Commander. I look forward to our next meeting with great anticipation."

Once she had taken leave of Vittorio, Irina made her way out to the stables, where Inessa and Galina waited in a finely painted horse-drawn carriage. As the carriage pulled out into the street and clattered through town, she feigned attention, nodding and occasionally murmuring agreement as Inessa prattled on about various bits of gossip concerning one noble family or another. Not even the bustling early evening activities of Gogoleth captured her attention. Instead, the majority of her thoughts were focused on what had most certainly been a threat from Commander Vittorio: Ensure Sebastian's continued cooperation, or things would get unpleasant.

This was comforting knowledge, inasmuch as all knowledge was to some degree an assurance. She now knew Vittorio to be a snake, and that the commander could in no way be counted upon for any kindness that did not in some way further his own purposes. For her son's sake, as well as her own, she would need to form other alliances to fall back upon should the need arise. Alliances that could not easily be broken.

"What a dear thing Galina is," she said, cutting short Inessa's moment-by-moment account of a recent event at the Grand Northern Ballroom.

"Sorry?" Inessa blinked in confusion for a moment at the sudden change in topic. Then she looked at her daughter, who sat scrunched into the corner of the carriage with her face in a book as if the rest of the world didn't exist, and her expression became even more confused. "*My* Galina?"

"Yes of course, silly." Irina smiled. "A precious flower among weeds."

"She's a clumsy, galumphing beanpole, too long of limb and narrow of chest. I keep telling her that if she only smiled now and then, she might catch *someone's* attention. She does have a pleasing face, after all. But as you can see, it's always buried in her precious books."

Irina affected surprise. "You mean to tell me that she has no suitors?"

"Not a one!" Inessa began wringing her hands, a forlorn look marring her painted beauty. "Oh, Irinushka, it's such an embarrassment. You would not believe how often it comes up in conversation. At every party!" Her eyes narrowed resentfully. "Lady Volkov, Lady Gusin, even Lady Ovstrovsky! You'd think they'd stop inquiring by this point, but they never fail to mention it, the scurrilous harpies! It's enough to make a mother weep."

Indeed, Inessa's eyes did seem to be tearing up. Irina supposed that to someone like her, it might truly seem like a profound burden.

"I apologize for bringing up such a tender subject, Ina," she said. "I suppose I am only surprised because I am certain Sebastian would adore her."

"Truly?"

Conflict washed across Inessa's face, as if she was trying to decide if Irina was only saying it to be polite, or if the statement could be taken in earnest. Poor Inessa. Even after a lifetime among the nobility, she didn't understand that nothing could ever be taken at face value.

"My goodness, yes!" Irina let out a wistful sigh. "I love my son more than life itself, of course, and it's true that his abilities make him a tremendous asset to the empire." She gave Inessa a plaintive look. "But you've met the poor boy. So thoughtful and shy, without any experience in courtly graces. And I can never decide which is more delicate, his health or his heart. He has far too many qualities of the dreamy poet, and not nearly enough of the gallant gentleman."

Inessa's expression took on what passed for a shrewd look on her part. "Those society girls would eat him alive. You remember how they can be."

"Precisely!" said Irina. "No, I can't allow that. He'd be simply miserable. But I fear that unless he finds another gentle soul with whom he can entrust his tender emotions, he will live and die a lonely bachelor, and I will never be a grandmother."

"There, there." Inessa leaned across the carriage and patted Irina's hand comfortingly, although the shrewd look had not left her eyes. "You still have Sonya to provide grandchildren."

Irina's bitter laugh was genuine. "I'd have more luck hoping for a midwinter thaw."

Inessa made a show as if an idea had just occurred to her. "Wait a minute, my dearest Irinushka! What if we were to put our two unconventional young people together? Do you think it might lead to something . . . *romantic*, thereby solving both our woes?"

Irina pretended to consider that a moment. She glanced over at Galina, who seemed so engrossed in her book that she appeared oblivious to the fact that they were discussing her future. But for a moment, her eyes flickered to Irina's, and a rosy blush crept onto the girl's cheeks. In extolling Sebastian's "flaws" within earshot of Galina, Irina hoped she had in fact listed the young woman's most valued attributes. She was pleased to know she still had a good eye for character.

This might just work. Sebastian, like all young men, could use a woman to ground him. And a familial alliance with the Prozorova family would be invaluable, should the relationship with Commander Vittorio sour.

Irina beamed at her host. "Why, Inessa, what a splendid idea!"

13

Dead already, *Lisitsa*? That was quick."

Sonya opened her eyes and found herself kneeling on the banks of the Eventide River, which she had not seen since her initiation as a Ranger of Marzanna. As before, the surrounding area was a drab, featureless gray shrouded in mist and possessing an unnerving stillness. It was neither dark nor light, but instead existed in a hazily unreal twilight somewhere between. It was not cold or hot. Or perhaps it was both at once, one rendering the other meaningless. Her keen sense of smell could not find purchase anywhere. Smell required air, and air was for the living.

She looked down into the dark, still waters of the Eventide River and saw in place of her own reflection the terrible, sublime beauty of the Lady Marzanna. The Lady's skin was white as snow, while her eyes and hair were black as midnight. Her arms were long and thin, with hard jagged fingers like icicles. She wore a crown of bare, leafless branches on her brow that curved out to either side like antlers, and a flowing white robe that glowed as brightly as the moon.

"I had expected you to entertain me a bit longer," Lady Marzanna continued in a voice as swift and cutting as a winter wind. "And getting sidetracked by your family problems? That was not what we had discussed at all. You are meant for a greater purpose."

"I've failed you, my Lady."

The Lady cocked her head to one side. "I didn't say that. It's far too early to say that. In fact, some things that you have set in motion, intentionally or not, look very promising. But they will need your continued involvement to come to fruition."

"Oh."

"Yes, my *Lisitsa*. I do not permit you to stay dead."

Sonya was of course relieved. A Ranger of Marzanna did not fear death, but that didn't mean they longed for it. Even without a family, she wanted to see more of the world, to feel the surge of her blood during the hunt, and taste the pleasures of life. But along with her relief, Sonya also felt a deep trepidation. The gifts of Lady Marzanna came at a great price.

"What will you take this time, my Lady?"

Lady Marzanna considered for a moment. "Your ears, I think."

"Both of them?"

"Of course. What would be the point of one ear? But don't worry. Better ones will replace them. Ones more . . . suited to you, *Lisitsa*."

Sonya felt sick with dread, but her voice did not falter. "Thank you, my Lady."

"You are most welcome, my child."

Lady Marzanna's long, spindly hands emerged from the black water of the Eventide River, but no ripples marred her beauty.

Sonya closed her eyes and steeled her heart. Hunters might strike with efficiency, thereby sparing their prey undo pain and suffering, but creatures of the wild did not take into account such things. And certainly Lady Marzanna, Goddess of Winter and Death, was not a creature that could ever be tamed.

The Lady did not move swiftly or with any compassion as she took hold of Sonya's ears. Her grip was colder than ice and harder than metal. Sonya clenched her jaw and forced herself not to flinch as her ears slowly grew black and shriveled with frostbite. The sharp, chilling pain brought tears to her eyes, but she did not cry out.

Then, Lady Marzanna began to unhurriedly wrench Sonya's ears off at the root, as if savoring the action. The pain flared up white hot so that guttural noises escaped Sonya's throat, and her fingers dug into the icy mud of the riverbank, but she did not pull away.

The last threads of blackened flesh snapped free and the Lady drew the ravaged ears into the river. The raw stumps of Sonya's ears did not bleed, but neither did the pain stop. In fact, it spread down into the rest of her body, a rolling shock wave of agony that reached all the way to her fingers and toes. It felt as though something *essential*, something even more important than blood, was being drawn from her veins.

Sonya screamed like an animal, a piercing ragged sound that burst from her throat.

"There, there, my adorable *Lisitsa*. It's time to get more serious about your duties," chided Lady Marzanna. "I expect better results by the next time we meet, or I won't be so . . . gentle."

"Yes, my Lady," sobbed Sonya as she pressed her forehead into the mud. "I swear!"

"Good. Now go."

14

"Ah. I believe she's coming around," said a familiar, kindly old voice. "Welcome back to the land of the living, my child."

Sonya's pain was gone. In fact, she felt warm and comfortable, lying on a soft bed beneath a heavy wool blanket. When she opened her eyes, she saw the old apothecary, Velikhov, smiling down at her from one side of the bed, while Jorge looked worriedly down from the other. There was little else in the tiny room besides heaps of books stacked on the floor, and a small table with a number of potions on it.

"How...did I get here?" Her voice was scratchy.

"Your horse brought you back here a few days ago," said Jorge.

She smiled tiredly. "The apples. He came back for the apples." Then she paused. "Did you say *days*?"

"You've been unconscious for quite a while," said Velikhov. "And you were in terrible shape when you arrived. Bringing you back to good health was a challenge even for one of my skill. To be perfectly honest, there was a moment I thought you'd died on us. But I suppose God must still have need of you."

Someone does, anyway, thought Sonya. The memory of her meeting with the Lady Marzanna was disjointed and blurry, like a dream. She could not even say for certain what the Lady looked like. But she remembered enough.

"Wait..." She lifted up her arm. It was no longer broken. Even her split lip was healed. "Wow, you *are* good, Master Velikhov."

94

Jorge beamed. "He is the *best*."

"Now, now." The old man's cheeks flushed. "Healing potions just happen to be my specialty. I'm little more than competent in other areas of potion-making."

"Well, thanks, I—" She sat up, and pain lanced through her body.

"Oh dear, please don't do that quite yet." Velikhov and Jorge eased her back down onto the bed. "You sustained a number of internal injuries, and those do take a bit more time to heal, even under my care. With a broken limb, I can apply strong salves directly to the damaged area, but with something inside the body, you have to let the medicines you ingest take their slow course. Be patient."

Sonya nodded as she rubbed her torso with both hands. "Yeah, I can be patient."

"Speaking of potions, it's time for another dose," said Velikhov. "I'm afraid the side effect is extreme drowsiness, so even though you've been sleeping for days, you will likely sleep quite a bit through the next few days as well."

"Whatever I need to be back to my old self," she said.

He nodded. "I'm glad I have a patient who is able to see the big picture."

He reached over and took a small glass vial filled with a thick, emerald-green liquid from the table. He measured out a few drops into a spoon and handed the spoon to her. She appreciated that he wasn't trying to spoon-feed her while she was awake. She sucked the medicine down. It tasted predictably foul, reminding her of swamp grass mixed with the bitter, dank mushrooms that grew inside dead trees. For all she knew of potions, those might very well be the primary ingredients.

"I'll check back with you later." Velikhov slowly stood and left the room.

Sonya turned to Jorge. "I guess we're even now, huh?"

He smiled and nodded. "Did you..." He hesitated, as if unsure he should bring it up.

"Find my mother and brother?" she guessed.

He nodded.

"I suppose you could say that. I found people who *looked* like them, but didn't particularly talk or act like them. Although maybe they did, and I just hadn't seen who they really were before." She thought about it a moment. "Or hadn't wanted to."

"I'm not sure I understand," confessed Jorge. "Are they well? Are they safe?"

"They made the safe choice of joining the empire. My brother even enlisted as an officer of the imperial army."

"Sonya, we already *are* a part of the empire," said Jorge. "It's not like there's an alternative. What could one person do alone against such a powerful entity? It would be like a fly picking a fight with a horse. The horse might not even notice as it kills the fly with a single blow of its tail."

"Yeah...I suppose we'd need a lot more flies..." The potion was already taking effect. Her thoughts were beginning to feel as slippery as fish swimming upstream. Without meaning to, she let out a large yawn.

"I should probably let you sleep." Jorge stood and bowed. "I'm very happy to see you again, Sonya."

Then he left the room.

After a moment, Sonya tentatively brushed her dark hair back from her temples and felt for her ears. They were no longer empty stumps. Nor were they the ears she'd had before. Instead they were perhaps a bit larger than human ears, and came to a delicate point at the top. Her first visible mark of the Lady, the true sign of a Ranger of Marzanna. She felt pride, but also a sense of loss. It was said that with each "gift" of the Lady, a Ranger became less human, both in body and in mind.

Lady Marzanna had reprimanded her for getting sidetracked. Family or not, the empire had massacred the Rangers and banned her worship. That simply could not be allowed to continue.

But Jorge had a valid point. How could one person hope to make an impact on such a monolith as the Aureumian Empire? For more than a year she had been trying to strike out against them, hitting supply lines, stealing back tithes, and killing high-ranking officers whenever possible. But the empire didn't seem to even notice. Somehow, she needed to make a bigger impact. She needed to challenge them in a way they couldn't ignore. Surely even an empire feared... something...

She tried to turn the problem over in her mind some more, but the medicine continued to work its soothing magic and after only a short time, she slipped into a deep and dreamless sleep.

15

Rykov, do you know much about elemental magic?" asked Sebastian as he and his recently confirmed aide-de-camp stood once again on the banks of the Sestra River.

"Nope." Rykov's face was calm and incurious, his arms at his sides, one hand loosely holding a coil of rope.

Sebastian supposed some officers might be irritated by Rykov's apparent disinterest, but he found it rather soothing. Perhaps after a childhood in which his parents constantly focused their attention and expectation on him, it was a relief to speak and know that the listener would not be intensely scrutinizing every word that left his mouth.

"Not surprising, really." Sebastian gazed down at the swift gray waters of the Sestra. "Although it is the *oldest* known form of magic, it is the least understood. I have come across a few books written about the residual magic of Kante, and several about the expressive magic practiced in Raíz—have you ever seen a troupe of Viajero practice expressive magic?"

"Nope," said Rykov.

"They're extraordinary," said Sebastian. "One came to Gogoleth when I was a boy. It was one of the few times my father allowed us to travel to the city. Witnessing their...*performance*, I suppose you'd call it, although that word seems far too reductive, was easily one of the most impactful moments of my childhood."

"Okay."

"My point is, if one wishes to expend a little effort and money, it isn't terribly difficult to gain knowledge on either residual or expressive magic. There are some who consider apothecary to be a sort of *supplemental* system to magic, and there is an entire library dedicated to that subject right here in Gogoleth. Yet I have never found more than fleeting mention of *my* magic. I can only suppose the reason is because it's so rare."

"I guess you should write it," said Rykov.

"What?"

"The book on elemental magic," said Rykov. "If there isn't one, and you know about it, then you should write it. That's why books get written, isn't it?"

Sebastian's eyes widened. The idea seemed preposterous. Him? Write a book? "Why, Rykov, that's..." But was it really so absurd? He frowned thoughtfully. Obviously, there was still a great deal he had yet to learn. But if not him, then who? "Rykov, that's a wonderful idea. Once I've reached a level of mastery that I'm satisfied with, I will write the definitive book on elemental magic." He grinned, feeling a little giddy because of his bold declaration. "Rykov, it's such a blessing to have you around."

"Sure," Rykov agreed.

"Now, let's get back to work."

"Okay."

Sebastian gripped the diamond in one hand. After a few days' practice with this gem, he understood better that his intentions needed to be more specific. The more deliberate his forethought, the more effective the result.

Sebastian pictured a narrow bridge of ice that stretched across the Sestra. He constructed the image carefully, methodically, with thick round piers spanning every ten feet, and an elegant handrail that stretched across on either side to compensate for the fact that the deck itself was composed of such a slippery substance.

He designed this image carefully in his mind and focused it on the diamond. This was where the gem showed its superiority. Without any focal point, the result of his magic was only a momentary alteration. A gust of chilling wind, a slight cooling of the temperature, or something else nearly undetectable.

With metal, he could collect his focus on it to some degree, but at best it was a few moments before the material began to decompose, with or without the release of the magic. That was why Sebastian's intention had always been so rushed, and the results therefore less than ideal.

But with the diamond, Sebastian could take his time to construct exactly what he wanted, down to the last detail, and the gem could bear the magical weight of that sustained focus for as long as necessary.

Sebastian continued to grasp the diamond tightly in his right hand as he gestured toward the rushing Sestra with his left. Slowly, the bridge he had envisioned rose up from the river until it stretched from one side to the other. He felt a moment of dizziness, as one might after spinning around several times, but he quickly steadied himself.

"Now for the *real* test."

He held out his hand to Rykov, who gave him one end of a long rope. He had stayed up half the night studying the mechanical principles involved in designing a bridge, so he was fairly certain it would hold his weight. But if it broke beneath him, Rykov would be able to haul him out of the frigid waters with the rope before he was swept downstream.

Sebastian didn't trust the strength of his grip, so he wrapped the rope several times around his wrist. Then he took a deep breath, squared his shoulders, and stepped onto the ice bridge.

It held.

"Stay on the bank," Sebastian told Rykov. Then he slowly walked farther out until the rope was taut between them, nearly halfway across the river. The bridge continued to hold his weight. He stamped his foot down on the deck several times, each time with increasing force. Still it held.

Sebastian's heart surged. The potential benefits for this skill were almost limitless. Sure, this bridge would melt in the spring thaw. But this was only the beginning. Water and fire were the elements that came most easily to him. Once he was more confident with earth-working, he could make bridges of hard-packed mud, and eventually stone. And of course not just bridges, but *any* structure so long as he understood the engineering principles behind it, all within a matter of minutes. He would be able to rebuild an entire city in a day.

"Success!" he declared, and turned toward Rykov with a grin.

Commander Vittorio stood next to Rykov, his hat under his arm.

"Good day, Commander!" he shouted.

"Congratulations, Lieutenant," Vittorio called back to him.

"Thank you, sir!" Sebastian walked back carefully across the slippery bridge, then saluted to the commander. "Really, it's thanks to the diamond you gave me. I can say without fear of exaggeration that it has increased my ability to create complex structures a hundredfold!"

"Is that so?"

It was only then that Sebastian noticed that Commander Vittorio did not appear to share his happiness.

"Is...everything okay, sir?"

"I'm glad you have been applying yourself rigorously this past week, Lieutenant," Vittorio said gravely. "Honing one's skills is never a bad thing. But I did not go to considerable lengths and great expense to procure that diamond so that you could engage in civic improvement projects."

"Oh..." The giddy elation Sebastian had been feeling evaporated. "Sorry, sir."

"Surely you have not forgotten that the barbarous Uaine Empire and their horde of undead paces our western border, held in check only by the impassible wintry tundra?"

"N-no, sir."

"It looks increasingly likely that they will march with the spring thaw. Though I pray it never becomes so dire, there may come a time when the only thing standing between their hordes of undead and the fair city of Gogoleth is you. On that day, what will you do? Build bridges for them?"

"O-of course not, sir." A cold shame snaked through Sebastian. He had been so caught up in his own selfish interests that he had lost sight of the bigger picture.

Vittorio grasped his shoulder firmly. "Then by God, my boy, show me something I can use. Magic with *military* application."

"Military application. Y-yes of course..." It made perfect sense. Except Sebastian wasn't certain what that actually entailed.

Vittorio looked at him for a moment, then sighed. "Perhaps I have assumed too much. Did your father impart none of his knowledge of warfare to you?"

Sebastian's feeling of shame deepened as he wordlessly shook his head.

"I see." He placed his hat on his head. "Well, there's nothing else for it then. I'll need to instruct you on such matters myself. Follow me."

Half-anxious, half-thrilled, Sebastian followed Vittorio, who walked swiftly across the ice bridge without a moment's hesitation or any hint of concern. This was a true soldier, fearless and bold. Sebastian looked down at the rope in his hand and his shame deepened further. He quickly handed it back to Rykov, who followed wordlessly behind them.

Once they were across the bridge, Vittorio stopped and gazed out at the Pustoy Plains before them. Beyond the plains, Sebastian could just make out the dark line of trees that marked the beginning of the Stena Forest, and to the north loomed the black, craggy peaks of the Cherny Mountains. But directly before them and stretching several miles to the south, the Pustoy Plains were flat and useless for agriculture because of the rocky soil. It was a great swath of empty space that in the winter now appeared as an endless-seeming blanket of snow interrupted occasionally by a small cluster of fir trees.

Vittorio stretched out his hands. "Imagine a vast army of undead marching across these plains, Lieutenant! What do you do?"

"Well, I suppose—"

"Don't tell me, boy! *Show* me how you would wipe such a horde of abominations from our fair lands! Prove to me, here and now, that I did not seek you out and gift you with a priceless treasure in vain!"

Sebastian stared at Vittorio, but the commander's keen eyes did not waver.

"Has no one ever spoken to you like that?" asked Vittorio in a quieter but no less firm voice. "Has no one ever demanded more of you than you were easily able to give? Has no one ever *challenged* you as you deserve to be challenged?"

He waited, motionless, for a response.

Sebastian had never been allowed to use his magic in such a massive and sweeping way. "N-no, sir."

"Then it is well past time. How can you expect to achieve your full potential if you do not push yourself to the fullest expression of your gifts? I promise you that the great apothecary Stephano Defilippo did not cling to such safety. If you wish to follow in his footsteps and change the world, you must move beyond what you perceive to be your limits. Indeed, you must accept no limits at all. Only then will you know your true capabilities."

"I understand, sir. And...thank you."

Vittorio nodded, then turned to face the Pustoy Plains. "Picture it, Sebastian. A mass of slavering, shambling corpses coming toward us, intent on consuming the tender flesh of your mother and everyone you hold dear." He looked back at Sebastian with wide, haunted eyes, as if he was already picturing such a horror in his mind. "What will you do?"

Sebastian gripped the diamond tightly in his fist and stared out at the empty plains. No, not empty. Full of monstrous creatures that were an affront to nature and God. An endless wave of evil descending on the innocent of Gogoleth. He would wipe them from the face of the earth. He would cleanse the ground of their foul existence.

First he melted the snow, making it disappear like a blanket being yanked away. The liquid soaked into the thawing ground beneath until it was a sea of mud. But that was surely not enough to stop the undead.

Slowly the mud began to seethe and bubble. The grass and trees turned brown and shriveled with the heat, but he did not stop there.

He renewed his focus on the gem and increased the heat until the liquid boiled away, and the ground was nothing but a hard, barren mass of brown.

Even then he knew that wasn't enough. The undead could surely survive such a thing. He must try harder, push further.

He reached deeper, below the earth's crust to the bedrock. The weight of it pressed against his mind, the heaviness so palpable it became difficult for him to breathe. But he squared his shoulders, gritted his teeth, and pressed his focus further into the gem.

Sweat glistened on his brow as he heated the bedrock. It built up so much pressure that the ground beneath his feet began to tremble. He steadied himself and continued to make the ground before them hotter and hotter.

Suddenly, a font of bright orange magma burst through the ground and splashed across the plains, hissing spitefully as it scorched away any remaining life. Within minutes, there was only a mass of black, steaming sludge.

Exhaustion swept over Sebastian and he might have fallen if Rykov hadn't been there to steady him. He took a moment to catch his breath, his face and collar now drenched with sweat. When he finally assessed his work, he saw that there would be no life of any kind on those plains next summer. No grass, and therefore no elk to graze. No wildflowers or trees, therefore no birds or insects. Sebastian had made the Pustoy Plains truly dead.

He felt sick to his stomach.

"Wow," said Rykov.

"Indeed." Commander Vittorio turned to Sebastian with a triumphant smile beneath his mustache. His eyes glistened with unshed tears as he put his hands on Sebastian's shoulders. "That, by God, had military applications. And it was *beautiful*."

"Thank you, sir." Sebastian forced himself to smile, though he would have preferred to vomit. He understood that what he had done could be seen as useful to the military. He felt powerful, proud even, but he did not understand how such wanton destruction could be seen as *beautiful*.

"Oh, I almost forgot to mention," said Vittorio in a more casual tone as he went back to surveying the blighted plains with a satisfied expression. "The Lady Prozorova is hosting a party this evening at Roskosh Manor and your mother has requested your presence for the event." He gave Sebastian an amused smile. "And she made it clear that *this* time she would accept no apologies. So I suggest you go tidy up for supper with all due haste."

"Yes, sir."

The last thing Sebastian felt like doing right then was attending a formal social event, but it was clear he could not decline his mother's invitation yet again. So he saluted the commander, then headed back across his ice bridge to his quarters, the silent Rykov following behind.

16

"What did you think of it, Rykov?" asked Sebastian as he stood in his undershirt before the mirror and gently dragged the razor down his moistened cheek.

"Think of what?" Rykov stood nearby, cleaning Sebastian's green wool jacket with a coarse brush.

Sebastian looked at him through the mirror. "What I did out on the plains, of course."

"Oh." Rykov considered a moment. "Most impressive thing I've ever seen, I guess."

"Yes." Sebastian carefully scraped the razor along his neck. "I suppose it was."

He realized that might sound like bragging to some, but it didn't feel like bragging to him. If anything, it felt like an admission of guilt. His father would have been furious at him for such excess. Yet Vittorio and even Rykov seemed pleased by it. How could they be so happy about something that was so antithetical to life? This was clearly what the commander expected of Sebastian. Could he even do such a thing again? Well, with the help of the diamond he was certain he could. But should he?

There was a soft knock at the door.

"Please come in," said Sebastian as he wiped away the excess shaving soap with a towel.

Commander Vittorio stepped into the room. "Ready to depart, Lieutenant?"

"You're coming, too, sir?"

Vittorio smiled broadly. "I wouldn't dream of missing a delicious meal at Roskosh Manor. Have you eaten the food in the mess hall?"

Sebastian managed a wan smile as he pulled his green jacket back on. "It's *all* I've eaten, sir."

"By thunder, then you're in for a treat, my boy." Vittorio turned to Rykov. "Make certain the lieutenant's clothes are laid out for tomorrow, then you may have the rest of the evening off, Private."

"Thank you, sir."

Vittorio turned back to Sebastian. "Shall we then?"

The commander walked with a spring in his step as they made their way through the halls and across the yard to the carriage awaiting them at the entrance to the barracks. Sebastian couldn't decide if Vittorio's jovial mood was caused by his display of raw magical power or the promise of a sumptuous dinner at Roskosh Manor.

It had been a gray and overcast afternoon, so the setting sun was little more than a ruddy smear above the building tops as the carriage wound through the narrow cobblestone streets. During the short trip, Vittorio's exuberance continued as he listed the guests he anticipated would be in attendance, and the food he hoped would be prepared.

Roskosh Manor was as splendid as before, but it was also a lot more crowded than the last time. Everywhere he looked, he saw imperial officers or Izmorozian nobles chatting gaily and drinking small, stemmed crystal glasses of vodka. There was even a doorman who announced the arrival of Lieutenant Sebastian Turgenev Portinari and Commander Franko Vittorio. The imperial officers all saluted Vittorio, who nodded graciously in return. The nobles seemed to eye Sebastian with a mixture of curiosity and suspicion. He couldn't blame them. Technically, he was one of them, but he did not know or understand their world at all.

Sebastian's mother emerged at the upper landing, looking radiant in a long, flowing green gown, her pristine white hair artfully piled atop her head. She paused when she saw him, then smiled and continued down the staircase.

"What a pleasure to see two such gallant gentlemen." She held out her hand to Vittorio. "Good evening, Commander."

He kissed the top of her hand with the utmost solicitousness. "Delighted to see you as always, Lady Portinari."

Then she turned to Sebastian.

"And you..." Although she appeared quite cheerful, she embraced him with an unusual intensity. "I hope you haven't forgotten your dear mother."

"O-of course not, Mother." He felt a new pang of guilt. She had seemed to get along well with Lady Prozorova, but perhaps her stay at Roskosh Manor had been more lonely than he'd realized.

She took a step back and smiled as she placed her hand on his cheek. "Dinner will be served soon, but first there is someone I'd like you to meet." She turned to Vittorio. "I'm sure we'll see you in the dining hall, Commander."

Vittorio raised his eyebrow at the pointed dismissal, but then smiled and bowed his head. "I look forward to it, Lady Portinari. If you'll excuse me, my generals will likely have taken up their usual post at the bar, and I have found that the presence of their superior officer curtails any temptation toward excessive inebriation they might otherwise entertain."

Sebastian's mother politely inclined her head as Commander Vittorio made his way unhurriedly down the hall. Once he was out of sight, she turned back to Sebastian and took his hands.

"Are you well, my darling? Eating properly and brushing your teeth?" She pushed his bangs back, then tucked his hair behind his ears.

"Yes, Mother."

She smoothed the sleeves of his green jacket, though they didn't need it. "You do look rather dashing in your uniform, Sebastian.

So much like your father, it made me catch my breath when I first saw you."

"Thank you, Mother."

He wanted to tell her what had happened that day. He wanted to confess the doubts that filled his mind. Had his father been right? Should he have refused to enlist so that he would never be forced to unleash such destructive power? But he had already pledged his allegiance to the empress. To turn away from those vows now would bring nothing but dishonor and shame on them both.

But before he could broach the subject, she hurried him down one of the many hallways of the manor.

"Quickly, my darling. The call to dinner will chime soon, and there is someone you absolutely must meet first."

"Who is it I am to meet?"

She only gave him a knowing smile and said, "You'll see."

He wondered who this important person might be. A distant relative, perhaps? Or the head of an important noble family? It couldn't be his sister, could it?

That idea filled him with dread when he thought of what Vittorio might do when he saw her at dinner. After all, she was a murderer, and since her victim had been an imperial soldier, potentially a traitor to the empire as well. Punishment would be swift and brutal.

Perhaps Sebastian could convince Sonya to sneak out the back, or hide in a closet until the commander had left. She'd be furious, but if it meant saving her life, he would accept her ire. After all, it wasn't as though displeasing his big sister would be a new experience for him.

But when his mother guided him into one of the many small sitting rooms in the manor, he saw a young woman he did not recognize. She was about his own age and sat alone in a high-backed chair reading a book, oblivious to the party going on around her.

He noticed she was reading *An Air of Last Year's Spring*, a collection of poetry by Valery Lomonosov that he rather liked. The fingers that grasped the book were long and elegant, but faintly stained with ink. Her hands and wrists were thin and spare, calling to mind the delicacy of a bird. The sleeves of her gown only came three-quarters of the way down her arm, and seemed more ill-fitting than suggestive of an intentional style. And yet there was something captivating about the fair skin and fine white hairs of her forearms that they revealed. She had a long, lean frame, almost boyish, and thick, honey-blond hair that reached well past her slender shoulders.

A few moments after Sebastian and his mother entered the room, she looked up, and he was immediately struck by the solemn light that shone in her large green eyes. He felt at once that this was no frivolous noble, but someone who thought and felt things deeply. Perhaps even as deeply as him.

"Galina, this is my son, Sebastian Turgenev Portinari," said Sebastian's mother. "Sebastian, this is Galina Odoyevtseva Prozorova, daughter to Lord and Lady Prozorova."

Sebastian and Galina stared at each other. He had never looked at someone quite the way he looked at her now. It was as if he had lost all peripheral vision and could only see her. She was so pale and melancholy, like the ghost of a doomed princess from a fairy tale.

"Well?" Sebastian's mother nudged him with her elbow. "Say something, my darling." In a much quieter voice, she murmured, "A compliment wouldn't go amiss."

"Oh, uh... Good evening, Galina Odoyevtseva. I like your... book."

He had no idea why he'd blurted that out. It was the first thing he'd noticed and the first thing he said. His mother was looking at him with undisguised chagrin.

"Wh-what I meant to say..." He struggled with how to recover. "That is, I was—"

Galina interrupted him. "You're familiar with the works of Lomonosov?"

"Oh, well, of course..." There was now a sharpness in her gaze that made him even more self-conscious than usual. As he spoke, he felt as though he should do something with his hands, but he didn't know what that should be, so they merely flapped aimlessly at his sides. "H-his writings on the essence of nature have had an enormous impact on my work in elemental magic."

That sounded like bragging. Would she think him immodest? Or was that the sort of thing gallant and dashing soldiers did? A charming bit of bravado, perhaps?

She gave no indication regarding her preference either way, but only tilted her head to one side and asked, "How so?"

"Ah, well, you see, when exerting your will on the elements it is important to understand them scientifically. But I have found, at least for me, that it's just as important to understand them on…an *emotional* level, I suppose you could call it. And it seems to me that there is no better way to do that than through poetry. For example, in Lomonosov's 'The Song of River Angels,' he speaks of the sound that water makes as it moves over stones—"

"'It tumbles trippingly over rocks worn smooth with Nature's tireless progression, like children fleeing their schoolhouse on the first day of Spring,'" she quoted.

"Yes, that's…" He stared into her melancholy eyes. "You know it all by heart?"

"Important things are worth remembering," she said.

"I couldn't agree more," he said.

There was another moment of silence as they once again stared at each other, but Sebastian thought—or rather *hoped*—that this time, it was a warmer, more welcoming silence.

"Now then," Galina Odoyevtseva said. "Regarding Lomonosov's 'The Song of River Angels,' what—"

The bells chimed out in the hallway, a signal to guests that dinner was about to be served. She paused until the bells stopped ringing. Then she placed her book on the small side table beside her chair and stood.

"Perhaps, Sebastian Turgenev, we may continue this conversation at dinner?"

He smiled at her. The first genuine smile he'd mustered since he'd destroyed the plains. "It would be my pleasure, Galina Odoyevtseva."

She held out her pale, ink-stained hand to him, and he was not quite able to still the quiver in his own as he accepted it. It was soft and quite warm. Together, they made their way toward the dining hall, Sebastian's mother following silently behind.

17

Galina Odoyevtseva Prozorova was a great admirer of contradictions. If pressed, she might even go so far as to say that she distrusted anything that appeared uncomplicated. In her experience, nothing was ever truly simple, and anyone who presented themselves as such was either foolish or deceitful. Galina was pleased to find that Sebastian Turgenev Portinari was neither.

Galina's mother had made it abundantly clear over the course of the last few days that it would bring her great joy if Galina took a romantic interest in Lady Portinari's son. Lady Portinari's descriptions of him had sounded promising, but it was surely no difficult task for someone of Lady Portinari's intellect to guess which qualities Galina would find most pleasing. Besides, as the celebrated playwright Aleksey Kapnist once wrote, "One never truly knows whether a connection of romantic passion is possible until they meet the person's shadow." The likelihood of having such an experience at so contrived an event had seemed rather low, so Galina had more or less resigned herself to once again breaking her poor mother's heart.

But as Galina sat at the long banquet table in the dining hall and scrutinized the blond boy who sat beside her, she wondered if she might spare her mother yet. Sebastian was, if nothing else, a bundle of fascinating contradictions. He shifted constantly between arrogant and humble, awkward and charming, thoughtful and impulsive.

He had a slender frame for a man, and with his full rosy lips and pronounced cheekbones, was more pretty than handsome. Some girls might have found such a feminine aesthetic in a man distasteful, but appearing as it did in stark contrast to both his earnest gravity and his intellectual swagger, Galina saw it merely as another facet of interest in what might prove to be the most complicated boy she had ever met.

Vittorio's boorish generals dominated the dinner conversation, as they usually did. Their faces already flushed with drink, they held forth on any number of topics, from the length, intensity, and tedium of Izmoroz's winters compared with the vastly superior Aureumian weather, to the inferiority of the Uaine Empire, who they claimed were mere barbarians who had gained what little power they possessed by means of a pact with demons.

"It's well known," declared General Bonucci, a bullnecked man with a fringe of sweaty hair atop his shiny scalp. "Necromancy is no *human* magic. Surely they've sold their souls to a pack of demons in exchange for such hideous abilities."

"Hear, hear!" General Marchisio, a square-headed fellow with a luxurious beard, pounded his fist on the table in agreement.

Assuming what they said was even true, Galina wondered if these men would be so bold to decry such tactics if they knew that before imperial rule, Izmorozians had a long history of making pacts with supernatural creatures that could perhaps be described as "demonic." Of course, given their prevailing lack of respect for Izmoroz in general, they probably wouldn't have been concerned about giving offense, even if they had known.

"Gentlemen." Vittorio's stern voice broke into their rambling. "While I appreciate your patriotic enthusiasm, I must ask for a certain amount of decorum at Lady Prozorova's table. If you wish to pound your fists as if you were in the mess hall, you are welcome to go eat in the mess hall. Do I make myself clear?"

Marchisio blanched. "Apologies, Commander."

"It is not me to whom you owe an apology," Vittorio said.

"Lady Prozorova, I apologize for getting carried away." Marchisio lifted his wineglass. "May I drink to your health?"

Inessa blushed like a girl Galina's age. Not that Galina would have blushed at such a crude show of respect. "You may, General."

After Marchisio had drunk heartily to Galina's mother's health, Vittorio's third general, Zaniolo, spoke up. Although just as brusque and ill-mannered as the other two, Zaniolo never lost his composure and, of the three, seemed the most intelligent and perceptive by far. His black hair was grown long on one side and plastered across his scalp with hair tonic as if it somehow hid his baldness. But even if he was somewhat deluded on that count, there was little else that escaped his piercing blue eyes.

"If I may be so bold as to inquire, Lady Prozorova," said Zaniolo, "where is your dear husband? I do so miss his charming anecdotal descriptions of Izmorozian life."

"I'm sure Sergey would have loved to be here, General, but he had to leave town for a short time," said Galina's mother. "Like most men of idleness, he does dote upon his hobbies."

"Pray, in what hobby does Lord Prozorova indulge?" Zaniolo's expression was innocent enough, but the hair on the back of Galina's neck prickled.

"Oh, his beloved preservation of Izmorozian culture," she said. "Although, to speak candidly, it seems to me he's merely collecting silly children's stories."

Galina inwardly winced. She could not fathom why her father had ever entrusted such sensitive information to her empty-headed mother. Along with the extermination of the Rangers of Marzanna, a great deal of Izmorozian culture and folklore had been deemed seditious by the empress. For Galina's father to pursue interests even tangentially related to such topics was to invite sharp scrutiny, and there was already a great deal of tension between the imperial military and the Izmorozian nobility. In theory, the Treaty of Gogoleth allowed the Izmorozian nobility to maintain direct authority over their people. But the noble families had quickly discovered their sovereignty was in name only. The true ruler of Izmoroz was the imperial army, and by extension, its highest-ranking officer, Commander Vittorio.

General Zaniolo maintained his innocent expression, but his eyebrows rose. "Lady Prozorova, I had not realized the Izmorozian culture was in need of preserving. Is your husband unhappy with the generous freedoms that our benevolent Empress Caterina Morante has granted him and his people?"

Though she was reluctant to do so, Galina felt she must step in before her mother made things worse.

"Surely *all* cultures should be preserved from one generation to the next, General," she said. "The great Aureumian Empire has an army of scribes dedicated to recording each magnificent word the empress utters. My father was so inspired by the imperial archives during his visit to the great capital of Magna Alto that he longed to emulate such farsighted and lofty goals in his own humble way."

That was not entirely untrue. Her father *had* gone to Magna Alto and been deeply impressed by the imperial archives. But his actions were not so much in emulation of them as a way to protect Izmoroz from them so that his people would not have their history and culture recorded solely by their conquerors.

"Galina Odoyevtseva, that was very well said." Vittorio's keen eyes bored into hers with an interest she'd never seen before and did not like. "You so rarely speak up, and now I see that all this time you have been cruelly denying us the pleasure of your enlightened and thoughtful discourse."

Galina stared at him, unable to formulate a response that would not further pique his interest, which she decidedly wished to avoid.

"Now, now, Commander," chided Lady Portinari, coming to her rescue. "The poor girl finally comes out of her shell a little and you frighten her right back into it."

Vittorio turned and looked at Lady Portinari without expression. Lady Portinari held his gaze, smiling with an almost flirtatious challenge.

"I see," Vittorio said at last, then turned back to Galina. "Forgive me, Galina Odoyevtseva. My words were intended to be complimentary, but I fear my experience with the delicate sensibilities of adolescent girls is somewhat lacking."

Galina nodded. "I thank you for your kind apology, Commander. Though it was unnecessary, it is appreciated nonetheless."

Vittorio seemed satisfied, but Galina had the sinking feeling he would be watching her much more closely from now on. Of course, if she agreed to engage herself to Sebastian, that would be inevitable anyway.

Vittorio turned back to Sebastian's mother. "I am happy to report, Lady Portinari, that today our Sebastian has proven he is not only able to meet, but *exceed* my expectations."

Galina thought it strange the way the commander referred to "our Sebastian," as if Vittorio were his father, rather than the departed Giovanni Portinari. But naturally a woman of Lady Portinari's poise would never let any irritation show. Instead she merely smiled and said, "How wonderful."

"I cannot go into details of a sensitive military nature, of course," continued Vittorio. "But if he continues to develop at his current pace, we may all rest easy and be confident in the safety of Izmoroz, even if the Uaine Empire with their legions of undead are foolish enough to invade."

"I'm so very proud," said Lady Portinari.

Galina turned to Sebastian and was both surprised and intrigued to see that he did not seem proud, or even pleased by such a boastful declaration. If anything, he seemed saddened by it. That was the moment she decided that this boy was worth further examination.

She softly laid a hand on his sleeve. He looked up at her, surprise now mingling with his sorrow.

"I would not wish to distract you from your duties, Sebastian Turgenev," she said quietly. "But I hope that with all your preparation for the defense of our beloved Izmoroz, you still might find the time to call upon me so that we may speak at leisure in a less formal setting of our mutual appreciation for poetry."

His eyes widened. "Galina Odoyevtseva, I can assure you that such a meeting would not be a distraction from the defense of Izmoroz, but rather an inspiration to redouble my efforts."

"Then by all means," said Galina, "for the good of Izmoroz, I look forward to seeing you again soon."

18

After two days, Master Velikhov pronounced Sonya well enough to get out of bed and move around, as long as she didn't push herself too much or go too far.

Naturally, Jorge was very glad of that. But it did present some challenges for him. He knew that Sonya was accustomed to ranging far and wide in the wilderness. She no doubt felt frustrated to be sequestered so long in the small apartment. Unfortunately, her restlessness expressed itself primarily in interrupting him while he was trying to work, so it was difficult to truly feel sympathetic.

"Whatcha making?"

He snatched up the bottle of distilled flatfish oil that she nearly knocked off the lab table when she sat on the edge. Then he resumed his work grinding up foxtail and dried alpine rose petals with a pestle.

"Hopefully, a tincture that temporarily grants one increased resistance to cold temperatures."

"Huh." She looked impressed. "I didn't know that was possible."

"I'm trying to see if it is," he said. "Right now it's merely a hypothesis."

He began to count out teaspoons of the paste into a beaker already boiling with several other ingredients.

"By cold resistance, you mean protection from frostbite, hypothermia, stuff like that?"

"Yes, of course. Merely relieving the *feeling* of being cold would have little practical value..."

Jorge paused, realizing he'd just lost count of how much paste he'd put in the mixture. He'd have to start all over again, not just with the paste, but from the beginning.

He looked up at Sonya, and she smiled warmly back at him. He found that it was a smile he could not stay mad at. And yet, something had to be done, or he would get nothing accomplished during her convalescence.

"Would you care to go for a walk?"

Her eyes widened. "You sure old Velikhov won't get mad? I'm trying to be a well-behaved patient, you know."

"Just a short one," he said. "So you can express some energy."

"That would be great, Jorge. I'll be honest, I'm going crazy in this place."

"Yes, I noticed."

She winced. "Sorry, I'm being a pain, aren't I? Listen, I can just—"

"No, it's all right. I need to go get some more alpine rose at the market anyway."

Sonya only drew on her patchwork hooded cloak, but Jorge bundled up thoroughly, including gloves and his large fur hat. He'd been in Izmoroz nearly a year, but still hadn't acclimated to the cold yet. He wondered if using a tincture to temporarily increase resistance to cold would slow down the person's natural process of acclimation even further. Or would it speed the process up? Something to test later on, once he'd accomplished the initial goal of his experiments.

He and Sonya left the cozy warmth of the college and headed into the abrasive chaos of Gogoleth's open-air market. That was yet another aspect of Izmoroz that Jorge hadn't acclimated to. Back in his hometown of Colmo, the Raízian merchants tried to beguile passersby with charming, tantalizing descriptions of their wares, sometimes even singing to them. By contrast, Izmorozian merchants seemed to prefer intimidation, at times even physically accosting potential customers. The first time an older Izmorozian woman had grabbed his arm and yanked him over to her stall, he'd been so surprised he'd had to stifle a scream.

"Best meat in Gogoleth! Get it now!"

"Don't go anywhere else for fruits! Only buy mine!"

None of the merchants smiled. In fact, hardly anyone in Izmoroz smiled. Except Sonya.

He glanced at her as she walked beside him, and saw her smiling even then, her eyes wide as she took in the rambunctious energy of the market that surrounded them.

A large, bearded man stepped in front of her and shoved a necklace in her face. "Beautiful lady! Buy my jewelry!"

"Now see here . . . ," began Jorge.

But Sonya only chuckled and shoved the man aside. Surprisingly, the man seemed amused by this as well, expelling a short bark of laughter before kissing his fingertips. Jorge wondered if he would ever really understand the Izmorozian people.

At last they came to the booth where Jorge always bought his floral ingredients.

"Ah, Jorge," said the elderly woman. "Back again so soon?"

"I'm afraid so, Misha Bagrov."

"My fault, *babushka*," said Sonya. "I distracted him while he was working."

The old woman looked at Sonya, and her thin, wrinkled lips curved into a slight smile. "I bet you did, *devushka*."

"Ah, okay . . ." Jorge felt his face redden. "Misha Bagrov, I hope you still have some alpine rose in stock?"

"Of course. I only keep it for students of the college. Nobody else wants it."

"Really?" Sonya seemed surprised. "It's great for hangovers. Chew a few petals and your mind is clear again in hardly any time at all."

"I suppose . . ." Misha Bagrov gave her a skeptical look. "If you can choke them down." Then she turned to Jorge. "Another bunch will be ten copper."

"Oh, let me pay for this, Jorge, since it was my fault." She pulled out a large swatch of pure white mink fur from her satchel. "You do trade, right?"

The old woman's eyes lit up when she saw the mink, and her hand reached out longingly, almost as if on its own.

121

"May I?" she asked.

Sonya smiled knowingly. "Sure."

The old woman's bony fingers swept lightly across the fur and her eyes closed blissfully.

"Nice, isn't it?" asked Sonya.

The old woman nodded as she stroked the fur.

"There's enough here to line the inside of a pair of gloves easy. Imagine feeling that every day on your way to work."

The old woman smiled.

Sonya gently moved the mink out of reach. "Probably worth more than a bunch of alpine rose, I'd say."

Misha Bagrov's eyes opened, and her expression became wary.

"I'm not trying to swindle you, *babushka*," Sonya said. "I just want a fair trade. *Sdelka*, the old ways. I'll even let you decide what is fair. Seeing as how Jorge's a regular customer of yours, I know you'll do the right thing."

"Hmph," said Misha Bagrov, her eyes still wary. "Your Izmorozian is terrible, *devushka*. But at least you try. Few your age do. Okay. We have a deal." She turned to Jorge. "What more do you want, my boy?"

"Oh, uh . . . I suppose I could use some more blue fern?"

"Yes, yes. What else?"

"Really?" He thought a moment. Master Velikhov was a notorious miser, and as a student, Jorge rarely had money, so he usually only got by on the very basic ingredients. The idea of obtaining something that wasn't a necessity was a luxury he hadn't experienced since he'd left Raíz.

"Would . . . a bunch of emerald dandies be okay?"

Her eyebrows lifted. "Oho! Expensive taste for a student. Yes, fine, but no more. I call that a fair trade."

"Thank you, *babushka*." Sonya handed her the mink.

The old woman pressed it against her cheek and closed her eyes, a dreamy expression on her face. Then her eyes snapped back open and fixed on Sonya. "Some free advice, *devushka*. Be careful who you speak such words around. Not everyone in Izmoroz finds comfort in the old ways."

Sonya touched her forehead respectfully. "I'll keep that in mind."

Misha Bagrov gave the bundle of alpine rose, blue fern, and emerald dandies to Jorge, then he and Sonya continued through the market.

"I've never seen those emerald dandies in the wild," said Sonya.

"Oh, I should think not," said Jorge. "They are extremely difficult to grow, requiring the greatest care and skill."

"A plant that delicate, what's it good for?"

He grinned at her. "You'll find out at dinner tonight!"

"Is it going to set my mouth on fire?"

"No, no, this is actually an Aureumian seasoning."

"Really? You know, I'm half-Aureumian, and I don't think I've ever had any Aureumian food. My father never cooked and my mother only cooked Izmorozian food..." She frowned thoughtfully. "I wonder if he ever missed the food of his homeland."

"I'm certain he did," said Jorge. "Despite all my efforts to replicate the food of Raíz, they are a pale shadow compared to the meals I ate as a child, and some days I find I miss them even more than the weather."

Jorge led Sonya the long way back through the market, hoping that all the extra stimulation would leave her feeling less anxious by the time they got home. On their way, they passed the entrance to the Imperial Church, whose brightly painted wooden walls and square top contrasted strikingly with the black stone buildings with sloping roofs that surrounded it. It was nearly noon, so the priest stood out in front of the church, haranguing people as harshly as the merchants. Despite the similarity of tone, he was Aureumian. A tall, gaunt man in bright yellow-and-red robes, clean-shaven with sagging jowls and deep-set brown eyes.

"Come to pray! Come and beg God to protect you from the Uaine Demon Menace that lies at our doorstep! Throw your weak and foolish selves upon His mercy and He will shield you from the horrors to come!"

Sonya stopped and slowly turned toward the priest. There was an alarmingly mischievous glint in her eye.

"Uh, Sonya, perhaps we shouldn't antagonize him," murmured

Jorge. "Live and let live, you know. Everyone has their beliefs. I know the Aureumians can be a little...demonstrative about their religion, but it's not like they outlaw native religions."

"Maybe not in Raíz, but they do here." Sonya didn't take her eyes off the priest as she spoke. "Since the Rangers led the resistance during the Winter War, *any* worship of the Lady Marzanna is punishable by death."

"I hadn't realized there was a religious component to being a Ranger," admitted Jorge.

Sonya nodded slowly, her eyes still fixed on the haranguing Aureumian priest. "It's the most important part."

"I see...," said Jorge. "Still, it probably wouldn't be wise to draw attention to ourselves."

"I just want to ask him a question. That's all."

Jorge wasn't sure he believed her, but he followed nervously behind as she sauntered over to him.

"Priest! What do you know about these Uaine?" she asked in a tone that could not have been less respectful.

He loomed over her. "The greatest threat to our people since time began! Blue-skinned demons with spikes for hair who cavort with the dead! If you don't repent, they will come with their skeleton army and tear your flesh from your body until you are one of them, a slave for eternity!"

She smirked at him. "Uh-huh..."

This seemed to irritate him even more than a smart comeback might have. "You will know despair unless you place yourself in the protection of God and the great Aureumian Empire!"

"Nah," she said. "I'll take my chances, thanks."

He drew himself up to his full height, and a vein pulsed nastily on his forehead. "I would expect as much from an ignorant savage with the stink of the wild about her! Go back to your mud huts and hovels in the wilderness, you miscreant, and let the dead army of the Uaine have you!"

Sonya's grin looked almost feral, and took on a menacing edge. "Maybe I will."

Jorge took her arm and smiled weakly at the glowering priest. "My apologies, Holy Father. She is still recovering from terrible, life-threatening injuries and meant no harm."

The priest grunted. "Keep your filthy peasant girl under control, Raízian."

Jorge ignored that and gently led Sonya down the crowded street. She didn't resist, but she still had that unnerving grin, which made Jorge very uneasy.

19

It was a brilliant idea. Or a terrible one. Sonya couldn't decide which.

"Is everything okay?" Jorge looked apprehensive for some reason.

"You said before that there's no way I could get the empire out of Izmoroz on my own."

"Well, perhaps I meant—" he began.

"You said I'd be like a fly bothering a horse."

He winced. "I might have said that."

"And you're right. I've been striking at the empire as hard as I can for more than a year now and they haven't even noticed. Not a wanted poster or anything, which is a little discouraging."

"I'm sorry, you *want* to be a hunted fugitive?" asked Jorge.

"Maybe, just a little," she said. "You have to admit, it would be impressive. Anyway, my point is, I can't do this alone. I need help."

"But who could help? You said yourself that the other Rangers are probably all dead. All that's left are peasants, most of whom have little experience fighting, and no weapons, armor, or magic."

"Right. Which is why I was thinking of looking outside Izmoroz for help."

His eyes narrowed. "I thought you were merely antagonizing that priest, but you were genuinely asking about the Uaine?"

"The empire is clearly terrified of them. They've got my brother all worked up about it. He's convinced he's going to 'save' Izmoroz from an invasion—as if we haven't already been invaded, but whatever. And their priests are trying to work up a panic among the commoners about it, too. Clearly, they're gearing up for some kind of conflict, and they want to make sure the people of Izmoroz are on their side. Why would they care, unless they're concerned the Uaine might actually liberate Izmoroz from the empire!"

"You're making a pretty big leap there," said Jorge. "They might just take Izmoroz for themselves."

"I know, I know," she said impatiently. "But even if they aren't planning on liberating us, maybe I could strike a deal with them."

"What sort of deal could you offer them?"

"I could convince them that what they *really* want to do is invade Aureum. After all, Izmoroz is poor! Why would they want us?"

"It's not *that* poor," objected Jorge.

"Really? Have you seen much of it outside Gogoleth?"

"Well, no . . ."

"Trust me. It isn't nice like this. Anyway, if I convince the Uaine to go after Aureum, we could offer to let them use Izmoroz as a staging area for an invasion. Then they would be all set to go after the richest prize on the continent."

He looked skeptical. "And you could deliver that? The rest of Izmoroz would honor your offer to let them station a force here?"

She tried not to take offense to that. "Look, you're Raízian, so you don't really get it. Once we get rid of the empire and the people are allowed to worship the Lady Marzanna again, they'll look to Rangers for guidance like they did before the empire got here. If I tell them it's a good idea to help out the Uaine, they will."

He did not seem convinced. "If you say so . . ."

"And that's not all I would offer them," continued Sonya. "The empire won't expect them to invade before spring because they think crossing the tundra during winter is impossible."

"Isn't it?" asked Jorge.

"Not for a Ranger. I could teach the Uaine how to make a winter crossing, before the empire is ready. Help them launch a surprise attack."

Jorge still looked skeptical. "Okay, fine. Maybe you convince them. Or maybe since they are blue-skinned, spike-headed demons with an army of the undead, they just decide to kill you."

"I'm pretty hard to kill," said Sonya. "And even harder to keep dead."

"What does *that* mean?"

"It doesn't matter. The point is, I have to take that chance."

"Why?" Jorge looked like he was getting upset, though she had no idea why. He began pacing back and forth, his thick black eyebrows furrowed. "Why do you have to do *any* of this?"

"Because I swore an oath to the Lady Marzanna, and if I don't uphold that oath..." Sonya shook her head. She loved the Lady. She truly did. But Mikhail had told her some terrifying stories of the few Rangers who had broken their oaths. "Let's just say, there are fates far worse than death."

"Wait. You're telling me that this Lady Marzanna is...real? Like a real magical entity?"

"Of course. That's how I'm alive. Your Master Velikhov didn't actually save me. She did. That moment he thought I might be dead? I was."

Jorge's eyes were wide. "You...defied death?"

Sonya shook her head. "I *serve* Death. That's who Lady Marzanna is. And she decided I hadn't adequately fulfilled my oath to her, so she sent me back." Sonya brushed her hair back to show her ears. "The price for that boon was my human ears. Every time you ask something of her, she takes a part of your humanity and replaces it with something else. Something...well, let's just say it's not human."

Jorge seemed a little overwhelmed by all this. Maybe Sonya should have eased him into it all a little more gently.

"What..." He cleared his throat. "What does your Lady Marzanna do with the human parts?"

Sonya frowned. That question had never occurred to her. "Hell if I know. She never said. Anyway, I appreciate that you care, Jorge, but I swore an oath to get the empire out of Izmoroz so that people can worship the Lady freely again. Can you think of some other way to make that happen?"

"Well . . . I mean, not right this moment," he said. "But surely given enough time, we'll think of something."

"Nope. Sorry, Jorge. I'm not waiting around for some vague future promise. I found a solution and I'm running with it."

"You're leaving *now*?"

"Well, I thought I might stay with you one last night so I can try those emerald dandies you were talking about. But I'm leaving tomorrow at first light."

As soon as she said that, she felt a vast weight lift from her shoulders. A weight she hadn't even realized was there. Yes. She needed to get out of this suffocating, imperial-pandering city and back to the *real* Izmoroz. She had been here too long.

But Jorge looked at her with a sorrowful expression. "Is there anything I could do or say to convince you not to do this?"

"Nope."

The two stood there in the courtyard in silence as a gentle snow began to fall.

Finally, Jorge sighed. "Shall we go inside out of the cold?"

She shook her head. "You go on. I'm not ready to go back in there yet."

He nodded and reached for the front door. Then he paused. "Will you promise to say goodbye before you leave?"

"Don't worry, I'm not going to duck out on you like last time." She grinned. "If nothing else, you still have my saddlebags."

He gave her an even sadder smile. "Yes, of course."

Sonya stood in the courtyard and watched him enter the college and close the door behind him. She briefly wondered if there was something else troubling him. Then a snowflake landed on her nose, and all she wanted to do was stand with the snow falling all around her. The courtyard was much too sheltered. She needed to be higher.

She took her time, making her way more carefully than usual, not wanting to undo all the hard work Velikhov had put into getting her back into shape. Her bare hands were almost numb from grasping the cold black stones of the building by the time she made it to the slanted slate-covered roof.

She put her heels on the gutter edge and leaned back so that she was angled up toward the darkening sky as the snow began to fall more heavily. The air was crisper up there, the scents less muddied. She really had been too long in the city. It couldn't have been helped, of course, but there had been many moments these last few days when she'd felt a restless frustration creeping up within her, like a tiger pacing in its cage.

She closed her eyes. *Yes*, she thought. *Like an animal.* Mikhail had said that with each "gift" of the Lady, it became more difficult to rein in one's instincts. To keep the animal at bay. That was why he had only ever asked one boon of her. When the empress ordered that all Rangers be put to death, Mikhail asked the Lady to change his appearance, and paid for that boon with his human heart. That had been the only time he had asked the Lady for a boon in the many years he had served her. He had seen other Rangers lose themselves completely to their animal aspect and did not want to follow them into madness. He had urged Sonya to follow the same course. To never be too reckless or greedy, to never give *too* much of herself to the Lady.

Was Sonya being too reckless now? Were her thoughts already growing muddied with the instincts of the wild? It was impossible to say for certain, and second-guessing herself all the time would only drive her to distraction. She needed to stay focused and fulfill her oath.

Then she heard a soft scrape of shoe leather on cedar. She looked up and saw a figure in a gray wool cloak huddled on the rooftop of the next building over. Sonya was surprised that she could hear something so faint from such a distance. Perhaps her new ears had enhanced her hearing even further.

She watched the figure, idly wondering if the person was enjoying the snowfall as much as she was. She saw him slowly sit up and caught a glint of gold buttons and a green jacket beneath the cloak. Then he unwrapped a small crossbow from a wool scarf.

An imperial assassin? Maybe they *had* noticed her efforts after all.

She was vaguely aware that a little saliva leaked from the corner of her mouth as she leapt to her feet and sprinted across the slanted roof toward the assassin. He clearly had not expected her to rush him, and in his panic, he fired off a shot that went wide. Then he turned and ran, slipping and nearly falling off the roof as he fled.

Sonya easily cleared the gap between rooftops, while the assassin balked at jumping to the next. As she drew near him, everything else dropped away. All she saw was the sweat trickling down his temple, and the thud of his pulse in his neck. All she smelled was the sweet-salty tang of his panic. The thrill of the hunt burned in her veins as she licked her lips and pulled her long knife from its sheath.

The sight of her grinning, hungry visage terrified the assassin, and he finally jumped for the next roof. He caught hold of the edge, but was still hauling himself up when she landed on top of him. Her heels slammed down onto his forearms. She felt the bones of one arm give under impact and he screamed.

He began to fall, but she caught him and hauled him back up to the roof.

"Please . . . ," he whimpered.

He began blubbering about something, but all she could hear now was the hammer of his frightened heart as she held him close.

"One day I will return as you now return," she whispered in his ear. "Until then, I will travel light."

She drew her knife across his throat and felt the warm blood splash onto her hands and face. Then she laid her ear against the side of his neck so she could hear the frantic beat of his pulse peter out and grow still.

At last she released him and tilted her head back so that the falling snow cooled her hot face. She inhaled the smell of blood and piss and death that now permeated the air. The scent of victory.

During Sonya's initiation, Lady Marzanna had named her *Lisitsa*, which was the word for a female fox in Old Izmorozian. Foxes were cunning, swift, and without mercy. Perhaps Sonya really was becoming more fox-like in mind as well as body. But in that moment she did not care. Because it felt glorious.

20

Jorge was, on the whole, a sensible young man. Back in Raíz, his older siblings were known for their fiery passion and intense drive. Perhaps for that reason, Jorge had always striven to maintain a certain equilibrium. But after his conversation with Sonya, he was finding such composure extremely difficult to maintain.

He sat at the lab table, determined to get back to what he *should* be doing, working on his proposal, which the College of Apothecary had so generously accepted. That should be enough for him. A week ago, it *had* been enough for him. In fact, it had probably been the most quietly satisfying year of his entire life. But now? He didn't know what had changed. Or rather, he *did* know, but he didn't understand why. And that made it all the more frustrating.

Grinding up the alpine rose was actually somewhat satisfying. Taking the pestle and grimly crushing the delicate petals against the bottom of the mortar had a slow, implacable rhythm to it that suited his mood nicely. But once he had to focus on the careful measurements and precise timing of adding each ingredient at just the right temperature, skimming the froth off now and then without disturbing the sediment at the bottom...it taxed his patience to the point that he could barely restrain himself from flinging everything across the room.

"Jorge, my boy," called Master Velikhov from his habitual resting spot in the ancient overstuffed chair.

Jorge did not appreciate yet another interruption, and it was only a lifetime of being taught to respect his elders that enabled him to keep his tone civil. "Yes, Master?"

"Come sit by me."

Jorge closed his eyes and took a deep breath. He let the air out slowly, then said, "Yes, Master."

He made his way over to the sofa beside Velikhov, careful to keep his expression neutral. Once he sat down, his master gazed at him thoughtfully for a moment, tugging at his long, gray beard.

"Something is troubling you, my boy."

Jorge bowed his head. "Yes, Master. I apologize for not being in my usual good humor."

"There is no need to apologize," said Velikhov. "But I would appreciate it if you unburdened yourself to me. My responsibilities as your mentor do not end with the art of apothecary. So please, tell me what troubles you so much."

"Sonya is a reckless fool!" burst out Jorge.

"Well, yes, I would say that is fairly obvious," said Velikhov. "But I think in that respect she is refreshingly honest and makes no claim to be otherwise. So why does it suddenly bother you this much?"

"She has taken it into her head to throw her life away in pursuit of an impossible goal," said Jorge.

"What is this impossible goal?" asked Velikhov.

Jorge paused. Even though he was furious with Sonya, he didn't want to betray her confidence. "My apologies, Master. I do not think I am at liberty to share the details. But I can at least say that while her quest may be noble, it is foolhardy and will most likely end in her death."

"Oho!" Velikhov sat up. "A quest, is it? Perilous adventure? Travel to distant and dangerous lands?"

"Er...I suppose you could describe it like that..." Jorge had never seen his master's eyes sparkle quite like they did now.

The old man chuckled and gave Jorge a knowing smile. "It may be difficult to imagine, but I was not always the dull and complacent old apothecary you see before you."

"Master, I would not call you dull—"

Velikhov waved his hand dismissively. "Believe me, I'm happy to be so. At least now I am. Because I *had* my adventures when I was a young man." He leaned back in his chair and his eyes drifted toward the ceiling. "Ah, I would have followed Fyodor Atlasov anywhere. To the very shores of the Eventide River, if he'd asked. Such terrors we faced, but also such wonders!"

He grew silent for a moment, seemingly lost in old memories from a life Jorge could never have imagined. Then he looked at Jorge again, and his eyes were sharp and knowing.

"Tell me, are you mad at Sonya for going, or at yourself for not following?"

"Me? Follow her on this doomed quest?"

"It might be less doomed if you were there," said Velikhov.

"But..." Jorge struggled to voice the conflict within himself. "What about my studies? My training as an apothecary?"

Velikhov leaned over and smacked Jorge's knee. "It's called field-work, my boy! Do you think I became the world's preeminent apothecary on healing potions by sequestering myself my whole life in a stuffy college apartment?"

"Well..." That actually was what Jorge had thought.

"It's because my Fyodor was at least as reckless as your Sonya, and it seemed a day did not go by that I wasn't healing some sort of injury, often with limited means and in challenging environments. Such life-or-death experiences, where improvisation and ingenuity are essential, were invaluable to my development as an apothecary. I have no doubt that wherever Sonya leads you, it will be dangerous. She has the look of someone who thrives on such situations. And if that is more than you are willing to risk, you are welcome to remain here at the college and become the competent apothecary I have no doubt you can be. Or you could risk everything in order to become the greatest apothecary of your generation."

"Master..." Jorge knew which he wanted as soon as the options were laid out like that, but it almost felt unfair somehow. "How could I possibly refuse such a challenge?"

Velikhov chuckled. "Besides, what won't we do for love, eh?"

"L–love, Master?" Jorge's voice was embarrassingly shrill.

Velikhov laughed even harder. "Never mind, my boy. I'm only teasing. So you'll go?"

Jorge sighed. "I suppose I must. Not just for her sake, but for my own."

Velikhov slowly stood. "I think such courage deserves a reward of some sort, and fortunately I know just the thing."

He tottered slowly out of the room, leaving Jorge behind to contemplate the radical decision he had just made without a moment's hesitation. He'd barely survived a trek through Bear Shoulder Pass, and now he intended to accompany Sonya across the Great Western Tundra in the dead of winter into unknown lands to beg the aid of a mysterious people?

He'd promised his parents that he would not take any unnecessary risks. Did this count as a *necessary* risk? Certainly they wanted him to become the best apothecary he could be and bring honor to the Elhuyar name, didn't they? He would need to explain to them why they would not be receiving any letters from him for a while. He didn't wish to deceive his parents, but perhaps in his final letter before he departed, he would be … vague on the details and simply call it "fieldwork" as his master had suggested.

"Here we are!" Velikhov returned carrying a large, stiff rectangular leather backpack. He set it down upright on the table and unfastened the latches on the sides. The backpack opened up to reveal narrow shelves with vials, pouches, and a small, exquisite oil burner. "This is the mobile apothecary lab I took on my travels with Fyodor Atlasov. I will allow you to take it with you on your own travels."

"Master." Jorge approached the ingeniously made mobile lab, his eyes filled with wonder. "I cannot accept such a generous gift—"

"Nonsense, my boy. Besides, it's not a gift, it's a loan. So you must be sure to live long enough to return it to me once your quest is complete. Do you understand?"

"I understand completely, Master Velikhov. And I thank you for your generosity and wisdom."

"Well, I expect Sonya will want to leave sooner rather than later, so you had better make your preparations. And be sure to stock up on fresh ingredients while you have them readily available. Some of those vials haven't been opened in half a century."

Jorge went to work immediately, refreshing the mobile lab's supplies, and adding oil to both the burner and the spare oil jar. Then he sat down and wrote his final letter to his parents, apologizing that they would not be receiving his customary monthly letters for an extended period, but promising he would try to send word from "the field" whenever he could share in his discoveries.

He was just finishing when Sonya returned to the apartment, looking oddly relaxed. Almost lethargic. She flopped down on the sofa with a contented smile and closed her eyes.

Jorge walked over to the sofa and cleared his throat, but she didn't open her eyes.

"Sonya, I've made a decision."

She opened one eye. "Don't try to talk me out of this plan, Jorge."

"On the contrary, I would like to come with you."

She opened both eyes and sat up. "Are you serious?"

"Well, yes..." His resolve wavered in the heat of embarrassment. "That is, if it's okay..."

"Sure it is!" she said. "But why do you want to come?"

"Oh, er..." He suddenly recalled Velikhov's knowing smile and comment about love, and his face reddened. "You are very reckless, Sonya, and if you are going to be constantly injuring yourself, I should be there to make healing potions for you."

21

Galina read aloud in her soft, lilting voice, "'When I saw that tender shoot unfurl triumphantly through the snow, I at last saw the beautiful hand of Lady Zivena at work. O glorious Maiden of Spring, why must your bounty always be presaged by the death and suffering of your sister, Winter?'"

Sebastian had never been particularly enamored with the works of Konstantin Zhukov. But now, as he lounged on a bench in the gardens of Roskosh Manor with the rare winter sun bathing his face and Galina reading from the author's famous prose poem, *Hopeless, Victorious*, Sebastian thought the man a genius.

"Thank you for sharing that passage, Galina Odoyevtseva," he said. "I'm afraid I had not given Zhukov the attention he deserves."

Galina sat on the bench opposite him, her long hair seeming to glow as sunlight caught the wispy edges. She gently closed the book and laid it on her narrow lap, then treated Sebastian to one of her melancholy smiles.

"His form is at times inconsistent," she said. "But for me that only heightens the vulnerability of his sentiment. Much is made of perfect men and their unbreakable resolve, but I believe true courage derives from honesty and the acceptance of one's own foibles."

"It is not an easy thing to accept one's flaws," Sebastian said. "But I find my own disquiet greatly assuaged while in your tender presence."

Sebastian had been calling upon Galina every day since they met, partly because her presence did indeed soothe him, and partly to avoid the thing that troubled him most: fulfilling Vittorio's expectations of performing magic with "military application."

After a pause, Galina Odoyevtseva asked, "Sebastian Turgenev, will you share the worries that afflict you? Perhaps in doing so, you will be able to enjoy that ease beyond our brief times together."

"I don't wish to burden you," he said.

Her smile took on a surprisingly playful, almost teasing air. "Though my shoulders be slight, they can bear more weight than you might think."

"Well…" It was tempting to unburden himself to Galina. But he knew that proper soldiers were not plagued by doubts regarding their commanding officer's orders. Or if they were, they certainly did not confess such doubts to a charming young lady they admired.

Galina leaned across the gap between benches and laid her soft hand on the back of his. The warmth of her touch made his pulse quicken and his face feel hot.

As if seeing directly into his heart, she said, "You need not play the heroic savior of Izmoroz with me, Sebastian. Such tedious posturing is surely exhausting to one of your sensitive nature, and you should save such efforts for the barracks. I ask that when you are with me, you only be yourself."

This was the first time she had used only his given name. It was a bold acknowledgment of the growing familiarity he had been fervently hoping was growing between them. But it was also a challenge in a way. A clear statement that if he wished to maintain this intimacy, he must risk his heart and be honest with her.

He laid his hand on top of hers, feeling the hardness of her knuckles on the pads of his fingers. The heat on his face and neck increased and he could not quite meet her gaze as he spoke. "To me, magic has always been a means of communing with nature. Of sharing in its beauty and delight. I admit I sometimes feel a desire to show off. To bring forth something spectacular, you know? But never something destructive. Yet it seems that to save the empire, I must turn nature against itself. I must use the elements of life to destroy life so that I might protect life. I...cannot seem to reconcile this in my heart."

Once he finished speaking, he was at last able to look at her, his throat tight as he tried to gauge her reaction to his confession.

Keeping their hands joined, she moved over and sat beside him on the same bench. "It is a terrible dilemma you wrestle with, and you are right to be troubled by it. I would be a fool to think I could offer you a solution, but you may rely upon my support and comfort."

"Galina, I..." Emotion choked his voice. She had offered her sympathy without judgment or hesitation. He took a deep, shaking breath, praying that the tears in his eyes did not break loose. "I am so lucky to have met you."

"And I you."

They sat there holding hands, and stared into each other's eyes for some time. In that moment, Sebastian could not think of anything but her peerless beauty and tender heart. He could have sat like that all day. But then someone nearby cleared their throat. Sebastian and Galina both started and looked over to see Galina's maid, Masha.

"Apologies for the interruption." She bowed to them. "Lieutenant Portinari, Commander Vittorio wishes to speak with you immediately. If you will please follow me, I will take you to him."

"Ah." The warm glow Sebastian had been feeling now fled. "Thank you, Masha." He turned back to Galina. "I..."

"You must do your duty, Sebastian," she said. "I look forward to your next visit."

"As do I, Galina."

He stood and followed Masha out of the garden. He expected her to take him back to the study where he and Vittorio had spoken on the first day they met. It seemed to be his favorite room in the manor. But instead they found him in one of the many parlor rooms. It was the largest one, and contained a grand piano, as well as a number of sofas and chairs. Despite the numerous places to sit, Vittorio stood gazing out the window, his hands clasped behind his back.

"Lieutenant Portinari, as requested, Commander," said Masha.

The commander did not turn around. "Thank you, Masha. You may go."

Masha quickly left, perhaps sensing the tension between the two men that now filled the room.

Sebastian decided he might as well accept whatever punishment awaited him. He gave a sharp salute, even though Vittorio's back was to him. "I must apologize, Commander. I have been shirking my duties."

"I noticed," he said dryly, still not turning around. "And now I see why."

"Sir?"

"Come here." His tone was firm, but not harsh.

Sebastian's gait was awkward and self-conscious as he strode over to the commander. He looked first at Vittorio, then followed his gaze through the window out to the garden, where Galina could plainly be seen, still sitting on the same bench, now intently reading *Hopeless, Victorious*.

"She possesses a singular beauty," said Vittorio. "Perhaps not conventional, but captivating in a way that is uniquely her own. And as we recently learned, when necessary she can express herself most eloquently. I admire your choice."

"Sir, I—"

Vittorio held up his hand and Sebastian was silent. "A soldier is not a monk, Lieutenant. It is natural and healthy that you take an interest in such a remarkable young woman. Especially in such trying times, a woman can give comfort to a man's troubled heart like no one else."

The commander must have seen Galina comforting Sebastian just now. His face reddened at the idea, but decided it would be best to remain silent, no matter how embarrassing or uncomfortable it might get.

"And rest assured," continued Vittorio, "it has not escaped my attention that your heart *is indeed* troubled. It was evident to me that you did not share my feelings of triumph regarding our first successful test of offensive magic. That concerned me at first, but then I realized that I may have underestimated the profound influence your father has had on you."

"My...father?"

"When my men invaded your home, you could have easily driven them off with magic, yet you did not."

"My father would not let me."

"He preferred to die rather than allow you to use your magic in a violent way."

"I hadn't really thought of it like that, sir, but I suppose that could be true."

"Was he noble for doing so, or merely naive?"

"I...don't know, sir."

"Of course not. Because much as we would like to have clear answers to such challenging questions, there rarely are. You have a soaring intellect and generous heart, Lieutenant. I have no doubt that those qualities will one day make you an excellent leader. But for now, you are a soldier, and such vast philosophical questions will only hamper you. There is but one thing you need to concern yourself with at present."

"Wh-what is that, sir?"

"Look at that beautiful girl, sitting serenely in her garden of plenty. See how the sunlight rests gently on her fair countenance as she engages in that noblest of pursuits, the betterment of the mind. Would you want anything to disturb her?"

"No, sir."

"No?" Vittorio continued in a mild voice. "What about a horde of the undead spilling over the garden wall to assault her delicate frame? Imagine their skeletal fingers piercing her pale, tender flesh as they dine gluttonously upon her entrails. Imagine her screams of unbearable agony and horror. Would you allow that?"

Sebastian could only stare at the commander, who spoke so calmly of such a horrific scene.

At last Vittorio turned to him, his eyes burning with passion. "Wrestling with doubt and conscience is all well and good in times of peace, Lieutenant. But make no mistake, we are preparing for war, and that makes our choices very simple. We protect those we love by *any means* at our disposal, or we allow them to suffer terribly and die. Soldiers in wartime do not have the luxury of moral quandaries."

"I . . . see, sir."

"Look upon this peaceful maiden. Fix her image in your mind so that you may call upon it whenever doubt or worry begins to take hold, and remind yourself that the time may come when your hard work and unflinching resolve are the only things that stand between this young woman and an army of cruel and ravenous undead."

Sebastian turned and gazed at Galina Odoyevtseva Prozorova through the window. He had only known her a short while, but already he felt as if she understood him better than anyone else he'd ever known. The idea of not getting to know her more, of not being able to spend more time with her, seemed unbearable. He would protect her at any cost.

Part Two

The Wizard of Gogoleth

"And what of magic, that most alluring, frightening, and mysterious of arts? Perhaps we are fools to think that our will shapes such power. Could it not instead be the unknowable source of magic's power that shapes our will?"

—Pedro Molina, Raízian author of the play *Tonight, We Dance*, in a speech given at the Colmo College of Arts and Magic

22

Like many who traveled to Izmoroz from other countries, Jorge had taken the Advent Road that stretched north from Raíz, through the western region of Aureum, and cut up through the middle of Izmoroz to terminate at Gogoleth. The road was well traveled and scrupulously maintained by the empire, with imperial hostels placed evenly along its entire length. As such, Jorge had not actually seen much of Izmoroz during that journey.

Once Jorge had arrived at Gogoleth, his studies had kept him so busy, he had not had the opportunity to see much beyond the immediate surroundings of the city. In fact, when he'd crossed through Bear Shoulder Pass looking for foxtail, it was the farthest he'd ever gone from the city. In truth, he had not felt compelled to see more. Like most people from elsewhere, he thought of Izmoroz as comprising two things: the venerable city of Gogoleth, and the untamed and often inhospitable wilderness.

But now that he was traveling with Sonya, Jorge began to see that to know only Gogoleth was hardly to know Izmoroz at all.

They reached the small town of Vesely, a few weeks' travel northwest of Gogoleth on horseback, when Sonya decided she could don her Ranger garb without drawing unwelcome attention. Although Jorge discovered that out there they could count on a great deal of welcome attention.

It began with the children. From the moment Jorge and Sonya led their horses onto the frozen mud roads of the village, young people began spilling out of the small, sturdy wooden homes, skipping and jumping as they followed along beside them.

"Ranger! Ranger! Will you stay with my family tonight?" asked one shrill blond girl in a bedraggled fur wrap.

"She stayed with your family last time, Tasha!" objected a boy with red hair whose voice was beginning to squeak and warble with the onset of manhood. "Ranger, you should stay with *my* family this time! My mother makes such good food, you'll cry with joy!"

"*My* family has the softest beds in all Vesely!" claimed another boy.

"No, they don't," said the first boy. "Your beds are just like everyone else's!"

"No, they aren't," protested the second. "My father treats the hay so that it's soft as wool!"

"No, he doesn't!" said the first.

Sonya didn't reply, but only smiled and looked fondly down at the children as they rode through the village. She seemed to enjoy the attention.

Vesely was not large, and they soon reached the center of the village where several adults appeared to be waiting for them. An old man with long gray hair and wearing a long fur robe stepped forward and bowed his head to Sonya.

"You honor us with your presence, *Strannik* Sonya," he said in a quavering voice.

"It's good to be back, *Dedushka* Yuri," she said. "I can always count on a warm welcome here."

"How may we assist you?"

"My friend and I are just passing through on our way to the tundra."

The old man's eyes widened. "The tundra? At this time of year?"

She shrugged, as if it was nothing to be concerned about. Jorge was of course still very concerned.

"A Ranger goes where she likes" was all she said.

"Of course, honored *Strannik*. If you are staying the night, I'm happy to say that you arrived on *banya* day."

"Bathing day? That *is* lucky!" Sonya turned to Jorge. "I'll bet you've never experienced a traditional Izmorozian bathhouse, huh?"

"Eh, no, I haven't." In fact, he hadn't realized that there was any sort of bathhouse tradition in Izmoroz. The baths he had taken at the college had all been in a small, individual tub within the apartment.

She squeezed his shoulder enthusiastically. "Oh, you're going to love it. I promise, you'll feel like a new man after."

"Oh. Great." Jorge had a number of questions, one of which was whether bathing here was so rare, it was thought of as a special treat.

"So when's it start?" Sonya asked Yuri.

"The rocks have been heating since this morning, *Strannik* Sonya. If you would like to join my family for supper, the baths should be ready by the time we finish."

"Then by all means, lead the way, *dedushka*!" said Sonya.

Sonya and Jorge dismounted from their horses. When Sonya gave the reins of her horse over to a patient, middle-aged man, she had a great many instructions on how her Peppercorn was to be treated, and Jorge suppressed his amusement at her uncharacteristic seriousness. He suspected that the creature was not merely a means of travel to her, but also a traveling companion. During their journey, he'd caught her more than once whispering quietly to the horse in the same way he had spoken with the family cat at home in Colmo.

Jorge and Sonya followed Yuri into one of the wooden homes. It was pleasantly warm inside, with a small stone firepit crackling in the center. A large cast-iron pot bubbled over the pit and wooden benches surrounded it.

"Please, sit," said Yuri. "The food will be ready soon."

Sonya and Jorge sat on the benches while Yuri spoke to an old woman in a kerchief whom Jorge thought might be his wife. They talked in anxious tones and Jorge wondered if he and Sonya were being an imposition on them. After all, they hadn't been expecting company. Did they even have enough food?

"I must go and arrange some things," said Yuri. "Please, allow Yelena to offer you a drink while you wait for my return."

Yuri hurried out and Yelena came over with small wooden cups.

"Ah, *Strannik* Sonya," said Yelena as she handed them the cups. "I see the Lady has already blessed you."

"Oh, yeah . . ." Sonya looked a little sheepish as she tucked her hair back so that her pointed ears were more evident. "I'm surprised you noticed."

Yelena chuckled. "It's also in the way you carry yourself, young one. I've been honored to know several Rangers in my long life, and the hand of the Lady marks them in more ways than one." She paused for a moment, then said, "Please don't be in too much of a hurry in asking for her favors."

Sonya smiled at her. "No, *babushka*. I promise."

Yelena patted her cheek. "That's what I like to hear. Now drink up."

The liquid in the cup appeared to be water, but when Jorge brought it to his mouth, he could smell that it was in fact a generous pouring of vodka. He glanced at Sonya, who drank it down in one gulp. Jorge wasn't much of a drinker, but his work with potion-making had already begun to dull his sense of taste. So he thought he could follow her lead without much trouble. But perhaps he had not taken into account the less refined distillation methods this far from Gogoleth, because it burned terribly going down, and he found himself blinking back tears.

When Sonya saw his face, she burst into laughter. She hooked one arm around his neck and drew him close. It was clearly meant affectionately, but she squeezed so hard, it was difficult for him to breathe.

"Yelena, this is my best friend, Jorge," she said, still not releasing her hold.

"Nice to meet you, Jorge," said Yelena.

"Likewise." Jorge rubbed his neck as Sonya finally released him.

He was struck by Sonya's pronouncement that he was her best friend. After all, they had only known each other a month. Perhaps it meant that he was her *only* friend. As affable as she was, it was clear she spent a lot of time alone, and if everyone in these villages treated her with such reverence, it might be difficult for her to make real connections with people.

"Ah! Where is my favorite *Strannitchka*!" came a rumbling voice outside. Then the door burst open and a round, bearded man in thick furs stomped in holding a steaming iron cauldron by the handles with his gloved hands. His eyes lit up when he saw Sonya. "There you are, baby Ranger! How I have missed that devilish smile!"

Sonya grinned at him, then turned to Yelena. "You see how Dima disrespects me?"

"I can't help myself!" declared Dima as he set down the iron cauldron. "A *Strannik* should be a terrifying servant of Death Herself! People should grovel and beg for mercy before you! But you are beloved by all you meet, as feisty as a pepper and as sweet as a plum. I ask you, what kind of Ranger is that?"

"The young kind," said Yelena gravely. "All too soon, these days will seem like a distant dream and you will not be able to imagine ever having spoken to her with such familiarity."

"All the more reason to enjoy it while I can!"

Dima lifted Sonya into a crushing hug that left her feet dangling in the air. Jorge was alarmed by the act, but Sonya had an oddly satisfied expression on her face so he said nothing. After all, it wasn't as if she needed him to stand up for her.

Once Dima set her back down, she asked in a teasing tone, "Are you drunk already, Dimishka?"

"Well, of course! It's bathing day, isn't it? My old man, rest his soul in the bosom of the Lady, said the only thing better than a scalding-hot bath is being drunk in a scalding-hot bath!"

Jorge was growing nervous about this bathing day activity. The word *scalding* seemed particularly worrisome. He hoped Dima was exaggerating, but feared he was not. Leave it to Izmorozians to turn a pleasant, relaxing activity into a test of courage and mettle.

"Drunk or not, thank you for coming, Dima," said Yelena.

He shrugged. "A Ranger has to keep up her strength, and you old people peck at crumbs like birds. My wife's cooking is exactly what she needs."

Sonya frowned. "What about your own family, Dima?"

"Yuri is working it out," he said. "A little from here, a little from there. Don't you worry, *Strannitchka*. It's bathing day. No one will go to bed with an empty stomach."

"Still, before we leave tomorrow morning, I'll go out and find you some game."

"We won't say no to that, will we, Yelena?" asked Dima.

"One does not say *no* to a Ranger of Marzanna," agreed Yelena.

"Now that's settled, let's eat!" said Dima.

Jorge found the food bland but filling, which he supposed was something he needed to get used to out in these less developed parts of Izmoroz. Eventually Yuri joined them, looking tired but pleased. They drank quite a bit of vodka, and Jorge, afraid to offend anyone, kept up as best he could.

Finally, Yuri said it was time for bathing.

Jorge looked nervously at Sonya. "How does this work, exactly?"

"Oh right. This is your first time! " She grinned, her cheeks flushed with drink. "It's simple. I'll show you."

"Sh-show me?"

Jorge let Sonya lead him out of the house and down the narrow road, with Yuri, Yelena, and Dima following behind. He'd heard that out in the more rural areas of Izmoroz, much of societal decorum was abandoned. If men and women bathed together, could he refuse? If he did, would he offend people? The Elhuyars were by no means the most religious family in Colmo, but even they had limits.

Much to Jorge's relief, and possibly a little to his disappointment as well, the large wooden structure Sonya led him to had separate entrances for men and women.

"Dimishka, you take care of Jorge," said Sonya. "He's from Raíz, and they don't do this down there, so ease him in gently."

"You can count on me, *Strannitchka*," Dima said. "Come on, Jorge. Let's go cook ourselves!"

"O-okay." Jorge had grave doubts that Dima understood the concept of easing someone into anything gently, but he followed the heavyset Izmorozian into the men's entrance.

It seemed as if every man in the village was there. The tub in the center of the room was massive but Jorge wasn't convinced they'd all be able to fit. Certainly not comfortably. And they were all stripping down naked as casually as if they were merely taking off their hat and coat, proudly showing large, pale, hairy bellies. Jorge was not accustomed to such casual nudity even among other men, but he forced himself to strip down as well, keenly aware of how thin, hairless, and brown he was by comparison.

As he feared, the water was painfully hot. And with so many men climbing in at the same time, easing in slowly was not possible. He gritted his teeth and followed behind Dima and Yuri, feeling as though his skin would be boiled off the bone at any moment. He was grateful for the vodka, which he suspected at least dulled the pain somewhat.

Since Yuri was the village elder, others respectfully made way for him, allowing the three a slightly less crowded section of the tub that was closest to the wall that divided them from the women's bath. They sat side by side on the narrow ledge that lined the inside of the tub. Jorge was just beginning to acclimate to the heat and embarrassment when he heard a female voice.

"Ranger Sonya is here!"

He turned and realized that the dividing "wall" was merely a heavy leather curtain.

Dima laughed. "Don't get any ideas, Jorge."

He quickly turned back around. "N-no, of course not."

Another female voice said, "Oh, Ranger Sonya! How did you get that scar?"

"Aha!" came Sonya's voice, sounding pleased that she'd been asked the question. "This was from when I wrestled the great Bear spirit during my initiation. Hooked me with one of his terrible claws right in my belly!"

Dima nudged Jorge and gave him a knowing look. "It does fire the imagination, though, doesn't it?"

"Oh, I . . . well . . ."

Dima laughed again. "I never met a Raízian before, Jorge, but you seem all right. What're you doing in Izmoroz?"

"I'm studying at the College of Apothecary in Gogoleth," he said.

"Oh." Dima nodded. "I hear it's real nice there."

"You've never been?"

"Why would I go? Nothing but imperials and their lackeys."

"There are actually quite a few Izmorozians in Gogoleth," said Jorge.

Dima snorted. "Nobles suckling at the teat of the empire."

"I'm fairly certain it's more than just nobility."

"That's worse then. Common folk joining up with the empire?"

Yuri, who had remained silent until then, spoke up. "Have a more forgiving heart, Dima. Many have no choice. A soldier's pay can feed a lot of bellies back in their home village."

Dima grunted, then nodded slightly, as if grudgingly admitting the point.

Yuri turned to Jorge. "Some years, Lady Zivena blesses us with a bountiful harvest, and the cost of the empire's tithes are not too difficult to bear. Some years, Lady Zivena does not see fit to bless us so. Thankfully, Ranger Sonya brought back our tithe this year after the empire had claimed it."

"Was that why you were so adamant on feeding her this evening?"

Dima chuckled. "You *always* feed a *Strannik*, unless you want to displease the Lady Marzanna, and none of us can afford to do that. It's bad enough that we cannot pray to her in public anymore."

"I'd never even heard of Lady Marzanna before I met Sonya, and I'd been living in Gogoleth for over a year," said Jorge.

"There are many ways to conquer a people," said Yuri. "You can force them to submit by the sword, but that will only get you so far. To truly conquer them, you must make them forget who they are. Little by little, they chip away at what it means to be Izmorozian. My children remember. My grandchildren know the stories. But how well will my great-grandchildren know them? And their children? Unless something changes, there will one day be no such place as Izmoroz."

Jorge was embarrassed to admit, even to himself, that he'd never given much thought to such things.

After a moment, he said, "Well, at least you're still allowed to have these baths." Now that he had become more accustomed to the heat and nakedness, he could feel the water relaxing his muscles in a way he hadn't felt since leaving the college, as if soaking away weeks' worth of travel grime. "Or, sorry...*banyas*? Is that the right word?"

"You would be wise not to use that word in Gogoleth, I think," said Yuri. "But yes, we are grateful for the *banyas* and other small miracles we're allowed."

"A *banya* purifies the soul as well as the body," said Dima. "And those who bathe during winter find favor with Lady Marzanna and don't get sick."

"Interesting." Jorge could smell certain herbs and minerals in the water and wondered if that had something to do with the protection from illness. Was it some folk remedy that he could use in his apothecary work? Perhaps Master Velikhov's "fieldwork" was already paying off.

"Of course," continued Dima, "there is one more thing to do for it to be a true *banya*."

"What's that?"

"Why, cool off in the snow, of course!"

"Wait, what?"

Jorge watched with growing horror as the two men climbed out of the tub and made their way toward the door.

"Wait...," Jorge said again. "*Naked?*"

23

$\odot$n your way to Roskosh Manor, Lieutenant Portinari?"

Sebastian was about to climb into a carriage when he heard General Savitri Zaniolo's voice. He turned to see the thin, black-haired man strolling toward him, a pleasant smile on his face, but an odd gleam in his eyes.

"Good afternoon, General." Sebastian saluted him sharply.

Sebastian wasn't sure what to make of the general. He seemed a clever man. Perhaps a little unnervingly so. It was as if no matter what he said, he was also thinking something else. Commander Vittorio had told Sebastian that Zaniolo was, among other things, in charge of intelligence gathering for the imperial army in Izmoroz. Sebastian supposed that his unnerving presence might then merely be an unavoidable aspect of his job. In that case, the man could hardly be blamed for it.

"You've been spending a lot of evenings at Roskosh Manor lately, Lieutenant," said Zaniolo.

Sebastian could feel his cheeks reddening. "Oh, yes, well the commander said it was fine if—"

Zaniolo waved his hand dismissively. "I'm certainly the last person to criticize anyone for their preoccupation with the fairer sex, and Galina Odoyevtseva is one of the most striking beauties in all Izmoroz. Besides, I see you out there in the yard every day practicing your magic or assisting General Marchisio with cavalry drills. Your diligence puts a poor rogue like me to shame."

"With respect, General, Commander Vittorio speaks most highly of your invaluable contributions to the empire."

"He is too generous, I'm sure." Zaniolo's smile did not quite seem to reach his eyes, and once again Sebastian felt as though he did not know what the general's true thoughts were. Then he patted Sebastian's shoulder. "Well, good luck to you tonight, Lieutenant."

"Why would I need luck, sir?"

"Hadn't you heard? Lord Prozorova has returned from his travels. Tonight, you will dine with Galina Odoyevtseva's father for the first time, and I don't need to tell you what an *important* event that will be."

Sebastian felt a chill run down his spine. "I-important, sir?"

"Why yes. You have been courting Lord Prozorova's daughter for over a month without his consent, so you will have to work doubly hard to impress him now."

"I had not realized…that is to say, the word *courting* hadn't really…"

Zaniolo looked surprised. "Oh? Are you saying your interest in Galina Odoyevtseva is merely as friends? Fellow appreciators of literature?"

"Well, no…" Now Sebastian could feel his skin warming. Hot, cold, why couldn't he keep his emotions in check?

"Then, my boy, don't be disingenuous." He gripped both of Sebastian's upper arms and gave him a hard look. "Call it what it is, Lieutenant. A proper, gallant courtship."

"Y-yes, sir."

"And if I may speak frankly, you had better impress his lordship this evening if you wish to *continue* courting her. Do you take my meaning?"

Sebastian's throat felt dry and he had to swallow before he could respond. "Yes, sir."

Zaniolo beamed at him and this time the smile seemed quite genuine. "Wonderful. Now, go forth!" He spun Sebastian around and pushed him toward the carriage.

"Thank you, sir," Sebastian said over his shoulder. "I appreciate your advice."

"Not at all, Lieutenant. And do remember you represent the entire imperial army."

Sebastian froze, a foot on the first rung. "U-understood, sir..."

Zaniolo laughed. "I'm only teasing, Lieutenant. Now be off with you."

Sebastian tried not to fret too much during his ride to Roskosh Manor, but it was nearly impossible to refrain. He didn't even know what sort of man Lord Prozorova was. Surely an intellectual, if Galina was any indication. And perhaps a scholar, since Sebastian recalled that his lordship had been away all this time collecting legends and folklore throughout Izmoroz. Sebastian had always considered himself to be an intelligent person. Now, for the first time in his life, he wondered if he was smart enough. But how did one prove their intelligence without coming across as boorish and arrogant, or else desperately insecure?

By the time Sebastian reached Roskosh Manor, his anxiety was nearly at a fever pitch and his jaw was quite sore from tension.

"Lieutenant Portinari?" Masha stood in the doorway looking concerned. "Sir, is something the matter?"

"N-no, Masha. Th-thank you for your concern. May I see Galina?"

"Of course, sir. Right this way."

Sebastian followed Masha with a stiff gait. He knew he must relax. How could he impress Lord Prozorova if he couldn't even get out a clear sentence? But how did one force themselves to relax?

When he saw Galina sitting in her favorite drawing room, book in hand, the lamplight illuminating her long, golden hair, he felt his chest loosen. That's when he understood. One relaxed by finding comfort in the presence of those they trusted.

"Lieutenant Portinari to see you, miss."

Galina, though always sweet and gentle, was typically restrained with her affections. But when she heard Masha's announcement, she immediately came to her feet, pressing the closed book to her chest. Her large eyes sparkled with pleasure and her smile was so broad he could see her tiny, white teeth.

"Sebastian! How wonderful you're here!" she said. "I have a present for you!"

"A present? For me?" He had never given her a present. If he was courting her, shouldn't he have done that by now? Flowers at least? Why was he such a *fool*?

"You may go, Masha," said Galina.

"Yes, miss." The maid looked amused for some reason as she left.

"I'm sorry, Galina," said Sebastian. "I should have … why did I not consider a gift for you…"

She laughed. "Don't be silly. A true gift comes from knowing a person and wanting to help them in some way."

Sebastian knew she was trying to make him feel better, but it only made him feel worse. Did he not know her well enough? Why wasn't he constantly thinking of ways to help her?

"Dearest Sebastian." Her cool hand rested on his burning cheek. She seemed amused by his anguish. "Stop internally berating yourself so that I may give you this gift, or I shall become cross."

He took a deep breath and smiled sheepishly. "That is rather ungracious of me, isn't it?"

"Truly." But the sparkle of amusement remained in her eyes. "Now, several days ago, you were bemoaning the lack of knowledge that could be found on elemental magic. Do you recall?"

"I recall every word of every conversation we have ever had, Galina," he said earnestly.

She seemed to find that amusing as well. "As you should. Now, I happened to mention your quandary to my father and he reminded me of a book he had given me as a girl."

She held out the thick tome she had been clasping to her bosom. Sebastian accepted it and looked at the title on the spine.

"*The Age of Wizards?*" he asked.

"The title *wizard* is used by many cultures to refer to elemental magic users. It's apparently derived from the Aureum peasantry as a contraction of *wise lord*."

"I see." He began flipping through the pages. The paper was dry and delicate, suggesting it was quite old. An entire book about elemental magic users? Who knew what wisdom it might contain ...

"If I recall, it's a collection of various folktales and legends about elemental magic users found throughout the civilized world," said Galina. "That includes of course Izmoroz, Aureum, and Raíz, as well as the independent country of Kante, which lies to the east of Aureum. There's even a tale from a land south of Raíz across the Sea of Charmed Winds called Victasha that I confess I know little about."

"Astonishing ..." Sebastian didn't know what to say except, "Thank you, Galina. This ... this is a treasure to me."

Galina suddenly looked a little embarrassed herself now, a blush creeping onto her cheeks. "Yes, well, I doubt you'll find much *practical* information in there. But as my father says, folktales often focus on the underlying moral dilemmas we all face at some point in our lives. Perhaps you will find insight into your own internal struggles."

The warm glow of gratitude that had been building in Sebastian's chest was abruptly strangled by Galina's mention of her father. "Yes ... er ... Galina, what kind of man is Lord Prozorova?"

Galina gave him a long look, one eyebrow arched speculatively. "Is that what has you all twisted up? Meeting my father?"

He dropped his head. "I'm afraid so."

She took his chin between thumb and finger, then lifted his head. "I'm certain he will adore you."

"Truly?"

"Of course. Just don't be alarmed if he remains reserved, or even aloof, throughout supper. That's merely his nature. Answer any questions he puts to you with your habitual sincerity and I'm certain he will be pleased." She considered for a moment. "And perhaps only speak of military matters if he brings it up first. He is not ... overly interested in such things."

Sebastian sighed. "Just knowing that you have confidence in me soothes my anxious soul."

That evening, everything was exactly as Galina said. Lord Prozorova was a small man with a neatly trimmed beard, thick spectacles, and a detached, almost uninterested air. Had he not been warned,

Sebastian would have thought the man already loathed him. But now he could see it was merely the distraction of a great mind. Lord Prozorova did seem curious about Sebastian's thoughts on the connection between poetry and elemental magic, however. And, thankfully, Sebastian was savvy enough to mention how grateful he was for *The Age of Wizards*.

It all went by in such a blur, Sebastian could not have said what he ate or drank, and before he knew it, the ordeal was over and Galina was walking him to the door.

"Did…did I please him?" Sebastian asked, feeling somewhat dazed.

"The important thing, dear Sebastian, is that you pleased me," she said.

"O-of course, Galina!" he said quickly.

"But yes, I think he was quite satisfied. As am I."

She leaned forward and before he even understood what was happening, she pressed her soft, warm lips to his cheek. He stared at her, his eyes wide with wonder.

She smiled at him with wry amusement. "Good night, Lieutenant Portinari."

As Sebastian left Roskosh Manor, his hand pressed to his cheek, he walked three blocks in the wrong direction before realizing that he had left his carriage behind.

24

Sonya was alone in Izmoroz's lush pine forests. That was where she was happiest. She crouched low in snow that came nearly to her knees, blending into her surroundings. Her breath was slow enough that no telltale plume of steam escaped from her lips, and she held her newly carved bow with an arrow nocked but not drawn.

When the Lady Marzanna had first accepted her as a Ranger, it had taken weeks to adjust to her heightened senses. Every sound, every flicker of light, and especially every new smell, had stunned her as sharply as a blow to the face. Without Mikhail's patient guidance, she might never have learned to cope with the overwhelming amount of input she received. He was the one who taught her how to dampen it when necessary, when to allow it all in, and how to sort through it all when she did.

Now information streamed in through her senses. The flicker of shadow in the branches above, the crunch of snow, the hiss of the wind, the smell of fur, food, and scat. She did not consciously choose which to focus on, but instead allowed herself to simply exist with it all, floating down a stream of impressions that created a vast picture of the forest surroundings composed of the feedback from all her senses. By keeping such an image in her mind, she could easily tell when something new introduced itself.

The unexpected sharp crack of a stick echoed a hundred and fifty yards away. That was all it took for her to become aware of the lone caribou bull that drew near. Without turning toward the sound, she listened to him trudge through the snow, then begin to scrape the dense green lichen off a tree with his hoof.

So slowly that it would have been difficult for human eyes to observe, Sonya rotated her body around, drawing the arrow back as she did. The caribou's ear twitched as her new bow creaked, but her quarry didn't bolt.

The caribou was slightly quartering away from her, almost an ideal angle for a quick, clean kill. Or as quick and clean as it could be at a hundred and fifty yards. She took a slow breath, drew the rest of the way to her anchor point, aimed, then released her arrow on the exhale.

The faint twang of the bow was enough to alert the caribou. In the moment between when the arrow left her fingers and reached its target, the caribou bent his legs to spring away, which lowered his body and changed the height of the target point. Of course, Sonya had anticipated that movement and adjusted her aim accordingly. So the arrow pierced the caribou's side, punctured both lungs, and exited the other side. Muscles already coiled, the caribou leapt forward toward the nearest snow-covered thicket, but instead of landing gracefully, it crashed into thin, bare branches with a gurgling wheeze.

Sonya sprinted through the snowdrifts as fast as she could. When she reached the dying caribou, he was still thrashing and spilling red blood all over the white snow. She knelt down and gripped his muzzle. His wide eyes gazed up at her in mute suffering.

"One day I will return as you now return. Until then, I will travel light," she intoned. Then she quickly slashed his throat and ended his pain.

This was what separated her from the beasts, Sonya decided. She recognized that death was an essential part of existence, but needless suffering was not. Animal predators did not care at all if their prey suffered.

Once the caribou had bled out enough to not leave a trail behind, Sonya dragged him through the snow to where she had left a small sled. She secured the caribou, strapped on her snowshoes, and began the long trek back to the village of Zapad, where Jorge waited.

Zapad was the last village before the forest began its transformation into the vast tundra that comprised the westernmost region of Izmoroz, so Sonya and Jorge had stopped to rest and gather supplies. Preparation was perhaps the most essential aspect of crossing the tundra in winter.

Supplies were scarce, however. Zapad was the smallest, poorest, and most remote village in all Izmoroz. Even a humble village like Vesely or Istoki seemed quite comfortable by comparison. As Sonya dragged her caribou sled through the small village, children wrapped in torn furs appeared, their grimy faces eager for any break in the routine. They trailed along behind her like a pack of fox kits, throwing out a barrage of questions that she did her best to answer.

"Ranger, Ranger! Where'd you get that bull?"

"The forest."

"But it's winter. How'd you find any animals?"

"You have to look for the lichen. It's like a moss that caribou eat in the winter. It can grow on tree bark, rocks, or just about anything, even in winter."

"Do you know that because you're a Ranger?"

"Yes, but now you know it, too. Remember it for when you're old enough to hunt."

"When I'm old enough to hunt, will you marry me?"

She laughed. "Rangers don't marry. Our lives are already committed to the Lady Marzanna."

"Have you ever met her?"

"Lady Marzanna? Twice."

"Is she scary? My mom says she's terrible mean."

Sonya thought of the Lady's long, jagged fingers emerging from the black water of the Eventide River to tear off her ears.

"She can be. But she's also beautiful beyond description."

"Is that why you married her?"

Sonya smirked at that. She'd never thought of it that way, but the analogy wasn't entirely wrong. "Perhaps."

"Can *I* marry the Lady Marzanna and become a Ranger?" asked one little boy.

Sonya stopped and looked down at him. "Once we have driven the imperial invaders from our lands, I will make certain there are more Rangers. As for whether *you* could be one of them..." She raised an eyebrow and he shrank back. "That will depend on you. Never take the easy way with something, always help others, and always respect the gifts of nature. Do all of that, and you stand a good chance."

He grinned up at her, showing a large gap in front where he'd lost his baby teeth. "I will, Lady Ranger! I promise!"

She nodded and resumed dragging her caribou through the village. There really wasn't much to Zapad. Just a cluster of homes around a well, and a tannery a little set apart on the western edge where the tundra began. The buildings were all quite small and plain, but it was clear that a great deal of effort had gone into constructing them. That was how things usually were. People who had the least valued it the most. She thought back to the opulence she'd seen in Roskosh Manor, each room as big as one of these houses, yet most of them unused, except perhaps for the occasional social event. Once the empire was driven out of Izmoroz, her next focus would be on decreasing the sharp divide between the classes. The people only needed someone to lead them, then the nobility would see where the *real* strength of Izmoroz lay.

She stopped in front of the centermost building, which was where the village elder lived and where she and Jorge were staying while they made preparations for the next leg of their journey.

"What's all this?" She gestured to the line of people standing in the cold before the door.

"Your brown friend is making people better," said the boy who wanted to be a Ranger.

"My brown friend has a name. Jorge Elhuyar."

"Sorry...," the boy said sheepishly. "Jorge Elhuyar is making people better."

"He is, is he?" She smiled. "Watch this bull for me until I get back and I'll let you have the pelt."

The boy's eyes widened. At his size, that might be a whole new set of clothes. "You bet I will, Lady Ranger!"

Sonya eased her way past the line of people, who all bowed their heads respectfully to her. She opened the door, feeling the first true blast of warmth she'd felt all day, and slipped inside before it all escaped.

Jorge sat at a table in the center of the room with his travel apothecary lab opened. His dark brows were knit together in concentration as he mixed up some sort of tonic for the sallow-looking old woman who waited patiently nearby. Once he was satisfied, he sealed the clay jar with a piece of cork and handed it to her.

"One tiny sip a day. That should have you feeling better. At least for a while."

"Lady Zivena bless you, young man." She clutched the small jar as if it were gold and hurried out.

"What was wrong with her?" asked Sonya.

"Only malnutrition," he said sadly. "That's true of nearly all of them. I'm only giving them supplements."

"It's very kind of you."

"It's not enough."

"It'll get them through the rest of the winter. And then they'll be able to get proper nutrition."

"Until next winter." His tone was bleak.

"Yes," she agreed. "Still, I'm grateful you did what you could, and so are they."

It was clear that Jorge had lived a sheltered life even before he moved to Gogoleth. As they'd traveled from town to town, then village to village, she'd watched him observe the increase in poverty the farther they got from the imperial garrison with growing discomfort.

"In Raíz, those in need can request aid from the local imperial station," said Jorge. "But I haven't seen a single imperial soldier this far out, much less an actual station. It really does seem like they don't care about the people here. Why even bother annexing this land if you plan to let it languish?"

"Who knows what their empress thinks in her distant tower," said Sonya. "I'm sure she has little grasp of the plight my people suffer."

He was silent for a moment, staring at the door. "Perhaps that's true of a great many."

"I took down another caribou today. Once I strip the meat off it, we should have enough to start into the tundra."

Jorge nodded. "I better see to the rest of these people then."

25

It looked like the end of the world: Heavy purple clouds flashed furiously with lightning. The Sestra River boiled. The black crusty surface of the land beyond the river split open like a lanced boil and oozed seething orange-and-red lava.

It gave Sebastian no pleasure to know this all happened by his will, but he was at least satisfied that his hard work during the past couple of months had paid off. Anyone who dared threaten the peace of Galina Odoyevtseva would truly find Hell on earth.

He lifted the diamond and again focused his will into it. Once he released his intention, the skies cleared, the river settled down, and the earth beyond quieted. Of course there were new scars in the land that still glowed a sullen red. Fish that had cooked alive in the river now floated to the top. Regrettable but inevitable casualties of war, or so he'd been assured.

"Well, Commander, are you satisfied?" He glanced back at Vittorio, who stood over his left shoulder.

"I am." The curled tips of his mustache twitched with pleasure as he turned to the three generals who stood openmouthed behind him. "And what about you, gentlemen? I believe this is the first time you've witnessed a full demonstration of Lieutenant Portinari's power."

"Astonishing, Commander!" General Marchisio's eyes were wide as he stroked his thick beard.

"Yes, indeed!" said General Bonucci, his brow furrowed beneath his sweat-slicked scalp.

Unsurprisingly, General Zaniolo was able to maintain his composure. His eyes were narrow as he smoothed down his black hair. It was an unconscious habit that probably sprang from the fact that it had a tendency to curl up and reveal his baldness. Sebastian had noticed he usually did it when he was deep in thought and about to say something surprising.

"Truly, Commander. We are lucky to have the lieutenant." Zaniolo frowned thoughtfully. "Something occurs to me...I have seen this young man work diligently every day for months now, either on mastering his own awesome power, or assisting General Marchisio and General Bonucci so that he might better understand the complexities of military strategy. I wonder...have you considered promoting young Portinari here to the rank of captain?"

Vittorio's eyebrows rose. "An interesting suggestion. He is quite young, but I agree he could serve as a great inspiration to our troops." He turned back to Sebastian. "What do you think? Ready to take a more direct role in leadership?"

"If it will enable me to better protect the people of Izmoroz, I will accept any responsibility you deem me worthy of."

"Well said." Vittorio nodded. "Report to my quarters tomorrow morning and by the powers invested in me by Her Imperial Majesty, Empress Caterina Morante the First, I will officially bestow the rank of captain upon you."

Sebastian saluted sharply. "Thank you, sir. It is an honor."

"That is all, gentlemen. You are dismissed. Please return to your usual duties."

Once they dispersed, Sebastian made his way toward headquarters with Rykov following silently behind as usual. He felt fatigue from the demonstration, but he'd grown accustomed to that. A brief rest, a bit of broth, and he'd be completely recovered.

"Well, that should help out some," Zaniolo said quietly as he caught up with Sebastian.

"Sir?"

"A captain's pay is significantly higher than a lieutenant's," said Zaniolo.

"With respect, General Zaniolo, money doesn't hold much interest for me."

"A noble outlook, to be sure," said Zaniolo. "But I promise you that the Prozorova family cares about money a great deal, and it is plain to anyone with eyes and a knowledge of men's hearts that you care a great deal about Galina Odoyevtseva Prozorova."

"I'm...not sure how those two things are related, sir," admitted Sebastian.

"You have been officially courting Galina Odoyevtseva for some time now, have you not?"

"I have."

"As an Aureumian gentleman, I am not an expert on the customs of Izmorozian nobility. But my understanding is that it's high time you asked Lord Prozorova for her hand in marriage."

"M-marriage?" Sebastian nearly stumbled when he heard the word, as if the ground had dropped out beneath him. Rykov's hand shot out to steady him.

Zaniolo looked surprised. "Are you opposed to the idea?"

"Of course not!" said Sebastian. "It's just...I suppose I hadn't given it a great deal of thought."

They had reached headquarters by then. Zaniolo opened the door and gestured for Sebastian to enter first. "Were you planning to string the poor young woman along indefinitely?"

"Not at all!" Sebastian said as the two men walked side by side down the hall, Rykov following behind. "I care for no one else but her."

"That *is* a relief, since Galina Odoyevtseva has been patiently waiting to learn if you are serious in your suit, all the while no doubt turning away other potential suitors."

"Other potential suitors?" Sebastian stopped in his tracks, and his heart nearly did, too. Of course a woman as exquisite as Galina would be highly sought after. Why had that fact never occurred to him?

"Perhaps you begin to perceive that there is some...*urgency* in the matter?" suggested Zaniolo.

"I still have a great deal to learn," agreed Sebastian. "Thank you once again, sir, for your timely advice."

"Think nothing of it, Lieutenant." Zaniolo smiled. "Or I suppose I should get accustomed to calling you captain, eh?"

"Thank you for suggesting my promotion to Commander Vittorio as well, sir," Sebastian said quickly. "It seems I owe you a great deal."

Zaniolo waved that away as they began walking down the hall once more. "I'm certain the commander already had your promotion in mind and was merely waiting for one of us to propose it so that it didn't seem like he was spoiling you. You *are* his favorite, after all."

"I am?"

Zaniolo let out a surprisingly rich and hearty laugh. "You *do* have a lot to learn, don't you, Portinari. Never mind, the other generals and I will keep an eye on you. It's up to us officers to look out for each other, after all."

They reached Sebastian's room and he gave Zaniolo a sharp salute. "I am grateful for your mentorship, General. I look forward to the opportunity when I can repay your generosity."

Zaniolo nodded. "Good luck with your new post, Captain." Then he turned and continued down the hall.

Once he was gone, Rykov said, "I don't trust him."

"No? Why not?" asked Sebastian. In theory it was terribly rude for a private to criticize a general, and he knew he should not encourage it. But Rykov so rarely expressed any opinions at all that he was curious.

Rykov shrugged. "Not sure. He's one of those guys who have plans inside of plans. Who knows what he's really after."

"Still, he's not wrong," said Sebastian as they entered his quarters. "If Galina is waiting on me to make the next move, I cannot disappoint her. I'm not entirely sure how to proceed, though. Perhaps I should ask my mother for advice."

"She settled into her new place yet?" asked Rykov as he took Sebastian's jacket and carefully hung it up.

"I haven't checked in on her since the move," said Sebastian.

Rykov only had to give him a look.

Sebastian winced. "Yes, all right. It's been far too long. I might as well call on her now, see how she's faring, and ask what I should do about Galina. I can also tell her the good news about my promotion."

"You want to wear your uniform?" asked Rykov.

"She does seem to take pleasure in me wearing it," said Sebastian. "It reminds her of my father."

Rykov nodded. "Let me brush it out first."

"I'm grateful for all your help," Sebastian said as Rykov took a brush to the wool coat. "I fear I would not be able to function properly without your ministrations."

"You wouldn't," agreed Rykov.

Once Sebastian's jacket, hat, and boots had been tidied up, he gave Rykov the rest of the day off, then took a carriage through Gogoleth to his mother's new home.

The townhome was just down the street from the Prozorovas', and although it was not nearly as magnificent as Roskosh Manor, it was still far nicer than the farmhouse he and his mother had called home for much of his life.

When he knocked on the red front door, it was answered by a man in his midtwenties dressed in a tight-fitting red jacket and cravat, and cream-colored trousers tucked into shiny black boots. His bright coppery hair and beard were carefully combed and neatly trimmed. At the insistence of both Lady Prozorova and Commander Vittorio, Sebastian's mother had agreed to hire on a valet, and presumably this was the fellow.

"Lieutenant Portinari, welcome home." The valet bowed, then moved aside so Sebastian could enter.

"I don't believe we've met," said Sebastian as he stepped into the foyer.

"No, sir. But her ladyship was most exact in her description of you, so I recognized who you were the moment I saw you. I am Dmitry Kuvaev and it is an honor to serve your family."

"Thank you, Dmitry. Is my mother home?"

"Yes, if you would kindly wait here, I will inform her of your arrival."

"Very well."

As Dmitry hurried away, Sebastian examined the oil paintings that hung in the foyer. One of them looked a great deal like a much younger version of his mother. Sebastian suddenly wondered whether his mother had possessed the painting this whole time, and if so, why she hadn't hung it in their old home.

"Lady Portinari will see you now, Lieutenant," Dmitry said. "This way, please."

Sebastian followed him down the hall into a small but nicely decorated drawing room. His mother sat on a plush sofa dressed in one of the gowns that she now wore daily, despite never having worn them on the farm. He supposed farms were simply not the appropriate place for such finery. Had she missed such luxuries during his childhood?

"Sebastian, what a pleasant surprise," said his mother. "Please sit. Would you like some wine? Or is it vodka the officers drink?"

"Tea would be wonderful, Mother. Thank you."

"As you wish. Dmitry, please see to it."

"At once, your ladyship." Dmitry bowed and left.

Sebastian noticed his mother's appreciative gaze as she watched Dmitry leave and with a mild shock realized it was possible she had selected him for more than just his ability to run a household.

"Well, darling," she said once she had turned away from her valet's backside. "What do you think of our ancestral home?"

"This is ours?"

"Of course," she said. "You didn't think a home like this in the finest neighborhood in Gogoleth would be something one could simply purchase at one's convenience, did you?"

"I hadn't really thought about it."

She sighed. "As usual. If the topic isn't magic, the military, or Galina Odoyevtseva, you barely acknowledge its existence."

"Mother!" he objected.

"I'm only teasing. Still, if you had come around more often, you'd have known that I've been endeavoring to make this place livable again since our arrival in Gogoleth. It had been left to gather dust for over a decade and was in a frightful state."

"We had no other family to live here?" asked Sebastian.

She shook her head. "I'm afraid you, your sister, and I are all that is left of the noble house of Turgenev."

"But you always talked about your older sisters. What happened to them? And your parents?"

His mother's face grew sad as she smoothed out her skirts. "A topic for another time, perhaps." Then her face suddenly brightened. She had always been mercurial, but the sudden shifts in mood seemed to have become more pronounced since their arrival in Gogoleth. "Now, what brings you here, my darling one?"

He cleared his throat uncomfortably. "Well, uh, I *did* want to see how you were getting on after the move."

"I do appreciate it, dear," she said. "But I doubt that's your only reason."

"Yes...well...one of my fellow officers happened to ask me when I was thinking of...*proposing* to Galina, and, er, I hadn't given it much thought, but I suppose that is the next step in our relationship."

"Yes, dear," she agreed. "If that is what you want."

"It is!" He found himself leaning forward, his hands gripping his knees. He knew he must look like a lovesick schoolboy but he couldn't help himself. "She makes me happy as no one else. Every time I leave her presence, I feel renewed—no, *improved*! As if some small part of her astonishing kindness and intellect has been passed on to me simply by speaking with her. If I were to...well, *live* with her...if I could come home after an exhausting day and be in her comforting presence every night..." He shook his head. "I cannot think of anything more wonderful."

His mother's smile was beatific. "I'm so happy to hear that, my darling. Well, if that is the case, we have much to do in order to make your dreams come true."

"Oh, and I have other news that will please you," said Sebastian.

"Is that so?"

"Yes, the commander has decided to promote me to captain."

"How wonderful, darling. Congratulations."

"Yes, it's the strangest thing. General Zaniolo of all people suggested it. Honestly, even after all this time, I still don't know what to make of him."

"I grant that he has an...oily sort of personality. But he also strikes me as the only one out of the three generals with any real intelligence." She placed her hand on his and looked firmly into his eyes. "He could be an invaluable ally to you, my darling. Even within such a rigorously disciplined organization as the imperial army, you will find true allies to be both rare and precious, so you should not squander them."

This was one of those times, which had become more frequent since they arrived in Gogoleth, when his mother spoke with a gravity that implied important things left unsaid. He felt he rarely grasped her full instruction in those moments, but also felt compelled to pretend that he did. "I understand, Mother."

She smiled again. "Wonderful. Now, let's start planning the ball we'll be throwing to impress Lord Sergey Prozorova enough that he will be willing to relinquish his only daughter to you."

"Shouldn't I ask Galina first?" he asked.

She laughed merrily. "My darling boy, it is entirely unnecessary. But I suspect it is precisely such thoughtful and solicitous concern that has won her heart, so by all means, speak to her first."

26

Galina sat in one of the smaller drawing rooms, reading a collection of essays by Iosif Kantemir concerning the purpose of Man, Nature, and Governance. It was one of her favorite rooms, largely because of its soothingly warm brown and beige tones, and the smell of lemon and vinegar that always seemed to permeate the wood. That particular book she was less fond of, but likened reading it to eating one's vegetables. A necessary and healthy, if not altogether pleasant, enterprise.

"Captain Portinari here to see you, miss," Masha said from the doorway.

Galina closed the book as she looked up from the high-backed chair in which she sat. "*Captain?*"

Sebastian stood behind the maid, shifting his weight back and forth and displaying what Kantemir, with his insistence on using the vernacular of the peasantry, would have likely described as "a shit-eating grin." Either Sebastian was immensely pleased with his promotion, or his expression was indicative of an even more exciting development. As Sebastian had never before expressed a desire for promotion, she suspected it was the latter.

"Thank you, Masha, that will be all," she told the maid.

Masha bowed and took her leave as Sebastian entered the room. He appeared barely able to contain his excitement, and yet there also seemed to be a great deal of anxiety. Galina could think of only one thing that would produce such a conflicting state. But she would wait for him to broach it.

She smiled. "Congratulations, *Captain*."

"Oh, yes, thank you," he said distractedly, as if he'd already forgotten about the promotion. "Listen, Galina, I hope you will forgive my forwardness, but as you know, I find it difficult not to speak my heart to those I care deeply about."

"I am pleased to know I am numbered among such a cherished group of people."

He dropped suddenly to his knees and took her hands, his own trembling with emotion. "That's just it, Galina. There is no one in the world I treasure more than you. Your intelligence, beauty, and kindness are unmatched, and I want nothing more than to spend every day for the rest of my life with you. And so I've come... to ask... if you will marry me."

And there it was, just as she'd suspected. Certainly both their mothers had been planning it all along, but poor, sweet Sebastian presented the proposition as if it was some wildly impulsive notion. She wondered if he would always be stumbling around in the dark, ignorant of the fact that his life was mostly determined by those around him. Perhaps one day he would find his own way. Until then, she would have to protect him as best she could. Really, it was going to be a great deal of work, but that was likely the trade-off when avoiding marriage to one of the arrogant, pig-headed fools that composed the majority of the male Izmorozian nobility.

"Have you approached my father yet?" she asked.

He blinked. "Er, no... I thought it best to ask you first."

"Indeed so. Very insightful. That gives me time to prepare him." Now that the engagement was official, there were a great many things that needed to happen. Her thoughts began running in several directions at once, like children on a scavenger hunt.

Sebastian grew increasingly pale, and his hands trembled more intensely. "So... Galina... wh-what is your answer?"

She looked at him. "Hmm?"

"W-will you marry me?"

She laughed gaily and pressed her hand on his suddenly flushed cheek. "Silly boy, there is no one else I *would* marry."

"R-really?"

"In fact, I'd already decided months ago."

"You...had?"

"That day in the garden when you confessed your trepidation regarding the use of sweeping power. Do you recall?"

Relief washed over his face. "Of course! I felt the same! I had never known such acceptance, such comfort from another soul. I had not believed it even possible." He winced. "Should I have asked for your hand then?"

"No, my sweet Sebastian, that would have been far too abrupt, even for you." She stood, bringing him up with her. "Now, presumably you've spoken to your mother about this already?"

"Er, yes."

"And she is poised to begin preparations for the traditional engagement ball?"

"So it would seem."

"Wonderful. Tell her I will speak to my father at once. I expect to have no trouble putting him in a favorable mind, especially since my mother has no doubt already spoken to him about it."

"She...has? But how could she have known?"

She smiled fondly at him as she brushed an errant curl from his forehead. "Did you think it a coincidence that two people so well suited for each other just happened to meet? Our mothers planned this from the very beginning."

He looked shocked. "That's just..."

"It may not be as romantic as a meeting fated by the hand of Lady Zivena," conceded Galina. "But it does express how well our mothers know us, and how deeply they care for our happiness."

He sighed and gave her a rueful smile. "I suppose that's true. Galina, you look at everything with such a clear eye, while my vision is always clouded by passion."

"True. But without you, I have a tendency to withdraw too deeply into my own mind. We really do bring out the best in each other."

His eyes glistened with tears as he smiled at her. Then he suddenly stepped forward, closing the short distance between them, and pressed his feverish lips to hers. Galina was not used to being taken by surprise. Nor was she accustomed to the sudden flood of heat that swept through her. Her lips parted slightly and a thick desire welled up within her, reaching all the way down to her heels. For just a moment, she lost all sense of balance, and when she stumbled, his arms encircled her. Should she tense up? Push away? But no, this was her sweet Sebastian, who treated her with a tenderness and consideration she had rarely known. In his arms, she felt safe. Even when at last the kiss ended, she did not pull away, but instead rested her cheek on his shoulder.

"Galina, you have made me so happy," he whispered into her hair.

She allowed herself another moment to luxuriate in the tender warmth of his embrace. Then she took a slow, deep breath and at last disengaged. "And now, my darling, there is a great deal of work to be done. Go and speak with your mother, and I will speak with my father."

"Yes, of course." His eyes still glistened wetly as he gave her one last bright smile, then hurried away.

She watched him go, allowing her own aroused body to slowly cool off, and her pulse to return to normal. It was just as the poet Boris Rodionov had described. "What animals we are, what slaves to passion, when our heart bursts free for the first time." Was it love? She could not say. It was, at the very least, a potent combination of fondness and lust, and successful marriages had been built on less.

She smoothed her hair and skirts, then went in search of her father. If there was any impediment to this engagement, it would be him. But she was ready to counter any argument he might have.

It was not difficult to find Lord Sergey Bolotov Prozorova. For months after one of his "folk story hunts," in which he traveled from town to town, recording the local legends in terse shorthand as people recounted their stories to him, he would sequester himself in his study, expanding those notes into lucid and engaging prose.

She knocked gently on his closed study door.

"Ah, Galina, my love," his voice came through the door. "Come in."

She smiled as she opened the door. He'd always been able to recognize her knock somehow.

"Papa, how is your work progressing?"

Sergey was a slight man, short and thin like Galina, with the same large, melancholy eyes. Two stacks of paper lay on the desk in front of him, one blank, one filled with his cramped, jagged handwriting. He pushed up his glasses and rubbed his eyes, then stretched his arms over his head.

"Well enough, I suppose. Quite a few dark tales this time, Galechka."

"Intriguing," she said. "Perhaps I might assist you with transcribing as I did last time?"

He swiveled his chair around and smiled. "Only if you promise not to be frightened by what you read."

"I can't promise that until I've read them, Papa, by which point it would obviously be too late."

"Fair enough. I was only teasing, of course. Naturally I always welcome the assistance of the brightest young scholar in Gogoleth. Now, since you've sufficiently endeared yourself to me, was there something you needed?"

"I do apologize for interrupting you in your work, Papa, only there's something important we need to discuss."

"Oh? And what is that?"

"Sebastian Turgenev plans to ask you for my hand in marriage."

"Is that so?"

"Don't pretend ignorance, Papa. I'm hardly a little girl."

"My apologies."

"Besides, I already know what you will say."

He smiled at her. "Do you?"

"Certainly. It's unlikely you'll object on financial grounds. Between the yield of the remaining Turgenev estates and Sebastian's new promotion to captain, I am confident he will be able to provide me with the lifestyle to which I am accustomed. And while it's true the Turgenevs no longer have a great deal of influence among the nobility, they more than make up for that by having the nearly undivided attention of Commander Franko Vittorio, arguably the most powerful man in Izmoroz."

"All of that sounds very sensible," he agreed.

"But it is this last aspect that gives you pause. No doubt you are leery of allowing your only daughter to marry a man who is half-Aureumian and seems for all intents and purposes to be a puppet of the empire."

He nodded, looking impressed. "And since you knew what I would say, presumably you have already prepared your rebuttal?"

"I have indeed, Papa," she said primly as she picked a piece of lint from the shoulder of his jacket. "Regardless of his apparent subservience to Vittorio and the empire, I know him to be a thoughtful man of deep personal conviction. He serves the empire because he believes that is the morally correct course of action. Once we are married and I am able to spend more time with him than the commander, my influence over him will grow and I will slowly, gently guide him away from the misapprehension he currently labors under and show him the truth about the empire. His heart is tender and sincere, and I have no doubt that once he fully understands the scope of the empire's crimes, he will join with us in saving this blessed, suffering land."

"That is a magnificent rebuttal, my darling." He looked at her for a moment, his expression serious but kind. "Yet I fear you've missed one crucial element."

"Oh?" A jolt went through her. She had been so certain. What had she missed? Had she bungled the entire thing?

He stood up and put his hands on her shoulders, then looked deeply into her eyes. "My Galechka. From what I have seen and heard of Sebastian Turgenev, I have little doubt you can mold him to be whatever you wish. What I want to know—what is most important to me— is this: Will he make you happy? Think carefully before you answer."

Lord Sergey Bolotov Prozorova was not a perfect man. Stubborn, obsessive, intellectually vain, and impatient with those he deemed not worth his time. But underneath it all, he was also a tremendously kind and caring father. Sometimes she forgot that.

She smiled at him. "I can say with certainty that he makes me happier than any man I've yet encountered. Excepting you, of course, Papa. When I am with him, I feel alive and hopeful in a way I have never known before. Whether that is love, or merely the enthusiasm of my youth and inexperience, I cannot say. But I find his presence a great relief from the loneliness that plagues me when you are not here, and for the first time, the idea of sharing my life with someone else does not seem repugnant to me."

"And there's also the kissing," he said with a sly grin.

"Papa!" She felt her cheeks flush.

"Your lips are a bit redder than usual, my darling. It was fairly obvious. Forgive my crude stab at humor. I have been among peasants so long, I fear they have made an impression on me."

Now her ears reddened. "Yes, well, now that you've had some fun at my expense, what is your answer?"

He sighed and dropped back into his chair. "I would love to say, 'No! I must have my beautiful, brilliant daughter by my side forever!' but then I would be a terrible father. And if you are half as fond of Sebastian Turgenev as you seem, you'll at least be happier than your mother and I. So while it pains me to say this, I promise you I will give Sebastian's proposal my blessing."

She leaned forward and kissed his cheek. "Thank you, Papa!"

He smiled sadly. "Naturally, this is all on the condition that whenever your mother is being tiresome, I can come and stay at your home."

"Naturally, Papa," she agreed.

27

Sonya paused when she reached the top of the snowdrift and took a deep breath, enjoying the sharp bite of arctic air as it entered her lungs. She stared through the slits of her goggles at the vast expanse of white that lay before them. The sky overhead was thickly clouded, but still bright, so it almost seemed like a continuation of the frozen tundra beneath. Even the mountains that rose in the distance were blanketed with snow. Out here, the world was serene and quiet.

Except of course for the young Raízian man who puffed and panted his way up the slope behind her. One of the few things she hadn't considered when preparing for this trek was just how shockingly out of shape Jorge was.

"These shoes . . . ," he huffed when he finally reached the top. "Take some . . . getting used to."

"They do." She vividly remembered the first time she had walked in the wide flat shoes that prevented one from sinking into the snow. It had been exhausting hauling the extra weight, and challenging to adjust one's gait to accommodate the odd shape of the shoes. Of course, she'd only been seven at the time, and she'd hoped an adult male might be able to handle it a little better.

"Catch your breath and have something to eat," she advised. "Your body burns a lot more nutrients in low temperatures like this."

He let out a short burst of laughter as he slipped his pack off and fished around for provisions. "I don't *feel* the cold right now at all."

"Aren't you glad I made you leave behind that ridiculously thick fur coat?" she asked.

"It was rather expensive..." He gnawed on a piece of cured venison as he looked down at the less fancy but far more practical lightweight wool coat the chief had given him in exchange.

"But now you see what I was talking about, right?" she asked. "It would have made you sweat too much and that would have lowered your body temperature. So in the end you would have been more at risk of freezing to death in that big thing."

He tapped his own snow goggles, which she had carefully carved from soft wood for him before they left. "These make more sense now, too. I took them off a little bit ago just to see what it was like, and my eyes immediately began tearing up. I don't think my vision would have lasted more than an hour in this glare."

She nodded. "The days are shorter in the winter, but it's still enough light to make you go blind. And speaking of shorter days..." She pointed to a lone pine tree off in the distance, partly buried in the snow. "I think I've spotted a good place to camp tonight."

"Already? It's only midday."

"Distance can be deceptive out here. It'll take us hours to get there. And it's a good idea never to pass up a tree like that if you can help it."

"If you say so." He pulled his pack back on. "Okay, I'm ready."

They continued down the slope and across the field, their feet crunching softly in the snow. As Sonya had predicted, the sun was already beginning to set by the time they reached the tree.

"What's so great about camping next to a tree?" asked Jorge.

"Simple. The tree's already done most of the work for you."

She untied the shovel from her pack and started to dig about eight feet from the tree. Taking turns, Sonya and Jorge dug down and cleared out a small cave at the base. The branches closest to the bottom were the largest, and since they were below the snow line, made an excellent roof for their cave, while the trunk provided a strong support for one of the walls.

They sat in the small, dark space, surrounded by the smell of pine sap, their knees touching as they gnawed on dried venison.

"We're both going to, er, sleep in here?"

"It'll be snug, but that'll help us keep warm. It's already dropped about ten degrees up there, and it'll go even lower. Snow is an excellent insulator, and the more body heat we can keep trapped down here, the better."

"It's just..."

Sonya had better night vision than most, but even so she could only see the vaguest outline of his face down in the unlit cave. He sounded nervous.

"Just what?" she asked.

"We'll be practically on top of each other when we lie down."

"Oh, sure, that's part of the fun!" she said.

Jorge did not reply with words, but she clearly heard him swallow hard.

"Wait...Jorge, are you a prude?"

"A prude?"

"It's okay if you are," she said quickly. "My mom is a prude. But she has a lot of great qualities, too."

"Well, I've, er, never thought of myself as a prude."

"You just don't sound like you like the idea of us snuggling close tonight. Wait, is it my ears? Do they gross you out or something?"

"No! God, no! I hadn't even..." He paused for a moment to collect his thoughts. "No, nothing about you grosses me out."

"Then what's the problem?"

"In Raíz, a man and a woman do not...*snuggle* like that unless they're married."

She laughed. "Oh. I guess because it never gets so cold down there you'd freeze to death if you didn't."

"Er, yes, I suppose that's part of it." He paused a moment. "Wait, you're saying that if we don't, we might freeze to death?"

"Probably not tonight," she said. "But we won't be as comfortable, which means we won't sleep as well, which means we won't be in great shape for the next day of the trek. In the tundra it's best to utilize every resource you have, and that includes other people's body heat. I mean, if you really aren't comfortable with it, we can dig the cave out some more—"

185

"No, no. If you think this is our best chance at survival, then I would be a fool to ignore your advice. Besides, I came to Izmoroz to experience another culture, and that is what I plan to do, even in those times when I feel a little uncomfortable."

"Great," said Sonya. "I mean, it's not like we're stripping down naked this time."

"Yes, exactly, it's—wait, *this time*? Are there times when one *does* strip down naked?"

"Sure, if you're going into hypothermia, skin-on-skin contact is the fastest, safest way to warm up."

"Oh, I see."

"Also, you know, it's great if you just want to have sex."

"Oh. Right."

He sounded even more nervous, and a suspicion grew in Sonya's mind.

"Jorge, have you never had sex?"

"Um, well, you see…it's another one of the things in Raíz that we only do after marriage."

"I think the Izmorozian nobles are the same way. I don't get what the big deal is, though. Can you explain it?"

"Umm…" He cleared his throat. "I, uh, I suppose the idea is that there should be an emotional connection when making love. It should be special."

"I usually feel emotional when I have sex," said Sonya. "I wouldn't do it with someone I didn't have some sort of connection with."

"Okay, sure, but there should be a…you know, sense of commitment as well."

"Why?"

"Well, I suppose I can really only speak for myself here. It's…just what I want, you know?" His voice was quieter now. More relaxed. "I…long for it, I suppose. A unique connection with a special person who sees *me* as special as well." He paused for a moment, then laughed nervously, as if he'd suddenly become self-conscious again. "Perhaps that sounds foolish…"

She reached into the darkness and squeezed his shoulder. "No,

Jorge. It doesn't sound foolish. It sounds like you. I think I understand a little better now." She pinched his cheek. "I promise I won't go tearing your clothes off in the middle of the night."

"Er, thanks..."

"No problem. Now, let's settle in before it gets any colder out there. I don't know about you, but I could use some sleep."

Sonya laid down a thick blanket, then they wedged themselves in together on top of it, Sonya behind Jorge. It took them a few awkward moments to work out where everyone's arms and legs were going, but at last they were both situated.

"Perfect fit, if I do say so myself." She pulled the ends of the blanket overtop both of them.

Jorge was tense at first, but after a few minutes, with the heat building up nicely, he began to relax.

"Not so bad, huh?" she asked.

"Mmm," he said sleepily. "I might even go so far as to call it toasty. Who knew one could find such comfort at night in a winter tundra."

"Now you're getting it. Sleep well, Jorge."

"You too, Sonya."

Sonya lay in the darkness for a little while and listened as Jorge's breathing slowed. She savored the feel of his lean body pressed against her. She had promised to behave herself, but that didn't mean she couldn't appreciate what was already there.

Mikhail once told her of a village that had been decimated during the war. By the time he had arrived, it was little more than a burned-out husk. At first he had thought there were no survivors, but then he had found a little boy who had hid himself in the rubble. Mikhail had offered the boy some dried venison, but instead of taking the food, the boy took his hand and pressed it against his ash-stained cheek. That was when Mikhail had understood that perhaps human contact was a physical need, like breathing or sleeping. And no matter how strong or stoic or brave a Ranger was, they must accept that aspect of life.

Sonya had understood the idea intellectually before, but this night, with her body pressed firmly against Jorge's, she finally understood it in her heart. There was a comfort to be had in the embrace of a cherished friend that went beyond sexual gratification. She had been pushing herself hard since they'd left Gogoleth, but she knew that the wounds left by the betrayal of her brother and her mother had not yet healed; she could use all the comfort she could get.

She was just beginning to drift off when a strange scent jerked her sharply awake. She lay completely still, her senses on full alert, but a moment later it was gone. It had definitely been animal, possibly mammalian, but beyond that she couldn't say, which was strange.

Something unusual was out there. Whatever it was, it was keeping its distance for now, but she would need to stay on her guard.

28

Irina Turgenev Portinari leaned back into the sofa as Dmitry Kuvaev slowly pushed her skirts up her smooth, pale legs. His neatly trimmed beard tickled the inside of her thigh as he softly kissed her skin. His hands gripped her knees while she gently took hold of his ginger curls. He worked his way patiently toward the center with his warm lips and flickering tongue. Patience was something Giovanni had never possessed, particularly as a lover. Making love to him had been like riding a thunderstorm. Loud and thrilling, but also exhausting and lacking in nuance. Dmitry was more like a gentle rainfall whose delicate kisses cooled her skin like drops of rain even as his deft fingers stirred her body like a light summer breeze, leaving her quietly vibrating in a state that hovered between anticipation and bliss.

Her breath grew shallow and she pressed her thighs against the sides of his head. Her back arched as waves of pleasure radiated outward through her body like the ripples of a pebble dropped in a pond. She abandoned herself to the feeling in a way she had never allowed herself during her many years with Giovanni. As her body slowly relaxed, she wondered why it was easier now.

Then the doorbell rang.

Dmitry lifted his head and gave her a sheepish smile. His hair and cravat were disheveled, and his beard visibly moist. "My lady."

She returned his smile. "You may wish to freshen up before you answer the door, Mitya. I'm sure whoever it is can wait."

"Yes, my lady." He stood, bowed, and left. She liked that he never forgot his place, even in such intimate moments.

She allowed herself a few more moments to luxuriate in postcoital bliss, then sighed and stood up. She smoothed down her skirts and adjusted her hair in the mirror. The sofa was a bit damp, and she could use a change of scenery, so she made her way out to the terrace, which overlooked Nadezhda Square. She enjoyed watching the bustling commerce below. Merchants hollering, children frolicking, horses pulling carts laden with any number of luxuries she had never allowed herself back on the farm.

They had lived a simple, almost austere life, and she had not really minded. After such a decadent childhood, it had felt good to purge herself of all those supposed "needs," and Giovanni had a gift for romanticizing their more humble existence. And of course, the children had both been such a handful, most of the time the very idea of bothering with a formal gown would have seemed onerous to her. Those had been uncomplicated times, really. Full of modest pleasures, unhindered emotions, and a great deal of quiet.

But now she was returned to society and she enjoyed that boisterous complexity as well. She knew her children struggled to adapt their conception of her in this new environment, but that was a healthy learning experience for them as well. One should never presume they knew a person in their entirety. Not even someone they'd known their whole lives. Irina felt that both the best and worst thing about humanity was its endless ability to surprise.

"My lady," Dmitry said from the doorway, looking entirely composed now. "Commander Vittorio is here to see you."

"Really?" She frowned thoughtfully, wondering what his purpose might be. "Very well. I'll see him here."

"Yes, my lady."

As Dmitry went to fetch Vittorio, Irina continued to gaze out at Nadezhda Square, sorting through all the reasons the commander might wish to speak with her. Perhaps he objected to the impending engagement because he feared it would distract Sebastian from his duties. Or perhaps he had already caught on that this marriage would grant Irina and Sebastian some independence from him.

She would have to handle this carefully.

"Lady Turgenev, may I present Commander Vittorio."

Irina turned from her view of the square to Vittorio, spotless as ever in his green uniform, his hat under his arm.

"Welcome, Commander," she said. "May I offer you some refreshment? Wine or vodka perhaps?"

Vittorio shook his head. "I'm afraid I don't have leisure to stay long, Lady Portinari."

"As you wish, Commander. Thank you, Dmitry, that will be all."

"Yes, my lady." Dmitry bowed and left.

"To what do I owe the pleasure of your visit, Commander? Presumably something pressing, if it has taken you away from your busy schedule."

"Exactly so, my lady," he said. "I do wish I had the luxury of calling upon you earlier, but tensions with our neighbors to the west are rising, and I fear we will be engaged in conflict no later than midsummer."

"That is dire news indeed," said Irina. "Is there some way I can assist in this stressful time?"

He smiled. "In a manner of speaking, yes. I spoke with your son yesterday after one of his many visits to Roskosh Manor, and he seemed to be almost drunk, except I could not smell even a hint of liquor on his breath."

"Sebastian has never had much interest in drinking, or really in any sort of gluttonous activity."

"Yet another admirable character trait no doubt passed along to him by you and his father." Vittorio certainly was studious about slipping in compliments whenever possible. "At any rate, it did not take long to ascertain the cause of his elation. He is to be married to Galina Odoyevtseva."

"The engagement has not been formalized yet," said Irina. "I have sent the proposal to Lord Prozorova but I am still planning a great many details for the ball."

"So you have not committed your resources yet?" asked Vittorio. "Excellent. I'm glad I spoke to you as soon as I did."

"And why would that be, Commander?" Irina asked carefully.

"So that I might offer my own support, financial and otherwise."

Irina was not one to show surprise. Indeed she was not one to even be taken by surprise very often. But perhaps her eyebrows bounced once at Vittorio's reply.

"You are not opposed to the engagement?"

"Good heavens, no," said Vittorio. "A man needs a good woman to come home to. A soldier doubly so, especially if he must go to war. I hope you will forgive me, but in the absence of a family I can call my own, I confess that I have taken a paternal fondness toward Sebastian. Especially since he is now without a father of his own."

A father killed at your command, thought Irina, but her face expressed only gentle concern as she said, "I'm certain it must be lonely at times to have no family of one's own."

He nodded gravely. "It is indeed, my lady. And that is why I am resolved that Sebastian be engaged, and ideally married, with all due haste. In my experience, a soldier may fight with passion for his empire and his sovereign, but the truest commitment comes from a man fighting to protect a beautiful woman and achieve the peace that will allow him to return to her arms."

"A commendable view," murmured Irina, "but I would expect no less from you, Commander."

"It is a conclusion I have drawn after a number of years observing the sustaining power of love. Admittedly, I don't quite understand young Sebastian's fondness for this *particular* woman. If you'll permit me to say so, I find Galina Odoyevtseva to be a strange and mousy little thing bereft of her mother's charms and handsome figure. But thankfully, each man judges beauty on his own terms, and in doing so guarantees that there is indeed a match for everyone. I had only to observe the manner with which the young captain treats her for a few moments before I recognized that she is quite a suitable match."

"I am glad we are in accord on this view," Irina said with genuine warmth and perhaps a little relief.

"Indeed. And to make certain things move smoothly in the negotiations with Lord Prozorova, I would like to offer my aid. I am aware that the Turgenev family is presently not at its peak, and your resources are limited. At the risk of sounding boastful, my means are considerable and it would please me greatly if you would allow me to arrange the finest engagement ball yet seen in Gogoleth. I intend that no expense be spared in this, one of the most important and impactful events in the life of our young Sebastian."

"Your generosity overwhelms me, Commander." Irina's expression was appropriately fawning even as she fought back the bile that crept up her throat. *Our* Sebastian again? The man was truly insufferable.

He gazed out over the square, looking quite pleased with himself. "I would hardly call it generous, my lady, since his happiness benefits both me personally, as well as the entire empire."

"Truly said, Commander."

"So it's settled, then? Wonderful. I will of course consult with you on all pertinent matters." He bowed to her. "Now, I'm afraid I must be getting back to the garrison, so I'll take my leave."

"Good day to you, Commander. And thank you for coming."

"It was my pleasure, Lady Portinari. I look forward to working with you even more closely on this, the newest chapter of Sebastian's life." He bowed again and left.

Irina waited until she heard the door close. She turned and watched the streets below until Vittorio's carriage pulled away. Only then did she let out a harsh sigh. She could not have credibly refused Vittorio's offer, but with him footing the bill, he would also likely intrude on the negotiations with Sergey, and temper any efforts she made that might guarantee their independence from him.

"Shit," she muttered aloud.

"My lady?" Dmitry, ever attentive, stood in the doorway looking concerned.

"Get word to General Zaniolo through the usual channels. Tell him the plan has changed and I need to speak with him at his *earliest* convenience."

"Right away, my lady."

29

At Commander Vittorio's suggestion, Sebastian refrained from calling on Galina in the weeks leading up to the engagement ball. During that time, he suffered from frequent stomachaches and headaches, and each morning he woke up with his jaw unpleasantly sore. Perhaps the cause was being suddenly cut off from the most soothing presence he had ever known. Or perhaps he felt the subtle but inescapable expectations from everyone around him more keenly than he realized. In every conversation he had, no matter how short or who it was with, the other party felt it necessary to mention his impending engagement. Officers he barely knew stopped him in the hall to offer a hearty congratulations and a knowing wink that he only vaguely guessed the meaning behind.

"You worried about the engagement ball?" Rykov asked as he carefully trimmed the back of Sebastian's hair, which Commander Vittorio pointed out had grown too long.

"Wh-why do you ask?" Sebastian sat in the chair, shirtless, his bare shoulders slumped forward as he listened to the slow snip of Rykov's shears and felt the locks of hair tumble down his back.

"Gray hair." Rykov held it out for him to see.

"On me?"

"Yep."

"I don't think people really go gray from worry," said Sebastian. "Is there some evidence for it?"

"It's just what I was told." Rykov didn't sound like he cared much if it could be proved.

They were quiet for a moment, with only the quiet rasp of the shears. Then Sebastian said, "I suppose I am a little nervous. Do you know what happens at these balls?"

"I don't know how you nobles do it," said Rykov.

"I wasn't *raised* as a noble, Rykov. I don't *feel* like one of them, you know? Tell me what happens during the engagement balls you've been to. I'm sure things can't be that different."

"Well, it's not too complicated." Rykov continued to trim Sebastian's hair as he spoke. "The groom's family throws a big party. Everybody eats and drinks a lot. The bride and groom dance in front of everyone to show how great they look together. Then everyone else joins in the dance while the parents go off somewhere private and work out the deal."

"The deal?"

"Usually the bride's parents give the groom's parents a dowry of some kind. Most engagements I've been to, it was pigs or sheep or something like that. Probably for nobles it'll be something fancier."

"I'm not sure Galina's family has any pigs or sheep," agreed Sebastian.

"Well no, but the farms they own probably do." Rykov brushed the loose hair from Sebastian's neck and back, then handed him a clean undershirt.

"The Prozorovas have farms?" Sebastian pulled the shirt over his head.

"I'll bet the Portinaris do, too," said Rykov. "Or the Turgenevs at least. How else do you think your mother pays for her food and that pretty-boy valet of hers?"

"Well, we have *our* farm…I mean the one we lived on when I was a child. But you think there are others?"

"Probably." Rykov handed Sebastian's jacket to him.

"Huh." Sebastian considered that possibility as he buttoned up his jacket. His mother had never mentioned it, but then again, she'd never said anything to the contrary, either. Increasingly, he had begun to see that there were a lot more layers to his mother than he'd realized.

Perhaps a part of growing up was recognizing your parents as more complex entities, rather than simply someone who existed to fulfill your needs.

Then an altogether different thought occurred to him.

"Wait...did you say there will be *dancing*?"

"You don't know how to dance?" asked Rykov.

"I've never danced in my life," said Sebastian. "Can you teach me?"

"I only know peasant dances. You'll need to ask one of the officers to show you how fancy people dance."

"I see...," said Sebastian.

Rykov patted his shoulder comfortingly. "You've still got a week before the ball. I'm sure the commander would let you out of your regular duties to practice dancing so that you don't make yourself, him, and the entire empire look bad at your own engagement."

Sebastian glared at him.

Rykov shrugged. "Just trying to help."

He could never tell if Rykov was truly that dense, or merely teasing him. He suspected the latter.

Sebastian was still pondering his dancing dilemma as he made his way to the mess hall for lunch. It was a separate one-story building across the yard from headquarters, wide and squat, with a number of windows, and twin chimneys that spewed thick black smoke unceasingly.

All soldiers ate in the mess hall, but the officers ate in a separate area near the front, as far from the kitchen and chimneys as possible. Additionally, while the enlisted men were required to stand in line to get their food from large troughs, the officers were served at their tables. The menu was ostensibly the same for both enlisted and officers, although it was fairly evident that the choicest cuts of meat and freshest vegetables were set aside for the officers.

It was early in the lunch shift, and there was hardly anyone sitting in the officers' section. Sebastian sat down at an empty table and a few moments later, a girl brought him a plate with pickled beets and a generous slab of roast pork in gravy. Vittorio had been correct in saying that the food wasn't nearly as good as what was served at Roskosh Manor, but it was roughly comparable to the food Sebastian's mother had made back at the farm. She was many wonderful things, but "chef" was not among them. Still, there was something comforting in eating the bland, greasy food of his youth with the quiet murmur of male voices in the background.

"You look troubled, Captain Portinari," General Zaniolo said cheerfully as he approached the table.

"Ah, General. Please join me."

"I presume you have some anxiety regarding your upcoming engagement ball. Is there anything I can do?"

"Perhaps there is, General. I have been informed that there will be dancing?"

"Yes, indeed." Zaniolo seemed to enjoy the look of trepidation in Sebastian's eye.

"And there is…no getting around that, I suppose?" Sebastian asked tentatively.

"Thank you, my dear," Zaniolo said to the serving girl when she brought him a plate of food. Then he turned back to Sebastian, looking amused. "Captain, I'm surprised at you. Would you truly want to deny all the men at the ball the divine experience of watching Galina Odoyevtseva dance?"

"I fear the beauty and grace she exhibits will be marred by my own clumsiness."

"Ah." Zaniolo took on a more kindly expression. "If that is the only thing troubling you, I have good news for you, my dear young Captain. I happen to be a consummate dancer. In fact, I wager there is no dance known to imperial society that I cannot teach you. We shall begin immediately after lunch, for there is not a moment to lose."

30

Sonya decided not to tell Jorge that something was stalking them as they made their way across the tundra. It would only worry him, and she didn't have much to tell him anyway. Throughout the next day, she caught only the most fleeting of scents and she still couldn't decide whether it was merely a curious fox, or something much larger and less friendly.

That night, she stayed awake after Jorge fell asleep, and around midnight she heard the muffled crunch of something in the snow near the entrance to their tiny cave. Judging by the sound, it was fairly large. A smallish bear, perhaps? Or a person with snowshoes. The trouble was, she still couldn't identify the scent, other than that it was mammalian. Or was it avian? So strange that she couldn't quite decide. Whatever it was, it was big enough to pose a potential threat. She would need to address it sooner rather than later.

The next night, they couldn't find any trees, so they had to dig out their cave completely on their own. That took a fair bit longer, and required more care to make certain there was no danger of the cave collapsing on them while they slept. And then Sonya began to dig a narrow secondary exit tunnel just big enough for her to wriggle through.

"Why are you making another tunnel?" asked Jorge as he helped her toss the excess snow out through the main entrance. "Won't that let more heat escape?"

"It's part of my plan to catch whoever or whatever is stalking us," she said as she continued to dig.

"Wait, something is *stalking* us? For how long?"

"I first noticed two nights ago. They're keeping their distance, but I've caught the scent a few times and last night they came right up to our cave to sniff around."

"Oh, God, you don't think it's a polar bear, do you?"

Sonya could faintly see the concern in his expression from the bit of moonlight that spilled into the cave.

"Don't worry." She paused her digging to pat his arm reassuringly. "I'll take care of it tonight."

"How?"

"I'm going to dig this tunnel to come up a little farther downwind but not break through completely, so it looks like there's still only one way in or out. Then, when our stalker comes to investigate again, I sneak up behind them."

"And I'm the bait," he said gloomily.

"Mmm, delicious Raízian boy!" She pinched his cheek. "Who could resist?"

He did not seem to find that as funny as she'd hoped.

"I promise I won't let anything happen to you, Jorge. But it wouldn't be safe to ignore this problem."

"You're right, of course. I put my faith in you to sort it out."

"Thank you."

Jorge settled in for the night while Sonya stayed crouched by the second tunnel.

After a few moments, he said, "You were right, it's nowhere near as warm without you."

"Told you," she said.

"Good night, Sonya."

"Good night, Jorge."

Jorge lay down and closed his eyes, although Sonya could tell by his breathing that he wasn't sleeping. She waited patiently, as a proper hunter was wont to do, crouched at the entrance to the second tunnel with her knife held loosely in one hand. At last she was rewarded around midnight with the heavy crunch of steps near the entrance. Once again she caught that curiously unfamiliar smell. Now was her chance.

She clenched her knife between her teeth and quickly wriggled up the tunnel. It rose at a slight angle, so that by the time she reached the end of it, she was nearly thirty feet downwind of their stalker. Unless of course the wind had shifted since she'd dug the tunnel, in which case she might be in big trouble. But there was no time for doubt. If she didn't move fast, the stalker would retreat again, and she'd have to do the whole thing over again tomorrow night.

She used her knife to clear away the last portion of the tunnel and broke the surface. Slowly, silently, she pulled herself up until she was lying facedown in the snow, spreading her body out as widely as she could so she didn't sink down too far. In the distance, a figure crouched near the main entrance to the cave. The moonlight revealed it to be a person wearing a hooded leather coat lined in white fur.

For a moment, Sonya was too shocked to even react. Could there be another Ranger of Marzanna out here? Maybe they could help her recruit the Uaine—

Then a knife blade touched her throat, and a strong hand pressed down on her back.

A growling male voice said, "Not bad, little cub. But it appears you didn't consider that there might be more than one of us."

Sonya couldn't believe her luck. *Two* Rangers living out here?

"Thank you for this lesson, *Uchitel*," she said.

"A little presumptuous to call me teacher, don't you think?"

"Someone who teaches you something is your teacher, isn't that so?" she asked.

She still couldn't see him, but she heard and felt him sniff closely a few times. Then he grunted.

"Fox cub. Should have known, you cheeky little thing. What are you doing out here?"

"My friend and I are going to find the Uaine. We're going to enlist their aid in liberating Izmoroz from the empire."

"That so?" He didn't exactly sound supportive of the idea, but maybe he was just jealous he hadn't thought of it first.

"Sure," she said. "You could come with us, you know."

He didn't respond directly, but he did at least remove the knife from her throat and take his hand away so she could stand. Once she was back on her feet, she was finally able to get a look at this Ranger. He was an older man, though not quite as old as Mikhail had been. He was tall and thick, with a burly white beard and small brown eyes that looked like a bear's.

"Tatiana!" he called to the Ranger who still crouched near the entrance. When he spoke, Sonya could see his large, sharp canines. "Leave that one and come here."

Tatiana swiveled her head without moving her body, reminding Sonya of an owl. Then the rest of her body followed as she stood. "Ah, I see you were right, Andre. She *was* on to us after all."

"Little foxes like to play games," said Andre.

"Yes, and old bears like to grumble," said Tatiana teasingly as she walked toward them.

"And fussy owls think they're better than everyone else," retorted Andre.

"That's because they *are*, my dear." As Tatiana drew near, Sonya saw that she was around the same age as Andre. She walked with a curious, birdlike strut, and her large owl eyes almost seemed to glow in the moonlight.

Sonya sighed happily at the sight of two Rangers with such bold favors from the Lady. "It's so good to see more *Strannik*. I worried that I was the last of us."

"Who was your *uchitel*, fox cub?" asked Tatiana.

"Mikhail Popov Lukyanenko."

"Mikhail Popov survived the war?" Andre looked surprised. "I thought he was captured and put to death by the empire."

Sonya shook her head. "He posed as the stable hand for a farm outside Gogoleth." She didn't want to deceive these Rangers, but she also thought perhaps it was best not to bring up the complicated relationship between Mikhail and her father until she got to know them better.

"You see, Anya?" asked Andre. "A similar fate would have awaited us if we hadn't fled."

Tatiana merely shrugged.

"So you both have been out on the tundra since the war?" asked Sonya.

"Anatoly as well," said Tatiana. "But he is older than us, and these last few years have been hard on him. He does not hunt very often anymore."

"You mean not at all," said Andre.

Tatiana opened and closed her mouth rapidly a few times, making a sharp clicking sound with her teeth, then said, "What can we do if the Lady is not done with him yet?"

She reached out and brushed Sonya's hair back to reveal her pointed ears.

"So young and already you bear the Lady's favor. Interesting...," she said in a way that sounded neither judgmental nor particularly complimentary. "Did you ask for a boon, or merely die before you had fulfilled an oath?"

"I died," admitted Sonya.

"It is the way of foxes," said Andre. "Always reckless and too clever for their own good. This one thinks she will bring foreigners into Izmoroz to help her drive out the empire."

Tatiana again merely shrugged.

There was a quiet hiss as snow tumbled from the lip of the cave's main entrance. All three Rangers turned to see Jorge's head peeping out of the hole.

Tatiana laughed, a loud and shrill birdlike sound that again showed just how much more of the beast these older Rangers had taken in than Sonya. "What an adorable little lemming you bring with you, *Lisitsa*. Are you saving him in case you run out of provisions?"

"Jorge is my *friend*," Sonya said. "He may not be a Ranger, but he has a vast knowledge of herbs, potions, and medicine."

"I can see how that might be handy." Tatiana beckoned to Jorge. "Come, little lemming. I promise we won't hurt you. Bring your packs and we will take you to our cave, which is much nicer and more spacious than this."

"Really?" demanded Andre. "You trust them so soon?"

"She bears the Lady's favor. What other proof do you need?" asked Tatiana. "Besides, a bad storm is coming." She yanked playfully on Sonya's ear. "And I would not see our little *Lisitsa* beg another favor of the Lady quite so soon."

31

As Sonya might have expected, the entrance to the Rangers' cave was undetectable until they were nearly on top of it. They had been walking for over an hour through the glittering, moon-drenched snow when they suddenly came upon a hole in the ground. It was not even a particularly big hole. In fact, it looked barely large enough to accommodate Andre.

"I thought she said this cave would be bigger than ours," Jorge whispered to Sonya.

"They can hear what you're whispering," Sonya whispered back.

Jorge suddenly looked panicked, which again sent Tatiana into shrill peals of laughter.

"Fear not, sweet lemming," she said. "The passage widens out."

Then she slipped into the hole. Sonya followed, with Jorge quickly behind her. Andre brought up the rear.

The tunnel continued at a gentle decline into the darkness. The temperature noticeably rose the deeper they got, and after a few minutes, she could see faint, flickering lights ahead.

"Don't be alarmed by all the unfamiliar smells, Anatoly," Tatiana called. "We're bringing guests."

"Guests?" came a rumbling, nearly unintelligible voice. "What sort?"

"A little *Lisitsa* cub of our very own, if you can believe it."

"Foxes?" There was a noise that could have been a cough or a sound of disgust. "The worst."

"Now, now, *Rosomakha,* you sound just like Andre," chided Tatiana. "Foxes are quite charming and you know it. Here we come, so behave."

Sonya didn't know what she'd expected. Perhaps merely a larger, more carefully dug out ice cave. But they emerged from the narrow snow tunnel into a massive rock cavern. The floors and walls were covered in grimy fur rugs made from caribou, and a few made from bears. There was no furniture to speak of, but there were a number of thin wooden and bone structures from which curing meat and hides hung. Fat tallow candles guttered in small clusters here and there, and a small cooking fire danced merrily in the back. Judging by the way the smoke went straight up, Sonya guessed there must be a small vent in the rocks. Off to one side, a tiny stream trickled over a collection of carefully arranged colored pebbles.

"It's beautiful!" said Sonya.

There was another cough or sneer and Sonya turned to see a small figure hunched over in the corner that she assumed must be Anatoly. He was mostly wrapped in a ragged wool blanket patched with strips of leather. *Rosomakha* meant *wolverine* in Old Izmorozian, and with his beady dark eyes, long black snout, and protruding canines, he looked more like that fearsome animal than a human.

She touched her forehead. "Thank you for welcoming us into your home, *Uchitel.*"

"Bah, I'm not your teacher, cub."

"Never mind, Anatoly," said Andre as he climbed into the cave behind Jorge. "She has a liberal conception of that word."

"Well," Tatiana said brightly, "why don't we eat while you tell us all about what's been going on in the world."

"I'm afraid we don't have enough rations for an extra meal," Sonya told her.

"Of course, of course. You may have some of ours."

"May they?" demanded Anatoly.

"Ignore him," said Tatiana. "He doesn't even do the hunting anymore, so he hardly has room to complain."

Anatoly growled but said no more. He crawled on hands and knees to the center of the room. Tatiana joined him and motioned for Sonya and Jorge to sit next to her. Andre took a bundle wrapped in leather from a stack in the corner, then sat down beside Anatoly and unwrapped the bundle to reveal slabs of smoked salmon.

Sonya couldn't help letting out a little gasp of delight. "I haven't had smoked salmon since last winter! Mikhail was always better at smoking meat."

Anatoly looked over at her, showing interest for the first time. "You were taught by Mikhail Popov?"

"I'm so glad you all knew him." She snatched up a piece of smoked salmon and began to gnaw on it as she talked. "I was afraid I was the only one who carried his memories."

"Some of them I would like to forget," said Andre. Now that his hood was pulled back, she could see that he had long, shaggy white hair and short round ears that stuck out the sides.

"Hush." Tatiana's hair was just as white, but rather short and fluffy. She took a piece of smoked salmon and snipped off a corner. "So tell us, *Lisitsa*, how bad has it become out there?"

"I-I'm sorry to, er, interrupt," said Jorge timidly. "But why do you call Sonya that?"

"*Lisitsa?*" asked Tatiana. "It means female fox or vixen in Old Izmorozian."

"Listen, human," said Anatoly. "When a person is deemed wor-thy by the Lady Marzanna, they pledge their life to her. In return, she grants them the blessings of the animal that most suits their nature. And I can already tell that this girl is the most fox-like fox I've seen in half a century. Not since Nikita." He looked at Andre. "Remember her?"

"Of course." Andre chewed thoughtfully on a piece of smoked salmon. "I was young then, but I remember being terrified of her. You never knew what she was going to do from one moment to the next."

"That...*does* have a familiar ring to it," admitted Jorge. "Sorry, this is just...a lot to take in."

Anatoly let out one of his gravelly coughs. "I don't know why you're traveling with this human, *Lisitsa*. He isn't even Izmorozian. How could he possibly understand?"

"But he *is* Izmorozian," protested Sonya.

"With that brown skin and black hair?" asked Andre.

"It is true I am from Raíz, sir," said Jorge.

"Yeah, but he *lives* in Izmoroz," said Sonya. "He calls it his home so that makes him Izmorozian."

"Nonsense!" said Anatoly. "An Izmorozian has to be *from* this land. He has to have it embedded in his bones and steeped in his blood."

"But—" began Sonya.

"What is it you seek, little fox?" interrupted Tatiana. "Andre said you plan to ask foreigners for help?"

"Yeah, I'm going to cut a deal with the Uaine to help me get the empire out of Izmoroz."

"Necromancers?" asked Anatoly. "As a servant to the Goddess of Death you want to ally yourself with those who *defile* death? That's blasphemy! It's heretical! It's—"

He broke into a long, painful-sounding coughing fit. They all sat and waited, but once he was done, he merely gulped down some water and scowled at her.

"So then what's your idea?" Sonya asked.

"My idea? About what?" he asked.

"Liberating Izmoroz, of course."

He pulled his blanket more tightly around him. "There is no liberating Izmoroz. The sooner you accept that, the better."

"What..." She couldn't believe she was hearing this from a Ranger. "What do you mean?"

"We serve the Goddess of Death," said Andre. "Our responsibility is to facilitate death and change, to make way for something new. Not just the death of people, but the death of countries and cultures. The Lady Marzanna has made it clear that it is time for Izmoroz to die."

"No..." Sonya shook her head. "No, that can't be right. Why do you think she brought me back? She wants me to save our people!"

"None can truly know the will of the Lady Marzanna," Tatiana said. "And you should not speak so loudly with so many sensitive ears, little fox. You are our guest, and it is not seemly." She looked reproachfully at Anatoly, then at Andre. "And you two should not crush the idealism of youth so callously. You were both young yourselves, once, though you may pretend not to remember. It is late, we are all tired. Now that our bellies are full, we should rest."

Jorge touched Sonya's hand. "I'm very tired, my friend. Let's call it a night."

Sonya took a slow breath, then nodded. She turned to the older Rangers. "I apologize for my outburst. I'm sure that once I've had some sleep, I'll be in a much more respectful frame of mind."

Little else was said as the candles and fire were extinguished and everyone stretched out on the thick fur rugs and fell asleep.

Sonya was up before anyone else. She quietly woke Jorge and indicated that it was time to go. He looked confused, but nodded. They collected their packs, then climbed up the tunnel and back to the surface.

The first pink rays of dawn stained the horizon as they continued their trek west across the tundra.

"I'm sorry that didn't go well for you," Jorge said after they had been walking for some time. "You were so excited to meet other Rangers at first."

"Those aren't Rangers," she said quietly. "They're cowardly ghosts haunting the tundra."

32

Sebastian trained with General Zaniolo for hours a day. To avoid the ogling of the men, they practiced in Zaniolo's spacious quarters. Sebastian was grateful for that, because after five days, he was only marginally better at executing the sweeping steps of the popular dances of Izmorozian society. Sebastian didn't blame the general, of course. He had always been clumsy, a failing that his sister had never passed up an opportunity to ridicule when they were children.

Now he recalled some of those embarrassing childhood memories as he sat next to Commander Vittorio in the carriage that conveyed them to the engagement ball. Amid the ebb and flow of his anxiety, he was able to appreciate the fact that at least his sister wouldn't be there to laugh at him.

That thought reminded him of something he'd been meaning to ask the commander. "Sir, has there been any news of my sister?"

The commander gave him a somber look. "I suppose it is natural on this momentous day for your thoughts to turn to those family members who will not witness it. I had meant to put off telling you until after this evening, but I suppose it is better for you to hear it from me first, rather than some tipsy officer at the ball. Shortly after your sister murdered the patrolman, I sent several men to search Gogoleth for any sign of her. One of them never reported back."

"You mean…"

"Some time later, his frozen corpse was discovered on a rooftop near the College of Apothecary."

"Perhaps he merely froze to death?"

The commander shook his head. "I'm afraid not. His arm had been broken, and his throat slit. Presumably by your sister when she was discovered."

"How terrible..." Sebastian still found it difficult to think of his sister as a cold-blooded murderer. She'd had a temper, certainly. And during their childhood she had been mean to him on any number of occasions, but he'd always assumed that to be the typical cruelty of an older sibling toward their younger sibling. Had she been harboring something darker all along? He'd never understood why she'd spent so much time with Mikhail. Sebastian hadn't been close with the man, but he'd always seemed a rather harsh fellow. Perhaps he had been the one to take her down so sinister a path.

Vittorio smiled and placed his hand paternally on Sebastian's shoulder. "It is indeed terrible. But every family has its black sheep, so I do not hold you or your mother accountable for your sister's crimes. Today is a day for celebration, so let us put aside such grim matters for now."

"Yes, sir."

Engagement balls were traditionally held at the groom's family's main estate, but since the Turgenev estate was relatively humble, Commander Vittorio had generously offered to hold the ball at Her Imperial Majesty's Grand Northern Ballroom.

The ballroom had been constructed shortly after the Treaty of Gogoleth and the end of the Winter War. Its main purpose was to offer an appropriately lavish and stately location for Her Imperial Majesty to entertain, should she decide to visit the newly acquired northern region of her vast empire. She had not yet deigned to do so in the twenty years that followed, but the ballroom was always kept at the ready, immaculately clean and fully staffed, just in case.

Sebastian had never actually seen the Grand Northern Ballroom before, and when the carriage drew near, he was awed by its immensity and grandeur. It was the largest single building in Gogoleth, with the possible exception of the venerable College of Apothecary. It was made not of the black stone that was so prevalent in Gogoleth, but a beige, almost white stone that had been transported at great expense from Aureum. Set among the dark buildings around it, the Grand Northern Ballroom seemed almost luminescent beneath the light of the full moon that shone overhead.

The carriage stopped at the bottom of the white stone stairs before the front entrance. Commander Vittorio stepped out first, followed by Sebastian. In addition to his green jacket, cleaned and brushed to perfection, and his tall, polished black boots, Sebastian wore pristine white gloves and a white cape with green trim over one shoulder.

He followed Commander Vittorio up the stairs and through the main doors into the spacious foyer, where an army of well-wishers descended upon him, most of whom he did not recognize.

After nodding, smiling, and shaking hands for what seemed an eternity, Vittorio finally managed to extract Sebastian from the group and lead him into the ballroom. There he was accosted by an even larger group of guests.

He did his best to appear gracious, but there was so much going on in that magnificent ballroom, he could barely focus on the person in front of him. Five crystal chandeliers, each with four tiers, were evenly spaced across the ceiling, glittering with countless candles. Tables lined the sides of the ballroom, laid out with nearly every type of food he could think of, from whole roast boar to a three-tiered chocolate cake slathered in vanilla icing. Servants weaved through the crowds holding aloft trays of wine or vodka. A small chamber Aureumian orchestra was tucked away in one corner, the trembling sound of strings wafting through the air as enticingly as the food.

"There you are, my darling boy!"

Sebastian turned eagerly toward the sound of his mother's voice. She was dressed even more splendidly than he'd seen her before, with a wide hooped skirt and sleeves bordered in exquisite lace.

"Ah, Lady Portinari, you are a picture of loveliness," said Commander

Vittorio as he kissed her hand. "I'm so pleased that the gown I sent over suits you as well as I'd hoped."

She smiled warmly at him. "A most generous gift, Commander. I thank you."

"My dear lady, the only thanks I need is to see you wearing it on this most auspicious day."

Sebastian's mother turned back to him. "And don't you look handsome, my son. If only your father were here to see you."

Sebastian glanced over at Vittorio to see if he was offended by that statement, but the commander beamed broadly, as if it had nothing to do with him.

"Captain Portinari, man of the hour!"

General Zaniolo appeared, a glass of vodka in his left hand, a shy young woman half his age on his right arm.

"It's good to see you, General," said Sebastian.

"It's nearly time for you to show off all that hard work you've been putting in this week," said the general.

"Er...yes, I suppose it is...," said Sebastian.

"Hard work, my darling?" asked his mother.

"General Zaniolo has been kind enough to give your son a quick introduction into the intricacies of courtly dance," said Vittorio.

"Oh, how wonderful," said his mother. "My thanks, General. I fear Sebastian had little instruction in such niceties as a boy."

"That was readily apparent, my lady," Zaniolo said cheerfully. "But between my vast knowledge and his sincere efforts, I think we've at least managed to guarantee he will not trip and fall headfirst into the cake."

"No man can be master of all skills, my lady," Vittorio said earnestly. "And as we all know, Captain Sebastian has a great many other talents."

"Speaking of which," said Zaniolo, "I'm curious to see how he fares at command. Have you assigned his unit yet?"

Vittorio shook his head. "As you know, the poor fellow has been absolutely beside himself with anticipation for this day, so I thought it best to wait until the engagement had been settled before throwing him into such a challenging and important role."

Zaniolo nodded sagely. "As usual, Commander, your wisdom out-shines us all."

"Now, now, Savitri," chided Vittorio. "If you keep up such lavish praise, I might begin to suspect that you are drunk."

"Perish the thought, Commander," said Zaniolo, then tipped his glass back and drank the remaining vodka in one gulp.

Vittorio sighed ruefully, like a father who is slightly disappointed in his son. But then he looked across the room, and suddenly smiled.

"Well, my boy. I believe it's time."

Sebastian followed the commander's gaze and saw Galina stand-ing on the other side of the crowd. She wore a sleeveless white lace gown with gloves that reached up to the elbow so that only her upper arms were bare. Her long, honey-colored hair, usually left free of all constraints, had been artfully braided and piled atop her head, which displayed her thin, graceful neck to great effect. Her large green eyes were fixed on his, as if nothing else in the whole world existed but him, and her delicate lips curved upward into a gentle smile. He had never seen anything more beautiful in his life.

Behind Galina stood Lady Prozorova, her expression one of abso-lute rapture, her cleavage nearly bursting out of the pale pink gown that contained it. Beside her stood Lord Prozorova, looking less aloof than usual. Sebastian might have imagined it, but there even seemed to be a slight smile on his lips.

Perhaps a signal had been given, or perhaps the connection between Sebastian and Galina was simply that palpable. Whichever it was, the chamber orchestra stopped playing, then the guests quieted down and parted to either side so that the space between him and his bride-to-be was clear.

"Forward march," murmured Vittorio as he gave Sebastian a gentle but firm push.

Sebastian suddenly began to doubt his ability to walk in a normal fashion. It felt as though he tottered forward on stilts, his arms stiff at his sides. His mother and Commander Vittorio followed behind him. Galina and her parents also began to walk forward so that all six met in the center of the room.

Lord Prozorova began. "We thank you, Lady Portinari, for inviting us to partake in the generosity of your..." He paused and glanced around. "Home." The words were part of the formal engagement ceremony, and apparently could not be changed to match the situation.

"We thank you, Lord and Lady Prozorova, for accepting our invitation," Sebastian's mother intoned. "I give my only son, Sebastian Turgenev Portinari, this ring, which is a symbol of our commitment to his pledge." She handed the ring to Sebastian.

"Lo—" Sebastian cleared his throat. "Lord and Lady Prozorova, with this ring I pledge my heart, my honor, and my life to your daughter, Galina Odoyevtseva, so that we may be bonded for this life and the next in eternal matrimony. May she wear it as proof of this commitment?"

"She may," replied Lord Prozorova.

Sebastian held out the ring, his eyes locked on hers. "Galina Odoyevtseva, do you accept this ring?"

Galina held his gaze as she extended one of her gloved hands. "I do."

He gently slipped the ring onto her finger.

"Let all here witness the promise made this day between Sebastian Turgenev Portinari and my daughter, Galina Odoyevtseva Prozorova!" Lord Prozorova said in his deep, dry voice.

"*We witness.*" The sound of so many voices speaking at once boomed like thunder. Then everyone burst into applause.

Sebastian stood, red-faced and lock-kneed, his eyes clinging to Galina's soft smile like a man about to drown. The only time he'd felt more overwhelmed was when he'd first released the full force of his magic on the Pustoy Plains.

The six of them stood there until the applause began to die down. Then Lord Prozorova signaled to the orchestra and they struck up a tune that sounded surprisingly like an Izmorozian folk song, rather than an imperial courtly air. The musicians, all Aureumians, were clearly struggling with the unfamiliar piece, but they plunged gamely on.

"Well, Sebastian?" said Galina. "Shall we dance?"

Sebastian swallowed hard and held out his hand. When her slim fingers touched his, he drew her in until their torsos were nearly touching.

"I'm afraid I'm not very good at this," he whispered in her ear.

She grinned. "Did you think I was?"

"What shall we do, then?"

She shrugged. "The best we can, I suppose. If we are able to avoid stepping on each other's toes, I shall call it a success."

And so they began their awkward, four-legged gait around the open space in the center of the room, with their guests smiling politely all the while.

At first Sebastian felt painfully self-conscious, but as they danced, his attention was drawn to just how close Galina was. His hand was pressed against her lower back. He could feel her muscles shift beneath the fabric of the dress, and feel the heat from her skin through the thin material. He could feel the softness of her cheek as it brushed against his, and see the throb of her pulse in her elegant neck. What did he care what others thought when he held this beautiful, perfect woman in his arms?

"There they go," she whispered sadly in his ear.

He turned to see her parents, his mother, and Commander Vittorio quietly slip out through a door in the back.

"I do dislike the transactional nature of this ceremony," she told him.

"Yes."

"However, there are some aspects I like quite a lot."

"Such as?"

She flashed a surprisingly wolfish smile. "Well, for starters, you are expected to kiss me as often as conveniently possible. So why don't you do that now?"

They gave up the pretense of dancing, and instead he took her face in his hands and drew her in for a kiss. She returned it with a fierceness that surprised and delighted him. She grasped his back with both hands and pulled him closer so that their bodies were pressed together, and his head was swimming in a rapture he had never known before.

Silently, he renewed his vow to protect Galina Odoyevtseva no matter the cost. Nothing would take this happiness away from him.

33

As Sonya and Jorge continued their trek west, dark clouds covered the sky, changing the tundra snows from sparkling white to drab gray. It was nice that they didn't have to wear snow goggles as they trudged along, but it cast a dreamlike gloom over their surroundings that made it difficult to distinguish where the land ended and the sky began. It reminded Sonya unpleasantly of the banks of the Eventide River.

The clouds also brought a noticeable drop in the temperature. The storm Tatiana had mentioned would be here soon. She could already smell it on the wind.

"We better stop and make camp here," she told Jorge.

"So early?" he asked. "Why?"

"There's a bad storm coming. We need to take some extra time now to dig out as sturdy a shelter as we can, because we might be stuck there for a few days."

"A few *days*?" His eyes widened.

"Aw, don't be like that, Jorge." She grinned at him. "I don't smell that bad, do I?"

"You probably smell better than me. Not that I could tell…" He frowned and his eyes grew distant, as if that had given him an idea, perhaps for some new potion. Then he shook his head. "My concern is that if we have to wait out a storm for several days, we might not have enough food to get us to the other side of the tundra."

"True. That's why we veered northwest instead of due west yesterday when we started out."

"We did?" Apparently he hadn't noticed. "But how does that help?"

"Because now we're nearly to the White Sea. There isn't much inland hunting on the tundra during the winter. Most mammals have either migrated to another area or started hibernating. But there's still plenty of fish in the sea. We lost about a day coming this far north, but as Mikhail Popov used to say, better to lose one day than all of them."

"The White Sea?" Jorge squinted as he scanned the muddled gray horizon. "It's really that close?"

"Trust me. I can smell the salt. It's less than an hour's walk north of here. You start on the shelter and by the time you're done, I'll have some fresh fish for us. Or maybe even a nice fat seal!"

"I've never actually seen a seal," said Jorge.

"And you won't today even if I catch one," she said. "Something like that is too big to drag for an hour through the snow. I'll just cut off as much meat as I can carry and leave the rest for scavengers."

She dropped her pack and took out the few items she would need for ice fishing.

"Make the shelter bigger than usual so we can actually move around if we're stuck down there for a little while."

Jorge nodded. "Good luck."

"Who needs luck when you have skill."

Then she pocketed the hooks, line, and bait, slung her ice cleats over her shoulder, and started north.

The transition from tundra to ocean shore was almost unnoticeable, given how much of it was frozen over at this time of year. It wasn't until she was some ways out on the ice that she was able to see the black, rippling waters of the sea. The ice was thinner that far out, so it would be easier to break through.

She cleared a small area of snow, then changed from snowshoes to ice cleats. The bottoms of the cleats were lined with a jagged layer of tiger teeth, which prevented her from slipping. Then she drew her knife and began the slow, tiring work of chiseling a hole in the ice that would be big enough to pull a fish through.

Once she could see the cloudy black water, she pulled out her fishing line, tied one end to a small hook carved from whalebone, and baited the hook with a bit of meat. She slid the baited hook into the water, twirled the fishing line around her gloved hands, and sat down to wait. To Sonya's mind, fishing was merely another form of hunting. Like hunting, it required patience and absolute focus. One might have to wait in stillness for hours and then suddenly spring into action before the fish stole her bait.

By carefully reading the vibrations of the line, Sonya was able to catch a small pile of fish in a relatively short amount of time. She strung them all together with a rope through their gills, which would make them easier to carry back to the shelter.

The wind was stronger on the coast, bringing with it a sharp salt tang that never failed to soften her heart. As she sat and waited for the next bite, she wondered what it would be like to live life on the sea in one of those huge ships Mikhail had sometimes spoken of. Perhaps when she had liberated Izmoroz, she would find out.

She noticed that she hadn't had a nibble in a little while. She wondered if the fish had wised up. She had caught enough already, but there were still probably a few hours before the storm hit, so she decided to enjoy the solitude a little longer.

Occasionally, she felt a faint vibration beneath her feet, as if someone was dragging something across the surface of the ice. But when she looked around, all she could see was black rippling water on one side and rolling, uneven snowdrifts on the other. She was alone, and she was content.

It wasn't until the water in her fishing hole begin to bubble that she understood the danger. She had just enough time to grab her rope of fish and jump clear of the hole before the massive head of a black-and-white orca whale burst through.

The orca paused for a moment, showing a gaping mouth so wide it could have easily bitten her in half. Then it slipped back into the water, leaving a hole much bigger than the one she'd carved out.

As she lurched to her feet, she felt the ice vibrate again. The whale was moving, circling beneath her, no doubt getting ready for another pass. She had to get off the ice before it struck again. But she didn't have time to change back to her snowshoes and she cursed in frustration as her legs pushed against the snow with agonizing slowness.

The whale smashed through the opening again, this time widening it enough that it could fit its entire body through. It landed so heavily on the ice that it sent Sonya sprawling into a drift. Its black-and-white hide was scarred in half a dozen places, and it was over thirty feet long, far bigger than any orca had a right to be.

Sonya had heard of such a beast. People called it Lord Massa. Larger, smarter, and more aggressive than any other orca, some said it had lived so long that it had grown wise to men's tricks and perhaps had even come up with a few tricks of its own. Others said that no whale like this could exist in nature and that it must have been enhanced by some sort of magic. Still others whispered that it was a Ranger of Marzanna who had given up so much of his humanity that he was now indistinguishable from the beasts.

If it was indeed a Ranger, he no longer recognized the garb of his fellows. Sonya's stomach gave a sharp lurch when he fixed his hungry black eyes on her. His cavernous, toothy mouth snapped open and closed as his tail slammed into the ice over and over and he inched his massive bulk toward her.

The ice quaked with each blow, making it difficult for Sonya to regain her footing. She lurched forward, forcing her way through the drifts as fast as she could. She silently prayed that she would reach solid ground before the ice broke apart.

But the Lady Marzanna did not hear her prayer, or chose not to grant it. With a thunderous crack, the ice beneath Sonya split open. Snowdrifts slid into the dark water, dragging her down with them.

The moment she entered the water, her body seized up from the shock of the cold. Her clothes took on water, growing increasingly heavy. She fought against the weight and the numbness of her limbs as she swam toward the surface. But the current had swept her under a portion of unbroken ice. She hacked at it with her knife, but it was so thick that she barely made a dent, and every blow against the ice made her want to take a breath.

She saw a cloud of bubbles and pushed away from the ice in time to avoid the snap of Lord Massa's jaws. The orca began to swim languidly around her in a circle, biding his time, toying with her, knowing he now held a supreme advantage over his prey.

Then Sonya spotted an area a short distance away where the ice appeared to be broken enough for her to exit. She wanted to swim toward it as fast as she could, but knew the orca would be more quickly drawn to such prey-like behavior. So even though her lungs were burning for air and she had to clench her teeth to stop from involuntarily taking a gulp of water, she swam slowly, almost peacefully toward the break in the ice.

It wasn't until she was almost in reach of the opening that the orca understood that his prey was not merely drifting in the current but making her escape. He launched himself toward her, but she grasped the edge of the ice and hauled herself up before he could reach her.

She gasped for air but was unable to take a deep breath, and her body shivered uncontrollably, both potential signs of hypothermia. Her head was growing foggy, as though she were drunk. She wanted nothing more than to merely lie there in the warm snow, but she forced herself to stand up.

Lord Massa burst from the water once again, his mouth open wide. He was so close, she could smell his foul, fishy breath. She stumbled backward and one of the straps on her ice cleats broke. She tore it off her foot and hurled it at the orca. Its tiger teeth embedded in his snout, and he made a strange sound somewhere between a whistle and a groan. As he tried to shake the claw off, Sonya pulled off her other cleat and threw it at his eye. This time, he bellowed in unmistakable rage. She lurched over to her snowshoes and forced her unfeeling hands to strap them onto her feet. Then she grabbed her line of fish and ran. Soon she was well out of Massa's reach.

But she was now running headlong into the oncoming storm.

Her body felt rubbery, and her coordination was failing her. She fell several times. Each time it was harder to get back up, and each time she ran more slowly. After a while, running became impossible. Even when walking, she continued to fall, until at last she could no longer get up at all. She managed to roll over onto her back before her strength gave out completely and she grew still.

She didn't know how long she lay there in the snow, but at last the snow began to swirl all around her. The storm had arrived.

In her increasingly addled state, Sonya could no longer feel the cold, and her circumstances were unclear. What was she doing out here in this storm? Should she try to find shelter? But she was so tired, and the storm was so beautiful. The air was thick with dancing snowflakes, and the purple clouds overhead writhed sensually. The wind sang its song of savage freedom, lulling her to sleep. She was so warm and comfortable. And so very weary. It was time for her to rest...

"My darling *Lisitsa*, you are as vexing as you are endearing," said a voice as swift and cutting as the wind. "Did you think you were finished with your task?"

"No, my Lady...," Sonya whispered.

"Good."

Pain lanced through her eyes, shocking her back awake. But when she opened them, all she saw was darkness. It felt as though hot pokers were being driven into her skull. She screamed with a raw animal anguish as she clapped her gloves, now stiff with ice, over her face. The brutal cold had returned, and her body felt like it was on fire. She screamed again, so long and loud she was left gasping for breath.

"Sonya!"

It was Jorge's voice.

Hands grabbed under her arms.

"My God, your clothes are stiff as a board!"

He dragged her through the snow and into the shelter he had dug for them. Once inside, he stripped off her icy clothes.

"Okay, hypothermia...skin to skin contact...," he muttered. "It's fine. This is necessary..."

He hurriedly pulled off his coat, then his shirt. Bare-chested, he lay down on a blanket, pulled her in close to him, and wrapped the blanket around both of them. The warmth of his skin spread across her body like a salve and she sighed. The burning sensation lessened, as did the shivering, until at last she drifted back into unconsciousness.

She woke some time later to find herself sandwiched between two blankets, while still being wrapped in a third. The shelter was impressively large. Big enough for several people, in fact. Jorge was roasting the fish she had caught over a small cooking fire near the exit where the smoke could escape into the night air. Outside, she could hear the howl of the storm as it raged.

"If you're going to insist on keeping that fire, we'll need to make sure the storm doesn't completely cover the vent," she told him in a soft, scratchy voice.

He turned and looked at her for a moment, then smiled sadly. "I'm glad you're feeling a little better now."

"Yeah," she said. "To be honest, there were a couple moments where I didn't think I was going to make it. I guess this time you really did save my life."

His smile faded. "I'm sorry, Sonya. I don't think so."

"What do you mean?"

His eyes cast about the space until they fell upon her knife. He unsheathed it and held the flat of the blade toward her so she could see her reflection.

The golden eyes of a fox stared back at her.

34

Sebastian stood in the yard and stared at the twenty cavalrymen saluting him, most of whom were older than him, and all of whom had more military experience.

Rykov leaned over and whispered, "Probably want to let them stand at ease."

"Oh, right," he muttered. Then to the soldiers, "At ease, men."

They dropped their salute with obvious relief. He had clearly made them hold it too long. Did they resent him already? Their expressions were carefully neutral, but their eyes glanced to each other frequently, as if silent commentary about their new captain was passing between them. It must be plain as day to them that Sebastian had neither the experience nor inclination to lead. He'd been pleased by the promotion initially, especially once Zaniolo had pointed out that it would help him marry Galina. It wasn't until the engagement ball, when Zaniolo had asked Vittorio if Sebastian had been assigned a unit, that the idea even entered his mind that he would actually have to lead people. And frankly, he'd had a lot more pressing expectations in that moment, so the idea hadn't found a great deal of purchase in his mind.

That changed a few days later, when Commander Vittorio led him to this group of soldiers and informed all present that Captain Portinari was henceforth in command of the 404th Imperial Cavalry. All had saluted the commander with a sharp "Yes, sir!" Vittorio had nodded in satisfaction, and then walked away without giving Sebastian any additional guidance.

And here they all stood.

"Yes, well...," said Sebastian. "I look forward to working with you all."

Again they all exchanged silent, judging glances.

Not knowing what else to say, he concluded with, "Er...that is all. You are dismissed."

The soldiers quietly dispersed, stealing glances back at their new young captain. One whispered to another, "What are we supposed to do now?" The other shrugged. "Hell if I know."

"What indeed!" said Sebastian that evening after recounting the entire awkward situation to Galina. "What am I to do with twenty soldiers?"

"You will think of something, darling." Galina sat and watched as he paced anxiously around the room, nearly tripping over a pink upholstered ottoman in his distress. "Or perhaps this is an indication that the commander intends to assign your first mission soon. All you've been doing these past months is magic training and assisting the generals. Surely you are ready for something more substantial, my *volshebnik*."

Volshebnik was an Old Izmorozian word Galina had adopted as a pet name for him. It meant wizard or sorcerer, but could also mean someone who was enchanting or charming. His betrothed delighted in such wordplay, and normally he didn't mind. But on this occasion, the nickname rankled.

"I can assure you, my soldiers did not find me charming in the least," Sebastian said with more rancor than he'd intended. He stopped his pacing, took a moment to compose himself, then sat next to her. "I'm sorry, my love. It's just...even if the commander does assign me a mission, those men don't want me as their leader."

"Why should they, when you have not yet shown them what kind of leader you are?" she asked. "And how can you do that until you decide what kind of leader you want to be?"

"What kind of leader?" he asked.

She gave him a patient smile. "As you know, my *volshebnik*, I have no military experience. But I have read a number of volumes written by famous and respected leaders throughout the known world. Perhaps their collective wisdom might aid you in sorting out this dilemma."

"Perhaps . . . ," he said dubiously.

She considered for a moment, then said, "I believe it was the Aureumian General Matteo Fontanelli who wrote in his memoirs, 'A commander's men are an extension of his will. If his conviction is strong, and his goals are clear, his men will be inspired and gratefully accept any direction he gives.'" She brushed back Sebastian's bangs, which had fallen in his agitation. "Despite all the doubts and misgivings you expressed to me when we first met, I have seen your conviction grow stronger with each passing day. You have found a passionate cause that inspires you. Can you not share that passion with your men? Can you not inspire them as you are inspired?"

He considered that a moment. The root of his conviction, of course, was to protect Galina and those he loved at all costs. Surely each of his men had someone they also cared deeply about. Could it be that simple?

He pressed his lips to her hand. "My Galechka, you are a treasure without equal. I will do exactly that!"

The next day, he asked Rykov to assemble his platoon at the riverbank. They again stood before him, neutral expressions and flickering gazes. Each man had been told to bring an unlit torch with them, and they held the thick, rag-tipped sticks awkwardly, clearly unsure of their purpose. There was a moment when Sebastian felt the squirm of embarrassed discomfort, but he was able to push it away by fixing Galina's patient smile in his mind.

"Gentlemen," he said in a firm voice. "I welcome you to the new Four Hundred and Fourth Cavalry. I value candor above all else, and I will prove that to you now by telling you about myself. That way there will be no doubts regarding the man who leads you."

Galina's suggestion that he write out the speech and memorize it ahead of time had also been wise. He didn't mumble, stammer, or trip over his words as he was sometimes wont to do in high-pressure situations, and instead spoke clearly and effortlessly.

"My full name is Sebastian Turgenev Portinari. While it is true that my father was the renowned Aureumian Commander Giovanni Portinari, my mother is a descendant of one of the oldest families in Izmoroz. Like you, I have grown up here and consider myself an Izmorozian. You are no doubt aware that a great evil is looming on the western horizon. The foul and unholy Uaine Empire, along with their legion of undead, seek to claim our people and our land for themselves. I have been recruited, and this unit has been formed, for the express purpose of combating that dire threat."

He gazed out at them and for once they were not looking sidelong at each other, but instead looking with increasing worry at him. As he'd hoped, this sounded like a far more daunting task than they'd anticipated.

"We all want to protect our homeland, of course," he continued. "But in the dark times ahead, as we face horrors beyond imagining, it will be difficult to sustain our resolve merely with high ideals." He took out the gold locket that hung around his neck and opened it to show the tiny portrait of Galina that had been her engagement present to him. "This is my betrothed, Galina Odoyevtseva Prozorova. No matter what else might happen, or how terrible things might get, I will protect her and keep her safe to my dying breath. Any who threatens her will know my wrath."

He held out his torch and Rykov lit it, as he had been instructed beforehand. Sebastian watched the flames grow for a moment, then took out his diamond.

"This is what my wrath looks like."

He focused his will on the diamond, then hurled the torch across the river. As it sailed in a high arc, he made it burst into a giant blaze that momentarily lit up the overcast sky.

As Sebastian had hoped, the men's eyes went wide at the fiery display and their worry was now mixed with awe. They probably hadn't seen much magic, if any, in their lives, and even this small demonstration was impressive to them. It had to be small, because he planned to do it twenty more times.

"You, step forward." He pointed to one of the soldiers.

The soldier flinched, but then gathered his nerve and stepped in front of Sebastian. He was half a foot taller and nearly twice as broad in the shoulders, but now Sebastian didn't feel intimidated.

"What is your name?"

"Bogdan Vishneva, sir!"

"And who is it you wish to protect more than anyone else in the world?"

"I...suppose my niece, sir. Sh-she's only four, bless her, and as sweet as an angel. I couldn't stand it if anything bad happened to her."

"What is her name?"

"Tamara Vishneva, sir."

"Light your torch."

Bogdan obediently lit his torch from Rykov's.

"This will be our wrath to anyone who dares threaten Tamara Vishneva. Throw the torch."

Bogdan threw the torch, and Sebastian made it explode just as he had the first one.

"Well done. You may step back in line."

Sebastian brought them up one at a time and asked them who they most wished to protect. A wife, a sister, a younger brother, a mother, an elderly father, the range was wide. He committed the person's name to memory, then demonstrated that they were also under his protection. He had to improvise a little bit when one soldier, Leonid Lopokova, confessed he had no one. But Sebastian had done over half of them by then and was so swept up in his enthusiasm and the warming looks of his men that he handled it rather well.

"I might have said the same thing before I met my betrothed a few months ago," he told Leonid. This was a small lie. He would have said his mother. "But there will come a day when you see your true love and you will know, as I did when I first laid eyes on Galina Odoyevtseva, that she is the person you will dedicate your life to protect. Be assured, we will not allow the filthy Uaine to take her life with that promise unfilled!"

He continued until he had spoken to every one of his men. After flamboyantly combusting twenty-one torches, Sebastian was feeling very light-headed. But he managed to finish his speech.

"Make no mistake, the task before us is daunting. But with such precious souls under our protection, how can we fail!"

He lifted up the fist that held his diamond, and was both surprised and delighted when they lifted their fists as well and cheered.

"You are dismissed," he told them.

They all dispersed, looking far more lively than when they'd arrived, chatting with each other, asking each other more about the person they'd chosen to protect. Sebastian decided that this could be the beginning of something truly grand.

Then he swayed slightly, and Rykov caught his shoulder.

"Maybe you should lie down for a little while."

"Good idea," he said.

With Rykov's help, he tottered back to headquarters and into his room. The anticipation of telling Galina about his success with his men kept him too excited to fall asleep, but Rykov brought him some broth. They had learned after many days of rigorous training that when he overexerted himself like this, the hot, salty liquid helped more than anything else.

He was just beginning to feel better and was contemplating taking a carriage to Roskosh Manor, when a young boy in uniform appeared at his door, breathless and looking a little wild-eyed.

"Captain Portinari, sir!" The boy saluted.

Sebastian sat up. "What is it?"

"Commander Vittorio requests your presence in his quarters immediately, sir."

"I take it this is urgent?"

"It is, sir!"

"Lead the way, then."

Sebastian followed the boy through the halls to Vittorio's quarters. As always, he found the commander's living quarters to be inexplicably soothing. Hunting trophies hung from the walls, along with a portrait of Empress Morante somehow looking both stern and serene. The furniture was made of a light cedar wood and stuffed soft leather that had been shipped up from Aureum. There was a curious musky, spicy smell that always seemed to linger in the air. Somehow this combination of elements lent the entire room a sense of calm masculine authority. It was no exaggeration to say that this room was the true seat of power in Izmoroz, and it was comforting to find its occupant always thoughtfully attending the needs of his people. As exciting and flashy as Sebastian's earlier effort had been, he understood that *this* was what true leadership looked like.

At present, the commander sat behind his desk, frowning thoughtfully at a grimy piece of parchment marked with a messy, almost childlike script.

"Ah, Captain, come in," he said when Sebastian arrived. "Have a seat."

"Yes, sir."

"Roloff, it's going to be a long night, I fear," he said to the boy. "Go get some food in the mess hall, then bring a plate back for me."

"Yes, sir!" The boy saluted, then scampered off.

Sebastian sat down in the wooden chair in front of the commander's desk. "Is there something I can assist with, sir?"

Vittorio placed the parchment on the desk, then steepled his hands and smiled wearily at Sebastian.

"Indeed there is, Captain…" He frowned. "Have you lost weight?"

"Me? I…don't think so…"

"I shall speak with Rykov to make certain you are eating three square meals a day, as a young man should. And speaking of food, I suspect you were planning to enjoy supper at Roskosh Manor tonight?"

"I was, sir."

"Sadly, I will have to deny you that chiefest of pleasures this evening. I've just learned that the workers of Bledney Mines have revolted." He tapped the parchment. "The situation sounds most dire. The crew chief and boss have been taken hostage, and the miners have issued a number of demands. I need you to assemble your unit, travel to Bledney Mines, and restore order, preferably with as few casualties as possible."

"I—I see, sir." Sebastian had never considered that he might need to take action against his own people.

Vittorio frowned. As if reading Sebastian's thoughts, he said, "Soldiers must not only protect the peace of our borders, Captain. We must also keep the peace within our borders. Bledney Mine is a vital resource for the imperial army. Without the ore it provides, we would be hard-pressed to equip our soldiers properly. Would you want to send the brave men of Izmoroz against a horde of undead unarmed?"

"Of course not, sir."

"Good. So you understand what is at stake here?"

"I do, sir."

"Excellent. Once you have ended the revolt, I would then ask you to investigate the cause. It has been my experience that such things only happen when men are pushed beyond their capacity. It is true that the miners have broken the law and therefore must be punished. But if the owners have abused their authority, you are also authorized to punish them in whatever way you see fit. As with all things, the empire must approach this unfortunate incident with a fair and unbiased hand."

"Y-yes, sir."

Vittorio gazed at him for a moment, his eyes clear and strong. "This is your first mission, Captain. Do not disappoint me."

232

35

The Bledney Mines were located northwest of Gogoleth at the base of the Cherny Mountains. Sebastian was not as good a rider as his sister and had never felt comfortable on horseback. But a captain was expected to ride with his men rather than in a carriage, so he managed as best he could, hoping no one noticed the awkwardness with which he held his reins or the stiffness of his posture.

The landscape north of Gogoleth was flat, with sparse copses of pine dotting the white powdery fields. The Cherny Mountains loomed in the distance, seeming to get no closer, while Sebastian's thighs, groin, and rear grew increasingly sore. He knew he couldn't show weakness to his men, so he clenched his teeth and bore the pain silently. Unfortunately, this meant that by the time they reached the mines near midnight, his jaw was sore, he had a raging headache, and combined with his weariness, he was in a foul mood.

Ten gaunt, filthy men stood at the entrance to the mine. Their clothes were ragged and stained with dirt, and they were armed with shovels, pickaxes, and the occasional knife. The idea that they could stand up to Sebastian's twenty trained and well-armed soldiers was so preposterous, he nearly laughed with relief. But he reminded himself what Vittorio had said about men being pushed beyond their capacity. They probably deserved his pity, not his mockery.

He halted his men a short distance from the miners and prodded his horse a few steps closer so that he was in front.

"We come in the name of Her Imperial Majesty, Empress Caterina Morante the First, to restore the peace." He tried to make his voice sound as commanding as possible. "Lay down your weapons and your lives will be spared."

A bald miner, so pale and thin he almost appeared to be a skeleton, spat on the ground. "The damn empire sends *children* to punish us, huh? Well fuck you, pretty boy. We're sick of it."

Sebastian stared at him, not quite able to fathom what had just happened. Even though the odds were clearly in Sebastian's favor, this man was not only defying him, but insulting him.

Rykov pulled his horse up beside Sebastian and drew his sword. "You want me to teach this guy a lesson about respect?"

The miner eyed Rykov's gleaming sword, but did not back down. Instead he gripped his pickax with both hands. "We ain't going to surrender. I promise you that."

Sebastian was tempted to let Rykov handle it. But he knew his standing with his own men was still tenuous. Pretty speeches were nice, but a soldier proved their true worth by their actions. Besides, this man had insulted him directly. He needed to decisively show his men that they could count on his firm leadership.

"That won't be necessary, Private." He grasped his diamond, which hung from a leather thong around his neck. "This fellow will soon regret being so hot-blooded."

The human body contained a vast amount of fluid. Not just blood, but sweat, saliva, tears, and urine as well. Sebastian would have to be extremely careful here or he would instantly cook the man alive. This was a lesson, after all, not an execution. A few degrees should be enough to get the message across.

He focused his will into the diamond, then let it out slowly. The miner gasped as his face began to flush bright red. Sweat broke out on his bald scalp, cutting through the grime in streaks as it trickled down his face and neck. His lip curled into a snarl as he glared up at Sebastian.

"Magic, is it? You can't even fight me like a man? You prissy imperials disgust me!"

More insults. Right in front of his men. Sebastian couldn't believe the gall of this man. Who did he think he was? Didn't he understand how easy it would be for Sebastian to end his life in a blink?

"Have a care, *old man*. I made an effort to be gentle with you, but if you continue to irritate me, I may forget my control."

"You don't scare me, you little piece of shit. I've had *hangovers* that felt worse than this."

Sebastian's face flushed with frustration and embarrassment. He was giving this man every chance to back down, and all he got in return was more insults.

"Is that so? Well, then I'll raise it a few more degrees!"

He increased the heat of the liquids coursing through the miner's body. The man grunted with pain. He didn't release his pickax, but at least he dropped to his knees. Perhaps now the idiot understood how hopeless his situation was.

"That's more like it," said Sebastian. "You've learned some proper respect."

"I'll...never respect...the likes of you."

Sebastian stared in disbelief as the man used his pickax to push himself up off his knees. His eyes were bloodshot, and blood leaked from his nose. His ragged trousers were damp with urine but he looked at Sebastian as if *he* was the disgusting one.

"You entitled...spoiled little brats...think you own us." He spat out the words as his body shook with pain. "I'd rather be dead...than bow to a cowardly little weakling like you!"

"So be it!" Sebastian shouted, then released the rest of his will at once.

The miner froze, his eyes bulging and his mouth open in a silent scream.

Then he burst apart, spraying a steaming pulp of blood, meat, and bones into the cold night air.

The other miners, now covered in the still-hot remains of their leader, gaped first at the red-stained snow where he had just stood, and then at Sebastian, whose hands shook with the shock of his own actions, and the thrill of newfound power. Maybe *now* they would respect him.

But incredibly, one of the miners stepped forward, his face twisted into a mask of rage.

"You monster! How could you—"

That miner also froze, but only for a moment. Then he exploded as well.

"Anyone else?" Sebastian asked through clenched teeth. There was an odd eagerness in his voice that he didn't quite understand.

The rest of the miners threw down their weapons.

"Good," he said, although he felt a brief flash of disappointment. "Private, see these men are restrained."

"You got it, sir," said Rykov.

It was, Sebastian realized, the first time his aide-de-camp had addressed him properly. It made sense. Exploding torches were impressive, perhaps, but they had just learned what Sebastian was truly capable of when his patience was tested. Perhaps he hadn't known himself. Now there could be no doubt from anyone present that Sebastian was a force to be reckoned with.

Once the miners were chained up, Sebastian left a few soldiers to guard them. The rest dismounted and followed him into the mine.

"There might be a few more miners lurking in here, sir," said Rykov as they strode inside, holding the darkness at bay with torches.

"I've made my point," said Sebastian. "You can take care of any stragglers."

"Very good, sir," said Rykov.

There were a few more miners scattered about, but as soon as they saw Sebastian and his men bearing down on them, they realized their main force had already been neutralized, and surrendered immediately.

At last they reached a large, open shaft where two miners held a finely dressed man at knifepoint. Or rather, the man would have been finely dressed if his luxurious mink coat hadn't been caked with dirt and blood. His lip had been split, and one of his eyes was dark and swelling. But when he saw the orderly march of imperial troops, his face brightened.

"Oh, thank God you're here, Captain!"

"Stay back!" said one of the miners who held him.

Sebastian held up his hand and his soldiers halted. Behind him he heard one of them whisper to his fellows, "Like it matters how far back we stand." Several snickered quietly in response. They were breaking rank, but Sebastian allowed them that moment because they were reveling in his power with him. They felt themselves under his protection. One of *his* men. And that made him feel even more powerful.

"What is it you want?" asked Sebastian.

"W-we demand better working conditions!" said the second miner.

"Such as?"

"Only twelve hours of work at a time!"

To Sebastian, twelve still sounded like a long time to perform such grueling work. "How many have you been working?"

"Uh..." The miners looked at each other. Then the first one ventured, "Fifteen? Sixteen? It's hard to say for sure exactly."

"Sixteen-hour shifts? And how many days off?"

They stared blankly at him.

"You've had no days off, then," surmised Sebastian.

"Captain, why are you even listening to these fools?" demanded the captive, looking both nervous and offended.

"Shut up," Sebastian told him. Then he turned back to the miners. "What are your other demands?"

"If the foreman beats a man to death, the man's wife and children are still entitled to the money he earned!"

They nodded to each other, like they thought that such a thing would be a huge victory to achieve.

"And why is the foreman beating people to death?" Sebastian asked.

"Oh, well..." Again they looked at each other, as if hoping the other would be able to provide the answer. "I reckon because he wasn't working fast enough? Or he fell asleep on the job? Something like that. The foreman has a nasty temper so it could be anything, really."

Sebastian stared at them for a moment, marveling at how matter-of-fact they were about such terrible working conditions.

"Let me see if I have this right," he said at last. "After working sixteen hours, a man falls asleep and this is considered punishable by death? And your request is not that these appalling murders cease, but merely that the widow not be cheated out of the money?"

"Uh...," said one of the miners. "Yeah?"

"Why not just quit?" asked Sebastian.

"And go where? The next closest mine is a hundred and fifty miles away."

"I...think I understand now."

When the commander had said these men might have been pushed beyond capacity, Sebastian had thought he knew what that meant. Now he saw that he had not. These men were being horribly abused. No wonder the ones out front had been so suicidally defiant. They were truly in a desperate situation. Did that mean that Sebastian should have treated their leaders more kindly? But they had disrespected him. All they would have had to do was explain the situation as these men were now doing rather than hurl insults at him. Then he would have understood from the outset.

"Captain, I must insist you punish these men at once," said the well-dressed man.

Sebastian regarded him for a moment. "You...*insist*?"

"Clearly you're new to the post, so let me tell you how things are—"

"What is your name?" Sebastian spit the consonants out sharply. More disrespect? And this time from the mine owner? When would people finally understand that he was not to be crossed?

"S-Stalik Nazarov Vysotskaya." The man looked less sure of himself now.

"You are the owner of this mine?"

"I...am." Vysotskaya squirmed under Sebastian's unfriendly gaze.

"And you allowed the foreman to occasionally beat your workers to death?"

Now Vysotskaya looked genuinely worried, and his expression became almost fawning. "Please, Captain. I beg you to understand, these are hard and stupid men. Discipline must be maintained with a firm hand. Examples had to be made to keep the rest in line."

Sebastian felt another pang of remorse. He had done the same thing with the men out front. But what else could he have done? If only they had been smart enough to see that he had not been the enemy, but an arbiter of justice. As the commander had said, he must have a fair and impartial hand. He had been harsh with the miners, now he must be harsh with the owner.

"And what was your rationale for refusing to pay the widows what their murdered husbands had earned?" he asked Vysotskaya.

"Well...I mean...*they* didn't earn it, did they?"

Sebastian shook his head in disgust. "I see that you have no remorse for your grotesque negligence. I hereby charge you with the murder of..." He looked to the miners. "How many?"

They shrugged.

"The exact number of murders is still to be determined. Rykov, arrest this man."

"See here now! This is private property! I can do with my workers as I please!"

"It is, in fact, no longer private property," Sebastian told him. "By the authority invested in me as a duly appointed representative of Her Imperial Majesty, Empress Caterina Morante the First, I strip you of your ownership of Bledney Mines."

"For what cause?" demanded Vysotskaya.

"For inciting unrest in the populace and creating an atmosphere of rebellion. As of this moment, the empire will assume direct control of Bledney Mines."

"Don't you know who I am?" demanded Vysotskaya as Rykov pushed the stunned miners aside and took hold of his arm. "I'm one of the wealthiest men in Gogoleth! You can't do this to me!"

Sebastian's gaze was piercing, and a strange, terrible eagerness once again welled up within him. "*Please* say that again. Tell me what I can and cannot do."

Vysotskaya was clearly more perceptive than the miners had been because he immediately fell silent.

Once they were back outside the mine, Sebastian realized they should have brought a jail wagon to transport all their prisoners back to Gogoleth. Vysotskaya's carriage was nearby, so they stuffed him and as many miners as they could fit into the carriage, then put the rest on horses with his soldiers.

During the long ride back, Sebastian finally had the opportunity to consider his own actions more carefully. He had lost his temper with the miners. There was no doubt of that. And a leader should never lose their temper. Had it blinded him to other potential solutions? Could there have been a way for him to retain the respect of his men without killing those two miners? And why had he felt that strange eagerness after their deaths, as if he wanted to kill more? The second miner had called him a monster. Was he?

Loaded down as they were, the return trip took longer. It was after sunrise by the time Sebastian trudged wearily through headquarters to make his report to Commander Vittorio. He found the commander in his quarters, stripped down to his undershirt as he meticulously shaved his cheeks and chin with a razor.

"Ah, Captain. Come in," Vittorio said cheerfully. "I trust your first mission went well?"

"I . . . I'm not sure, sir," Sebastian admitted.

"Oh?" asked the commander. "Why don't you tell me what happened and then I can be the judge."

So as Vittorio continued to shave, Sebastian told him everything. He spared no details, not even his anger at the miners, because he felt he needed an honest perspective on his actions.

"So you see, sir. I fear I made a mess of things," he said finally.

The commander had finished shaving by then and was in the middle of buttoning up his jacket. He paused in mid button and looked incredulously at Sebastian. "A *mess*? Nonsense, my boy. Quite the opposite!"

"R-really, sir?"

"It was a very tricky situation I sent you into, but I knew you could handle it, and you did even better than I imagined. You put down a violent revolt with only two casualties, arrested a man who was grossly abusing his power, *and* obtained direct ownership of the largest mine in Izmoroz for the empire!" He stepped over to Sebastian and grasped both his shoulders. "Captain Portinari, I couldn't be more pleased. Job well done!"

Sebastian hadn't expected such praise, and he was muddle-headed from hunger and lack of sleep, so it was difficult to determine if it was warranted. The commander was not the sort to placate his men or try to spare their feelings. He was a strong man who expected his men to be strong as well. And yet...

"Captain, you still seem distressed." There was a glint of warning in the commander's eyes.

Sebastian shook his head and forced a smile. "No, sir. I'm merely tired. It's been a trying night. I'm pleased that you consider my first mission a success. It means a great deal to me, sir."

Vittorio nodded in satisfaction. "Excellent. You are dismissed. Go get some well-deserved rest."

"Thank you, sir," said Sebastian as he tried to quiet the unease in his heart.

36

The thing that had surprised Galina most since her engagement to Sebastian was the improvement in her relationship with her mother. She and her mother had never been particularly close. Their temperaments and values were strikingly different, and had been even when Galina was young. Her mother had always acted as if this disparity was somehow a failing on Galina's part, and Galina, not wishing to cause a scene that would inevitably make her father's life more difficult, had never argued the point.

Fortunately, all of that conflict appeared to be in the past. In fact, it was now a common occurrence for the entire Prozorova family to spend time together in the vast library that was her father's pride and joy. Little Vanya would sit on the rug by the fire and play with the toy imperial soldiers that Commander Vittorio had given him on his last birthday. Galina's mother would stretch out on the sofa with her knitting and talk in a gentle and bubbly stream about the latest society gossip, while Galina and her father sat nearby at the large maple desk, murmuring occasional sounds of assent in her mother's direction as they worked. Very occasionally, Galina's mother would pause in her ramblings to say in a dreamy voice, "Oh, my beautiful Galechka, how we shall miss you when you leave us..." Galina would look up from transcribing her father's work, and smile at her. Then Galina's mother would sniff a few times, dab at a nonexistent tear, and continue her rambling.

It was fairly obvious that her mother's change in attitude stemmed from the realization that once Galina married Sebastian and left Roskosh Manor, she would no longer have to compete with Galina for Lord Prozorova's affections, a contest that had rarely come up in her favor. But Galina was grateful for this new peace, regardless of its cause, because it allowed her to focus on helping her father with the great work of preserving Izmorozian culture.

While Galina felt that her work with her father was of profound importance, she was also committed to her other great work, gently guiding her betrothed, and all the power he possessed, away from the empire and over to the side of Izmoroz and its people. Though she had vocalized it to no one, not even her father, she sometimes fantasized that with her intellect and his magic, the two of them might be able to finally liberate Izmoroz from imperial rule. Galina was honest enough with herself to admit that such potential was at least part of why she found Sebastian so appealing.

When Masha entered the library, apologizing for the intrusion and asking if Galina was free to speak privately to Captain Portinari, she did not hesitate to comply. In her mind, she was performing her duty both as future wife and future savior of Izmoroz.

But Galina paused when she entered the drawing room where Sebastian waited for her. He hadn't noticed her arrival yet and he was pacing uneasily back and forth in the small room. His blond hair was more unruly than usual, and his military coat, which he typically took such impeccable care of, was streaked in dirt and grime, as were his usually spotless boots. When he turned to her, his face was gaunt and lacking its usual olive-tinged glow. His eyes looked bleary, with dark, heavy lids, as if he had not slept in quite some time.

"There you are, my dearest Galechka!" He took her hand and stroked it tenderly but anxiously, as though it were a beloved cat that was known to be fickle in its affection. "How are you feeling today, my love?"

"Very well, my sweet *volshebnik*, except for my present concern for you. Have you been pushing yourself too hard?"

He laughed, but it was only a short burst, and seemed more uneasy than mirthful. "I suppose I have, my love. It...has been a difficult night."

"You mean *day*, my dearest?"

He blinked at her in confusion for a moment, then gave another quick laugh and nodded. "Yes, I suppose I do."

"You mean to say you did not sleep *at all* last night? Please, my dear *volshebnik*, come sit with me. Rest your weary head." She gently led him over to the nearest sofa.

"I am a bit tired," he admitted as he sat down next to her.

"Come, I insist." She pressed his head down into her lap. For a moment he resisted, but then it was as if all the anxious energy he had been expressing suddenly left him and his head weighed heavily on the tops of her thighs.

"There now, isn't that a little better?" she asked as she stroked his hair.

"It is." He closed his eyes.

"Now, won't you please tell me what troubles you? I could not bear it if my own sweet *volshebnik* were to hide things from me."

"The life of a soldier is...filled with profound hardship, my beloved Galechka."

She wondered if he was already nearing his breaking point. It would be an additional challenge, not to mention exceedingly awkward, should he leave military service before the wedding, considering Commander Vittorio was paying for a great deal of it. But she was confident that with her father's support they could make it work, albeit with far less pomp.

"I can only imagine the challenges you must face daily, my dearest," she said. "But know that as your betrothed, I am here to support you, no matter what."

He turned his head slightly so that he could look into her eyes without lifting it from her lap. "I cannot tell you how grateful I am to hear that, my love."

"My darling, our lives are now so entwined that they are as one. What troubles you, troubles me. Do not hurt me by saying otherwise."

"Yes of course, I would not dream of it." His hollowed eyes drifted away from her to stare into empty space. "As you know, I could not join you for dinner last night because of a pressing mission given to me directly by Commander Vittorio."

"Yes, your first official mission as captain, my *volshebnik*. Though it saddened me to be denied your company, I was so proud to hear that the commander has begun to put his trust in you so fully."

"It was a...delicate mission, as it dealt with a revolt here in Izmoroz."

"A revolt? Like...some sort of uprising?" Naturally, the peasants would be nearly as dissatisfied with imperial rule as the nobility. Had they already grown so miserable that they were preparing to throw off the domination of the empire? And had such a demonstration already shaken Sebastian's faith in his beloved Vittorio? This could be even better than she'd expected.

Sebastian said, "I suppose you could call it an uprising of sorts... but that seems far too grand a word for it. The men at Bledney Mines had grown weary of the terrible conditions in which they'd been forced to work."

"Oh, I see. It was merely a workers' dispute." Galina strove not to express her disappointment. "Were you able to get everyone to come to terms?"

"Yes, I was, although unfortunately at...some cost." Sebastian was silent for a moment, then said, "You needn't worry, my beloved. Commander Vittorio was most pleased with my work, and insists that the benefits far outweigh the costs. In fact, he called the costs negligible and not something to which I should give another moment's thought. And yet..."

He trailed off. His eyes still stared unseeingly at the space before him. Galina allowed him several moments of silence.

"And yet?" she asked, when it seemed he might not continue at all.

"And yet, I still see their faces in my mind. Especially that first one. He was so defiant. So angry. I didn't understand why at the time. I thought he was merely being disrespectful and provocative to impress his fellows. Later I learned about the cruel conditions under which they were suffering, and I suspect it was that which drove him to such foolhardy desperation. But of course by then it was too late."

There was something unsettling about the way he said it, but she forced her question to carry no tone of judgment. "Too late for what?"

"I killed them, you see." His expression was disconcertedly tranquil now, as if merely recalling a dream. "Two of the miners. I boiled their blood until their bodies burst from the pressure. And it had been nearly... effortless."

Galina forced herself not to stiffen or pull away, even as her stomach clenched and grew cold. Her betrothed had settled a worker's dispute by brutally murdering the leaders. She was not surprised the commander found that an acceptable solution, but how could the sweet young man she had promised her life to even be capable of such an act? Had she so misjudged his character? Or was Vittorio's influence over him even more profound than she realized?

Sebastian's eyes suddenly focused on hers.

"Am I a bad person?" he asked.

Galina knew she could not hesitate in her response for even a moment, or else her silence would be its own reply. She also knew what his pleading, exhausted eyes really wanted. Not judgment, but absolution. On some level, perhaps beneath his own awareness, Sebastian knew that he had done wrong. Yet he was desperate for someone he trusted to confirm the commander's pronouncement that his actions had been justified.

If she were to tell him the horrible truth, she would be placing herself in direct conflict with Vittorio for the battle over Sebastian's soul. It was a battle she had hoped to wage later, when she was in a better position. She needed to be married to Sebastian, to live with him and have his heart and his trust so fully that her presence seemed as necessary to him as air. If she challenged Vittorio too soon, she stood a strong chance of losing not just Sebastian, but all her hopes and dreams for the future. Her parents might even suffer for her actions. They could be stripped of their titles, their lands, their very name. As courteously as Vittorio behaved, Galina had no doubt he harbored a terribly vindictive nature beneath.

There was also the matter of this sweet suffering boy who currently rested his head in her lap. Galina was fond of contradictions because they existed within her as much as those she admired. She was as romantic as she was pragmatic, and when she looked down into Sebastian's anguished gaze, she simply could not cause him further pain.

This all swirled through her mind in the instant between his question and her answer:

"Of course you are not a bad person, my sweet *volshebnik*. You are the protector of Izmoroz and I have no doubt that every choice you make is for the greater good of its people."

Sebastian looked up at her for a moment, his eyes glistening. "Thank you, my love. Thank you."

Then he closed his eyes and tears coursed freely down his cheek, where they soaked into the fabric of Galina's gown.

The two remained silent for several moments. Then Sebastian began to quietly snore. As Galina stroked his hair, she realized that with her absolution, he had at last been able to fall asleep. There was a strange sort of power in her position, but also a terrible responsibility. One which she was not sure she could bear alone.

37

Sonya and Jorge stayed in their shelter for two and a half days before the storm moved past. When they finally emerged, the sky above was a cloudless, bright robin's-egg blue, and any sign of life on the rolling tundra had been completely erased. There was nothing but pure white snow and clear skies as far as Sonya could see. Snowstorms were fierce and deadly things, but the tranquility they left in their wake was one of the Lady's greatest gifts.

The glare on the snow didn't bother Sonya as much as it had before, but she put her goggles on anyway, just to be safe. It had been easier for her to see in the dimly lit shelter as well. It troubled her that she'd had to lose another piece of her humanity, but her new eyes certainly had advantages. Her biggest concern now was that it would be difficult to pass as a regular person in crowded, urban areas like Gogoleth. The ability to finally walk freely and proudly as a Ranger was now a more personal and pressing reason to rid Izmoroz of the empire.

Two days of confinement had given Sonya and Jorge a lot of time to talk. Mostly they had shared childhood memories. Jorge had talked of his siblings, Maria and Hugo, and his parents, who seemed like sweet and doting people. He had also spoken of Colmo, the city in Raíz where he had grown up. It sounded like a strange, almost other-worldly place, with endless heat, palm trees, beaches, and clear blue oceans. Perhaps once Izmoroz was free and her work was done, Sonya would see its beauty for herself.

Sonya had surprised herself by talking mostly of her early life on the farm, before her brother had started displaying such a talent for magic. She felt a warm nostalgia for those childhood memories now, perhaps because life had been so simple and unconstrained by expectation. She wondered what the rest of her life would have been like if her brother had not been a gifted magic user. She might have been happy but dull, marrying some boy from a neighboring farm and popping out children who did not appreciate her. If so, perhaps she should thank the little empire-loving brat.

Having talked so much in the shelter, Sonya and Jorge now walked southwest across the bright tundra in a comfortable silence. The snow-covered ground gradually sloped downward until pine trees could once again be seen half buried in the drifts. As they pressed on, the temperature began to rise, the snow thinned, the trees grew more numerous, and a small, narrow mountain range came into view. After a few more days, they reached the base of the mountains, and followed it south, looking for a passage to the other side. That night, the snow was too shallow to dig a proper shelter, but they found an outcropping at the base of one of the mountains that provided some protection from the cutting winds.

They continued south the next morning, and finally around midday found a narrow pass through the mountain range. The pass gradually descended into a valley where the snow was little more than a dusting. Once they took off their snowshoes, they were able to move a lot faster.

The trees grew more dense the farther they went into the valley, and the snow gave way completely to a coarse yellow grass and low shrubs. Sonya began to spot signs of animal life. Tracks that looked like they came from something like caribou, but smaller, and scents she found familiar but not identical to those she knew.

That afternoon, as she was daydreaming of stalking one of these curious new animals, she caught a brief but unmistakable whiff of human sweat. She stopped and grabbed Jorge's arm.

"Sonya, what's—"

She covered his mouth with one hand and pushed back her hood with the other. Her fox eyes scanned the trees and her pointed ears strained to hear the slightest movement. Her bow and arrows were stowed away in her pack, so the only accessible weapon she had was her long knife. She slowly moved her hand down and loosened the blade in its worn leather scabbard.

Then she caught a slight creak of leather, and movement in one of the thick juniper bushes nearby. The only way someone could have gotten there was if they'd been lying in wait for some time. Sonya and Jorge must have been spotted when they first entered the valley. Were these bandits preparing for an ambush? If so, they were about to learn that sneaking up on a Ranger of Marzanna was impossible.

"Don't move," she muttered to Jorge.

Then she launched herself toward the bush. The figure startled and lifted their head slightly. Sonya leapt over them as she drew her knife. Then she spun around, shoved her knee into the person's back, grabbed them by the chin, and pressed her knife against their throat.

In response, five other people, all dressed in drab gray and green wool clothing, rose from nearby bushes. Some held javelins, others longbows, and all were now aiming at Sonya. She'd caught other scents as she'd leapt toward her prey, so she was not taken completely by surprise. But she was impressed that so many humans had concealed their presence from her as long as they had.

"Blue skin!" called Jorge from the path. "It's the Uaine!"

Sonya looked down at her hostage. It was not a blue-skinned demon, but merely a young woman with blue paint smeared on her face. The "spikes" were simply hair cut short and shaped into points with some sort of clay or mud. She imagined the paint and mud had obscured their scent to some extent, which was why it had taken her so long to get a whiff of them.

"*These* are the Uaine?" She'd been hoping for actual demons, of course, and felt a little let down.

The Uaine shouted at Sonya in an unfamiliar language. She understood the threatening tone, though.

"Back off!" she told them, but that only made them yell at her again even more forcefully.

"Remember we're here to make friends, Sonya!" said Jorge. "What you are doing does *not* look like friendship."

"They were trying to sneak up on us!"

"Perhaps they merely wished to observe us."

"They're pointing arrows at me!"

"Possibly because you have your blade at their comrade's throat."

Sonya ground her teeth in frustration. When she'd come up with the idea of allying with the Uaine, she hadn't counted on a language barrier, but of course it made perfect sense. Why would the enemy of the Aureum Empire bother to learn the imperial common tongue?

"Hullooo, hullooo!"

A sixth Uaine rose up from the bushes. He was a tall, muscular young man with wavy, dark blond hair that hung nearly to his shoulders. Unlike the others, he wore a heavy chain mail shirt over a padded coat. He was armed with a long sword, but it remained sheathed at his hip. In fact, he was grinning excitedly at Sonya and Jorge. There was something both warm and a little reckless in his blue eyes that Sonya couldn't help liking.

"Ya' tell me y'r is friend?" he asked in a thick, guttural accent that added an odd trill to the *r* sounds.

"Yes!" Jorge said immediately. "We're friends!"

The Uaine man kept grinning, but he raised his eyebrow and gestured to Sonya. "Thess friend?"

"Sonya, put the damn knife down!" said Jorge.

"But..." If she did that, she wouldn't be able to jump clear before the others filled her full of arrows and tiny spears.

"Hokay, hokay." The man's tone sounded reasonable. Cheerful, even. He nodded, then walked over to stand between Sonya and the arrows. Then he tapped his chest. "Jest me now. Stell scared?"

She glared at him. "I'm not scared!"

He laughed. "Hokay, shoore!" Then he gestured to Sonya's captive. "Free friend?"

It was a risk, but she knew that the whole idea of coming here was one big risk. She met his smile with one of her own and shrugged as if it was no big deal. Then she sheathed her knife and let the Uaine girl at her feet go.

That Uaine girl immediately spun around and tried to stab her, but Sonya grabbed her wrist and twisted her arm behind her back, forcing her to drop the knife. Sonya kicked the weapon away, then twisted the Uaine's arm more so that she was forced to drop to her knees. To further drive home the point, Sonya pressed her foot down on the woman's back until she was bent forward with her face in the dirt.

Sonya nodded to the woman who struggled to get out from under her boot and looked at the man in chain mail. "Friend?"

He laughed even harder that time. "Aye, aye. Hokay." He waved to the other Uaine and they lowered their spears and bows. He said something to the Uaine under Sonya's foot, and she immediately stopped struggling.

"Friend?" he asked.

Sonya sighed and released the woman. This time she staggered to her feet and glared at Sonya for a moment as she rubbed her arm. Then she stalked over to join the others.

The man's smile finally faded and his voice took on a more serious tone. "What friend want?"

"I want to offer an alliance to your emperor."

"Em-or-ror?" he asked, rolling the *r* sound in a particularly drawn out manner. "What es thess?"

"Emperor. Your leader."

"Oh, *leader*. Aye, Tighearna Elgin Mordha a' Clan Greim es now... eh...lord o' war?" He frowned thoughtfully and muttered something in his own tongue. "No, he es *warlord* of all Uaine. Thess make sense t' ya'?"

"Yeah, that sounds right," said Sonya. "I want to talk to him."

The man's grin returned as he said, "No."

"No?"

"I say no," he agreed. "But ya' fight me. If ya' win, I say *yes*."

"Really?" asked Sonya. "That simple?"

He nodded. "But ya' will lose. Because I es good."

Now she laughed. "Not good enough to beat me."

He laughed along with her. "Oh no? We see. Aye, we see."

"We will," she agreed.

He drew his sword and held it aloft with two hands. It was bigger than any Sonya had ever seen, but the weight didn't seem to hinder him at all. "I am Blaine Ruairc, captain a' Clan Dílis. Y're honored t' fight me."

She held up her knife. "I'm Sonya Turgenev Portinari, Ranger of Marzanna. And the honor is all yours."

His eyes widened as he looked at her knife. "That it? Ya' sure?"

She flipped the knife into a reverse grip and nodded. "This is all I need."

"Uh, Sonya..." Jorge looked very nervous. "Remember we want him to be a friend, so don't kill him."

"Kill me?" Blaine asked Jorge incredulously. He gestured to Sonya with the tip of his sword. "Lettle girl wi' lettle blade. Na' killin' me."

Jorge winced and looked pleadingly at Sonya. "*Please* don't kill him."

"Don't worry, Jorge. I'll just make sure he understands what a stupid thing that was to say."

She lunged toward Blaine, but he slashed his massive blade with impressive speed. She deflected the blow with her knife and used its momentum to alter her course down and to the right. She rolled over one shoulder when she hit the ground, pivoted, and tried to trip him with a scissor kick, but he leapt back and out of the way. Despite his heavy sword and chain mail, he was quite nimble. But in leaping back, he had put enough distance between them that she was able to safely regain her footing.

She feinted another attack at his legs, then when he lowered his sword to guard, she somersaulted over the blade. That would have put her in striking distance, but he dropped backward until his shoulders hit the ground, then used his sword as a pivot on the ground so he could bring his feet up to kick her head. She caught his ankle with her hand before the hard leather boot could strike and spun around his leg like a pole, maneuvering so that her heel was aimed right at his pretty head, which was pressed against the ground with nowhere to go.

He saw where she was going and twisted his torso so that his leg yanked her to one side and sent her into another dive roll. They both regained their footing at the same time and attacked again.

They were well matched. What Blaine lacked in speed, he made up for in force, and he continued to display impressive reaction time. Sadly for him, though, he did not consider his surroundings as much as he should have.

While Sonya didn't manage to land a blow, all her acrobatics pushed him back farther and farther into the trees until at last she had him in a section that was too dense for him to properly swing his massive sword. She made an obvious lunge at him with her knife, and when he tried to block it, his blade slammed into the trunk of a nearby pine. Sticky pine sap welled up from the gash as he tried to yank his sword free, but it was already too late. Sonya closed the distance and jammed the pommel of her knife just hard enough into his neck for him to choke and release his sword as he gasped for air.

Then she casually lifted one foot, took careful aim, and kicked him in the face so hard it broke his nose. He fell backward as blood gushed from both nostrils. The moment his back touched the ground, she pounced on him.

She crouched on top of him, her toes pressed into his stomach and her hands gripping his broad chest, which heaved beneath the chain mail. She smiled sweetly down at him and asked, "Do you say yes?"

He grinned back at her, his mouth and beard wet with the blood that still welled from his nose. His eyes were slightly glazed from the kick to the head, and were beginning to swell. "Aye. I say *yes* to anythin' ya' ask."

She leaned back so that her hands could grip his strong thighs and she leered at him. "Anything?"

"Anythin'," he repeated.

She chuckled. "Well, now. I'll remember that." Then she leapt off him and held out her hand to help him up. "But for now, take me to your warlord."

PART THREE

THE WARLORD OF THE UAINE

"Death hungers for Life, and Life requires Death to give it meaning. To step outside this endless cycle is to finally know the gods in all their capricious cruelty."

—Translation of ancient Uaine text, author unknown

38

Galina had discovered that one could be haunted by images they had never seen. Sebastian's description of how he had killed those miners had not been particularly detailed, but it had been enough for her fertile mind to extrapolate such a vision of horror that it troubled her sleep for several nights after.

Pedro Molina, the famous Raízian playwright, once wrote, "Minds unburdened find clarity, and anxieties shared become mere problems to be solved." Galina needed to talk to someone, but was undecided with whom to share her burden.

She would usually seek out her father's counsel, but she worried that once he heard of Sebastian's actions, he would break off the engagement. While she appreciated her father's desire to protect her from hardship, she felt certain that her betrothed was not yet a lost cause.

Galina's mother would be far less likely to call off the engagement. Galina suspected that nothing short of violence to her person would incite her mother to end it. And perhaps then only if it was excessive. Yet Galina had a hard time imagining what sage advice, or even thoughtful comfort, her mother could provide.

No, Galina needed someone intelligent and altogether less frivolous who also valued Sebastian and the engagement. And that was how, dressed in a shawl, gloves, and mink fur hat, she ended up before the red door of 821 North Veter Street across from bustling Nadezhda Square.

She let the brass door knocker fall several times, then waited patiently, her wool shawl held tightly around her shoulders with one hand to ward off the biting winter wind that swept through the square.

After a few minutes, a handsome young man with a neatly trimmed beard and fitted jacket answered the door.

"May I help you?"

"Please tell Lady Portinari that her future daughter-in-law, Galina Odoyevtseva Prozorova, begs an audience with her."

He bowed. "At once, Miss Prozorova. Won't you please come in out of the cold while you wait?"

"Thank you," she said. "That's very much appreciated."

She stepped into the narrow foyer and examined the paintings that lined the walls while the servant hurried off. She had never been to the Portinari home, and as she looked around, it occurred to her that soon this would be her home. If the foyer was any indication, it was rather small, and the cornices were somewhat plain. The rug beneath her feet was likewise an unremarkable shade of brown. But everything was clean and well kept, and she supposed that was preferable to the inverse. After all, as Monsignor Salvador Musso, Aureumian prelate of Magna Alto, once wrote, "Cleanliness without ostentation may suggest frugality or limited means, but ostentation without cleanliness suggests the most grotesque form of indulgence." Once Galina moved in, perhaps she could persuade Lady Portinari to add a few more decorative touches.

After a few minutes, the servant returned.

"Her ladyship will see you now, if you would kindly follow me."

The parlor he led her to was equally modest yet neat. But what beauty the parlor lacked was more than made up for in the grace and poise of its inhabitant. Lady Irina Turgenev Portinari sat in a high-backed chair with her hands resting in her lap. She wore a rose-colored gown, with her long, silky white hair, pure as fresh snow, loose upon her bare, delicate shoulders. Few women could manage to look regal with their hair down, but Lady Portinari was one of them.

"Galina Odoyevtseva, what a lovely surprise," said Lady Portinari. "To what do I owe the pleasure?"

"I pray you will still look upon me with such fondness once I disclose the worries that preoccupy my mind," said Galina.

"I see." Lady Portinari raised a single eyebrow. "Thank you, Dmitry, that will be all. I will ring if you are needed."

"Yes, my lady." The servant bowed low, and left.

"Won't you sit, child?" Lady Portinari gestured to the sofa nearby.

"I prefer to stand, my lady."

She inclined her head. "As you wish."

Galina walked over to the glass doors that led to the terrace, which overlooked Nadezhda Square. She could not see the square below from where she stood, but the thin cloud covering above was a radiant smoky gray. Why was it that Galina always felt such days were even brighter than those that allowed the sun to shine freely?

"Lady Portinari, have you ever known your son to be cruel or violent?"

"Not in the slightest," said Lady Portinari. "If anything, his flaw is a too-tender heart."

"Rest assured that I feel the same, my lady. From the moment I met him. Yet, have you observed your son to be . . . *changing* these past few months?"

Lady Portinari was silent for a moment. "In what way?"

"What is your opinion of Commander Vittorio, my lady?"

Another pause. "I am grateful for all he has done to benefit my son."

It was an elusive answer. Galina wasn't surprised. After all, she and Lady Portinari didn't know each other well and openly expressing dislike of the most powerful man in Izmoroz was a dangerous proposition. So they were at an impasse that would only be resolved if one of them risked speaking the truth. And since it was Galina who had broached the subject, she knew it must be her.

"I am of course grateful for much of what the commander has given Sebastian," said Galina. "Military leadership has provided him a focus and determination that he might have otherwise lacked. Yet I fear that either the influence of the military, or else the commander's direct influence, has also affected Sebastian in a negative way as well."

"My child, you seem to be skirting around a topic that is difficult for you to broach. I pray you speak candidly and know that I am as fond of you as if you were my own daughter. If you express yourself honestly and intelligently, you will find neither judgment nor condemnation here."

Galina turned from the windows and gave Lady Portinari a smile. She wasn't sure she completely believed the assurance, but she appreciated the gesture nonetheless. "Thank you, my lady. Please know that what I say next is out of a deep concern for Sebastian and a desire to see him become the best man he can be."

Lady Portinari nodded, but said nothing.

Silence hung in the room. Galina was surprised at her own nervousness. She took off her fur hat, which had grown intolerably warm now that she was inside, and placed it on the sofa. Then she took a deep, fortifying breath.

"Sebastian recently recounted the events of his first official mission as an imperial captain, in which he was ordered to broker peace for a workers' dispute at Bledney Mines."

"I believe he mentioned it to me," said Lady Portinari.

"Did he expound on the means by which he settled the dispute?"

"He did not."

"I am sorry to be the one to tell you, then, that he killed two of the miners by boiling them alive with their own blood."

"I see" was all Lady Portinari said.

Her expression did not change. In fact, Galina could not discern even the slightest emotional reaction. Was Lady Portinari truly so poised that *nothing* visibly unsettled her? Or did she simply not care? Some mothers did not like to acknowledge any faults in their sons and would grow angry if any were brought to light. Galina suddenly wondered if she'd made a terrible mistake in coming there. But she was unsure how to break off now without making things worse, so she plunged on.

"Sebastian came to me soon after the mission in a state of great distress. He was...unkempt, which as you know is very unlike him, and it was clear he had not slept in some time. His actions troubled him greatly, but he was attempting to...*console* himself with the commander's assurance that he had handled the situation perfectly. And well...I could sense he was looking to me for affirmation..."

Lady Portinari slowly stood and walked over to Galina. Her expression did not change, but she took Galina's hands, which Galina had not realized she had been wringing, and held them gently but firmly.

"Speak, child. You are safe here."

Galina hoped that was so. Clearly it was too late to turn back now.

"He asked me if...Sebastian asked me...if he was a bad person." Galina vividly recalled his haunted expression, and was surprised to find her eyes filling with tears. "H-he was suffering so, my lady, that I...I could not find it in my heart to condemn his actions, despite the suffering he had inflicted on those poor miners."

"Ah, I understand now."

Lady Portinari guided Galina over to the sofa. Galina wasn't sure what her future mother-in-law understood, but she allowed herself to be pulled down until they were sitting side by side, their knees almost touching. Lady Portinari took out a lace handkerchief and handed it to Galina.

"Thank you, my lady." Galina dabbed at her eyes.

"Selecting you for Sebastian's wife was perhaps one of the wisest choices I have ever made. Be at ease, my child, because you have done exactly the right thing. Condemning Sebastian in that moment would have accomplished nothing except drive a wedge between the two of you. And he *needs* you. Surely you know that."

Galina nodded.

Lady Portinari continued. "I cannot say if it is the commander specifically or the military as a whole that brings such a troubling influence on our beloved Sebastian. His father was so profoundly affected by his own service to the empire that he forbade Sebastian from enlisting. And perhaps he was more right than I realized."

Lady Portinari was silent for a moment, her eyes trailing away, possibly distracted by some memory of her deceased husband. Then she turned back to Galina, her expression firm.

"Regardless, I feel certain that if the two of us work in concert, we can at least soften the hard lessons he is being forced to learn. In the end, that is a woman's job, after all. To act as a counterbalance to man's darker inclinations. Do you understand?"

The tension in Galina's face eased and a cold calm settled over her. "Yes, my lady."

What she understood was that she had not found an ally here. She was on her own.

39

Sonya and Jorge followed Blaine and his blue-painted, mud-haired Uaine through the widening valley for several days. The sky remained a sodden gray, but the temperature grew warmer, and the rough yellow grass and pines were replaced by lush green meadows dotted with white and purple flowers, and the occasional clusters of maple or oak. Birds flew overhead, filling the air with their song, and from the tall grass came the buzz of insects. Sonya had become so accustomed to the silence of the tundra that she found this new cacophony of noise both thrilling and a little overwhelming to her sensitive ears.

In stark contrast to their surroundings, the majority of the Uaine were a quiet and grim-faced lot, keeping to themselves and only occasionally muttering to each other in their rolling, guttural speech. The sole exception was Blaine, who seemed to relish Sonya and Jorge's company, and chatted intermittently in his broken and at times nearly incomprehensible accent about the weather, the landscape, and various plants and animals around them.

"How did you learn to speak Aureumian?" Sonya asked after listening to what she was fairly certain was a description of what this valley would look like when summer came.

"Aye, 'twas old Angelo teach me," said Blaine.

"Angelo sounds Aureumian," said Sonya.

Blaine nodded. "He old soldier who hates hes people now."

"A deserter?" asked Jorge.

Blaine gave him an odd look. "Dessert? No have now."

Then it was Jorge's turn to look strange for a moment before understanding the miscommunication. "Deser*ter*. It means someone who abandons their army."

"No, no," said Blaine. "He just *change* army." Then he gave them a mischievous grin. "To *good* side."

"I hope so," said Sonya.

Blaine narrowed his eyes. "Why ya' want talk t' Elgin Mordha?"

Sonya wasn't sure about the protocol for diplomatic discussion, or if the Uaine even had any protocol, but she figured she might as well tell Blaine. His reaction in a less formal setting might help her fine-tune how she discussed it with the warlord, and he might end up needing to translate anyway.

"The empire has conquered my people, and I want your help to free them."

"Your people?"

"I'm from a country across the tundra called Izmoroz." She decided not to complicate things by mentioning that her father was Aureumian.

"Hmm." His eyes narrowed as he considered that. "Oh, aye. Iz-mo-roz. That was war Angelo left."

"Really?" That sounded promising. Perhaps this Aureumian deserter had already laid the groundwork and made the Uaine sympathetic to her people's plight.

"Aye," he said cheerfully. "Losers wha' could na' protect their own."

Sonya's eyes widened in outrage. "That's not—"

She felt Jorge's hand on her arm. He gave her a pleading look. He was right, of course. She was trying to make friends, not start more fights.

She sighed. "That's one way of looking at it, I guess."

In the afternoons, several of Blaine's Uaine would range out to hunt for that night's meal. After the first day, Sonya insisted on joining them. A new landscape bristling with new game was too much for her to resist. Initially, the others didn't seem pleased that she was tagging along. In fact Blaine had to speak to them in a rather stern tone before they finally agreed. But once she tracked a large buck and took it down with a single arrow, they began to warm to her. Perhaps true hunters didn't require words to win each other's respect.

At night they sat around the campfire and roasted that day's catch on sticks while Blaine played lilting and often sorrowful tunes on his wooden flute. Sometimes his fellow Uaine would even sing along. It reminded Sonya of stories Mikhail had told her about the old days in Izmoroz before the empire came, when the people felt safe in their beliefs, and would spend many evenings singing songs to Lady Zivena and dancing in the town squares.

After several days' travel, the valley opened up onto a vast plain that stretched for miles to the north and south. Far to the west was a mountain range so tall, its snowy peaks were hidden in the slate-gray clouds that never seemed to leave this land beyond the tundra.

About a mile north of where Sonya stood, two small rivers joined, and at the confluence was a large settlement of tents. It looked to be semipermanent, with muddy strips between clusters of tents that suggested frequently trod paths, and a tall, iron-wrought frame in the center that looked like it would be challenging to transport on a regular basis. People could be seen moving about the settlement, though none of them had the blue paint or spiked hair. A number of horses were tethered at one end, and a sizable pen of pigs at the other.

"*This* is the mighty Uaine Empire?" Jorge muttered to Sonya.

"They look to be a nomadic people, so probably not the whole thing," said Sonya. "Although I agree the word *empire* is a bit of a misnomer."

"You think?" he asked dryly.

She shrugged. "I don't really need an empire. If they have even a small army filled with warriors who are as skilled as Blaine, that'll be plenty."

"I'm not seeing any undead shuffling around, either," said Jorge. "Maybe that was a false report as well. Like the demon rumor."

"Un-dead?" asked Blaine, who was several feet away but clearly had sharp ears. "What es?"

"The dead who walk again," said Sonya.

"Oh. Aye." Blaine nodded, but said no more. Did that merely mean he understood what she was saying? Or was he confirming that there were indeed undead at their command? She was tempted to press him for answers, but decided that for now she should focus on meeting the warlord.

"Does this Elgin Mordha live here?" she asked.

"Aye," he said. " 'Tis Clan Greim before ye."

"Oh, see, Jorge? This is only one clan of the Uaine. And Blaine, what's the name of your clan again?"

"Clan Dílis." He grinned at his fellow Uaine. "The *best* clan."

"Really?" she asked.

He shrugged, then stroked his short blond beard. "Sure the handsomest, I think."

She laughed. "It'd be hard to be more handsome."

He nodded sagely. "True ya' speak, Sonah."

"Son*ya*."

He tried again. "Son-ee-hah?"

"We'll work on it," she said.

They walked on for a little while in silence.

Then Jorge asked, "So what's this warlord of yours like?"

"No es handsome es me," Blaine assured him. "But more smart and more..." He thought for a moment. "Mean."

"Wonderful..." Jorge gave Sonya a worried glance.

She slapped his shoulder good-naturedly. "It'll be fine. Worse comes to worse, I'll just have to fight him, too. Right, Blaine?"

Blaine's cheerful demeanor evaporated completely for the first time since they met. His expression was grave, and even a little concerned. "Sonah, ya' would no' ha' so easy a time wi' the Tighearna Elgin Mordha. He warlord for a reason."

40

One reason Tighearna Elgin Mordha was warlord might have been height. He was larger than any man Sonya had ever seen. He towered at least a full head above Blaine. The lower half of his face was covered by a massive auburn beard that reached halfway down his broad chest. The upper half of his face was an uneven relief of scars and pockmarked skin, most likely left behind by the pox that had ravaged every country on the continent not under the Aureumian Empire's protection. Piercing green eyes watched with interest out of the mass of scar tissue as Blaine led Sonya and Jorge into his tent.

The tent was large, with crackling fire braziers, and furs stretched across the ground that dispelled some of the lingering wet chill, which seemed to cling to these lands of the Uaine.

Blaine dropped to one knee before the Tighearna and spoke rapidly in their language. The Tighearna listened, and occasionally nodded, without betraying any emotion. Then at one point, the thick hairy ridge of his scarred brow rose and he interrupted Blaine with a question. Blaine's expression became sheepish when he replied, and Sonya wondered if he had just gotten to the part where he'd been beaten by a "little girl with a little blade."

Elgin Mordha laughed heartily at the response, loudly declared something, then dropped his massive hand on top of Blaine's head like a benediction. Blaine's face reddened, and he became even more embarrassed as he mumbled another reply. That made the Tighearna laugh even harder. He leaned down, grasped Blaine by his shoulders, yanked him up onto his feet, then embraced him.

"Is...that a good sign?" Jorge whispered to Sonya.

"I hope so..." Sonya cleared her throat. "Blaine? Is everything okay?"

"Es okay!" Elgin Mordha thundered as he clapped Blaine on the back hard enough to make him stumble. "You okay!"

"You speak Aureumian, too?" Sonya asked.

Elgin Mordha shrugged and held his thumb and forefinger near each other. "Little bit. Now sit! Drink!"

He clapped his hands loudly and shouted something, then dropped down onto the fur rug. Blaine did likewise, so Sonya and Jorge followed suit. The four sat in a loose circle as a boy hurried in holding a small wooden cask in his arms. Elgin Mordha pried the cork free from the cask as the boy hurried out of the tent and returned with four small wooden cups.

The Tighearna filled each of their cups from the cask, then jammed the cork back into the hole. Sonya took a precautionary sniff and found the aroma very strange. The smell of strong alcohol was similar to vodka, but there was an unfamiliar smoky quality to it as well. When she took a sip, the flavor was even more pronounced.

Jorge immediately began coughing after he took a sip. His eyes became watery and it was clear he was striving valiantly to keep a neutral face.

Sonya grinned. "I thought apothecaries lost their sense of taste, Jorge."

"*Eventually,*" he said. "I've only been studying a few years."

"So!" Elgin Mordha had a volume and presence that seemed to immediately take control of any situation. "Bhuidseach Sonah! What es you want?"

Sonya looked questioningly at Blaine. "Bhuidseach?"

"Et mean...eh...wizard? Or girl is...witch?" He pointed to his eyes. "You ha' the witch's mark."

"Oh, my eyes. And that...doesn't bother you?"

"No, no!" Elgin Mordha cut in. "Bhuidseach honor Clan Greim with visit! Bring...eh...how ya' say *good luck*? Aye! Good luck!"

"Oh. That's great." Sonya couldn't help wishing her own people were so open-minded. She suspected that once she returned to Izmoroz, even some who claimed to follow the old ways would be uncomfortable with her beast marks.

"Ya' not yet say, Bhuidseach Sonah," said Elgin Mordha. "What ya' want."

"I want to form an alliance with the Uaine."

He shook his head. "That what ya' seek. What dya' *want*?"

Despite his thick accent, that seemed to Sonya a rather nuanced understanding of the language. She would need to keep in mind that he might understand a lot more than he could express.

"I want to rid my country of the Aureumian Empire."

He nodded. "Tha' good want. An' ya seek help?"

"The empire thinks you might invade my country this spring or summer, when the tundra is easier to traverse. Their standing army in Izmoroz is small, and if we cross *now*, we can surprise them and take control before reinforcements from Aureum arrive."

"An' then?" asked Mordha.

"Well obviously, I would expect you to swear on your honor that you would not try to take power in Izmoroz. Instead, we would give you a staging ground to invade Aureum. Surely your Angelo has told you all about the endless wealth in Magna Alto."

"Oh aye," agreed Mordha. "Only one problem, Bhuidseach Sonah. We canna' cross in winter. Less ya have magics can get us there?"

She shook her head. "Better than magic. I have knowledge and skill. I can teach you how to cross the tundra, show you how to make shoes that will let you walk on top of the snow, and how to protect your eyes from snow blindness. I can teach you how to find shelter and where to hunt."

"Tha' good." Mordha nodded. "Buh no' enough."

"What do you mean?" asked Sonya. "I swear I can guide your people safely across the tundra with minimal loss."

"People, aye. Buh no' the sluagh gorta."

"Sluagh gorta?" asked Sonya.

"What ya' call un-dead," said Blaine.

"So you really do have an army of the walking dead?" asked Jorge.

"Sluagh gorta no walk in snow," said Mordha. "Too cold." He held his arms out and moved them stiffly up and down. "No' fight. Just break."

"I see . . ." Jorge's brow furrowed in thought. "They don't have an internal body temperature, do they?"

Mordha looked baffled.

"No heat inside?" Jorge asked.

"Ah!" said Mordha. "Aye, only cold inside."

"That makes sense," said Jorge. "Without a consistent internal body temperature, there's nothing to prevent them from freezing solid. Within a day on the tundra, they would either be unable to move, or their limbs would start breaking off."

Mordha nodded. "Just so."

"I hadn't thought of that," admitted Sonya. "And you need these . . . sluagh gorta?"

"Oh aye. Canna' fight wi'out 'em. Make ancestors angry, they no' fight."

"These sluagh gorta," said Jorge. "Do they feel pain?"

"Sluagh gorta feel no pain, feel no fear, feel no doubt," Mordha said proudly. "Someday we *all* be sluagh gorta."

There was a curious reverence in his tone that made Sonya think that the Uaine considered becoming a sluagh gorta after death to be a great honor.

"I have been working on a . . . well, let's call it a salve," said Jorge. "Something that will keep a person warm even in extremely cold environments. However, I've hit a formidable problem in the development of this salve because while it *does* protect a person from the cold, it also causes an intense pain that makes the person feel as though they are burning alive."

"For how long?" asked Sonya.

"For as long as the salve is in effect," admitted Jorge.

"Yeah, that's a problem," she agreed.

"But," said Jorge, "if these sluagh gorta don't feel pain, then we could apply the salve to them without worry, and it would provide the internal temperature they lack to prevent them from freezing." He turned to Mordha. "Does that make sense?"

But Mordha was already staring at him with a grin so broad they could see his teeth within his massive beard. "Ya' can do thess?"

"Well, I won't know for certain until we test it," said Jorge. "And I probably don't have enough ingredients with me to make enough salve for an entire *army* of sluagh gorta. Perhaps we can find materials with similar properties that grow nearby. Of course that would slow development down somewhat, but—"

"But ya' can do et?" Mordha's massive hands seized Jorge's thin shoulders.

"Y–yes, I think so."

Mordha embraced Jorge so fiercely Sonya was worried he might break the frail apothecary. He laughed and pounded on the poor man's back, then embraced him again. "Tha' good! Very good!"

"So do we have a deal?" asked Sonya.

Mordha released Jorge and turned to her. "Ya' help us cross snow. We help ya' free yer people. Ya' help us invade Aureum."

"That sounds about right."

"Deal." He spat into his drink and handed it to her.

She stared at it, unsure what to do.

"Ya' spit in yer drink and give et to the Tighearna," said Blaine.

Sonya took the offered cup in one hand, then spat in her own drink and handed it to Mordha. Mordha held it up, then drained the entire thing in one go. He sighed happily, wiped his beard with his forearm, then looked expectantly at Sonya.

Years of drinking bad vodka with Mikhail had prepared her for this particular ordeal. She raised her cup to Mordha, then drank it down in one large gulp. She felt the searing burn of the liquid as it made its way down her throat and into her stomach, but she didn't show any outward discomfort.

Mordha's eyes widened and he nodded, looking impressed. Then he nudged Blaine with his elbow and said something in their language that caused Blaine's face to turn red again.

"Okay!" said Mordha. "We ha' accord. Now we celebrate!"

"If there's this much drinking in serious discussion," murmured Jorge, "I wonder how much there will be when they celebrate."

"We're about to find out!" said Sonya, already feeling her limbs begin to loosen and buzz.

41

It was impressive how quickly the Uaine could mobilize for a large-scale celebration. It hadn't seemed like there were many people in the settlement when they arrived, but now the muddy pathways were teeming with them, and they were already working passionately toward the goal of getting drunk. After knocking back that drink in Mordha's tent, Sonya felt as though she was already halfway there herself.

Mordha led them toward the center of the settlement while boisterous revelers cheered and stamped their feet as they passed. Apparently among the Uaine, this was preferable to bowing, and Sonya found she rather liked that. In fact, the more she saw of these Uaine, the better she liked them. They were a welcome respite from both the rigid formality in Gogoleth and the placid domesticity she'd grown up with on the farm.

Soon they reached the large iron structure in the center of the settlement. Sonya hadn't been sure of its purpose, and thought it might simply be a sculpture of some kind, perhaps for religious worship. But as she watched the Uaine fill it with wood and light it on fire, she began to suspect that its sole purpose was to facilitate the quick and easy creation of bonfires.

"We call et An Dannsair," Blaine told her as they watched the fire spiral up inside the iron frame, bathing them all with a flickering heat that drove away the seeping damp chill of the early evening air. "The...Dancer, I think ya' say."

"Because flames seem to dance inside it?" asked Sonya as she watched.

"Aye, thas one reason," Blaine agreed.

A group of Uaine gathered nearby with drums, flutes, fiddles, and an odd instrument that looked like a bag with several large flutes sticking out of it. After a loud and heated discussion in their language, they seemed to finally agree what song they were going to play, and began. The drums kept a brisk pace, while the flutes and violins played harmonies that sounded lively, even though they were in a minor key. Then the man with the odd bag instrument broke in with a melody that was harsh and proud, yet haunting in a way that Sonya had never heard before.

Blaine pulled off his heavy chain mail and tossed it to the ground with a clatter. His thin wool undershirt fitted tightly enough for Sonya to see the outline of the large slab-like pectorals she'd felt at the end of their fight. And it was short enough that she caught a fleeting glimpse of the pale, flat abdomen beneath.

He held out his hand. "Bhuidseach Sonah. Will ya' dance wi' me?"

She had absolutely no idea what sort of dancing the Uaine did, but she wasn't about to let that stop her. She peeled off her thick Ranger coat and dropped it on top of Blaine's chain mail. The cold breeze blew through her thin cotton shirt, but the drink Mordha gave her had kindled its own kind of warmth, so she barely felt it.

She grasped his hand and allowed him to pull her close.

"I have no idea what I'm doing, so you'll have to lead this time," she said.

He grinned, then spun her around so that they were each at arm's length, then brought her back in, holding her hip to hip and cheek to cheek as they skipped around the roaring Dannsair. Shouts rang out among the Uaine, and soon others joined in, skipping briskly around the fire in pairs as the band continued to play.

Again and again, Blaine spun her away, their shared heat dissipating in the evening chill, then reeled her back in again so she never quite grew acclimated to the feeling of flesh against flesh. The heat of the fire, the heat of his body, and her own heat soon had her so drenched in sweat that when they pressed together, she could easily discern the solid curve of his muscle through their damp shirts. His grinning face gleamed with sweat as well, and the ends of his wet hair, free from any sort of binding, flung out in all directions as he moved. Her pulse pounded in time with the drums, and her heart soared with the rough, poignant sound of the bag and pipes instrument.

Then she caught sight of Jorge, who stood at the edge of the crowd of people watching the dancers. He had a fixed smile on his face as he carefully nursed the same cup he'd been given in Mordha's tent.

"I think Jorge is feeling left out," she told Blaine.

His smile returned with renewed vigor. "We canna' have that!"

He spun her over to Mordha, who stood nearby. The Tighearna was not dancing, but instead drank deeply from his cup as he looked out at his dancers with great satisfaction, rather like a father contentedly watching his children play.

Blaine shouted something in their language to him over the music. Mordha gave an enthusiastic nod and took Sonya by the shoulder.

"Come! Drink wi' me, Bhuidseach Sonah!"

"Wait, what?" She bewilderingly accepted a cup as Blaine slipped away.

Mordha roared something as he lifted his cup. The Uaine around them also lifted their drinks and shouted something back. Then they all drank. Mordha looked expectantly at Sonya.

"What did you just say to them?" she asked.

"Here's ta all the drinkin' an' dancin' an' fuckin'."

She laughed. "I'll drink to that!" And she downed her drink.

"There they go." Mordha pointed to the dancers, and Sonya was amazed to see Jorge now dancing with Blaine just as intimately as she had been.

She looked around and noticed there were other couples composed of just men or just women. "Is that normal for Uaine?" she asked. "Men dancing together?"

"Aye! Angelo say et not so in Aureum."

"Or Izmoroz, I suppose." She'd never actually been to a proper Izmorozian ball so she couldn't say for sure. Certainly, it would have been frowned upon in peasant dances. The thought that her people might not be as open-minded as the Uaine troubled her. Perhaps once she'd vanquished the empire, then lessened the divide between peasants and nobility, that would be her next goal. Helping her people understand how beautiful it was for all people to love as they wished.

And it was beautiful. Sonya watched Blaine spin Jorge around the Dannsair. He was grinning just as wildly as when he'd been dancing with her, but Jorge looked utterly baffled, as if he had no idea what he was doing or how he felt about it. Yet his confusion didn't hamper his movements, and they were surprisingly graceful. During their time waiting out the storm, Jorge had told her that dance and artistic expression were profoundly important to the Raízian people, so perhaps despite his bookish personality, such things came naturally to him. Blaine had apparently convinced him to take off his coat as well, and Sonya was able to appreciate his long, lean body as he danced. It was not the large and heavily muscled physique so valued in Izmoroz, but something more lithe and elegant. Even as his face continued to express the greatest confusion, his body moved nimbly, his long black braids stretching out as he twirled in Blaine's arms.

"I canna' understan' why no allow," said Mordha. "Clan es clan, beauty es beauty, an' fuckin' es fuckin'. All es good."

"I'm starting to see why you're in charge," Sonya told him.

He let out a booming laugh and pounded her on the back some more, then filled their cups again.

"Where is this Angelo who taught you and Blaine our language?" she asked.

"He wi' Clan Dílis right now."

"That's Blaine's clan, right?"

"Aye. Ya' see 'im when I summon all the clans together." He held up his cup and smiled grimly. "Then we go ta' war wi' the empire."

"That easy?"

"That easy," he agreed.

They both drank deeply to that.

42

Sebastian rode out of the imperial garrison of Gogoleth shortly after daybreak with his men. A fierce blizzard had passed through the region the day before, covering everything in a fresh blanket of white. As his eyes swept across the unblemished landscape, he found it a little easier to believe in the hope of redemption.

No matter what Commander Vittorio said, Sebastian knew he had gone too far with those miners. There must have been a way to settle the dispute without death, but his anger had prevented him from thinking of it. His beloved Galina has assured him that this didn't make him a bad person. That he was, like all people, merely imperfect. Fallible. He would do better next time. He would hold himself to an even higher standard than the one the commander expected. The wizard of Gogoleth must strive to be beyond reproach.

Fortunately, his current mission was much less complicated than the previous one. A group of river bandits had been terrorizing the passage between Gogoleth and the town of Otriye near the southern border of Izmoroz. The commander had explained that while Otriye was small, it was a vital stop on the trade route between Gogoleth and the Aureumian capital of Magna Alto, so it must be protected at all costs.

Protecting the inhabitants of a small Izmorozian town from the cruelty of bandits was such a noble goal that Sebastian was certain even his sister would have approved. She had such a narrow view of the empire, it might have even surprised her to know that imperial soldiers were willing to put their own lives in danger to protect simple peasants. Why could she not see that there was so much good that could be done with the empire's resources?

Of course, it probably didn't matter anymore. His sister's actions had made reconciliation impossible. But he reminded himself that even if he had lost his sister, and barely recognized his mother in looks or speech, he had a new family: the noble Commander Vittorio, the wily General Zaniolo, the stalwart Rykov, his loyal men, and of course the beautiful and gentle Galina Odoyevtseva, who comforted him when the burdens of leadership grew heavy. He was not alone.

The 404th rode south along the western bank of the Sestra River, the icy winter winds lashing their faces. A full gallop would have been impossible with the newly fallen snow, so they kept to a swift canter, stopping occasionally to rest their steaming mounts. Finally near sunset they reached the town of Otriye.

Sebastian decided that *town* was a generous word for the loose collection of wooden shacks nestled against the riverbank. The largest structure was a sawmill, whose wheel turned endlessly with the strong current of the Sestra. Sebastian would have thought that such a resource could make a place quite prosperous, but the homes looked so old they might collapse under the weight of the snow on their cedar roofs. The few people he saw about were gaunt, dirty, and dressed in ragged, poorly cured leathers and furs.

When Sebastian and his men reached the edge of the town, he called for a halt.

"I had thought we'd stay at an inn once we arrived, then get started on our bandit hunt first thing in the morning," said Sebastian. "But I don't see any inns."

"We don't need an inn," said Rykov. "We'll have to split up, but peasants are supposed to house imperial soldiers when needed."

"Really?" asked Sebastian. "That sounds...invasive."

Rykov shrugged. "That's how it's done. Right, boys?"

There were several nods in the group.

"You have more experience in these matters than I, so we'll do it that way," said Sebastian. "It isn't like we have a lot of options. I suppose it'll at least give us a chance to ask the locals if they have a guess where the bandits are lurking."

"Good idea," said Rykov.

"So..." Sebastian looked around at the cluster of shacks. The few people who hurried past studiously ignored them. "How do we go about it, exactly?"

"Knock on doors. Tell 'em we're staying the night," said Rykov. "We'll find the nicest one for you, sir."

"Oh, er, thanks..." Sebastian wasn't sure there would be much difference. "Can you handle it, Private? I'm not certain what the protocol is."

Rykov dismounted, strode up to the first door, and pounded on it with his massive gloved fist.

"Open up in the name of the empire!" he called.

After a few moments, an old man answered the door.

"Y-yes, sir?"

"Four Hundred and Fourth Imperial Cavalry on official business. We require room and board for the night. How many can you accommodate?"

"Uh..." The old man looked at the twenty mounted men and winced. "Two, I suppose."

"Legkov and Stepanova," Rykov called. "This one is yours."

The two soldiers dismounted, tied their horses up in front of the house, and went inside.

The platoon continued from house to house like this, leaving two at each place until it was clear that two at each place would not be enough. Then Rykov stopped asking how many they could accommodate and merely informed the homeowner they would offer room and board for three.

Finally it was only Rykov and Sebastian remaining. Rykov indicated the house beside the sawmill. "I saved this one for us, since the mill owner is probably the wealthiest person in town."

"I suppose that makes sense." Sebastian felt a little bad about taking the best for himself, but he supposed it was expected of the leader. If he didn't, all manner of conflict and jealousy could arise between the soldiers.

Rykov knocked on the door and a large man of perhaps thirty years with a thick neck and droopy eyes opened the door.

"I reckon you need room and board," the man said dryly. "We heard you coming door to door."

"You have the honor of welcoming Captain Portinari into your home," said Rykov.

The man looked at Sebastian. "We haven't got much, but it's yours, Captain. We're just sitting down to supper. Come inside and my wife will fix you a plate."

Since Sebastian had grown up on a farm, he considered himself comfortable in rustic settings. But as he walked into the small wooden house, he realized that his experience of rural living was very different from this one. It was as cramped as any apartment in Gogoleth, perhaps even more so, since every inch of nonessential space seemed to house some sort of tool, utensil, or item of clothing.

But at least it was warm. And it did have a cozy, cheerful atmosphere that places like the stately Roskosh Manor lacked. In one corner was a potbellied stove, and in another were two beds. In the center of the room was a large table, and seated at that table was a plain-looking woman in a faded pink blouse, and a boy of perhaps six.

"Everyone, this is Captain Portinari," said the man. "And..."

"Private Rykov," said Rykov.

The man nodded. "I'm Igor. This is my wife, Catherine, and my son Luka."

"Please have a seat while I get you some food, Captain," said Catherine without enthusiasm as she got up from the table.

"Thanks..." Sebastian sat down next to Luka. While Igor and Catherine seemed to accept his presence with weary resignation, the boy was staring at him with something between fear and awe.

Rykov sat on his other side, and they waited in an awkward silence as Catherine filled two plates with sour bread and boiled potatoes, a meal Sebastian had not eaten since that fateful night imperial soldiers invaded his childhood home.

Sebastian cleared his throat. "I apologize for our imposition, but we have been tasked with flushing out a group of bandits who have been terrorizing merchant ships on the Sestra between Gogoleth and Magna Alto, and our intelligence suggests their hideout is nearby."

Igor nodded, but said nothing. A few moments later, Catherine brought their plates, and they all began to eat.

"Perhaps you've heard about these bandits?" pressed Sebastian. "And might have some idea where we can find them?"

"Never heard of any bandits around here," said Igor. "Not much to steal."

"Yes, but there is plenty to steal on this river, and since your mill is also on the river, perhaps you've at least seen a suspicious boat pass by?" suggested Sebastian. "By all accounts, it's a rowing barge that sits low in the water, but is fairly wide, with plentiful storage to accommodate the cargo stolen from the merchant ships. I should think it would be difficult to miss."

Igor shook his head. "Sorry. Haven't seen anything by that description."

"*I* have," said Luka.

Both Igor and Catherine flinched. Then Catherine gave Sebastian a nervous smile. "I apologize for our son. He still hasn't quite got the hang of his manners yet. Please ignore him, I'm sure it's just his imagination. Little boys live half in dreams, you know."

"I do not!" protested Luka. "I seen 'em more than once! A boat just like the one the captain described!"

Igor's face darkened. "Luka—"

"Please." Sebastian held up his hand. "I know it is tempting to dismiss the words of a child, but we have little to go on, and it could be he *has* seen something." He turned to the boy. "Tell me everything you know."

"Yes, sir!" The boy gave him one of the sharpest, most enthusiastic salutes he'd ever seen. "I seen 'em just a few days ago in fact. Boat was so low in the water, it looked like it might sink. Bunch of guys on there, all with bows and swords and axes and things, lookin' real tough, so I followed them along the riverbank."

"Of course," said Sebastian. "I was a curious boy as well. If I'd seen a group of fierce-looking men, I would have done the same."

The boy seemed delighted by that affirmation. "Right? So I stayed low, in case they were bad guys, and followed them to a spot a little ways downriver, where it splits into the Syn and the Doch. Right at that split, there's a big hill with a bunch of bushes along the bank. And you won't believe what they did."

"I can't wait to find out," said Sebastian.

"Well, Captain, they moved some of the bushes, and there was a *cave* set into the hill. They unload the boat, take all the stuff into the cave. Then some of the men stayed in the cave, and the rest went down the Doch River with the boat."

He grinned expectantly at Sebastian.

"Luka, that was some excellent work," said Sebastian. "Perhaps when you grow up, you can come to Gogoleth and work for imperial intelligence."

"Really, Captain?"

"I know the head of the intelligence division personally and I'd bet he's always looking for smart, curious young men who are willing to put forth the extra effort." Sebastian turned and smiled at Luka's parents. "You should be very proud of your son. He may very well have saved countless lives and helped secure the river from these dastardly bandits."

Igor and Catherine both had tense smiles fixed to their faces.

"Yes," said Igor. "We're very proud."

43

Despite Sebastian's protests, Igor and Catherine insisted he sleep in their lumpy, straw-filled mattress bed. They laid out some furs on the ground near the stove, and assured him they would be quite comfortable. Perhaps it was Sebastian's imagination, but it seemed that after Luka's report, their entire tone had changed from resigned indifference that had bordered on rudeness to a tense but thoughtful generosity. Perhaps they hoped that Sebastian could help Luka get a job for the intelligence division in Gogoleth. He wasn't certain he could, but promised himself he would mention it to Zaniolo when he returned.

That resolution made him feel a little better about taking their bed for the night, and soon he drifted off to sleep.

But he was awakened a few hours later by a shout of surprise and the sound of a struggle. The only illumination in the room was the moonlight that streamed in through the windows, but the reflection off the fresh snow outside had amplified it, so he was able to see Rykov on the floor by the door holding Igor in a loose choke hold.

"Sasha, what are you doing?" demanded Sebastian.

"He was trying to sneak out," said Rykov.

"Why would you sneak out of your own house in the middle of the night?" Sebastian asked Igor.

Igor glared at him, but remained silent.

"To warn those bandits we were coming, I'll bet," said Rykov.

"And why on earth would he do that?" asked Sebastian.

"Probably because he works with them," said Rykov. "Maybe he spots likely targets for them as they come up the river."

"But why would..." Sebastian shook his head, then walked over and crouched next to Igor so they were on the same level. "What do you have to say for yourself? Anything?"

Igor said nothing.

"What are you doing to my daddy?" Luka was awake now. He jumped out of his little bed, but before he could come over, his mother grabbed him and yanked him close to where she still sat on the furs by the stove.

"Hush yourself," she told him. "Don't say another word or so help me I will slap you into next week."

Luka's eyes widened but he clamped his mouth shut and pressed himself against his mother's side.

"I'm...sorry about this," Sebastian told her. "I truly am. But he's not giving me any choice. My mission was clear. Subdue or kill all the bandits. I'll have to take him back to Gogoleth."

He didn't say what would happen after that, but the charge of banditry was quite serious and frequently led to execution. The look she gave him back said she already understood how much harder her life was going to be from now on.

Sebastian turned back to Igor, but his eyes were on his wife, as if silently pleading for forgiveness. Perhaps he had gotten greedy. The income from the mill hadn't been enough for him, so he decided to get some money on the side by helping the bandits. Maybe he'd justified it by thinking how much it would help his wife and son. Only now did he understand that he'd only made things more difficult for them.

No one got any more sleep that night. They tied up Igor and kept him apart from his wife and son. By the time the sun rose, they were all exhausted from the lack of sleep and the tense silence.

Sebastian apologized to Catherine again, though she didn't seem to hear him. Instead she sat on the bed and held her son, her eyes not looking at him, or her husband, but somewhere else entirely. Perhaps thinking of her new life without a husband.

They brought Igor out with them and secured him to Rykov's horse.

"You're lucky the captain doesn't make you walk behind on a tether," Rykov told Igor as he tied his legs to the stirrups and his hands to the horn.

The other soldiers eyed Igor curiously as they emerged from the homes they'd stayed in, but no one asked any questions.

"We've got a lead on the whereabouts of the bandits," Sebastian told them.

"Want me to scout ahead, Captain?" asked Zagitova, easily the best rider in the unit.

"Yes, thank you for volunteering, Zagitova," said Sebastian. "Their hideout is downriver in a cave at the confluence of the Sestra, Syn, and Doch. The entrance to the cave is apparently concealed by some bushes."

Zagitova saluted. "I'll check it out, Captain."

"Be careful," said Sebastian. "And don't engage before we arrive."

"Yes, sir!"

Zagitova kicked his horse's flanks and took off, quickly speeding up to a gallop, despite the snow, and soon was out of view. Sebastian and the rest of the unit followed behind at a slower pace. Since she was bearing the weight of two large men, Rykov's poor mare could barely manage a slow canter.

They rode along the bank until they reached the point where the Sestra split to either side of a large, snow-covered hill. To the left was the larger, stronger Syn River that continued all the way down to Magna Alto. To the left was the smaller Doch River, which looked shallow enough to ford just past the split. A bit of flat land jutted out at the split, and beyond that was a ring of bushes at the base of the hill. A section of the bushes had been pulled away to reveal a narrow cave entrance.

"Is that Zagitova's horse?" asked one of the men.

Zagitova's chestnut roan, riderless, was ambling slowly along the bank near the cave entrance.

A chill swept over Sebastian, though he couldn't say why. There was just something unnerving about seeing the horse without its rider. He called for the unit to stop.

Rykov, who was sitting behind Igor, grabbed him by the ear. "What do you know about this?"

Igor said nothing.

Something had happened to Zagitova. Sebastian was sure of it. He'd never lost a man before, and the feeling of helpless anxiety was excruciating. "Plotnikov and Shipulin, go check it out. But be *careful*, and keep your eyes open."

"Yes, Captain," said Shipulin.

The two urged their horses forward and across the Doch River, while the rest waited in strained silence. Plotnikov and Shipulin dismounted, drew their swords, and moved cautiously toward the cave entrance. They stopped about ten feet short of the entrance, and stared at something for a few moments as they spoke to each other. Then they remounted and hurried back across the river to where the unit waited.

"Zagitova's dead," Plotnikov said grimly. "Pit trap."

"Shit," Rykov said.

"What's a pit trap?" asked Sebastian.

"They dig a large hole in the ground and line the bottom with sharpened stakes," said Rykov. "Then they cover the hole with something that camouflages it but doesn't hold a lot of weight. Zagitova probably walked up to the entrance, maybe to check if he could hear anyone inside, and fell right through." He yanked on Igor's ear hard enough to make him wince. "I bet they got all kinds of nasty surprises in there. But our *friend* here is going to tell us about them."

"No. We can't trust anything he says." Sebastian felt a cold fury well up within him as he turned to Igor. "One of my men is dead, and you could have prevented that. You are unarmed and defenseless, so I will not kill you. But I want you to see what happens to anyone who dares harm those under my protection."

Sebastian guided his horse toward the shallow crossing point in the river. "Rykov, come with me, and bring Igor. The rest of you remain here."

"You sure that's a good idea, Captain?" Plotnikov asked nervously.

Sebastian ignored him and continued toward the cave entrance. Once he drew close, he dismounted and walked over to the hole. There was just enough space on either side to pass by and enter the cave, so it was likely that the pit trap was always in place, and the bandits habitually walked around it. A simple but efficient strategy.

When he looked into the hole, he saw poor Zagitova, impaled on a number of blood-drenched stakes. One appeared to have gone through his neck, so at least he hadn't suffered long. But it was cold comfort. The fact was, one of Sebastian's men had died under his watch and the shame of it choked him like fingers around his throat. He remembered that Zagitova had a younger brother named Kazimir who looked up to him. What would happen to Kazimir now?

"What's the plan, Captain?" asked Rykov, still astride his horse with Igor.

"Bring me a lit torch, and bring Igor over, too. I want him to hear this. I want him to ... *smell* it."

Rykov dismounted, lit a torch, then untied Igor and yanked him out of the saddle and walked him around the pit trap to join Sebastian at the cave entrance.

"Our orders were to subdue or eliminate the bandits," Sebastian told Igor. "I'm not about to risk any more of my men, so I guess the only one we'll be subduing is you."

He took the torch from Rykov, then took out his diamond. Lately he had been practicing how to control two elements simultaneously. He began now by strengthening the wind, bending it so that it funneled into the cave. Then he took all the anger he felt at the death of his man, the guilt, the shame, the frustration, and he poured it onto the torch like a bucket of oil. The wind swept it into the cave as a swirling, crackling funnel of fire.

As loud as the fire roared, it could not drown out the screams of the men inside the cave as they were burned alive. One staggered into view, lighting up the dark cave with his burning hair and clothes. The whites of his eyes and teeth were stark against his blackened skin and an animal-like keen escaped his throat. He made it a few steps toward the entrance of the cave before he collapsed. The funnel of wind died away, and the smoke began to leak out of the cave, bringing with it the stench of burned flesh.

Sebastian turned to Igor. All the defiance had been wiped from the man's expression. His face was ashen, his eyes were wide, and his mouth gaped like he wanted to retch. Sebastian found it oddly satisfying.

"You could have avoided this, if you'd only told us about the traps. Remember that." Sebastian turned to Rykov. "Now let's go find that barge. My torch is still lit."

44

Sonya was teaching a group of Uaine how to make snowshoes when she heard the deep, mournful call of a horn. She paused in midsentence, her pointed ears twitching.

"What was that?" she asked.

The Uaine looked at each other in confusion, then turned to Blaine, who was acting as Sonya's translator.

He shrugged. "I not hear anythin', Bhuidseach Sonah."

The horn sounded again, but louder. Along with the horn, Sonya now heard the higher-pitched trills of bagpipes and the low thrum of drums.

"Ah!" said Blaine. "I hear et that time."

The rest of the Uaine seemed to hear it as well. Several broke out into smiles, and they began talking excitedly to each other.

"What is it?" asked Sonya.

"One o' the other clans has answered the Tighearna's call t' fight."

"People seem relieved," she said. "Was there some doubt?"

"A' course," said Blaine. "People respect the Tighearna, but he es nah emporor. He canna' command anyone outside his own clan."

"That seems like it might be a problem..." Sonya had already been concerned about numbers. Although the Uaine seemed to be hardy and skilled warriors, there were only about a hundred members in Clan Greim, and she had been told it was the largest clan. That meant no more than six hundred warriors in total. But if not all the clans joined the battle, it would be even less. Could they prevail against even the small standing army at Gogoleth with so few warriors?

"No problem at all, Sonah. Et means when they come, they come because they wan' t' fight. Because they believe we win. No Uaine wi'out heart can win."

"I guess that makes sense. Do you know which clan is coming?"

Blaine shook his head, then grinned. "Less go see!"

Sonya followed Blaine as he wound his way between the tents of Clan Greim toward the sound of the horn. When they reached the edge of the settlement, Sonya looked south across the rolling meadow and saw a mass of people marching toward them out of the mist. Most of them were on foot, but a few rode small, sturdy-looking ponies. There were also oxen slowly pulling wagons stacked with wooden crates.

Blaine squinted hard at the group. "What can yer witch's eyes see, Sonah?"

"A big group of people coming toward us. There's an old man with a big white beard riding a pony in front. He has a pennant fixed to the back of his saddle that depicts a silver snake swallowing its own tail on a field of dark green."

"Clan Dílis!" said Blaine.

"That's your clan, right?"

"Aye. And that's me dad, Chief Albion Ruairc!"

"Your dad is the chief of your clan?" asked Sonya.

Blaine looked even more boyishly enthusiastic than usual, which was impressive. "Come, let's go meet 'em!"

He took off at a run toward the approaching clan, and Sonya kept pace with him.

When they were still a little ways off, Blaine waved his hand over his head and shouted something in the Uaine language. His father lifted his hand to halt the march of his clan, then shouted something back to Blaine and spurred his pony forward. When the two met, Chief Ruairc leapt from his mount with surprising nimbleness for an old man. The two kissed each other on the lips, then heartily embraced. Sonya tried to imagine her father and brother expressing such unselfconscious affection for each other, but could not. It was simply too far beyond either of them.

Blaine spoke to his father in an excited torrent of words, and his father's reply was just as enthusiastic. Finally, after several moments during which it seemed they were speaking overtop each other, the elder Ruairc turned and waved back to his approaching clan. "Angelo!" he bellowed.

Another old man on a pony came forward. Sonya wondered if only the old people were given ponies? She supposed that made sense. The Aureumian deserter was dressed in the same woolen clothes as the Uaine, but he was clean-shaven, which was an unusual sight among Uaine men. His eyes widened when he saw Sonya.

"An Aureumian?"

"Half," Sonya said quickly. "My mother is Izmorozian."

"A child of the war, then," he guessed. "Where did you grow up?"

"Izmoroz."

He dismounted and offered her his hand. "I'm Angelo Lorecchio. I take it you're the one who's managed to convince the Tighearna to march on the empire?"

"I've asked for his help to liberate Izmoroz from the empire, and offered a staging ground for a campaign against Aureum."

"And if the Uaine then invade Aureum, it would alleviate any concerns you might have of the empire attempting to retake Izmoroz," observed Angelo. "Not a bad strategy."

"I merely wish to free my people," she told him.

"Your father served in the war?"

"He did."

"What was his name? Perhaps I knew him."

Sonya hesitated. She wasn't sure she trusted this Aureumian. But she didn't really have a reason. Was she merely prejudiced? He had rejected the empire and was now helping the same people she was forging an alliance with. They were allies and she should treat him as such.

"Portinari," she said finally. "My last name is Portinari."

Angelo stared at her. "As in Commander Giovanni Portinari?"

"The same," she said. "I take it you knew him?"

"I served under him for years," said Angelo. "I take it he's dead?"

"Slain by imperial soldiers," said Sonya.

"I...see. You have my condolences. He was a remarkable man."

"He was," agreed Sonya.

Chief Ruairc said something to his son and Blaine nodded. "We best continue. Me dad an' the Tighearna want ta' speak, and we best start ta' teach Clan Dílis how ta' make snowshoes an' snow gog-els."

Ruairc remounted his pony and called for his clan to advance. They moved at a slow pace, with Blaine and Sonya walking beside the two old men.

"I haven't seen eyes like yours since the war," Angelo said in a deliberately casual tone. "And pointed ears as well. The markings of a Ranger of Marzanna, if I'm not mistaken."

"That going to be a problem?" asked Sonya.

"On the contrary," he said quickly, "it will be nice to have one of your kind as an ally for once. It's just...I would never have expected Giovanni the Wolf's daughter to become a Ranger."

"It's...complicated."

Angelo might have rejected the empire, and they might truly be allies now, but he didn't need to know her family's business.

Thankfully, he didn't press the issue, and only nodded. They walked on for a little while in silence, with only the thud of horse hooves, and the quiet creak of the wagons loaded down with crates behind them.

"What's in the crates?" she asked Blaine after a little while.

He glanced back at the wagons. "The dead who will become slu-agh gorta."

"*All* of them?" There were at least two hundred crates.

"Aye."

"And each clan will be bringing that many?"

"Or more," he said.

Sonya grinned as she realized all of her earlier concerns about numbers were unfounded. They truly would have an army of the dead at their command. Not even her genius brother would be a match for that.

45

Jorge was aware that there was a lot of activity going on outside his tent, but he wasn't paying much attention to it. He had been given a challenging task as an apothecary—his first official commission, really—and he had thrown himself into the work completely. He found it a welcome respite from all the other aspects of his life that seemed so daunting. Sonya would poke her head in occasionally to make sure he was eating and sleeping, but she seemed to have learned the lesson that when it came to apothecary work, he preferred solitude, so she never stayed long. Considering she was one of the sources of stress that he needed respite from, he was very grateful for that.

Their months traveling together had not lessened his feelings for her. Not even when he'd learned that as a Ranger she couldn't get married. He supposed whether or not she could marry was somewhat beside the point anyway. After all, if she had been willing and able to marry, he certainly could not have competed with the more masculine and virile Blaine. Jorge had no illusions about that.

And then there was the matter of Blaine. It was not unheard of in Raíz for men to feel romantic love for each other, but such peculiarities were really only accepted among the Viajero. Furthermore, Jorge had never had such feelings for another man before. Yet that first night they arrived at Clan Greim, with the strong drink, the fire, and the dancing... The memories of it returned to him at unexpected moments, leaving him both unsettled and aroused.

Of course, in addition to his own personal worries, he was also still quite worried about joining a foreign army intent on invading Izmoroz. Sonya didn't seem concerned at all, and continued to assure him that because she was a Ranger, the people would welcome them with open arms. As much as he adored Sonya and apparently could not refuse anything she asked, he was certain that one day her cocksure arrogance would be her undoing.

Blessedly, all of those worries were mere flies batting against the windows of his mind now as he worked patiently on his long-gestating apothecary project. He had spent a week foraging through the wilderness with Blaine, and had brought back a number of unfamiliar but promising ingredients. He had then secluded himself in the tent Elgin Mordha had kindly provided, and thoroughly tested each one. None were perfect replacements, but he believed he had found a way to utilize a few of them to amplify the ingredients he had brought with him from Izmoroz, allowing him to stretch his meager supplies significantly further than would otherwise have been possible. He hoped it would be enough.

"Jorge Elhuyar?"

Jorge looked up from his work to see two people standing at the opening of his tent. One of them he recognized as the Aureumian, Angelo Lorecchio, whom he'd been introduced to a few days before. But the other person was new and entirely strange. She was tall for a woman, very thin, and dressed in a plain brown hooded cloak. Her somber eyes were almost colorless, and both her skin and long hair were an eerie bone white.

"What can I do for you, Angelo?" Jorge asked. He couldn't say why, but in his limited interaction with the old man, he felt unexpectedly at ease, as if he had known him for some time. Perhaps it was merely the more familiar reserved demeanor of an Aureumian, which contrasted so sharply with the Uaine, who were warm, but coarse and occasionally alarming.

"Actually, it's what I can do for you," said Angelo.

"Oh?"

"But before I get to that, I would like to offer my apologies for taking so long to place where I'd heard your family name before. The Elhuyars are, of course, one of the most powerful and respected families in all Raíz. I am honored to make such an acquaintance, señor."

Jorge winced. It had been a while since he had to contend with the expectations and assumptions that went along with being an Elhuyar. "Please, just Jorge, if you would."

Angelo bowed his head. "Again you honor me, Jorge. Now, I would like to introduce you to Bhuidseach Rowena Viridomarus. She does not speak the imperial tongue, so I have been asked to facilitate your discussion regarding the sluagh gorta."

"Bhuidseach? So she is a...witch?"

"We would probably call her a necromancer," said Angelo. "But the Uaine don't make such distinctions. Anyone with any sort of supernatural or preternatural ability is invariably given the title of Bhuidseach."

"I see. So she is in charge of...animating the dead?"

"Each clan has its own necromancer. Bhuidseach Rowena is the necromancer of Clan Dílis, and has agreed to act as your liaison with the other necromancers and apprentices."

"That's very kind of her. Please convey my thanks."

Angelo said something to Rowena, and she nodded to Jorge.

"Now," said Jorge, "do we have an idea yet of how many sluagh gorta I will need to treat?"

Angelo asked Rowena. The necromancer considered it a moment, then in a surprisingly gentle voice, given both her profession and the fact that she was Uaine, she replied at great length while Angelo listened attentively, nodding now and then.

"It's still too early to say," he translated. "We have a little over a thousand preserved corpses sealed in crates, but Bhuidseach Rowena says that not all corpses preserve successfully, so when they begin to open the crates, they may find some are simply unusable. Additionally, a small number fail to awaken during the process, which Bhuidseach Rowena tells me is an indication that they lacked the passion of a true warrior in life."

"I see..." Jorge wondered if that last part was objectively true, or if it was merely a belief the Uaine held. He suspected that with something like this, magic and religion were so intertwined that the practitioners might not make a distinction. Apothecaries in Raíz, such as they were, were often hindered by their own religious beliefs, which was why Jorge had insisted on studying at the college in Gogoleth, where logic and reason, not superstition, reigned.

Rowena said something else to Angelo.

Angelo nodded, then gave Jorge a good-humored smile. "Bhuidseach Rowena would also like us both to know that necromancy is a sacred tradition among the Uaine, and only spoken of with the greatest reverence. What we learn about must never be discussed with outsiders without the permission of a necromancer."

"Please tell Bhuidseach Rowena that I understand and respect her wishes and beliefs."

Angelo translated to Rowena and she produced a gentle smile that matched her voice. She inclined her head toward Jorge, then said something else and left.

Angelo looked startled. "I...guess they're starting right now. Bhuidseach Rowena has kindly invited you to witness the awakening before you return to your work."

"Yes, I suppose I shouldn't miss this." Jorge quickly packed away his lab equipment, then followed Angelo out of the tent.

Four out of the other five clans had answered the Tighearna's call to arms, which was apparently no surprise, as Clan Seacál was not known to get along with the others. With four additional clans present, Clan Greim's population had nearly quadrupled. Of course, each clan came with their own tents, so the settlement had quadrupled in size as well. In terms of size and population, it now rivaled a midsize city in the empire, and often felt just as congested.

But Jorge found it was not difficult to follow Bhuidseach Rowena even through the most crowded areas. When people saw her coming, they stepped aside and dropped to one knee, leaving a wide space behind for Jorge and Angelo as they trailed after her.

"They don't even give the Tighearna this much reverence," said Jorge.

"There is an axiom among the Uaine that, roughly translated, says, 'A man, though he be a lord, is still a man, while a god, no matter what kind, is always a god.' Since the necromancers are the Uaine's god's representatives on earth, they are revered accordingly."

"What gods do the Uaine worship?" asked Jorge.

"Primarily Bàs, God of Death."

"I should have known," said Jorge. "I wonder if he knows Sonya's Goddess of Death."

"The Lady Marzanna? I thought she was the Goddess of Winter."

"According to Sonya, she's both."

"I suppose that makes sense. Those things tend to go together, especially in Izmoroz. And I've seen the Rangers in battle, so I'm not surprised they worship a death goddess."

"Don't you find it strange?" asked Jorge. "Both of us abandoning our own people to ally ourselves with these death-worshipping cultures?"

"Not at all," said Angelo. "Having fought in the last war, I can say with confidence that death is the most sure and reliable thing in the world. Perhaps the *only* reliable thing."

Jorge gave him a wan smile. "That isn't a particularly comforting statement."

Angelo returned his smile. "It wasn't meant to be."

The caskets from all five clans had been gathered on a flat stretch of meadow just outside the settlement. Seeing them all lined up side by side, row after row, and imagining that each might produce a nearly indestructible and pitiless undead warrior was impressive, and a little disconcerting.

"Do they ever get out of control?" asked Jorge. "The sluagh gorta, I mean?"

Angelo shook his head. "I've never seen it. And the only time I've even heard of such a thing is in an Uaine folk song. Loosely translated it would be called "The Heart-Sworn Dead." Even then, it's not so much a case of necromancers losing control of the sluagh gorta as it is a tragic story about a man and woman who loved each other so deeply in life that when the necromancers from two warring clans awakened them from death and pitted them against each other on the battlefield, they remembered their love and refused to fight."

"Do the sluagh gorta actually remember things from their lives?"

"If they're awakened immediately after death, they can remember their life for a short time, but the memories start to fade within the hour. If they're awakened more than a few hours after death, they can't even remember how to speak."

"I suppose they still might remember things, but be incapable of expressing it," said Jorge.

Angelo shuddered. "I hope not. The whole point of the sluagh gorta is that they're pure. The perfect warrior who does not feel fear, doubt, arrogance, or fatigue."

"Sounds frightening."

"Wait until you see them in battle. Then all you'll feel is gratitude that they're on your side."

Bhuidseach Rowena was speaking to four other people, two men and two women, who were also dressed in brown robes.

"Are those the other necromancers?" Jorge asked Angelo.

"Her apprentices. Each necromancer has several."

"They lack the same . . . hue as Bhuidseach Rowena."

"The eerie white skin and hair?" asked Angelo. "They call it Urram Le Bàs, or Death Touched. Only the necromancer of each clan has it, and only they can awaken the dead. Receiving the touch is apparently quite the ordeal to go through, and most don't survive the process. The necromancer doesn't really choose which of their apprentices will succeed them. All the apprentices go through the process, and whichever one survives is the one Bàs has chosen to be the next necromancer."

"That is a harsh selection process. Has there ever been a time when none survived?"

"Clan Greim in fact currently has no necromancer," said Angelo. "You ask me, that's how Elgin Mordha managed to become so powerful. The necromancers tend to keep the ambitions of their chiefs in check, and without that, Mordha was able to press his clan into achieving a dominance over the other clans that hasn't been seen in centuries."

"But if the other clans have access to sluagh gorta and he doesn't..."

Angelo shook his head. "It's been considered taboo over the last five hundred years or so for a clan to send its sluagh gorta against another clan. Before then, it was apparently a terrible era for the Uaine. They were slaughtering each other with such ferocity, they nearly died out."

More brown-cloaked people had gathered around the caskets. The other necromancers, all three of them men, were easy to spot with their ghostly skin and hair, and Jorge was surprised to see that unlike every other Uaine male, they were clean-shaven. There were also about fifteen apprentices, all busily opening the caskets. Once they finished, the necromancers went to each of the four corners. Bhuidseach Rowena was the closest, and Jorge watched as she lifted one pale arm. When the sleeve fell back, he saw a number of thin, even scars that lined her forearm almost like stripes. Then she held up a small, silver knife with a ruby in its pommel, and carefully, almost reverently, cut a new line on her arm.

Jorge glanced at Angelo, his face no doubt expressing his concern.

"Just watch," whispered Angelo.

Jorge looked back at Rowena. She was now walking slowly down a line of caskets with her bleeding arm outstretched. She paused before each casket long enough to let a few drops of her blood fall within, then moved on to the next.

It did not take long for the dead to rise. As Rowena and the other necromancers worked down their respective lines, heads with long, stringy white hair began to emerge from the crates behind them. The skin of the sluagh gorta looked strangely shiny, perhaps from the preservatives, and it was a uniform slate gray. When they climbed laboriously out of their crates, he saw that they were dressed in simple brown tunics that offered little protection from weather or violence. But of course that was part of the appeal of the sluagh gorta. They didn't need it.

Each one stood in front of their casket, their yellowed eyes staring off at nothing, their gray mouths stretched into a ceaseless grimace. They did not move or make a sound, but waited patiently.

When the necromancers had finished their blood distribution, they gathered in front of their newly awakened army of the dead. The oldest of the male necromancers bellowed something in the Uaine language.

"Bhuidseach Hueil is welcoming the newly awakened sluagh gorta," said Angelo. "He says, 'You have been given the supreme honor of ensuring victory in a war that will make the Uaine the most powerful and feared people in the world. Other nations will tremble at the mere mention of our name'..." Angelo gave Jorge a sidelong grin. "And etcetera."

Angelo seemed not to take such hyperbolic language seriously, but as Jorge watched a thousand undead warriors stand in orderly rows in an unnatural and eerie silence, he thought perhaps it wasn't so far-fetched.

"Now he's telling them to present arms," translated Angelo.

As one, the sluagh gorta turned back to their caskets, reached down, and took up a weapon. Some had swords, others axes, maces, or spears. Each one brandished their weapon with an ease that suggested that if they remembered nothing else, they still knew how to fight. When they had retrieved their weapons, they turned back to face the necromancers and were still once again.

Bhuidseach Hueil shouted something in an even louder and more vehement voice.

"'Proclaim your dedication to Bàs, the Uaine, and victory,'" translated Angelo.

With perfect unity, the army of sluagh gorta raised their weapons and let out a shriek of noise that was more like a chorus of tortured beasts than a war cry.

Jorge could only shudder at the sight.

46

Galina stood in the cold, muddy training yard of the imperial garrison and watched as Sebastian's men performed drills, parading their horses back and forth in perfect tight formation at the order of Rykov, Sebastian's ominously hulking aide-de-camp. Her betrothed stood next to Rykov, observing the drills with silent gravity.

Galina watched from a little ways off, so as not to get in their way or disturb their fragile manly decorum. She shifted her weight slightly as the wet slush seeped into her soft leather shoes. If she was to make a regular habit of visiting the garrison, she would need more practical footwear. And she certainly intended to make a regular habit if it. Only by understanding the daily pressures her betrothed faced within the military could she hope to counter them.

When she looked at Sebastian now, she hardly recognized him. He was still just as handsome, although he looked as though he had not been eating or sleeping as much as he should. What she found even more striking, however, was the cold, hard expression on his face. There was no sign of the tender heart that had won her over all those months ago.

She supposed it was to be expected. Men behaved differently in the company of other men. As the great Lady Olga Bunich Fignolov once wrote, "He preens, or postures, or remains stoically reserved, whichever is dictated by the expectations of his fellow men. But never does he show that gentle aspect which a mother, or sister, or wife, or daughter knows to be his truest self." Galina used to consider the writings of Lady Fignolov to be overly harsh regarding the less fair sex, but every day now seemed to lend additional credence to her views.

"My, but the garrison seems brighter by several degrees, as if an angel has descended among us."

Galina turned to see General Savitri Zaniolo standing beside her, his eyes following the movements of Sebastian's troops, but his expression betraying a faint, teasing smile.

Galina did not like or trust Zaniolo. But Sebastian felt he owed the general a great deal, since it was he who had suggested the promotion to captain, prompted him to propose to Galina, and even taught him the necessary dance steps for the formal engagement ball. As such, Galina supposed she was indebted to him as well and should strive for at least a modicum of cordiality.

"Is a woman's presence at the garrison so unusual that it implies supernatural intervention, General Zaniolo?" she asked.

His smile broadened. "I'm afraid so, my dear. If it were up to me, I can assure you there would be women abounding in this place."

"Yes, just as I saw you *abounding* all over that young woman at my engagement ball."

It was a risk being so flippant with Sebastian's ally, but she had a feeling Zaniolo was the sort of man that the poet Valery Lomonosov described as "a rake so in love with his own notoriety, he delighted in being scolded for it." The general's quick laugh and cavalier shrug suggested she was correct in her assessment.

"And to what do we owe the rare pleasure of your feminine charms?" he asked.

"Merely a longing to see my beloved. He has just returned from a mission that took him away from me for several days and I simply could not wait until supper to see him. You know how weak willed and impetuous womenfolk can be, General."

He turned to her with a pained expression. "Galina Odoyevtseva, you may insult my morals as frequently as you like, but please do not insult my intelligence. You are neither weak willed nor impetuous. Furthermore, know that I am very fond of your betrothed and consider him almost a younger brother. Your presence suggests you have some concern for his well-being, and you may be assured that any anxieties you may harbor are mine as well."

His candor threw Galina a little off balance. Or at least his pretense of candor. He was, after all, head of the imperial spy network in Izmoroz. She would need to tread very carefully with him indeed.

"My apologies, General. As you are an intelligent man, you will no doubt forgive my initial evasiveness. I did not wish to express my concerns for fear they would cause an unfavorable impression upon my betrothed."

He inclined his head. "A reasonable fear when speaking to his superior. But I hope Sebastian has told you that I am a true ally, and I also hope you will consider me the same."

"You are most kind, General. If I may beg a further kindness, do you have any advice on what a woman might say to soothe the troubled thoughts of a man who is asked time and again to perform... difficult tasks in service to his empire?"

Zaniolo sighed in a somewhat overly dramatic fashion. "Alas, I fear when it comes to such trials, there is little succor to be had from mere words. What a man needs at times like that is the sweet embrace of his wife, and the adoring gaze of his children. *Those* are the comforts he craves."

There could be no mistake that Zaniolo was suggesting she shut up and prepare to start popping out babies. A spiteful anger rose up within her, despite her best efforts to suppress it.

"Alas, General Zaniolo, for you have neither a wife nor children."

The words slipped from her lips before she could stop them, and she winced at the possible ramifications of her barb.

But rather than get offended, Zaniolo merely nodded. "Too true, my dear. Too true."

There was an awkward, uncomfortably long silence.

Then the general said, "You remind me of my own innocent surety as a youth. I recall it perhaps better than most, as it was the impetus for both my greatest achievements and worst failures. What I say next, you will view however you wish, but I beg you to take it in the warmhearted spirit in which it is given. Do not pry too deeply into the difficult work a soldier must do for his country. A man hopes that there be at least one person in the world who still sees him in a good and pure light, and I have no doubt that is the cherished position Sebastian wishes for you."

Galina could not decide whether Zaniolo was once again advising her to shut up and make babies, or if he was suggesting that no matter what she did, it would not help Sebastian, and was therefore merely trying to save her the heartache. Regardless, she found his complacency irritating. This time, however, she was able to keep her temper in check.

"I am grateful for your considered advice, General," she said finally.

"I am grateful you took it as such." He bowed slightly. "Now, if you'll excuse me, I fear I must attend to other duties not nearly as pleasant as conversing with Captain Portinari's betrothed."

Galina nodded and returned to watching Sebastian. His men had stopped their parading and now listened intently while he extolled both their virtues and shortcomings. As she watched him give his stern lecture, she wondered if perhaps she'd had it wrong all this time. Was *this* the true Sebastian? Was the sweet, tender boy she knew a mere echo that remained more in her heart than in reality?

At last Sebastian dismissed his men and hurried over to her. As he approached, and she was able to look at him more closely, she observed that it wasn't merely that he was tired or had lost weight. He looked... worn. It had only been a few days since she'd seen him, but if she were to judge solely by his appearance, she might have said a few years. There were dark circles under his eyes, and the creases in his brow appeared more pronounced. Perhaps it was a trick of the light, but she thought she even saw a couple of gray hairs at his temples. She did not know what to make of this change in his appearance, but could not imagine that it boded well.

"My darling Galina, what a wonderful surprise!" Though his countenance was weary, his enthusiasm remained. That was some comfort to her. "Would you care to take lunch with me in my quarters? I fear the options are rather meager, but it would soothe my spirits greatly."

"I would be delighted, my *volshebnik*." She took his arm and allowed him to lead her inside. "But please tell me what has agitated your spirits so."

He nodded gravely as he led her down the hallway. "As you know, I have not been able to attend supper the last few nights at Roskosh Manor because I was called away on another mission."

"Yes, it was very thoughtful of you to send a message."

"I didn't want you to worry, my love. Especially after the . . . difficulties of my last mission."

"You said it was bandits this time, yes?"

"That's what I thought at the time," said Sebastian. "But it turned out to be much worse."

"Worse?" asked Galina.

"Here we are." Sebastian gestured to one of the rooms. "I don't believe you've seen my quarters before. It is only men here, so I hope you won't be too horrified."

She would apparently have to wait to learn more about his latest mission until after she had assured him that his bachelor residence was sufficiently masculine. She wondered if women ever needed reassurance of their femininity, or if this particular insecurity was exclusive to the male gender.

"Let us see these quarters of yours, my *volshebnik*. This should be most interesting."

In fact, the room was perfectly unremarkable. Neater than she might have expected, but not unnervingly so. It was not large, and there were very few decorations that might have added a personal touch. The only details of the room that indicated Sebastian lived there were a portrait of his mother on his desk, and a large stack of books, most of them concerning magic or the natural sciences.

"Oh, it's quite tidy," she remarked as she walked into the room.

Rykov had followed behind at a respectful distance but now stood in the doorway. "That's because I clean it."

Galina nodded. "I'm sure Captain Portinari has weightier matters on his mind."

"Ah, Rykov," said Sebastian. "Would you be so good as to fetch food from the mess for Galina Odoyevtseva and me?"

"Sure." Rykov turned without saluting and left. Galina was by no means an expert on military decorum, but she suspected that Sebastian let him get away with a lot of informalities.

"Please make yourself comfortable, my love."

Sebastian gestured to a stuffed leather chair. When Galina sat in it, the thing nearly swallowed her up. She gripped the thick armrests and pulled herself forward so that she could balance on the edge of the cushion. Sebastian brought a small table and his desk chair over, then sat down.

"I suppose it will do for an impromptu lunch setting," he said.

"I came for the conversation, not the decor, my *volshebnik*. Now, I believe you were telling me that your mission was worse than you'd anticipated?"

"Ah yes. You see, the commander tasked us with flushing out what we thought were a group of bandits who had been harassing merchant ships on the Sestra. It was my first time dealing with such fiends, and though I of course did not expect them to fight with honor, I was disgusted by just how low they were willing to go." He paused for a moment, and his face grew pensive. "I'm ashamed to say that their devious traps took the life of one of my men."

"Oh dear," said Galina.

"Indeed. Naturally, I did not hesitate to show my displeasure. We had them cornered in a cave, and rather than risk any more of my men to their diabolical machinations, I simply filled the whole thing with fire."

"The...cave?" Galina felt a cold chill in her stomach, but she strove to only allow an expression of confusion to show in her face. Perhaps she was misunderstanding. "With...the bandits still inside?"

"Of course," he said. "I doubt they would have come out of their own volition."

"But they did come out?" she pressed.

"Oh no. They all burned to death."

"I...see."

Galina strove not to show the horror that she felt, but she was no Irina Turgenev and her feelings must have been plain, because

Sebastian suddenly looked anxious. He leaned across the table to take her hand. He began to stroke it softly as he spoke.

"I—I realize that must sound rather *harsh*. And I confess I did have some feelings of regret after, concerned that I had once again let my temper carry my actions too far. But we did have one captive from the group, the local miller, and we brought him back to the garrison. That's when I was relieved to learn that my actions had been quite justified. You see, he confessed under intense questioning that they were not bandits at all."

"No?" She could not imagine what those men could have been that would justify their cruel fate. Mass murderers? Child rapists?

"They were rebel dissidents intent on overthrowing the empire!" Sebastian said grimly. "Can you imagine? That cave was a hornet's nest of extremist militant traitors who had no doubt been filling the minds of simple peasants with all manner of treasonous ideas. When this came to light, the commander told me it had been a godsend that I'd treated them so firmly. Had I shown them the slightest mercy, it could have emboldened other such fanatical groups to even worse acts of terrorism. I had no idea at the time, but apparently this was not the first rebel cell we have been forced to dismantle, and the commander firmly believes it will not be the last." He shook his head, looking wounded. "Here we are, ready to lay our lives down for the safety of Izmoroz, and instead of thanks, these people show us nothing but contempt. The commander believes they are resentful of our strength and their own weakness, and that is why they lash out so horribly."

Galina stared at Sebastian. It was true that she could be prideful at times, but she was humble enough to admit when she was wrong, and as she looked into the firm, unyielding gaze of her betrothed, she understood that she had made a terrible mistake. Perhaps she had overestimated her influence over Sebastian, or underestimated the commander's. Or perhaps underneath it all, he had been a lost cause from the beginning. Regardless, it was clear that accepting Sebastian's proposal of marriage had been the most foolish thing she had ever done in her short life.

He looked at her with renewed concern. "My love? Are you all right?"

And now she was presented with a choice. She could be honest with Sebastian, shatter this illusory calm, and denounce him for his barbarous actions and callous views. Such an act would likely satisfy the anger and disappointment that roared within her narrow chest. But what would that accomplish in the long run? It would break her heart, and his, and their parents' as well. And if it was inevitable that everyone would suffer, couldn't she find some good in all this? Some justification for the misery? The one glimmer of light in all this was that she now knew there *were* Izmorozians who were willing to fight for their independence. Surely such groups could find great use for the knowledge that could be obtained by the most trusted confidante of the imperial wizard of Gogoleth.

So she chose not to be honest. Perhaps she was not Irina Turgenev. Perhaps she did not want to be. But she could be just as strong. She would tear out the fondness she felt for Sebastian by the root and destroy it. Then she could use him as a tool, just as everyone else used him.

She carefully released the tension in her face, easing away the expression of her true feelings. Then she knitted her brow into merely the concern of a woman for her betrothed.

"Forgive me, my *volshebnik*. I confess I am stunned by the mere idea of rebel fanatics within the borders of Izmoroz. It is terribly shocking."

"Yes, it's an outrage," he said. "The Uaine and their hordes of undead practically at our doorstep and they want to get rid of the empire? It's sheer reckless nonsense. We must put a stop to this madness at once. The commander is deploying squadrons to every town in Izmoroz, and I will personally hunt down every lead or rumor of sedition we uncover."

Galina smiled. "How wonderful, my love. I am here to support you in whatever way I can, even if only as an ear to listen and a shoulder upon which to rest your weary head."

47

"Outrageous! I won't do it!" roared Lord Sergey Bolotov Prozorova as he paced back and forth in his study.

"Now, now, dear," Lady Inessa Odoyevtseva Prozorova said soothingly, although it was unclear whether that was directed toward the fuming Lord Prozorova, or to young Ivan, who sat next to her on the couch whimpering in fear from his father's sudden outburst.

Sergey shook the parchment in his hand. "Have you *read* it, Inessa?"

"Of course, dear." Her voice remained gentle as she continued to smile down at the sniveling Ivan and stroked his blond curls.

Galina paused in her transcription work and looked up. "*I* have not read it, Papa."

He held it with both hands at arm's length, as if it exhibited a foul odor. "It says, dear daughter, that our presence is requested—not merely *invited*, mind you—at the Portinari residence on 821 North Veter Street one month hence for an intimate family celebration of the Ascendance."

"I see," said Galina, and went back to her work.

"*Do* you see, Galina?"

She put down her quill and looked at him. "Do I see that celebrating an Aureumian high holiday this year is a clear indication that Commander Vittorio's influence over my betrothed and his mother continues to grow? Yes, I think I see that quite well. What's more, considering I am in regular communication with my betrothed, I am not particularly surprised."

"Well...I mean...it's just—"

"Which do you think will be more effective in protecting Izmorozian culture, Papa? To throw a childish tantrum and refuse to attend? Or to attend and do our best to keep Sebastian from completely succumbing to the will of the commander?"

He gaped at her for another moment, then regained his composure and bowed. "My daughter, I do believe you are maturing at an almost alarming rate." Then he raised an eyebrow. "Childish tantrum?"

She smiled sweetly. "Sorry if I have given offense, Papa. What description would you have preferred? Infantile outburst? Puerile paroxysm?"

He laughed, as she'd hoped he would, and held up his hands in surrender. "Very well, my dearest Galechka. We'll do it your way. For the good of Izmoroz, I will summon all the courtesy and aplomb I can muster for the night of the Ascendance celebration."

Galina looked over at her mother. "I hope I can count on you to assist in that effort, Mother. All Gogoleth knows of your gift with social graces, and without your aid, I fear the evening will be terribly trying for Papa."

Inessa attempted not to look too pleased by the compliment. "Of course, my beloved daughter. I will do everything in my power to maintain the peace in your engagement to Captain Portinari."

"You are most kind, Mother."

Galina had intended to return to her transcription, but noticed Masha waiting in the doorway. She carefully blotted her work, then began to put it into the drawer. "Now, if you both will excuse me, I must go out for a bit."

"This late in the day?" asked her father.

"Yes. Masha saw a pure white mink for sale at the markets and persuaded the merchant to set it aside until later so that I might come down and take a look when I had a moment." It was a necessary fiction. Her father would most likely agree with what she was doing in theory, but might object to the potential danger.

"Couldn't you have just had Masha pick this mink up for you?" he asked.

312

She smiled. "Why, Papa, what a terribly dull suggestion. Surely you understand that for a young woman, such a rare quarry must be stalked personally, or else there is no thrill in the hunt."

"I think a white mink hat would look lovely on you, my darling," said her mother. "Sebastian will be most pleased."

"I hope so, Mother."

Galina followed Masha out of the study and down the hall. The two did not speak until they stepped out of the manor house and onto the early evening streets of Gogoleth, which were still bustling with activity.

"Have they all gathered?" asked Galina.

"Yes, miss. Everyone I told you about is waiting to meet you at the Sturdy Sturgeon Tavern."

"That's quite a name," observed Galina.

Masha smiled apologetically. "It is our usual meeting place, miss, and I fear it is not up to your standards. You are the first noble who has expressed genuine sympathy for our cause, so we have never considered such things before."

"It's quite all right, Masha. I suspect I will need to become accustomed to such environments."

Masha had never been particularly good at keeping her personal views to herself, so Galina had always wondered if she was involved in some sort of anti-imperial group. Galina had only to make a few choice comments regarding her betrothed's fall from her good graces for Masha to seize the opportunity to recruit her. Since it was merely a gathering of peasants, Galina didn't have high hopes for this group, but it was a start. Perhaps they would be able to put her in touch with a larger organization, if such a thing existed. And if it didn't, perhaps she would be the one to gather all these disparate rebel groups together and make one.

It was a ways to the inn, but Galina insisted that they walk rather than take a carriage. The fewer people at Roskosh Manor who knew where she was really going, the better. Even the coachman could be a potential leak. And Galina suspected that in the coming months, she might be called upon to take far more arduous actions than a long walk, so it was best she grow accustomed to increased physical activity.

They eventually reached an area of Gogoleth that Galina had never seen before, where the cobblestones were mostly broken and the buildings weatherworn and grimy. The Sturdy Sturgeon Tavern was a stout black stone building that had survived the Aureumian invasion. Yellow light shone from the greasy, smoke-filmed window that filtered the chaotic sound of drunken voices down to a dull hum.

Masha led her around the side of the tavern down a narrow alley that stank of vomit and things even less pleasant. At the back was a separate door. There were no windows to show what lay inside, but it was much quieter at the back of the building.

Masha looked carefully around, then handed a white porcelain mask to Galina.

"Do I really need to wear this?" asked Galina.

"Miss, you promised! Your identity must remain secret, even from our compatriots."

"Don't you trust them?"

"With my life, miss. But I don't trust the imperial torturers."

Galina thought about the miller that Sebastian had arrested during his last mission. The one who had confessed he'd been part of an anti-imperial group. What her betrothed had called "intense questioning" had more likely been torture.

"Very well. I am not ashamed of what I am doing, nor am I ashamed of who I am. But I will do this for your peace of mind."

"Thank you, miss."

The mask was rather pretty. Pure white with rosy cheeks and elaborately made eyebrows, it covered her nose, but left her mouth free so she could still talk easily. She tied it on with strips of silk ribbon, and the sturdy feeling of it as it settled on her face made her think of armor. Her nerves had been steadily growing more taut during the walk to the tavern, but now they settled back down.

"Please lead the way, Masha."

"Yes, miss."

Masha opened the door, and the two entered what appeared to be a large storage room. The walls were lined with ale casks, wine barrels, and a number of crates and canvas sacks filled with all manner of goods. A large rickety table sat in the center of the room. Twenty or so people were crowded around it, their faces all looking expectantly at Galina. She had not anticipated quite so many to start with. It was more than a little daunting, and if it weren't for the comforting anonymity of the mask, she might have frozen. As it was, it took her several moments of conscious, steady breaths before she was ready to speak.

"Thank you all for risking so much to meet with me," she told them. "I have a great number of resources at my disposal, and perhaps more importantly, the trust of one of the imperial commander's inner circle. But I fear I know precious little about what actually goes on in our fair, downtrodden Izmoroz, and that is why I have asked you here. Perhaps together we might find a way to free our people with as little bloodshed as possible."

A young man hesitantly raised his hand.

"Yes?" asked Galina.

"Is it true the imperials have a wizard now?"

Galina nodded. "You may have heard about a rebel group being cruelly burned to death near Otriye by a wizard, and I'm sorry to say those rumors are correct. The imperial wizard is young and perhaps overly influenced by his commander. I suspect he genuinely believes he is doing what's best for Izmoroz, and I would like to think he would not willingly harm unarmed innocent people, but…" She felt her throat constrict as emotions unexpectedly suffused her. She had thought herself over the loss of her idealized version of Sebastian, but perhaps not completely. "Apparently I am wrong. So we will need to consider carefully how we might stand against such power, should it come to open conflict."

"Only thing I can think would stand against a wizard is a Ranger of Marzanna," said a middle-aged woman.

Galina knew of the fabled Rangers of Marzanna, of course. They appeared many times in Izmorozian poetry, and in the folk stories her father brought home from his travels. If what was said about them was true, they would indeed be a potent force. *If* it was true. And if any of them still lived.

"My understanding is that the Rangers had all been put to death at the end of the war," she said.

"Well, I seen one," said an old man.

"When was that?" she asked.

He shrugged. "Earlier this winter."

"Olin, I never took you for no liar," said another old man. "But you know as well as I do that what the good miss here says is true. There ain't any Rangers left. The empire made damn sure of it."

Olin scowled. "Liar, am I? Well, what of this?"

He held up what appeared to be a large bear claw. Several at the table gasped.

"I'm afraid I don't understand the significance of the claw," Galina confessed.

Masha explained. "It's said that a Ranger gives a bear claw to someone if they feel they owe them a debt. That person can then show the claw to any Ranger at any time, and the Ranger is honor bound to help them."

Olin nodded, looking proud. "She was banged up pretty bad. I helped her set her broken arm, and gave her a ride in my wagon, without even knowing who she was. But then she give me this."

He looked down reverently at the claw in his hand, while others leaned over him to get a better look at it.

"Where did you take this Ranger in your wagon?" asked Galina.

"To Roskosh Manor."

Galina took a moment to calm herself before speaking. Surely it was some strange coincidence. A Ranger had recently visited her home? It couldn't be possible. "You're certain it was Roskosh Manor?"

"I am."

"And...what did this Ranger look like?"

"Young woman. Real pretty, as I recall. Black hair, like an Aureumian, but skin as pale as any Izmorozian maiden."

"Well, I'll be," said Masha.

Galina looked inquiringly at Masha.

"Er...begging your pardon, miss. I work at Roskosh Manor."

"Is that so?" Since Masha insisted Galina conceal her identity, she had to affect surprise.

"Yes, miss. And right around the time Olin is talking about, there was a young woman who fits that description that showed up out of the blue."

"Who was she?"

"She claimed to be the daughter of Lady Portinari."

"Claimed?" Galina knew that Sebastian had a sister, but the idea of her being an actual Ranger of Marzanna seemed too strange to be believed.

"Well, miss, she didn't exactly look like nobility. Dressed shabby and all beat up." She looked at Olin. "If I remember, she even had some kind of strange brace on her arm."

"She used arrows to keep it steady, and tied 'em on with a bow-string. Just the sort of thing you might expect a Ranger to do."

"I...see." Galina looked at Masha. "And this young woman truly was the daughter of Lady Portinari?"

"Lady Portinari recognized her right away," said Masha. "Sonya Turgenev, that was her name. Lady Portinari dismissed me, but... uh." Masha looked a little guilty. "I wasn't eavesdropping, miss. It's just that the young woman looked a tad unsavory, and I feared for Lady Portinari's safety, so I didn't stray very far."

Galina raised an eyebrow but realized the reaction was lost beneath her mask. "Go on."

"Well, miss. Among other things, they did talk about the fact that Sonya Turgenev was a Ranger, trained by one of the farmhands who I guess was secretly a Ranger hiding after the war. I hadn't said anything, because I wasn't sure if I even believed such a thing, but if she gave Olin here a claw..."

"Then I suppose it lends credence to the claim." Galina struggled to keep her voice calm, and was very grateful that the mask hid her expression. Was it possible that Lady Portinari had been harboring an actual Ranger of Marzanna all this time? "This is...an astonishing revelation. And one which we must, for now, keep in strictest confidence." If the commander found out, not even Sebastian could prevent him from putting Lady Portinari to death and tearing Izmoroz apart to find Sonya Turgenev.

"Well, I reckon my cousin weren't as full of shit as I thought," said an old woman.

"How so?" Galina chose to ignore the peasant's coarse language. She was gaining a better understanding regarding what her father had said about their rough demeanor. For the common folk, foul language seemed as natural as breathing.

"Well, miss, every month or so, my cousin Gennady comes to Gogoleth from Zapad Village to trade furs and suchlike, and he always stays with me. On his last visit, he was going on and on about this young Ranger of Marzanna with black hair, white coat and all, who brought in enough game in two days to feed his whole village for two weeks—in the dead of winter, no less. I thought he was cracked, to be honest."

"What was she doing all the way out in Zapad, Mathilde?" asked the young man.

The old woman shook her head. "He said she was getting ready to head out into the tundra. Something about bringing back an army to drive out the empire, but that can't be right. What kind of army could you find in the tundra? It don't make no sense."

"Perhaps if one of us traveled out to Zapad Village, they might be able to find out more," suggested Galina. "I would go myself, but I fear my absence would be noticed, and my connection to the commander's inner circle jeopardized."

"I don't mind visiting my cousin," said Mathilde. "If someone else can pay for the horse."

"Of course," said Galina. "Masha will provide you with whatever you need. But do be cautious in making inquiries. Since the wizard discovered the rebel group in Otriye, I have heard that Commander Vittorio is deploying small detachments of soldiers to every town and village in Izmoroz with the intention of rooting out any additional sedition. It's possible they will reach Zapad before you."

"I got plenty experience avoiding soldiers, don't you worry, miss."

"I look forward to your report, then," said Galina. "Contact Masha as soon as you return."

"I surely will," said Mathilde.

"Meanwhile, I will endeavor to learn of additional raids on rebel hideouts and pass that information along to all of you through Masha."

"Much obliged," said Olin.

"Let us hope that this is the beginning of a union among all those who chafe at the empire's occupation of Izmoroz, be they peasant, noble, or Ranger."

Galina did not know if they could truly count on Sebastian's sister to fight against her own brother. But when she saw the hope that now sparkled in the eyes of the peasants before her, Galina understood that if there was even a chance of recruiting a Ranger to their cause, they must pursue it. Someone like that could galvanize the entire peasantry to action. Such a thing would be, in the words of Konstantin Zhukov, "a most fearsome blizzard of revolt."

48

The icy winds swept across the barren tundra landscape, but they did not trouble Bhuidseach Rowena Viridomarus. Those who were Death Touched did not feel cold, or if they did, they did not notice it, because no mere winter chill could hope to match the frigid grasp of Bàs, Lord of the Dead.

As Rowena strode through the camp, she wore only the brown hooded robes of her calling, and the awkward but useful snowshoes made by the Izmorozian beast witch Sonya. The sun still hung low on the horizon, but Rowena's countrymen had already burrowed down into the snow for the night as Sonya had taught them. All she could see were the thin trails of smoke that came from the openings. As she passed one, she caught the faint strains of a flute playing a light and merry tune. She was glad to hear it. They had been more than a week on the tundra now, and the arduous crossing had taken its toll. It was a curious thing she had noted about her people that in times of content-ment, they gravitated toward tragedy, but in times of hardship, they strengthened their resolve by fiercely seeking out joy whenever and wherever possible.

Rowena reached the end of the camp for the living, and there stood row after row of the mighty sluagh gorta. The pride of the Uaine were heedless of cold, hunger, or weariness. They merely stood and waited for the moment when they could contribute to the great glory of their people. The Raízian apothecary, Jorge, moved among them as he applied a new coat of the salve that kept their limbs from freezing. Like most foreigners, he had initially been quite fearful of the sluagh gorta, and it had clearly taken a great deal of courage for him to paint on his salve. But he had gradually become so acclimated that he now seemed completely untroubled to be among them. Not even Angelo was so at ease in their presence. Rowena considered that a fine indication of character.

He looked up from his work and gestured for her to come over. "Bhuidseach Rowena! Good, good! Come, please come!"

Jorge had been attempting to learn the Uaine language. At first, Rowena had encouraged his efforts, but Mordha had recommended she instead learn his language. She had no inclination to do so, but knew there was little choice, since she would be in the lands of the empire for some time to come.

"Hello, Jorge," she said as she walked over to him. "Please speak in your own language so that I may practice."

He nodded. "Okay, good!" Then he jabbered on for a little while in his own tongue much faster than she would have liked. She only caught about half of his words, but with the accompanying gestures, she was able to determine that he was concerned for the sluagh gortas' eyes. It was one of the few places he hadn't covered in his salve because he was unsure if it would make them permanently blind. He'd hoped treating the areas around the eye would be enough to keep them from freezing, but apparently that had only slowed it down. He was now asking if he should risk putting the salve on their eyes or let the eyes freeze over completely.

She told him to let them freeze over. It would make them blind for now, but they only needed to keep marching forward and they could do that without vision. They wouldn't need their eyes until the fighting began, and she had been told the climate would be more hospitable once they reached the other side of the tundra. Better to wait it out than risk permanent blindness.

He looked a little concerned, perhaps unable to fully accept that it would be no problem for the sluagh gorta to march blindly across the tundra for the remainder of the crossing. But he was a rather timid man, so after a moment, he nodded and began to seal up the bucket of salve.

"Good night, Bhuidseach Rowena!" he said in Uaine, then hurried off toward the burrow he shared with Sonya and Blaine. She watched him go, thinking how awkward it must be in that burrow. Blaine had told her that Jorge's religion frowned upon males having sex with each other, as well as sex outside of their official religiously sanctioned union of marriage. She thought it must be difficult to lie side by side in a small space with people you were strongly attracted to, unable to satisfy your desires. The Raízian gods must be cruel indeed. Rowena would have chosen to sleep elsewhere rather than torment herself so, but Blaine seemed to be enjoying the unnatural self-denial. He had always been a little strange.

Rowena heard Mordha approaching. It was impossible for the big man to sneak up on anyone out here in the crunching snow.

"Do you like that Raízian?" he asked.

She looked up into his scarred face.

"He is pleasant company," she said.

"You could make more of an effort to be friendly with him," said Mordha.

"You mean attempt to seduce him? His religion makes that a difficult proposition, and it's not really my skill set anyway. Besides, he's far more interested in Blaine and Sonya. Bàs knows why, because they're both idiots."

Mordha shrugged. "I don't think you need to compete with them, and there's more than one way to gain someone's trust. He views you as a colleague, an equal. I'm just asking you to make more of an effort to foster that relationship. He is clearly burdened by his desires for Blaine and the beast witch. Offer a sympathetic ear. Let him come to depend upon you."

"I see." She couldn't decide if that would be less work, or more.

"A man with his skills, knowledge, and connections would be invaluable, especially once we begin our campaign against Aureum."

"I am aware of that, Tighearna."

"Good."

They were silent for a moment, both staring at the unmoving rows of sluagh gorta, though Rowena considered it likely their thoughts were quite different.

Eventually she asked, "Do you think the beast witch can really rally her people to fight with us?"

Mordha scratched at his thick beard. "I hope so. It would be the ideal outcome, since it would reduce our costs."

"True," said Rowena. "Although it isn't necessary for our success."

"No," agreed Mordha. "It isn't."

PART FOUR

THE REBEL OF ROSKOSH
MANOR

"Identity is never isolated. We are defined not only by our own thoughts and actions, but also by our relationship to the world around us."

—Lady Olga Bunich Fignolov, *The Wife of Morning*

49

There it is," said Sebastian.

He and Rykov sat on horseback and gazed at the lone farmhouse that stood before them in the middle of a dark field. The 404th Cavalry waited quietly in formation behind them. The house was a few hours' ride from Gogoleth, and all around them stretched miles of farmland. The yellow glow of the house's windows shone like a beacon in the inky blackness.

"You sure that's the one?" asked Rykov.

Sebastian gestured to the emptiness that lay all around them. "You see any other farmhouses in this vicinity?"

Rykov shrugged. "Just saying. It wouldn't be the first time the general got it wrong."

"I understand your frustration, Private, but we must remember that espionage is not an exact science. Furthermore, General Zaniolo's intelligence network is stretched nearly to the breaking point trying to ferret out sedition across the entirety of Izmoroz. It's completely understandable that there would be a mistake here and there."

"I wouldn't call three in a row 'here and there,' " said Rykov.

Sebastian had no real argument for that, and as the superior officer, he shouldn't feel the need to argue. But in spite of that, he said, "Well, *someone's* in there."

He wheeled his horse around to face his men. They likely couldn't see him well in the darkness, but he didn't want to risk any light that might warn the occupants of the farmhouse.

"All right, gentlemen. Same as last time. Take as many alive as you can for questioning. Go."

His men nudged their horses past him and began to fan out until they surrounded the house. Once they were all in place, they slowly constricted their circle until there were two concentric rings. The outer ring held their position, while the inner ring approached the house. Sebastian found himself holding his breath, his pulse racing. He wondered if this was how the commanding officer had felt when they surrounded his own home all those months ago. Galina had asked him if he was ever troubled by the idea that he was now leading the same missions as the one that resulted in his father's death. He had said that, on the contrary, he hoped he could show the same compassion to his captives that his own captors had shown to him and his mother. She had told him that his magnanimous view of the world never ceased to amaze her. Then she had pressed her lips to his so intensely he'd nearly swooned.

Rykov cleared his throat. "Ready, sir?"

Sebastian guiltily pulled himself out of fond remembrance and scrutinized the house. No sounds or movement came from within, so he nodded. Rykov lifted a lantern and quickly opened and closed the shutters twice to signal the men of the 404th.

The inner ring of soldiers crashed through the doors and windows of the house, while the outer ring drew their sabers and held their positions. It was only a few moments before two of Sebastian's men came out of the house, half dragging a scrawny old man through the snow.

"Doesn't look like a group of dangerous dissidents to me," said Rykov.

"Damn," said Sebastian, then spurred his horse forward to meet them.

"Sir!" The two men threw their captive to the ground and saluted sharply as he drew near.

"I take it this was the sole inhabitant?" Sebastian asked them.

"Yes, sir!" said one of his men.

"Wonderful," muttered Sebastian. "Get him on his feet."

His men hauled the old man up.

"What's your name, old timer?"

"N-Nikolai, my lord!"

Sebastian sighed wearily. "I'm not a lord, I'm a captain."

"B-begging your pardon, Captain!"

"Why are you in this house?"

"I-I'm sorry, Captain! I swear, it won't happen again!"

"What won't happen again?"

"I know I have no right to sleep in a place that weren't mine, only it's terrible cold tonight and I thought, since there was nobody in there, it wouldn't harm nothing. Door wasn't even locked."

"I see." He looked at his men. "Any sign of anyone else?"

They shook their heads.

Sebastian pinched the bridge of his nose and sighed again.

"Here and there, huh?" said Rykov.

This time, Sebastian did not reply.

50

Captain Guido Pavase was quite certain that God was punishing him for the sins of his youth. First, by sending him to the brutal, backward territory of Izmoroz, where the winters were nearly as frigid as the women. In Gogoleth, he'd suffered under the command of the notoriously zealous Franko Vittorio, who acted as if his post were some great honor, rather than the punishment everyone in Aureum knew it to be after his embarrassingly public display of indiscretion regarding the empress.

To make matters worse, Guido and his men had now been stationed in a filthy, frozen mudhole called Zapad that was within spitting distance of the lifeless void known as the Great Western Tundra. There was no tavern in Zapad, and no women worth fucking. Guido's assignment was to keep the peace, which was laughable because he had seen Aureumian convents more unruly than Zapad. He was also supposed to look for possible sedition, which was even more ridiculous. The inbred hicks of Zapad could barely schedule their planting and harvesting seasons. The idea of them organizing some sort of rebellion was absurd.

Still, orders were orders, even if they came from the disgraced ex-Count Vittorio. So Guido sat behind an unvarnished desk in the repurposed ramshackle home that served as their station house, and interviewed every damn potato-brained peasant in the place.

"Name?" He didn't bother looking at the old man, and instead stared down at the blank parchment that would soon be filled with trivial information about another useless person.

"Gennady Shukhov Zworykin, sir."

"Occupation?"

"Fur trader."

"You're the one who takes the surplus furs to Gogoleth?"

"Yes, sir."

"Heard you had a larger haul than previous years."

"The Lady does provide."

Guido looked up from the parchment. "The Lady?"

Gennady flinched. "Begging your pardon, sir. Lady Zivena. She... well, you'd call her a goddess I suppose."

"I see..."

The peasant sank back farther into his chair. "Ain't no crime to keep the old ways."

"No, I suppose it isn't." It was, however, cause for suspicion. Could there really be a seditious element in this little mudhole? If he were to find a rebellion stronghold and bring it down swiftly, perhaps he could finally get Vittorio to promote him to colonel. "Are you married, Mr. Zworykin?"

Gennady shook his head.

"Who was that woman I saw you walking with yesterday, then?"

"Oh, that's my cousin, Mathilde."

"I don't recall seeing her before."

"She's just visiting, sir."

"From?"

"Gogoleth."

"For what purpose?"

"Purpose? Uh, just to visit, I suppose."

"Halfway across Izmoroz? Long voyage just for a visit. Expensive, too."

Guido watched the man tense up.

"I—I suppose it is, sir."

Guido let him squirm for a moment, then smiled. "Well, that's the love of family. Blood is thicker than anything, right?"

Gennady looked relieved. "Y-yes, sir."

"Thank you, Mr. Zworykin. That will be all."

"Anything else you need, be sure to let me know." Gennady stood and put his fur cap on. "Still have some furs in stock if you and your men start feeling the cold too bad."

"Thanks, Mr. Zworykin. I'll keep that in mind."

Guido watched the peasant hurry away, no doubt thinking he'd made it through the interview without arousing suspicion. That was good. If this Mathilde from Gogoleth was here on behalf of some rebellious sect intending to recruit the local idiots, she would no doubt bolt at the first sign of trouble. She probably wasn't of much value herself, but she might be able to give him a lead on someone higher up in the organization.

Assuming there *was* an organization. It could simply be boredom taking its toll on Guido and he was reading too much into things. But even if an investigation led to nothing, at least it was something to do. First he would ask around about this Mathilde. See if he could turn anything up that might lend even a little credence to his gut instincts.

"Fontana, I'm heading out for a bit."

"Yes, sir," said the soldier stationed by the door. "Would you like an escort?"

It might be too intimidating if he started questioning people with an armed grunt looming over his shoulder. "No. But I want everyone assembled and ready to deploy at a moment's notice."

"Sir?" Fontana looked surprised.

"Just a hunch. Don't get your hopes up."

"Yes, sir."

"But be ready, just in case."

"I'll notify the men right away, sir."

Guido nodded and stepped out into the brutal Izmorozian winter. The truth was, he wished he could wear some of Gennady's furs. Even his heavier wool uniform wasn't sufficient to keep out the cold. But furs were against regulation, and he wasn't about to jeopardize his career just for a little extra warmth. His men were fairly loyal, but when it came time for a promotion review, if Commander Vittorio pressed them—and he was known for pressing—they would probably relay even minor infractions. Vittorio had that kind of effect on people.

Guido walked briskly to stave off the cold as he wove between the dreary hovels that composed Zapad until he reached the rock pit where the children typically played. He knew from experience that children were generally an excellent source of information. They overheard a great deal but didn't yet have the guile to effectively deceive someone.

The children were playing some sort of game that involved taking turns throwing one stone on a pile of other stones. Guido was not surprised that he couldn't discern any rhyme or reason to their actions. There probably weren't any.

"Who's winning?" he asked cheerfully.

They all looked up at him, their eyes wary. "I am, sir," said one boy reluctantly.

"Excellent. What's your name, boy?"

"Boris, sir."

"Well, Boris, I'm glad you're keeping yourself amused. I'm really bored. See, my job is to keep this village safe, and talk to any new people who come here to make sure they understand the rules. But since nobody new ever comes here, I have nothing to do."

"But somebody came yesterday," piped up a girl.

The boy turned and glared at her. Clearly he had at least some idea what discretion was. Fortunately, the girl did not.

"Really?" He acted surprised. Then he put on a worried look. "Oh dear. If I don't talk to that person, I won't be doing my job and I'll get in trouble. Do you know who it is?"

"We don't know her," the boy said quickly.

"So it's a woman, then?" asked Guido.

The boy winced, realizing he'd just accidentally given away information.

"Anything else you can tell me about her?"

He kept his mouth shut this time. He was a surprisingly smart little inbred hick. But that could be useful as well.

"If you don't know, I suppose I'll have to question your mother." He didn't know who the boy's mother was, but that hardly mattered. Judging by the nervous look on the boy's face, he was as protective of his mother as most boys. And since he was smart, even an implied threat should be sufficient. "She's quite sweet, your mother. I do hope I don't have to be too firm with her."

"You don't need to ask my mom," he said quickly. "I know where you can find the woman."

Guido smiled. "Wonderful."

"She'll be down by the tannery right now."

Guido sighed. Of course, it made sense, what with her cousin being a fur trader. But the tannery was possibly the most awful smelling place he'd ever been forced to go near.

"You've both been most helpful," he told the children. They did not look pleased by that. Perhaps he would reward them later with candy or some other trivial item so they wouldn't be reluctant the next time he questioned them. All kids, be they Aureumian, Raízian, Kantesian, or Izmorozian, were stupid like that.

Guido returned to the station house and found his men waiting for him, their uniforms smart, and their swords polished.

"It is *possible* that there is a woman newly arrived in town who *might* be involved with some sort of rebel organization," he told his men. "We have no concrete evidence as of yet, but we would not be doing our duty if we didn't follow up on it. I will approach the tannery from the front entrance. You will all fan out and circle around. If she runs, we'll know she's at least hiding something. Do not allow her to escape, but do *not* kill her. We will need her for questioning."

"Yes, sir!" They looked a little overeager, but Guido could hardly blame them, given the many dull weeks they'd spent in this place. He just hoped they didn't kill her in their enthusiasm. Killing an old woman on mere suspicion of seditious activity was not the way to get a promotion.

Guido strode purposefully through the village to the tannery, which, because of its awful stench, lay at the edge of the village closest to the tundra. It was larger than the other buildings, though still made of drab, unpainted wood, with mud sealing the slats and thatch as a roof. He eased off his pace until his soldiers were in position, then headed straight for the front door, doing his best to breathe through his mouth. Unfortunately, as he got closer, he found that the air even tasted bad.

He banged on the door with his fist. No sense beating around the bush now.

"Open up, Gennady! I need to speak with your cousin!"

There was a great deal of shuffling and muttered curses behind the door. Gennady's strained voice lent additional credence to Guido's suspicions. "Uh...just a second, Captain, sir. I'm, uh...right in the middle of something."

This will be over before it's hardly begun, Guido thought sadly. Really, it was almost too easy. But at least he had the interrogation to look forward to.

He pounded on the door again. "I'm warning you, Gennady! You better open this door or I'm going to break it down!" He of course could not actually do that by himself. Whatever else they were, these little hovels were damn sturdy.

The door opened to reveal a flushed, sweating Gennady. His attempt at a smile was painful. "What can I do for you, Captain?"

"As I said, I need to speak with your cousin."

He gave a tremendously exaggerated look of regret. "Sorry, sir. You just missed her."

"Oh, I doubt that," said Guido.

There was a hoarse female shout from behind the building and Gennady suddenly looked very alarmed.

"Oh my," said Guido. "I wonder what all the commotion is. Shall we go see?"

Guido grabbed Gennady's arm and pulled him around to the back of the tannery. Beyond the building lay a few sparse trees that stuck feebly out of the snow before giving way entirely to the vast and open tundra. It was almost like a white sea, beautiful in its way, and perhaps just as cruel.

His men had caught up with the old woman just beyond the tree line. It appeared that in her panic she had attempted to flee into the tundra. She really must have something to hide if she was willing to take an action tantamount to suicide. After all, no one could survive the tundra in winter. Even now, the old woman was surprisingly lively as she bucked against the two men who held her.

"Well, well," called Guido as he drew near. "Mathilde, isn't it? I can't wait to hear what you have to say. Judging by your desperation, it might even be worthwhile."

"I'll never tell you anything!" the old woman hollered.

"Not right away, of course," agreed Guido. "But despite what old heroic legends might suggest, I've found that most people buckle under torture rather quickly."

"Please, sir! Have mercy on her!" begged Gennady.

"Mercy is not killing you for harboring a seditionist," Guido replied. "Now, Ms. Mathilde, shall we return to—"

Then an arrow pierced the throat of the soldier holding Mathilde's right arm. A moment later, the soldier holding her left arm fell as well, blood gushing from his neck.

"Where is that coming from?" demanded Guido as he crouched low to the ground.

His soldiers drew their swords and wheeled around, looking in every direction except of course the tundra.

The tundra.

Guido saw someone standing out in the middle of that vast snowfield. She was dressed in a thick leather coat lined with white fur, her black hair whipping in the wind as a cloud of steam trailed from her mouth into the frozen sky. In her hands was a longbow, and another arrow was already nocked.

"There! She's there!" he shouted. "Piazza! Return fire!"

His best archer fumbled with his bow and quiver, but before he could get an arrow nocked, the assailant buried one in his eye and he fell twitching.

"Damn it, take cover!" Guido shouted to the rest of his soldiers as he grabbed Gennady and pulled him forward as a shield.

Mathilde dropped to her knees, tears streaming down her smiling face as she watched the female archer approach. Then she turned to Guido.

"You're dead," she whispered serenely. "You're all dead."

"We'll see about that." Guido backed toward the tannery, keeping Gennady between him and the archer. The white fur lining of the archer's jacket suggested a Ranger of Marzanna. He'd been too young to fight in the war, but he'd heard stories about the Rangers from veterans. *Horror* stories. They were supposed to be extinct, though.

The Ranger, if that's what she was, walked unhurriedly toward them as she nocked yet another arrow. Then a tall man with long blond hair and a massive sword caught up from behind to match her stride.

"Thought ya'd take 'em all, eh?" Guido heard the man say cheerfully in a strange, guttural accent.

"Still think I might," replied the Ranger as she loosed an arrow that somehow found a gap between two stacks of crates to strike down yet another one of Guido's soldiers. "Better hurry."

"Damn ye, woman!" he shouted, then drew his sword and ran forward at a full sprint.

"Archers!" yelled Guido. "Fire!"

But his most skilled archer was already dead. The others were not a great shot at the best of times, and now they were thoroughly rattled. Most of the arrows missed their mark, and the one that could have struck true, the man batted aside with his sword.

"There's just two of them!" Guido said as he finally reached the relative safety of the tannery. "Engage! Engage!"

His soldiers drew their swords and charged forward. It was seven against one. Even if the archer picked a few more off, there was no way one man could possibly break through seven imperial soldiers. Or so Guido thought.

The man swung his massive sword with astonishing speed and agility. He beheaded one man, then used his momentum and balance to twist around and parry another soldier's attack hard enough to send him staggering backward. He slammed his pommel into a third soldier's head, then stabbed the one who had just recovered from his stagger. The combination of speed and power would have been wondrous if it hadn't been so frightening. Soldiers fell one by one from his flurry of attacks, and any who stepped out of his reach were picked off by the Ranger.

Guido concluded his men were all doomed. The priority now was to report back to Gogoleth about this new threat. He had to escape while his men were distracting the attackers.

He threw Gennady down and ran.

But pain lanced through his leg as an arrow embedded itself in his hamstring. He had no idea how the Ranger could shoot so precisely at such a range, but he gritted his teeth and continued on, dragging his leg. Until another arrow pierced his other hamstring and he fell to the ground. Still he tried to escape, crawling on hands and knees. Guido was nothing if not committed to self-preservation.

"Ah no," he heard the man with the strange accent say right behind him, and then felt a strong grip on his collar. "Me' friend Sonya like t' have a word with ye."

The man dragged him, seemingly without effort, back toward the tundra, past the bloody corpses of his men, and deposited him in the snow before the Ranger. She was with Mathilde, patting her on the back and talking soothingly to her in a quiet voice.

"Sonya, is it?" Guido said. "You'll never get away with this. Once Commander Vittorio gets word of this—and believe me he will—he will bring down death upon you and every damn rebel in this God-forsaken frozen hellscape."

Sonya seemed to think about it for a moment, then shook her head. "I don't think so. Because first we're going to bring death down on you, your Commander Vittorio, and every other imperial who refuses to get out of Izmoroz."

Guido let out a harsh laugh. "The two of you? Take on the whole empire?"

"Oh, no, don't be silly." She jerked her thumb over her shoulder back toward the tundra. "They're going to help us."

At first, Guido didn't know to whom she was referring. But gradually, as his eyes grew accustomed to the glare from the snow, he made out a line of soldiers marching toward him from the tundra. They were clothed only in robes, which was odd given the temperature. But as they got closer, Guido began to understand. Their yellow, veiny eyes were glazed, their skin a mottled, desiccated gray. Their noses were mere holes, and their lipless mouths showed teeth in an endless cold grin.

It was just as the priests had warned. The undead armies of the Uaine Empire had come. And they'd come early.

Sonya hunkered down next to Guido and smiled. Now that she was close, he could see she had pointed ears and the golden eyes of a fox. Beast marks, just as the old war vets had described in their tales of violence and cruelty that had seemed too monstrous to give much credence.

"Now, I've got a few questions for you," said the Ranger. "And if you answer truthfully, I'll make sure to kill you nice and quick."

Those stories seemed much more realistic now.

51

Sebastian had not felt this content in weeks. As the spicy mulled wine warmed his stomach, he gazed happily around the table. To his left, ever beautiful and poised, was Galina, followed by Lord and Lady Prozorova. To his right sat his mother, followed by Generals Zaniolo, Bonucci, and Marchisio. And directly across from him sat the regal Commander Vittorio. Everyone was chatting gaily as they ate roast goose with brown, crackling skin, and delicately braised salmon.

"Are you not hungry, my *volshebnik*?" Galina gave him a concerned look. "I do worry that you have been losing weight again."

He smiled. "I am feasting my eyes and feeding my heart, my beloved Galechka. Having everyone in the world who is dear to me, all in one place like this, is the greatest gift I could ask."

"Surely not everyone," she said. "Whatever else she may be, Sonya Turgenev is still your sister, and as such still deserves your love, does she not?"

"My dear Galina Odoyevtseva," said Lady Portinari. "Clearly you have never met Sebastian's sister. Ever the stoic, I fear she would not have enjoyed such an opulent and joyful feast. As such, there is no point in wishing for her presence."

"Among other reasons," Vittorio said quietly. But he did not elaborate, and for that Sebastian was grateful. The last thing he wanted was for the Prozorova family to learn that his sister was an outlaw wanted for multiple counts of murder.

"Now," Vittorio said briskly as he patted his lips and mustache with a cream-colored silk napkin. "The majority of people at this table have never celebrated the Ascendance before, so I thought I might speak a little about its origin and importance, both to Aureum and to the empire."

"An excellent idea," said General Marchisio as he poured himself some more mulled wine from the crystal decanter.

"It is an Aureumian high holiday, is it not, Commander?" asked Galina.

"Indeed, it is the *highest* of holy days, Galina Odoyevtseva." Commander Vittorio seemed a little more boisterous than normal, and his face was unusually flushed. As Sebastian watched him accept the crystal decanter from Marchisio and liberally fill his own glass, he suspected that the holiday had induced the commander to drink more than usual.

"And it is a celebration of the inception of the empire, Commander?" asked Galina.

Vittorio beamed first at her, then at Sebastian. "A fine and knowledgeable woman you've found, Captain."

Galina looked pleased. "Since my betrothed is half-Aureumian, I have endeavored to read as much about the country and culture as I could, Commander."

"Do you know the story of the Ascendance, then?" asked Vittorio.

"I have come across several iterations of it, Commander, but I would much prefer to hear your telling."

He nodded approvingly. "Quite right. A dry and musty tome can only teach so much."

Sebastian was concerned that even such a minor slight to Galina's beloved books would displease her. But she only smiled and humbly inclined her head. "Please honor us with your rendition, then, Commander."

Vittorio took a large gulp of wine, then cleared his throat. "Centuries ago, Aureum was like any other country. Weak, struggling, and above all corrupt, from the lowest thieves to the highest politicians. It was a republic back then, ruled jointly by a group of men called senators who constantly undermined each other, and spent more time worrying how to line their pockets than helping the people of Aureum."

He held up a finger and smiled. "With one exception. A young senator named Alessandro Morante understood that the once noble republic had fallen into dark and dreadful times. But when he urged his fellow senators to look beyond their own needs and consider the greater good, they mocked or outright rebuffed him. He did not give in to despair, however, and continued to press them until they at last grew tired of his idealism and conspired against him. Joining together in common purpose for the first time in decades, those pompous, self-serving senators captured Alessandro Morante, dragged him to the highest tower in Magna Alto, and threw him over the side. And do you know what happened then?"

The commander looked around the table, but everyone remained silent.

Vittorio raised his half-full glass of wine. "God did not allow Morante to fall to his death, but instead lifted him up to Heaven, where He bestowed astonishing gifts of intellect and wisdom upon him. Exactly one year later, Alessandro Morante returned to earth so that he might wrest control from the dissolute senators and rule Aureum with firm resolution and noble goals, as God intended. Thus the empire was born, and has, with a strict hand and the will of God, become the greatest power on earth, now led by the wise and beautiful Empress Caterina, great-granddaughter of Alessandro Morante!"

All three generals burst into applause. After a startled moment, the rest of the table joined in.

"A remarkable story, Commander," said Galina. "And your telling was filled with such passion that even I, who have not a drop of Aureumian blood, felt my heart stirring."

"Ah, but that is the beauty of the empire, my dear little Galina!" said Vittorio. "One need not be Aureumian to feel the stirrings of patriotism within their breast, because the generous Empress Morante embraces all, regardless of the culture or beliefs from which they come."

"Truly she is a magnanimous ruler," murmured Galina.

"Dmitry, clear the food please," said Vittorio. "No, you may leave the wine, isn't that right, Marchisio?"

"Hear, hear! What is the Ascendance without a bit of spiced wine?" Marchisio drained his glass, then reached again for the decanter.

"Once the table is clear," continued Vittorio, "we may begin a solemn Ascendance tradition. Each of you will be given a small piece of parchment and a bit of charcoal. The continued might of the empire is in part thanks to the firm will and intention of its rule. So that we might all live by that example, each year on the day of the Ascendance, every subject of the empire is expected to write down something they wish to accomplish in the coming year. You will then fold it and place it in the bowl." He gestured to the empty metal bowl in the center of the table. "Once everyone has placed their piece of parchment in the bowl, we will light it on fire, thus sending our declarations of intent for the coming year to God in Heaven, where He will most certainly hold us accountable."

Once Dmitry cleared the table, he distributed the parchment and charcoal. Sebastian knew what he wanted to write, but he thought for a few moments how best to phrase it. At last he settled on: *To protect Izmoroz and the empire from any who would harm it.*

As he folded his parchment, he glanced over at Galina and couldn't help but read her own goal, which read: *To serve my beloved Sebastian faithfully and completely in all things.* He quickly turned away, realizing it might not have been intended for his eyes, even as he felt a blush creep onto his face. But then he felt her light touch on his arm. When he turned back to her, she smiled at him as she folded the parchment and dropped it into the bowl.

"I do hope, Lord Prozorova," said General Bonucci, "that you are writing down a goal to achieve something of value, and not the indulgence of your little hobby of collecting Izmorozian children's stories."

Lord Prozorova's eyes widened behind his spectacles. "How da—"

"How *thoughtful* of you to remember, General," Galina said quickly. "Isn't that right, Mother?"

"What?" Lady Prozorova looked up from her still blank parchment, took in her daughter's expression, and then her husband's. Sebastian had never thought much of Lady Prozorova's intellect, but she seemed to comprehend the uncomfortable situation in an instant. "Yes, of course. Sergey, my dear love, I'm ever so sorry, but could you help me with mine? I can't think of a single thing to write."

Lord Prozorova ignored her and continued to glare at General Bonucci with what looked like open hostility. Sebastian supposed he couldn't blame his soon-to-be father-in-law for such a reaction. After all, no man liked to have his hobbies dismissed, even if they were silly and pointless.

Lady Prozorova pressed her powdered bosom against her husband's arm and tilted her head until it lay on his shoulder. "*Please*, my dearest?"

Lord Prozorova took a deep breath and nodded. "Yes, of course I will help you, my dear wife. I know how hard such things can be for you."

Once everyone had placed their folded parchment in the bowl, Commander Vittorio stood and walked over to the crackling fireplace. He lit his own parchment from the fire, then returned to the table and dropped it into the bowl.

"Not my will, but God's will be done," he intoned.

"Amen," said the generals.

They all watched in silence as the pieces of parchment blackened and curled into ash, smoke wending its way up toward the ceiling. Sebastian wondered if they should open a window so that it might find God sooner, but was still too unsure of his Aureumian heritage to suggest such a thing. He wondered why they had never celebrated the Ascendance when he and his sister were young. Had his father sworn off not only the imperial army, but its religion as well?

"Now, gentlemen," said Vittorio. "It is customary for us to adjourn to the study for a glass of grappa before the end of the evening."

The generals stood, and Sebastian followed suit a moment later.

"Lord Prozorova, will you be joining us?" asked the commander.

"I'm ever so sorry," said Galina, "but I must beg your kind indulgence in letting my father take me home early. I fear the spicy mulled wine, though delicious, was too much for my delicate constitution and I'm feeling somewhat unwell as a result."

"Oh, no, Galechka my love." Sebastian dropped to one knee and took her hands. "What can I do?"

She smiled and shook her head. "I'm certain it is merely indigestion and will pass by morning. I would be loath to disrupt this most important holy day any more than necessary, so you should continue with the commander and his generals."

"Quite right," said Vittorio. "No sense spoiling things for the rest of us." He bowed his head slightly. "Lord and Lady Prozorova, I bid you good evening. Galina Odoyevtseva, I hope you feel better soon."

Sebastian looked back at Galina and sighed. "I hate to imagine you in any discomfort, my Galechka."

"Then don't," she said gently. "Go and enjoy the rest of the evening with Commander Vittorio, and you can tell me all about it on the morrow."

"Yes, I'll come check on you first thing in the morning."

"Wonderful." She pressed her soft, cool lips to his cheek, her faint floral scent enveloping him.

"Coming, Captain?" Vittorio asked pointedly.

Sebastian rose quickly, feeling his face redden again. The generals seemed fairly amused as they waited by the doorway, but the commander looked decidedly grim.

"S-sorry to keep you, sir," he apologized.

Vittorio turned without reply and led the way down the hall to the study. It was quite a bit smaller than the study at Roskosh Manor, and frankly, Sebastian wasn't sure how they would have been able to fit a sixth man anyway. Vittorio took the chair by the fire, while Zaniolo took the one opposite. Bonucci and Marchisio shared the sofa, leaving Sebastian to sit on a small upholstered stool.

Zaniolo grinned at him. "Sorry, Captain. Seniority, you know. You'll have your time eventually."

Sebastian returned the smile. "Yes, of course, General. I'm happy merely to be here."

Dmitry appeared with two bottles of a yellow liquor called grappa that Vittorio had imported from Magna Alto for the occasion. He poured some into miniature wineglasses for each of them. Drink in hand, the men then began a far-ranging discussion of everything from the seemingly endless winter, to the possibility of an Uaine offensive in the late spring. None of it was really new information, and soon they began to harken back to their days in Aureum. Zaniolo talked with longing of the grand balls, while Bonucci recounted the incredible foods that could be cultivated in Aureum's more generous soil and warmer clime. Marchisio talked at considerable length about the legendary beauty of Aureumian women.

The only one who did not speak about Aureum, Sebastian noted, was the commander. He listened to the others intently, and even smiled indulgently at some of Marchisio's lavish descriptions, but he did not offer anything of his own. Finally, he stood up abruptly.

"I could use a bit of fresh air," he declared. "Sebastian, accompany me."

"Yes, sir."

The others glanced at him, then looked away. Was Sebastian in trouble? Had he done something wrong? He followed Vittorio out of the study and down the hall, anxiously trying to think how he might have displeased the commander. Perhaps it was Lord Prozorova's hostility he wished to speak about. While it was clear that Galina was doing everything she could to keep the peace, perhaps that was not enough for the commander. Perhaps he expected Sebastian, as the future son-in-law, to take things in hand.

Vittorio led Sebastian through the parlor to the small balcony that overlooked Nadezhda Square. It was quite dark out, with only a sliver of moonlight, and the stalls in the square were closed up for the night.

Vittorio rested one hand on the balcony railing and drained his glass of grappa.

"You know that I cherish my post here in Izmoroz, Sebastian," he said quietly.

"Yes of course, sir."

"But I confess that this one night of the year, I find myself fiercely missing the great city of Magna Alto."

"I hope to see it one day, sir."

He gazed up into the night sky. "Oh, you will. Of that I have no doubt. Once we have crushed the Uaine menace, we will be called back to that shining city to stand in the glorious presence of our empress. Her gratitude will be as generous as her displeasure is merciless. And then at last, all will be mended."

He fell silent, and after a few moments, Sebastian noted with surprise that the commander's eyes glittered in the faint moonlight with barely repressed tears. He had never thought of the commander as given to melancholy or sadness. In fact, it was the first time he'd ever seen weakness of any kind in the man.

"We will see her will done," Vittorio intoned almost like a prayer. "And she will welcome us back into her benevolent embrace."

"Y-yes, sir," said Sebastian, because he did not know what else to say. It was both comforting and worrisome to see one's heroes shown to be only human after all.

52

Galina and her mother listened patiently as Lord Prozorova vented his outrage during the carriage ride back to Roskosh Manor.

"*Little hobby?*" was the phrase he returned to again and again as his face changed from pink, to red, to an almost purplish hue. "Damn that ignorant Aureumian pig to an eternity of suffering!"

"Sergey, darling," soothed his wife as she stroked his trembling fist. "It's okay now, my love. It's over."

"Yes, you showed admirable restraint, Papa," lied Galina.

In fact, her father had shown the bare minimum of acceptable restraint, and if Vittorio hadn't been uncharacteristically dull and maudlin from too much drink, things might have gotten ugly. Still, it was too late to fix it now. Perhaps if they were very lucky, the commander would continue his trajectory into further inebriation and forget the entire exchange. That would be the best-case scenario.

The worst case would be that Vittorio forced Sebastian to end their engagement. Despite Sebastian's increasingly obvious subservience to the commander and his imperial mentality, Galina was surprised to find that she was still rather fond of him. Politically speaking, he might very well be beyond redemption, but she could not quite relinquish the belief that underneath it all, he was still a sweet and thoughtful boy. Besides, her daily communications with him provided information that had proven invaluable to her peasant insurgents. There had been several close calls, but thanks to her warnings, none of the rebel

groups had been killed or apprehended since Sebastian began searching for them.

When the carriage reached Roskosh Manor, it was clear that Masha
was anxious to speak to her, so after her parents were settled, she made
use of her earlier pretext of feeling unwell and bid them good night.

Once they were alone in Galina's apartments, Masha blurted out,
"Miss, Mathilde is waiting at the Sturdy Sturgeon Tavern with urgent
news. She says it's about that Ranger!"

"Really?" asked Galina. "And it's urgent?"

Masha nodded. "She wants to know if you can speak with her
tonight."

Galina considered it a moment. "I can't make an excuse of shop-
ping so late. Besides, I have already spoken of a stomachache twice
this evening."

"We could just try to sneak out, miss," said Masha.

"True, but knowing my father, there's a good chance he will soon
feel remorse for his outburst and come to apologize to me."

"But surely if you've said you're feeling unwell, he wouldn't try to
wake you if you don't answer the door."

Galina gnawed briefly on her lip, a nervous habit she'd picked up of
late, no doubt from the strain of keeping so many grave secrets. "He
can be a tad impulsive and has, on more than one occasion, forgotten
that I am now a grown woman and barged into my chambers, despite
my scoldings. No, I think you had better bring Mathilde here."

"But, miss, then she'll know who you are."

"There's a risk either way, and if I have to choose between the
possibility of overt discovery by someone who is not yet an ally, and
revealing sensitive information to a confirmed ally, I choose the
latter."

Masha clearly didn't like the idea, but she nodded. "As you say,
miss. I'll go fetch her at once."

"And if my parents ask who she is, tell them she's an herbalist you
are acquainted with who you hope will be able to soothe my unsettled
stomach."

"Yes, miss."

Once Masha was gone, Galina sighed and sat down in the chair next to the fire. She had been looking forward to shedding her corset and gown, slipping into a nightgown, and curling up in bed with a book, and perhaps a glass of warm milk. But at the same time, she could not deny the thrill she felt at this new element of intrigue.

Shortly after Masha left her chambers, her father arrived with the anticipated apology.

"I thought you were getting ready for bed, Galechka," he said when she answered the door.

"Masha has gone to fetch an herbalist, Papa."

His brow furrowed. "Oh, dear, is it that bad?"

"I'm afraid so, Papa." She made her way slowly back to the chair beside the fire. Having always been thin and sickly looking, people rarely questioned her claims of illness.

"Hopefully the stress of my near outburst in front of the commander and Sebastian's mother did not exacerbate your condition," he said contritely. "I know how truly fond you are of Sebastian, and that you would be greatly distressed if he was forced to break off the engagement for political reasons."

"Please don't worry yourself, Papa. I know you did the best you could."

He sighed and looked into the crackling hearth. "I still remember what it was like *before* the empire came. When the nobility truly had power in Izmoroz, rather than merely being figureheads for the commander and his lackeys to push around. When we lost the war, it was…a difficult adjustment. I thought it would get easier…" He glanced back at her, the glare from the fireplace gleaming in his glasses so that they masked his eyes. "But it hasn't. If anything, it grows harder each year."

Galina wished she could bring her father into her confidence. To tell him that she was at that very moment working on ways to free them of the empire. But to what end? What could he do to aid the cause? And in selfishly unburdening herself, she would be putting him at risk.

"Perhaps Izmoroz will be free again someday, Papa."

"Not in my lifetime, but perhaps in yours." He leaned over and tenderly kissed her forehead. "Well, good night, my dearest. I hope Masha's herbalist is able to give you some comfort."

Then he turned and left, closing the door quietly behind him. Her father did not often show such vulnerability, and when he did, it always struck at her heart. She promised herself that if there was any way she could free Izmoroz within his lifetime, she would do it. No matter the risk.

Some time later, there was a quiet knock on the door.

"Come in," Galina said as she closed her book in her lap and put it on the small table beside her.

Masha entered, followed meekly by Mathilde.

"Thank you for coming so late, Mathilde," said Galina.

"You...," said the old woman, her eyes widened. "I seen your face before. You're the young lady betrothed to that *wizard*."

"I am indeed," Galina agreed.

"That's how you always know when and where he's going to strike next."

"It is."

As Mathilde gazed at her, a strange sadness crept into her expression. "You still going to marry him?"

"I don't know," admitted Galina. "I will do whatever I think is best for Izmoroz."

Mathilde nodded, but the mysterious sadness remained.

"Now," Galina said briskly, "if you would, please tell me what is so urgent it couldn't wait until tomorrow."

"Uh, yes, miss." Mathilde began picking nervously at the hem of her sleeve. "I went to see my cousin in Zapad, just like you suggested. But them imperials had already set themselves up there, questioning everyone and pushing them around like they were expecting trouble."

"I've heard as much," said Galina.

"Well, I reckon I'm not really cut out to be a spy because it didn't take long for them to get suspicious of me. Nearly had me, too, except that Ranger we heard about came back just in the nick of time and killed all the imperials."

"By *herself*?" asked Galina.

"She had some funny-talking swordsman with her, but I reckon she could have done it alone, the way the two of them were treating it almost like a contest."

"I see. Go on."

"Well, miss, she started asking me who I was, and so I told her. And since it seemed like the thing to do, I told her about what we were trying to do in Gogoleth."

"How did she respond?"

"She said she wanted to set up a meeting with the person in charge. Like maybe you could work together. Wouldn't that be amazing, miss? Working side by side with a real Ranger of Marzanna?"

"And I take it after meeting her you have no doubt that is what she is?"

"Not a doubt in my mind," said Mathilde. "Has the Lady's blessings clear as day."

"The Lady's blessings?" asked Galina.

"When the Lady grants the Rangers amazing powers, she marks them with some features you might see in animals."

"Really? And this is considered a blessing?"

"A blessing and an honor, my lady."

Galina decided not to argue the point. "Very well. Let's meet with this Ranger, then."

"She said she'll be waiting for you in the town of Kamen three days from now at the Fox Tail Tavern."

"I see." Galina did not like that this Ranger, most likely Sonya Turgenev, simply presumed Galina would be willing to travel such a distance on short notice to meet with her. But the enthusiastic gleam in Mathilde's eyes reminded her just how much the peasants valued their Rangers.

"Very well. I shall devise some sort of reason for Masha and I to travel to Kamen that won't arouse suspicion, and hopefully when this

Ranger and I meet, we can forge an alliance that will hasten the liberation of Izmoroz."

"Yes, miss! Thank you! I don't doubt you will!" said Mathilde.

Galina hoped the old woman was right, but she had some reservations. After all, she'd yet to meet a Turgenev with whom she could truly find common cause.

53

"Another round for the Ranger of Marzanna and her allies!" a young man at the bar told the barkeep. Then he lifted his glass of vodka to the large table at the back of the tavern where Sonya sat with Jorge, Blaine, Angelo, and Mordha.

Sonya lifted her own glass and nodded, then the two drank.

"Yer people love ye," observed Mordha.

"Naturally. I'm very lovable."

She put her feet up on Blaine's lap, then leaned back so she was using Jorge's shoulder as a headrest. In retrospect, she should have done the opposite, because Jorge's shoulder was rather bony and not all that comfortable. It wasn't bad enough that she bothered to move, however.

"An' yer certain this woman will meet ye?"

"I'm not certain I *want* her to," said Sonya. "Jorge and Angelo are the ones who thought it was a good idea."

"I find it so strange," said Jorge, "that you were willing to journey across the tundra to enlist the aid of a foreign nation, but are reluctant to join with your own people."

"She isn't my people," said Sonya. "According to Mathilde, she's a damn noble."

"But isn't your mother a noble?" asked Jorge.

"Really?" Angelo looked astonished. "That old wolf Portinari settled down with an Izmorozian noblewoman? Must have been quite the beauty."

354

"Still is," said Sonya. "And she didn't act like a noble while I was growing up. Just...now that she's back in Gogoleth, I guess she has to fit in."

"Or she wants to," suggested Jorge.

Sonya grunted. She knew he was probably right, but even after all this time it still bothered her.

"Sonya, what ye have against No-bells?" asked Blaine. "They a nasty clan?"

"I told you, we don't have clans in Izmoroz," said Sonya. "And I guess you don't have nobility? Families who keep the power all to themselves even when they don't know what to do with it?"

"A chief that don't know what t' do with power gets it taken away," said Mordha.

"Not in Izmoroz," said Sonya.

"That's why ye lost the war, then," he told her.

Sonya winced, but she couldn't argue the point. If the nobility had been able to present a strong and united leadership, perhaps things would have turned out very differently. "Yeah, well, I tell you this. After we get rid of the empire, getting rid of the nobility is next on my list."

"Really?" Jorge looked dubious. "And without either the empire or the nobility, what system of governance will you install instead?"

"I haven't got that far in the plan yet," she told him airily. "Maybe you can come up with something."

"Right," he said dryly. "With my vast knowledge of political systems."

The barkeep brought over the round of drinks that the man at the bar had so kindly ordered for them. This was their third free round. The people were all so grateful that she'd gotten rid of the soldiers. She hadn't realized it had gotten that bad that quickly. Soldiers now infested every town and village like mice. But as Angelo had pointed out, it had made it a lot easier to prove to the people that the Uaine were liberators. They were still keeping the sluagh gorta away from the towns, however. Angelo had recommended they ease people into that idea a little more slowly, and the imperial presence in the towns they'd liberated so far had been quite small so they hadn't needed them anyway.

Sonya had grudgingly come to accept that Angelo was rather useful. Mordha seemed to have a good head for military strategy, but he was unfamiliar with both the terrain of Izmoroz and the tactics of the imperial army. Sonya was able to advise him on the former, but Angelo had become invaluable regarding the latter. She still didn't trust the ex-imperial, but he had yet to do anything that fed her distrust, so she was trying her best to keep an open mind.

They were still working on that third round of vodkas when Sonya saw Mathilde peer cautiously through the front door into the tavern. Behind her was another familiar face, Masha, the servant woman at Roskosh Manor. Next to Masha was a girl a few years younger than Sonya who seemed to think that wearing a plain, drab shawl and kerchief would hide the fact that she was a noble. The girl was incredibly thin and pale, with large, sad eyes. She made Sonya think of a fragile porcelain doll.

"Here we go, boys." She waved Mathilde over. "Our honored guests have arrived."

Everyone else straightened in their seats, but Sonya decided to remain lounging against Jorge and Blaine. She thought it would set the right tone for the conversation.

Mathilde led Masha and the camouflaged doll toward them, and Sonya could see the noble carefully assessing the situation while giving away no reaction. It reminded her a little of how her mother had looked at her when she'd come to Roskosh Manor, and for reasons she couldn't quite articulate, that annoyed her even more.

When they reached the table, Jorge and Angelo immediately stood and bowed to the noble, as if they simply couldn't help themselves. With her backrest gone, Sonya was forced to sit properly. She tried to hide her irritation, but knew that she was not nearly as good at masking her emotions as a noble. Blaine and Mordha gave her a questioning look to see if they should stand as well, and Sonya shook her head.

"Sonya Turgenev Portinari," said the noble in a voice as delicate and brittle as the rest of her. "It is a pleasure to meet you at last."

"You know me?"

"My name is Galina Odoyevtseva Prozorova of Roskosh Manor. My family has been deeply connected with the Turgenev family for generations. Indeed, before the war, my father courted your mother."

"Really?" Sonya found it hard to imagine her mother with anyone other than her father, but she supposed that was how most people felt about their parents. And the way Sonya understood it, betrothals among the nobility were more about politics than love anyway. Before the war, the Prozorovas had probably been very important, but once the empire took over, marrying a daughter to one of their war heroes would have been even more advantageous. Thank the Lady that Sonya never had to worry about nonsense like that.

"Have a seat," she told the new arrivals, mostly so that Jorge and Angelo would also sit back down. She managed to swallow her laughter when Masha made an attempt to clean Galina's seat with a handkerchief.

"So you're from Roskosh Manor," Sonya asked Galina. "I guess that means you know my mother."

"I am well acquainted with Lady Portinari, and..." Galina hesitated, her face creasing slightly as if she was deciding whether to continue. Apparently she wasn't quite as poised as Sonya's mother after all. Not yet, anyway. "And your brother as well."

"My brother." Sonya spat on the floor.

"You have a brother?" asked Angelo. "Giovanni Portinari had a son?"

"Yes," said Galina. "Captain Sebastian Turgenev Portinari."

"Captain already?" asked Sonya. "What a good little soldier he's turned out to be."

"Unfortunately, you are more right than you know," said Galina. "He has become so enamored with Commander Vittorio and the empire that I fear you would hardly recognize him now."

"He's always been a kiss ass little shit," said Sonya.

"When I first met him, I found him surprisingly thoughtful and sensitive for a man," said Galina. "Almost like a poet, really. But under Vittorio's influence, he carries out his orders with a cold efficiency, murdering defenseless peasants without remorse, using his considerable intellect to justify his actions in astonishing ways."

"Wait," said Sonya. "Murder? My *brother*?" That she found hard to believe.

"I'm afraid so."

"And how do you know this, Galina Odoyevtseva?"

"He confides everything to me," she replied. "Because I am his betrothed."

"Shit." Sonya considered that a moment. "And you've decided you don't like this new cruel streak of his, so you're betraying him? Is that it?" She was equal parts impressed and angered by the idea. On one hand, it was an admirably aggressive play for such a fragile little doll. On the other hand, Sonya knew that no matter what else her brother might be, he was a hopelessly romantic sap and when he eventually discovered Galina had betrayed him, he would be devastated.

"I do not do this lightly, Sonya Turgenev," Galina said sharply. "I reluctantly came to this decision after months of trying in vain to gently guide him down a better path. I even expressed my concerns to his—*your* mother, in hopes that she could get through to him when I could not."

"I can guess how *that* went," said Sonya. "You failed to realize that precious Sebastian is incapable of wrongdoing. It's inevitably everyone else's fault."

Galina smiled sadly. "Yes, that was more or less what I discovered. And so, when Sebastian calmly explained to me why it was necessary for him to massacre an entire group of rebels by burning them alive without warning or even the hope of surrender, I decided that for the good of Izmoroz, I could no longer sit idly by."

"You didn't just confront him?" asked Sonya.

"That would have compromised my position, which has enabled me to glean information that has already saved hundreds of rebel lives."

"You have a point," admitted Sonya. It still bothered her that Sebastian's betrothed was manipulating him, but there was no denying the potential advantage of having an informant like her.

"Is yer brother so fierce, then?" asked Blaine curiously.

"He uses elemental magic," said Sonya.

"Wha' es that?" asked Mordha.

"Controlling the elements of fire, air, water, and earth."

Mordha nodded, looking impressed.

"Additionally," said Galina, "Commander Vittorio has given him a gemstone that magnifies his power immensely. He can raze an entire field in mere moments."

"That's worrisome," said Jorge.

"I'm sorry, Sonya Turgenev," said Galina, "but would you mind introducing me to the rest of your allies?" There was a tinge of irritation in her voice that suggested this was something Sonya should have done already.

"Oh, sure. This is our apothecary, Jorge Elhuyar of Raíz."

"Elhuyar of Raíz?" Galina asked sharply. "Any relation to—"

"Yes, yes," Jorge said quickly, looking embarrassed. "The same."

"I...see..." It was clear Galina wanted to ask more, but it was just as clear that Jorge didn't, so she merely nodded. It made Sonya curious as well. Was his family important in Raíz? She'd have to bully him into some answers later in private.

"And these three gentlemen?" asked Galina.

"Angelo Lorecchio, formerly of the Aureumian Empire. He advises on imperial tactics."

"Very helpful, I'm sure."

Angelo still looked a little awed by the doll. And possibly nervous. He bowed his head stiffly and said, "I hope so, your ladyship."

Galina smiled gently. "Please, Mr. Lorecchio. I have no title yet, and even if I did, I would insist that my comrades speak to me more familiarly."

"As you say, Galina Odoyevtseva."

"And these two big bears are Blaine Ruairc, captain of Clan Dílis, and Elgin Mordha, chief of Clan Greim and warlord of the Uaine."

Galina's eyebrows jumped. "*Uaine?*"

"I needed an army to get rid of the empire, so I made a deal with them," said Sonya. "I'd get them across the tundra during the winter when the empire wouldn't be prepared, they'd help me drive out the empire from Izmoroz, and then I'd help them launch an invasion on Aureum."

"I...see." Galina's large eyes were even bigger now.

"And that's actually why I asked Mathilde to set up a meeting with you," said Sonya. "Armies need to be fed. Granted, the majority of my army is dead, so—"

"I'm sorry, did you say *dead*?" asked Galina.

Sonya was really enjoying watching her composure crumble. "Yeah, that whole thing about the Uaine having an army of the dead? Turns out it's not a myth."

"I..." Galina blinked rapidly several times, probably because those big eyes dried out quickly. "Very well. Please continue."

"We don't have to worry about feeding the dead ones, but there are still about five hundred living Uaine who need to be fed, and they have big appetites. Since we've been consolidating our base in these more remote, rural villages and small towns, they don't have the kind of food surplus we need." She narrowed her eyes and leaned forward. "As I'm *sure you know*, the common folk have to give a percentage to the empire *and* a percentage to the nobility, which leaves very little for them."

"Er...yes."

Sonya leaned back and smiled. "So when Mathilde told us that her benefactor was a wealthy noble, we realized that might solve our supply problems." Technically it had been Jorge and Angelo who realized it and had then convinced Sonya it was a good idea.

"I do not personally have access to the amount of funds that would require," said Galina. "I would need to convince my father to join us."

"Old Lord So-and-So of Roskosh Manor?" Sonya made a sour face. "Never met the guy, but I can't imagine someone like that risking not only his money but his neck, too."

Galina straightened, and her eyes narrowed. "I will forgive that comment because you do not know my father. Believe me when I tell you, there is no man who loves Izmoroz more than him. He has dedicated his life to preserving our history and culture."

Sonya did not care for Galina's tone of voice, and her amber fox eyes narrowed nearly to slits. But as she leaned forward, Jorge gently touched her shoulder. She glared at him, and he resolutely smiled back. They'd been friends long enough now that she knew what that meant. She took a deep breath and leaned back.

Jorge then turned his smile on the noble. "If I may ask, Galina Odoyevtseva, are you saying you feel confident you can persuade your father to our cause?"

"Yes, Señor Elhuyar, on the condition of our family's continued anonymity, I believe he will be overjoyed to take a more direct hand in saving our people."

"That is good news, Galina Odoyevtseva," said Angelo. "According to Mathilde there is already a large network of insurgents in and around Gogoleth. When we finally march on the garrison, can we count on their support as well?"

"I suspect they will find allying themselves with an army of the dead to be troubling," admitted Galina. She glanced at Blaine and Mordha. "No offense." Then she looked at Masha and Mathilde, neither of whom had spoken yet. "Would the presence of a Ranger of Marzanna offset their unease?"

"Begging your pardon, miss," said Masha. "I think it might be the only thing that would, and then only if it was clear that she is the one in charge."

Galina nodded.

"Well, I can't command the Uaine," said Sonya. "They like me, but not *that* much. What if Mordha and I were in joint command? Would that be enough, Masha?"

"As equals, Ranger Sonya?" Masha asked respectfully.

"Exactly."

"I..." She glanced at Mathilde, who seemed similarly unsure. "I think we'll have to ask others."

Sonya nodded. "Fair enough. We won't be marching on Gogoleth for a couple of weeks yet, so there's time. But we can count on the supplies at least, right, Galina?" Even Sonya knew she shouldn't speak so informally to her. Omitting her maternal name without permission was just plain rude, no matter what the social class. But she just couldn't help herself. She liked to watch Galina struggle to contain her reactions.

"Yes, *Sonya*," she said after a moment. "I will speak to my father as soon as I return to Roskosh Manor, and I have no doubt that I will be able to appeal to his deep sense of patriotism."

"Great. Can you do one more thing for me, Galina?"

"What is that, Sonya?"

"Nobody has actually taken my brother aside and just told him he's being an asshole, right?"

"I'm not sure I could—"

"No, I don't think you could, either. So help me think of a way to meet Sebastian face-to-face. No armies, just us. Maybe I can talk some sense into him. Even if I can't get him to join us, maybe I can at least convince him not to get in our way."

"If I may speak candidly." Galina's somber eyes did not waver as she looked at Sonya. "I have grave doubts it will amount to anything."

Sonya held her gaze for a moment, then sighed and closed her eyes. "Yeah, but he's my little brother. I have to at least try."

54

Ah! Lady Portinari! What a surprise to see you here!" exclaimed General Zaniolo when he came upon Irina sitting on a bench in the small green at the center of Nadezhda Square.

"Yes, General, I am surprised as well," she said grimly. She decided to keep her hands in their thick fur muffler rather than offering one to him.

He winced. "May I join you?"

"You may."

Once he sat down next to her, he said in a quieter, less jovial voice, "Apologies for asking you out on such a bitter cold day, my lady."

"While I enjoy the bustle of Nadezhda Square, I generally do so from the comfort of my balcony with a pot of hot tea."

"Again, I apologize. There is some urgency in what I need to communicate, and as we both know, it would be unwise for me to be seen making frequent trips to your home. A chance encounter in public seemed less suspicious."

She sat up a little straighter, but forced herself not to look around. "You think Vittorio's onto us?"

"I don't know," he admitted. "But things are getting…tense, and I don't think he would need a great deal of concrete evidence to start flinging accusations around at this point. I suspect that the only reason he hasn't done so already is because he has more pressing concerns."

"Oh? That's good, isn't it?"

"Unfortunately, those concerns pertain to your daughter."

"Ah." Irina was not so much surprised as she was disappointed. She had hoped, perhaps naively, that her daughter would slip away into the wilderness and live her strange little Ranger life far from imperial power. Irina had even hoped that years from now, when the fiery and conflicting ideals of her children had cooled, they might all be reunited. "She's causing more trouble, is she?"

"*Trouble* hardly covers it," said the general. "She's allied herself with the Uaine and somehow helped them cross the tundra in the dead of winter. Since then, they have been attacking the more remote western villages and towns, killing every imperial soldier they can find. At last count, she and her Uaine barbarians have at least five villages under their control."

"Dear God...," said Irina.

"The good news is that the Uaine don't seem to have brought their full force."

"So the empire should have no trouble driving them back," said Irina.

"Well, the bad news is that we cannot expect any reinforcements from Magna Alto until late spring at the earliest."

Irina looked at him in surprise. "None? Why on earth not?"

Zaniolo smiled bitterly. "Izmoroz is hardly Her Imperial Majesty's top priority. Perhaps you are not aware that the bulk of the empire's forces are currently engaged in a border dispute with Kante, its neighbor to the east."

"A border dispute?" asked Irina. "You mean they are attempting to *conquer* it."

Zaniolo looked surprised. "When did you gain a moral compass, my lady?"

"I don't care what the empire does with their neighbors," said Irina. "But I detest when people employ euphemisms in a pointless attempt to seem more civilized."

Zaniolo bowed his head. "My apologies. At any rate, if the *conquering* goes well, we can expect reinforcements to arrive before summer."

"And if the conquering does not go well?"

"We can expect nothing at all."

"I see. So what is Vittorio's plan?"

"He has just ordered all soldiers who were stationed at the remaining towns and villages to return to the garrison. He wants every available soldier here, in case your daughter attempts a direct assault on Gogoleth. Worse comes to worse, we hunker down and try to last until reinforcements arrive."

Irina closed her eyes, feeling perhaps more tired than she ever had in her life. How had Sonya developed such a knack for getting into trouble?

"Does Sebastian know?" she asked. "About his sister's involvement?"

"Vittorio is keeping it from him at present. He is…not sure your son is ready to confront his sister directly. No matter how loyal he is to the empire, anyone would have trouble engaging in battle with their sibling."

"I agree that Sebastian isn't ready, General," she said. "But for entirely different reasons. For the sake of all those who might get caught between them, keep my son out of it for as long as possible."

"Understood, my lady." He smiled then. "But it's not *all* dire news."

"Oh?"

"The coming conflict will decide Vittorio's status with the empress one way or the other. He is keenly aware of that, of course, and I fear the strain is already beginning to show."

"I fail to see how that is happy news, General."

"If we lose, Vittorio will be disgraced. But even if we are victorious, things will get quite stressful. It is likely that the commander's true nature will once again reveal itself in all its terrible, abusive glory, along with a few dead soldiers. If that happens, there will be no end to officer complaints and petitions for transfers. The empress will finally be forced to accept that Vittorio is the monster we all know him to be, and she will have to make an example of him. No more banishments or demotions. He'll be executed."

"So whether we win or lose, we will be rid of Franko Vittorio."

"In all likelihood. The man is simply not built for this kind of stressful engagement. Once he's gone, I will be named commander here in Izmoroz, and naturally I will ensure that Sebastian becomes one of my most trusted generals. Or your son may choose to transfer to a post in Aureum if he likes. After all, once we wipe out the Uaine, there really won't be much going on in Izmoroz, and while I have learned to appreciate peace, young men do crave action."

"And what of my daughter, General? What of Sonya Turgenev Portinari?"

"Ah." His smile faltered. "If I may speak bluntly, my lady, protecting your feral daughter was never part of our arrangement, was it?"

55

Sebastian stood in front of the mirror, as he often did before calling upon his betrothed. His uniform was clean and neatly brushed, and everything was perfectly in place, except...

He yanked out the gray hair. The sharp, fleeting pain was oddly satisfying.

"Another one?" asked Rykov, who sat in a chair nearby, giving Sebastian's boots a quick polish. "How many is that now?"

"I've lost count." Sebastian released the offending hair and watched it waft slowly to the floor. "You know that book Galina gave me? *The Age of Wizards*?"

"Not really."

Sebastian touched the skin around his eyes, which seemed to have lost some of its elasticity in recent months. Beneath the red-rimmed lids, there was a dark tinge to it, almost like a bruise. For a little while now, people had been expressing concern regarding his health. Had he lost weight? Was he sleeping enough? So he had been making a conscious effort to take better care of himself, and when he forgot, Rykov was there to remind him. Still he struggled to keep on weight. Still he struggled with a fatigue that crept up on him a little more each day. Then, not even seventeen years old, he'd begun getting gray hair. He'd been at a loss to explain it all. Until the previous evening.

"Last night I read a passage in the book," he told Rykov, "that makes reference to...premature aging among wizards."

"Oh?" Rykov looked up from his boots, his expression uncharacteristically concerned.

"Apparently, channeling the raw forces of Nature through one's body takes quite a toll. In one legend, a wizard claims to be thirty years of age, but has completely gray hair and appears to everyone as an old man."

"Is there any way to stop it?" asked Rykov. "Or at least slow it down?"

Sebastian smiled sadly. "Stop using magic, I suppose."

"Have you told the commander?"

"If he were to inquire, I wouldn't lie, of course. But I cannot think of a way to broach the subject that doesn't sound like I'm trying to shirk my duty."

Rykov nodded, and there was silence except for the rhythmic hiss of his coarse brush swiping back and forth across the toe of Sebastian's boot.

"You going to tell Galina Odoyevtseva?"

Sebastian continued to stare at himself in the mirror, trying to imagine how old and frail he might look in ten years, when Galina was a stunning woman in her prime. In twenty years...

Power had a cost. He would be a fool to think otherwise, but this cost seemed especially unfair.

"Perhaps I should tell her *before* we marry. In case she wants to..." Sebastian's throat seized up at the very idea that she might want to call off the engagement. "Well, I should tell her. It's the right thing to do."

Rykov handed Sebastian his boots. "If you say so."

Sebastian gave himself a hard look. A determined look. "Yes. I think it is."

He put on his boots in silence, then left the garrison for Roskosh Manor. Despite his resolution, he felt a hollow dread in his chest. His horse was quite familiar with the route by then, so he was able to focus on how best to broach the subject to Galina. He would need to do it in a way that did not make her feel guilty, should she choose to...

The very thought of losing his Galechka made his stomach plunge.

But deception by omission was still deception, and he could not break the sacred trust between them, no matter the cost.

Sebastian reached Roskosh Manor in time for supper. During the meal, he did his best to participate in the idle conversation at the table, but his forthcoming confession to Galina weighed heavily on his mind. It seemed that Lord Prozorova also had his thoughts elsewhere. His lordship barely spoke, and occasionally glanced over at Sebastian as if he were not quite certain who he was. It fell to Lady Prozorova and Galina to keep things lively, but if there were two women better suited to the task, Sebastian didn't know them.

Then at last the meal was over and Sebastian retired to the parlor with Galina to converse in private, as was their habit during his visits.

"How was your visit to...Kamen, was it?" He stood by the window that looked out at the gardens where the two of them first confessed their love.

"Very insightful, my *volshebnik*," she said as she sat on the sofa. "As you know, I've been assisting my father with his archival work, and there is a striking difference between transcribing my father's notes here in the comfort of my home, and actually listening to the peasants tell their tales. I find myself wishing there was some way I could capture not merely what they said, but *how* they said it."

"Indeed, that would be a challenge." He tried to sound interested, but the pressure of his looming confession was like a weight upon his chest.

She gave him an odd look. "Will you not come sit beside me, Sebastian?"

"I...have something I must tell you, and I think I would prefer to stand while I say it. And perhaps you might as well."

"Is something the matter?"

He still did not know quite how to begin. His mouth opened, but no sound came out.

"Have I done something to displease you, my betrothed?" She looked concerned.

Instantly he felt a pang of guilt. Here he was, so wrapped up in his own feelings that he had completely disregarded hers. He hurried over to her side and took her hands.

"No, my beloved. It's not something you have done. Indeed, I doubt you could ever do anything wrong. Instead, it is the cruel hand of fate that has wronged us both."

"Pray, tell me what troubles you, so that you no longer have to bear this burden alone," said Galina.

Sebastian took a deep breath. "I believe that the... *toll* my magic is taking on my body has been more exacting than I'd previously realized."

"You *have* seemed in poor health of late." Galina considered for a moment. "It's been such a gradual change, though, that I can't recall when I first noticed."

"It... it's worse than that, I'm afraid. The book you gave me suggests that elemental magic use causes premature aging."

"Oh?" Her large eyes grew wide.

"And so," he said, his throat tight with fear, "I leave it to you, my precious Galechka, to tell me honestly if you would not prefer to break off our engagement so that you might find a man who will age as you do and who will remain virile and hardy for many years to come."

He steeled himself, preparing for possibly the most heartbreaking moment of his life. But she surprised him by letting out a quick laugh that almost seemed relieved. "Don't be absurd, Sebastian. If your use of magic is what's causing this terrible affliction, then the solution is obvious. Simply stop using magic."

"B-but, my love..."

"Yes of course, it makes perfect sense!" He had never seen her so enthusiastic about something before. She was almost gleeful. "Surely if you explain this terrible predicament to Commander Vittorio, he will understand that you have no choice. You have so many other wonderful qualities that I'm certain he could find other ways for you to contribute."

"But, Galina, they're all counting on me! This is something only I can do! It would take an entire battalion to equal the power I possess. How could I ask all those men to risk their lives merely so that I might find some happiness?"

Her excited expression froze, which made it abruptly look more like a wince of pain. "*Merely?* Is happiness such a trivial thing to you?"

"It's not trivial, but surely you would agree that happiness is hardly the most important thing. I have sworn an oath. My men are counting on me. I *must* do my duty as an officer of the imperial army."

"I . . . see." She looked stricken, and turned away from him.

"I'm sorry, my Galechka. I . . . understand if you want to break off the engagement."

Her head snapped back toward him and a surprising anger glistened in her eyes. "If I urge you to stop using magic, it is not for my sake, but for *yours*. It is because I don't want you to throw your life away at the behest of some—" She broke off and took a deep breath, though it did little to ease the dark fury in her expression. "Do you think so little of me that you believe something as trivial as physical appearance would inspire me to break off our engagement? It was not your power, or your looks, or your virility that captured my heart, Sebastian. It was your thoughtfulness and tender sensibilities. *Those* are the qualities I value."

He stared at her, stunned into silence by her sudden wrath. He had never known her to speak so stridently.

She continued, her voice constricted to a hoarse whisper. "It would only be the loss of those cherished qualities that would induce me to break off our engagement."

Without another word, she left the parlor.

Sebastian's stomach twisted with shame. He dropped onto the sofa and stared down at the rug beneath his feet, his eyes absently tracing its intricate weave. Galina was right, of course. He had been speaking as if she was some vapid and frivolous courtesan who cared only about appearances, rather than the poetic, brilliant woman with whom he had fallen in love. His intentions had been sincere, but he had succeeded only in mortally insulting the most important person in his life. It felt as though the entire world fell away with that realization. Was it all broken? Had he alienated the one person who truly understood him? In that moment, he felt alone in a way that he had never known before.

"C–Captain Portinari?"

Sebastian blinked the tears from his eyes. He did not know how long he had been sitting there in the parlor wallowing in despair, but when he saw it was the servant Masha, he still felt too miserable to be embarrassed.

"Yes, what is it, Masha?"

"I . . . thought the young miss was here with you . . ."

"No, she left."

"Well, um, this is rather strange, but a message just arrived for you."

"For me? Who is it from?"

"The messenger wouldn't say and departed as soon as he handed it to me. It is addressed to you, and sealed, so I have no way of knowing."

"Was it a soldier who delivered it?" asked Sebastian.

"No, Captain."

"Let me see."

Masha meekly handed him the letter. She looked uneasy but he didn't blame her. He probably looked to be in a frightful state. Hell, he *was* in a frightful state.

When Sebastian turned the letter over in his hand, he didn't even have to open it to know who it was from. On the outside of the folded, sealed note, in a familiar slanted script, was written:

To Sebastian, Captain of the Imperials!

"Masha, you may go," he said quietly.

"Yes, Captain." She hurried out of the room.

His guilt and sorrow were suddenly drowned out by a combination of anger and unease. What arrogance—or perhaps even madness— could have induced his sister to contact him like this? Surely she must know that she was wanted for murder, and that as a sworn officer of the empire, he must report her.

He broke the wax seal and unfolded the parchment.

Hey, little brother. I hear you're getting married. Congratulations, I guess. Listen, before things get any more out of hand, I know Mom would want us to at least try to talk things out like the mature adults we've supposedly become. So how about it? No soldiers, no tricks, no bullshit. Just you and me, being reasonable human beings. Come to the town of Les, and if I see that you're alone, I'll show myself, and we can sort things out between us.

Love, Yasha

Sebastian crumpled the parchment, thinking of those poor soldiers she had killed before fleeing Gogoleth.

"Oh, you bet we'll sort things out, Sonya."

56

Sebastian rode west out of Gogoleth nursing an old, familiar resentment. Who did his reckless idiot of a sister think she was? He could practically hear the patronizing tone of her voice when he'd read her letter. What reason did she have to act so superior? Just because she was a few years older than him? Because she could ride a horse and shoot a couple of arrows? Maybe he had been impressed once, but now he found it laughable.

Of course, Sonya probably thought he was still sitting around making little ice sculptures in a bowl. He couldn't wait to show her what he could do now. That cocky attitude of hers would crumble and she'd have to acknowledge that he'd made the right choice to enlist in the imperial army. Then, as the final touch, he'd arrest her and drag her back to Gogoleth to await trial for her crimes. Freedom of choice was not freedom from consequence, and hers was long overdue.

He rode the rest of the day with those thoughts circling in his head like a cat chasing its tail. The longer he rode, the angrier he got, and the more eager he became to show her just what he was capable of now.

The town of Les was only about a day and a half ride from Gogoleth. He'd gotten a late start so he still had quite a ways to go when the sun began to set. He tried to push his horse to continue in the dark, but the roads in that direction were in poor condition, and after his horse stumbled, he reluctantly decided he would need to stop for the night.

There were no inns, but he'd been on enough missions with his men that he no longer hesitated to insist that a peasant provide him with room and board for the night. Normally he would at least try to get to know his hosts, but that night the idea of making small talk only irritated him further. Instead he ate with the peasant family in grim silence, still contemplating how he would punish Sonya, first for having the audacity to send a message to the home of his betrothed, then for her crimes against the empire. After supper, he lay in bed and allowed his mind to root through his memories of the last time he'd seen her in search of further fuel for his anger.

In retrospect, it amazed him how arrogant she had been. She had just strolled into his quarters, presuming that she knew what was best for him after their father died. She'd hardly been home for over two years. How could she possibly know about what was best for him? She didn't know him anymore. Perhaps her "rescue" had merely been her attempt to assert dominance over him, as she had when they were younger. She'd been shocked when he'd stood up for himself, as if she hadn't even thought it possible. Maybe it had wounded her pride to such an extent that she'd lashed out at two men who'd probably not even realized they were in peril until it was too late. She didn't look dangerous, but clearly all that time spent killing animals had made her quite deadly, and she had exploited that advantage without mercy.

At some point in his rumination, Sebastian drifted off to sleep. But he did not feel at all refreshed when he woke early the next morning. His head hurt, and his stomach felt sour. The thought of breakfast was unappealing, so he immediately continued on to Les, anger his only sustenance.

When Sebastian reached the town, he found it to be a predictably drab and unvarnished Izmorozian collection of wood and stone huts. During his recent expeditions to root out traitors, he'd seen many like it. Places half broken by a war that had ended twenty years ago, and yet the people still hadn't bothered to properly repair them. His father had built an entire farmstead in that time, so he wondered why they had done nothing. But when he looked at the dirty, ill-fed people who trudged down the cracked and uneven cobblestone streets, he was reminded of Commander Vittorio's statement that the Izmorozian people needed continued imperial guidance merely to survive. He'd thought the sentiment overly harsh before, but now he wondered if there might be some merit to it.

Sebastian led his horse to the main town square, dismounted, and waited for his sister to grace him with her presence. The townsfolk glanced at him, but when they saw his uniform, they quickly averted their eyes and hurried past.

Time crawled by and still his sister didn't appear. His frustration continued to grow as he waited, filling his stomach with a quiet, seething burn.

Finally he decided he'd had enough. He planted his feet in a wide stance and shouted as loudly as he could.

"SONYA! WHERE THE HELL ARE YOU?"

He shouted it over and over again, and he didn't care if people were staring at him.

At last she appeared. The bustling crowds that had been so studiously pretending to ignore him parted, and there she was, not twenty feet away.

"Stop being such an impatient child, Sebastian. I had to make sure you didn't have any lackeys hiding nearby."

It certainly sounded like her, but something was very amiss.

"What is wrong with your eyes?"

She smirked. "A blessing from the Lady Marzanna."

"You're joking."

"Didn't Mom tell you, little brother?" She looked very pleased with herself. "While you were playing around with magic, Mikhail trained me to be a Ranger of Marzanna."

"Right. You, a Ranger." He gave a short laugh, but she didn't join him. She was serious. He took a minute to consider that. "And... you're saying Mother knew about this?"

"She and Father both knew."

"Oh, come on, that's absurd. Father harboring a Ranger of Marzanna?"

"It went along with his whole thing about you not enlisting in the imperial army."

There it was. She was still resentful that he'd gone against her. "This again. I am a grown man, and I can make my own choices. This is the life I chose."

She narrowed her freakish amber eyes. "Yeah, you look like shit, by the way. Army food not agree with you, Bastuchka?"

She only ever called him that when she was trying to provoke him. He would show her he could rise above her pettiness. He took a deep, calming breath.

"Weren't we supposed to talk like mature adults?"

She grimaced and scratched her head in an unnervingly animalistic sort of way. "Yeah. You started by hollering like a brat and I just fell right into it."

"Oh no. *You* started it by sending that obnoxious letter—and to my *betrothed's* house, no less."

"I didn't think it would get through if I sent it to the garrison," she said. "Okay, maybe the tone wasn't great. I'm no writer. Sorry. I just felt I had to talk to you."

"Well, we're talking. Now what do you want?"

"I want to find out what's really important to you."

His eyes narrowed. She seemed sincere now, not teasing or patronizing. "How do you mean?"

"Where are your loyalties, Sebastian? To your family? To Izmoroz? Or to the empire?"

"They're all the same."

"No, Sebastian, they're not. You've been out among the people now. Surely you've seen it yourself. They suffer under the rule of the empire."

"I see bandits and dissidents causing problems. Once we get rid of them, and vanquish the menace of the Uaine Empire, the innocent people of Izmoroz will be able to live in peace and thrive with the empire's help."

"Okay, first of all, the Uaine are not really an empire. They're barely a country. And second, they aren't interested in Izmoroz because, let's be honest, there isn't much here. The Uaine want Aureum."

"And how would *you* know that?"

She paused. "Wait, did they not tell you?"

"Tell me what?" Sebastian asked uneasily.

"Oho! I guess *they're* worried about where your true loyalties lie, too!"

"Sonya, don't test my patience. What are you talking about?"

She nodded. "Sorry, sorry. You're right. I shouldn't gloat. I'm just surprised your commander hasn't told you that I'm the one leading the Uaine invasion."

He stared at her for a moment, hoping beyond hope that she would suddenly laugh and mock him for being gullible. But she didn't.

"You *what*?" His jaw felt like iron.

"I helped them cross the tundra. Now they're helping me drive the empire out of Izmoroz. And then we'll let them use Izmoroz as a staging ground for their invasion of Aureum."

Sebastian was so choked with outrage that he could not even form words. The murder of two imperial soldiers was one thing. He'd even been thinking he would plead for mercy at the trial on her behalf. But this...this betrayal was on a completely different scale. Once again she'd proven that no matter what he thought of her, she could sink lower. What she had done was unforgivable.

"Look." Sonya adopted a reasonable tone. "I'm not asking you to betray whatever loyalty you think you have with your Commander Vittorio. I don't expect you to fight with us. But I'm begging you—as your sister—to step aside so that when we liberate Izmoroz, you don't get killed in the process."

The fire that had been burning in Sebastian's gut spread out through his limbs. She still thought he was some helpless child. After everything he'd accomplished, she was still looking down on him. She thought she could brush him aside. That there was no one who could stop her from doing this terrible thing. He would show her just how wrong she was.

"Kill me? Who the hell do you think you are? Maybe you really are a Ranger, but so what? The empire beat them before and we'll do it again. You're just some backwoods, religious freak with delusions of grandeur like all the rest."

"Whoa, hey, I thought we were trying to be mature, here, brother."

He reached into the pouch at his hip and grasped his gem. Its familiar, comforting heft added to his confidence.

"And who do you think *I* am, Yasha? Certainly not your pushover little brother anymore. I've become a powerful wizard who could decimate your entire sorry army all by myself."

She let out a short hiccuping burst of laughter that she immediately stifled with a muttered, "Oops, sorry..." But even then he could see that damn smirk of hers. She didn't believe him.

He would *make* her believe.

He took the gem out of its pouch as he glared at her.

"You came to talk, but I came to see justice done for the men you murdered. This is your only warning. Submit willingly, or I will make you."

"Sebastian, let's calm down." She raised her hands in a placating gesture. "You really want to fight, fine, we'll fight. But there are a lot of innocent people here, so let's—"

"You think that will stop me? You think I can't do what needs to be done? You're a traitor and a murderer, Sonya, and I'm bringing you to justice."

"Come on, don't be ridiculous," she said. "Seriously. Look at all these people..."

But Sebastian couldn't see anyone except his stupid, arrogant, murdering, traitorous sister who would rather visit a horde of the undead upon Izmoroz than admit she was wrong. No one would be safe. Not his men, not his mother, and not his beloved Galina. He could picture her perfect, luminous face savaged by bony fingers, her delicate frame torn apart with mindless ferocity. She would die horribly and it would be his sister's fault. His sister with her revolting, beastly eyes.

"You...are a monster!" He lifted his gem. "And I am the only one who can stop you!"

He poured the rage that had been building up since he left Gogoleth into the gem and turned his attention to the earth beneath his sister's feet. He would make the world swallow her up. It would be like there had never been a Sonya Turgenev Portinari in the first place.

A thunderous detonation shook the ground beneath them.

"Sebastian? What did you do?" Sonya's stupid beast eyes were wide, and her face was as pale as milk.

"Oh, so you're finally taking me seriously?" Now it was his turn to smirk. A simple demonstration. That's all it had taken.

But the ground shook again, followed by another sharp report beneath the surface. Then a crack appeared in the cobblestones. It spidered out in all directions, growing wider, accompanied by a succession of detonations. People shouted in fear and horses whinnied as they staggered away from the fracturing earth. Sebastian's smug satisfaction was quickly swallowed up by a growing alarm. What *had* he done?

"Seriously, Sebastian." Sonya leapt with astonishing grace away from an approaching crack. "Whatever you're doing, it needs to stop before innocent people get hurt."

"I...I don't..."

The ground beneath them shook even harder and Sebastian had to grab on to his frightened horse to keep from falling. Nearby merchant booths tipped over. Buildings began to creak and groan under the strain. Shouts of alarm grew into screams of panic.

Then one of the buildings shuddered and collapsed. Several others followed. Shrieks of terror and pain came from within.

"Stop this, Sebastian!" Sonya yelled as she staggered toward him, her hands outstretched. "Please, I'm begging you! You have to stop it!"

"I...I *can't*."

Sebastian's anger must have magnified his intent, causing a chain reaction. The entire town was breaking apart, as if the earth intended to swallow not just his sister, but every single person there. Gaps spread in the ground and people disappeared into their dark depths. More buildings collapsed, crushing anyone who had thought themselves safe within their shelter. There was nowhere to hide, no place of safety. Everywhere Sebastian looked, people were suffering and dying. And it was his fault.

Sonya had left him and was now lifting a fallen cart to free the person trapped beneath.

No, this was wrong. This was not how it was supposed to go...

His horse screamed in panic, bringing him out of his horrified trance before he, too, was swallowed up. He jumped into his saddle, and doing his best to block out the calamity that surrounded him, he fled.

57

I'm sorry." Sonya dodged falling debris to yank a terrified man to safety.

"I'm so sorry." She hauled up an old woman who had somehow managed to cling to the edge of the still-widening cracks.

"By the Lady I am so sorry." She pulled a screaming woman from a collapsing house as she reached for the small arm of a child buried beneath the rubble.

Blaine and Jorge had been hiding in a nearby building while Sonya talked to her brother. Now they stepped into action. Blaine helped her rescue people and bring them to Jorge, who had set up triage in an old stone storehouse that was set back a ways from the town center and sturdy enough to withstand the quake. Jorge treated the injured as best he could with the meager supplies he had on hand, but they had not come to this meeting equipped for massive casualties. Perhaps Sonya had expected some conflict with her brother. Maybe she'd even been spoiling for it. But she could never have imagined him capable of such widespread devastation and death. Not in deed or intent.

The tremors at last died down and the earth grew still, but Sonya could still hear people screaming beneath the rubble. It was hours before she and Blaine cleared enough of it to rescue them. Some had been maimed, and now wailed in pain with a crushed limb. Many others had been killed. She and Blaine had only the most rudimentary knowledge of healing, but they assisted Jorge as best they could while he shouted instructions, never stopping until everyone who could be saved from death had been, and those who could not be saved had been made more comfortable with potions to lessen their pain as they died.

Finally, it was over. Sonya and her friends sat on the cold ground in front of the building, leaning against the icy stone that had saved so many, and looked out at the ruins of Les.

"Did *I* do this?" she asked quietly.

"Yer brother did et," Blaine said firmly.

"I know, but...did I *provoke* him?" She turned to Jorge, trusting that he would tell her the truth. "Did I make it worse?"

He sighed wearily. "I don't know, Sonya. On one hand, your mere presence probably provoked him. You knew it would. It might not have even mattered what you actually said. Siblings can be like that."

She nodded.

"But can I fault you for being the only person in the world who refused to give up on him? For believing that if he was just given the chance, he might make things right? If I had somehow gone down such a dark path, I would *hope* that my own big sister would be the one to slap some sense into me. Because siblings can be like that, too."

"Sometimes there's no good choices," said Blaine. "Ye do what ye can each moment, an' hope for th' best."

"I guess." Exhaustion was starting to set into Sonya's muscles. She laid her head on Blaine's thick slab of shoulder.

"But we *do* have a larger problem," said Jorge. "We knew your brother was powerful, but this was...*catastrophic*. He could swallow up half our army in an instant. Honestly, I don't know how we're going to win against that."

"Et's not all about power, Jorge," said Blaine. "Strategy ken go a long way."

Jorge smiled tiredly, and after a moment, allowed his head to rest on Blaine's other shoulder. "You, Blaine, of all people, telling me this..."

"I have strategy," Blaine objected mildly. "Lots o' et. An' so does Tighearna Mordha. We been fightin' our whole lives, ye know. Et never ends for the Uaine."

"I suppose that's true." Jorge's eyes slowly dropped closed.

"We need more help," said Sonya.

Jorge's eyes remained closed as he asked, "You mean in addition to the barbarians with their undead horde, and the cunning noblewoman who leads a secret rebel insurgency?"

"An' th' handsome potion maker from Rah-ez?" asked Blaine.

"R*aeez*," corrected Jorge, eyes still closed. "And thanks."

"Yes, boys, in addition to all that." Sonya slowly got to her feet. "I'm going to ask the Lady Marzanna for help."

Jorge finally opened his eyes. "You can do that?"

"I've never contacted her on my own. Usually she just finds me. But I watched Mikhail do it when he asked permission to train me to be a Ranger. It's a little involved, but I think I remember how it's done."

"How could she help us?" asked Jorge.

"She has more power than just bringing me back from the dead, you know," said Sonya. "A Ranger can ask for a boon. Some sort of extra ability. Mikhail asked to have his face changed after the war, so that none of the imperial soldiers who had seen him during his captivity would recognize him. He told me that his *uchitel* asked for the ability to communicate directly with animals. So hopefully she can give me something that would help against Sebastian's magic."

"And the price...would be the same?" Jorge did not look happy about it.

"Hopefully," she said.

He looked even more worried now. "Wait, it could be worse?"

"I'm sure it'll be fine." She didn't know if she was assuring him or herself.

"Ya' need any help?" asked Blaine.

She shook her head. "Only Rangers and those they plan to indoctrinate can witness it."

He nodded. "Ask her t' tell Bàs hello for me."

She smiled. "I wonder if they know each other."

"Why not?"

She hadn't really considered it before. She was of course certain of

Lady Marzanna's power. But clearly, the Uaine were harnessing some sort of power when they raised the dead. Why not this Bàs? The Lady and this Bàs might even be related somehow. Siblings perhaps? Or lovers? It was a strange idea, but she liked it.

"I better get started," she told them. "Have to go find someone worth killing."

"You have to *kill* someone to contact your goddess?" asked Jorge.

"Well, she is a goddess of death, after all."

58

Y ou bloody fool!" Vittorio's face was plumb-colored with outrage. "You child! You imbecile!"

Sebastian had never known Vittorio to be so furious. He stood in the commander's quarters and stared at the wooden slats of the floor as the insults rained down on him.

Then he heard a sudden crash and looked up to see that Vittorio had flipped his table onto its side, sending books, parchments, and other items across the room. Vittorio's shoulders heaved up and down, straining against his tight uniform jacket as he glared at Sebastian.

"Well? What do you have to say for yourself?"

"I—I know it doesn't change anything, but I'm so sorry. Such cataclysmic loss of life should never—"

"*What?*" Vittorio stepped in so close, Sebastian could hear the quiet whistle of air through his flared nostrils. "You think I care whether a bunch of useless, filthy peasants died?"

"Well, I—"

"Your damnable sister and her rabble of heathens are threatening everything we've worked for, and you pointlessly revealed our greatest military and strategic advantage. *That* is what I care about."

"Oh. I see…"

"*Do* you see? Do you understand that your sister will soon march on Gogoleth and until reinforcements arrive, we barely have enough troops to defend the city?"

"W-will we not ride out to face them?" asked Sebastian.

Vittorio sneered. "So that we can leave the city vulnerable to all those secret cabals of rebel insurgents who continually slip through your fingers? I thought you had some sense in you, Portinari. But perhaps I was mistaken. Perhaps you are nothing more than a weapon to be wielded."

"Wh-what can I do, sir?" Sebastian asked plaintively. "How can I make amends?"

"You can shut up, stop sniveling, and do what you're told. You will not act until I say you are to act. You will not speak unless I give you permission to do so. And you better pray that during the impending conflict you are able to kill your bitch of a sister so that I feel inclined to forgive you for acting like a reckless, idiotic, spoiled infant. Answer me now. Is that clear?"

"Y-yes, sir."

"Dismissed." Vittorio turned his back on Sebastian and shouted into the hallway. "Someone come and clean up this damned mess!"

Sebastian hurried out of the room, but once he was safely out of view, he stopped and leaned against the wall. He had managed to keep his composure in front of the commander, but now his breath came in ragged gasps and his hands would not stop shaking.

The hallway was filled with officers scurrying here and there, preparing for the impending conflict that was likely no more than a week away, two at the most. Sebastian wished he didn't look so frightened and foolish in front of them all, but he couldn't help it. He didn't know what to think anymore, or how to feel. He knew he shouldn't have killed all those people, but the man he admired most dismissed that as inconsequential. And yet that same man had just flown into a rage because Sebastian had compromised their strategy to the enemy. The enemy who was also his *sister*, and who had, in her own admittedly misguided efforts, been trying to find a way for the two of them not to fight each other. And now that had failed, and the only way for Sebastian to regain Vittorio's respect was to kill her.

He felt more sick, confused, and frightened than ever before. And what made matters infinitely worse, he longed for Galina to soothe his raw and miserable soul, but how could he do that when he'd insulted her so gravely, then fled her home?

"Dear Captain Portinari, are you well? You appear even more wan than usual."

Sebastian looked up to see General Zaniolo standing beside him with an expression of deep concern.

"Y-yes, General, I'm fine. I have . . . I've made a terrible mistake and the commander is extremely angry with me."

A burst of furious shouts from the commander's quarters echoed down the hall, followed by another crash and the splinter of wood.

"Oh dear." The general did not look particularly concerned or surprised. "I haven't heard him like that since we were stationed in Magna Alto. Terrible business, that."

"I'm not sure what you mean, sir."

Zaniolo glanced at the officers scurrying past, then said, "Follow me, won't you, Captain?"

Without waiting for a response, the general turned and walked down the hallway. Unsure how else to respond, Sebastian trailed after him.

Zaniolo led Sebastian out into the yard, which was even busier than usual. Several squads of infantry soldiers were drilling their formations, packed in so tightly they had to be careful they didn't collide with one of the other squads. A group of archers were fletching arrows off to one side. There was a long line of soldiers in front of Sergeant Costa's armory, waiting anxiously for repairs or new equipment. Costa had even asked if he could borrow Rykov until he'd caught up. Sebastian could see his aide-de-camp now, moving with surprising swiftness as he ran in and out of the small iron building carrying helmets, breastplates, swords, shields, and spears, sometimes all at once.

Zaniolo led Sebastian over to a corner of the yard that was a little removed from the hectic activity. He clasped his hands behind his back and gazed out at it all with a benevolent smile, as if it was under his direction.

"I probably shouldn't go into detail," he said quietly, "but it was exactly the sort of outburst you just encountered that landed Commander Vittorio in Izmoroz to begin with."

Sebastian frowned. "I...thought the commander chose this post."

Zaniolo gave him a pitying look. "My dear Captain, please don't take offense, but no sane Aureumian would choose a post in Izmoroz. Although I suppose technically it was a rank promotion, it would be hard to view moving from captain of the Imperial Honor Guard to commander of the empire's poorest and least advantageous territory as an advancement. Rather, it was the military equivalent of making him prince of a dung heap."

"I...didn't realize." Why had the commander lied to him? To spare his feelings regarding his homeland?

"In fact," continued Zaniolo, "the commander is exiled from the capital until the empress herself expressly commands his return."

"Really?" That certainly explained the commander's melancholy when talking about Magna Alto at the Ascendance celebration, but again he was troubled about being kept in the dark. It begged the question, just how well did Sebastian truly know Commander Vittorio?

Zaniolo smiled. "Still, you should count yourself lucky he didn't beat you to death. That's what happened last time. He must still be quite fond of you if he was able to rein in his temper that much. Although, I wouldn't count on it next time. When things aren't going his way, his... *episodes* tend to increase in intensity until he becomes quite out of his mind with rage."

"You can't be serious." Sebastian didn't want to believe such a thing, although after what he'd just seen, it didn't seem impossible.

Zaniolo's smile dropped away. "I'm deadly serious, Captain. I don't tell you all this because I enjoy gossiping. I tell you because I've grown rather fond of you, and the knowledge might just save your life."

As if to punctuate Zaniolo's point, Vittorio burst through the front doors of headquarters, roaring like a lion, his face crimson. Several officers scurried behind him as he stormed over to the armory and began shouting at Costa, demanding to know why his troops had not been properly equipped yet.

The old sergeant's face was expressionless as he stood his ground, weathering the storm of verbal abuse. But his calmness seemed to further infuriate Vittorio. The commander raised his fist as if to strike him. It was only then that Costa spoke. Sebastian couldn't hear what he said, but it brought Vittorio up short, his clenched fist raised in the air. The commander stood there a moment, as if frozen, then suddenly turned and struck one of the cowering officers nearby. Then he stalked back into headquarters, his face still livid.

"My God...," whispered Sebastian.

"You see what I mean?" asked Zaniolo. "The commander is an impeccable leader, so long as things are going his way. But I have learned that in battle, things rarely go one's way."

Sebastian felt as if the ground were dropping away beneath him. Could it really be true that this man, whom he had trusted to guide him, was unstable and given to fits of madness? If that was so, what did it say about the choices Sebastian had made? Had he been laboring under poor, possibly deranged guidance this whole time?

No, he assured himself. The commander's advice might now be somewhat suspect, but if Sebastian had truly done something terrible, his beloved Galina would have told him.

59

Sonya had some difficulty locating any bandits. She suspected that the coming conflict had driven most of them into hiding. But finally she got a lead from some villagers that there was a group holed up in the western foothills of the Cherny Mountains.

She didn't mind taking her time, however. She was fond of her allies, but it was wonderful to be back in the wilderness with no one but her faithful steed, Peppercorn, for companionship. Her beloved *Perchinka* had put on some weight while in the care of the villagers of Zapad. It was clear they had spoiled him outrageously with far too many apples and far too little exercise. As the steed of a Ranger of Marzanna, that simply wouldn't do, so she had run him pretty hard when she'd reclaimed him from their care. He'd seemed a little resentful at first, but it didn't take long for him to adjust.

She found some likely tracks and followed them through the snow into the foothills until she caught sight of an abandoned salt mine. She dismounted and tied Peppercorn to a tree near the entrance. Not because she was afraid he would wander, but because she knew he would try to follow her, and horses were not known for their stealth.

The entrance was fairly large, probably so that it could accommodate the wagons that once trundled in and out. There wasn't anyone guarding the entrance, but bandits rarely took such precautions, so that didn't mean it was truly abandoned.

She crept quietly into the mine and followed the main shaft as it slowly descended. It was dark, but her fox eyes allowed her to see well enough.

There were a few narrow tunnel branches from the main shaft, but none of them bore any trace of the bandits, so she kept moving forward and downward. For a while, the air grew steadily colder. But then she saw a faint, flickering light ahead, as if from a fire, and the air began to warm slightly.

Finally she reached a large open area roughly fifteen yards wide and thirty yards long. The smooth walls made it clear that this was not a natural cave, but had been laboriously hand dug over a number of years. To prevent a cave-in, the sides were stacked from floor to ceiling with wooden frames packed full of the loose rock that had been cast aside while mining.

Four men sat around a small cooking fire in the center of the space. They held skewers of meat on sticks over the fire, and the air was thick with the smell of hot fat. After observing them for a few moments, she realized that all her efforts to remain quiet had been pointless, because they were roaring drunk and probably wouldn't have noticed a bear.

"I tell you, we are missing out on the opportunity of a lifetime," said one. "When the fighting starts, there'll be looting for days."

"And I say we stay put until the whole thing blows over," said another. "We let 'em all kill each other, then scrounge around what's left."

"Sounds to me like you're scared," said a third.

"Damn right I am," said the second. "Soldiers, wizards, demons, necromancers. I hear there's even a Ranger running around out there. Anybody who's not afraid of all that is an idiot."

"You don't know if those things are really out there. You ain't seen 'em. You just heard stories. I bet it's all bullshit. There's no such thing as demons or necromancers, and there haven't been any Rangers since the war."

"Wrong," said Sonya.

The four men stumbled drunkenly to their feet. One fell back down immediately, clutching an arrow in his throat. The next one she shot in the eye, and the third she shot in the nose. She'd always wondered if an arrow could reach the brain through the nostril, but judging by the way he gurgled and thrashed around flinging blood everywhere, it appeared not. At least not at that angle. She shot him in the heart and he grew still.

The surviving bandit stumbled to his feet as Sonya calmly shouldered her bow and took a small leather drawstring sack filled with stones from her belt.

"What the hell you gonna do with that," he shouted with terrified bravado.

She began to twirl the small sack by the drawstring.

He seemed to realize even in his drunken state that this might be his only opportunity to counterattack, so he grabbed a sword that lay by the fire and rushed toward her, hollering in a way he probably hoped was intimidating.

Sonya watched him approach as she continued to spin her little sack of rocks. She waited until he lifted the sword to strike, then released the pouch so that it hit him square between the eyes. His momentum carried him forward, but she stepped nimbly out of the way and he dropped face-first to the ground, his sword clattering loudly as it flew out of his hand.

She crouched next to the fallen bandit and rolled him over. The skin of his face was a little scraped up, and a lump was already forming between his eyes, but fortunately, he was still alive. She didn't have a great deal of experience with rendering people unconscious, so she had been afraid she'd overdone it.

There must have been a fifth bandit off in the corner, perhaps relieving himself, and the smell of hot greasy fat from the cooking fire had covered his scent. Now she heard him drunkenly attempt to sneak up behind her. It was pitiful, but she didn't turn around immediately. Instead she waited until he was within reach, then drew her knife, pivoted on one knee, and stabbed upward, parrying the overhead blow of his ax and taking a few fingers as well.

He screamed and cursed as he dropped the ax and clutched his bloody hand. But then he looked at her eyes and seemed to forget all about his wounds.

"*Strannik...*" He jammed his wounded hand under his arm and began backing slowly away. "Please have mercy on me, Ranger! I keep the old ways! I swear it!"

"I did not realize that preying on the weak was one of the old ways," she said quietly.

"Never again! I swear by the Lady! From now on, I'll live right!"

"Tell everyone," she said. "Tell them the Rangers have returned to purge this land of any who would harm the people of Izmoroz, be they imperial or brigand."

He nodded his head jerkily and stumbled off down the dark mine shaft toward the exit.

Once she was certain he was gone, she turned back to the task at hand. She took the coil of rope she'd brought and tied one end to the unconscious bandit's ankles. Then she threw the other end over one of the wooden support frames and hauled on the rope, hand over hand, until the bandit was hanging upside down. She'd picked the smallest of the four, but even so he was heavy, and once she'd tied off the rope, she had to rest a few moments.

When she'd caught her breath, she left the mine to retrieve Peppercorn. She found the bandit who'd fled lying on the ground next to him, his skull kicked in.

"Did he try to steal you, my *Perchinka*?" Sonya scratched him behind his ears.

Peppercorn whinnied quietly, still looking a little offended.

She gave him a piece of carrot, then brought him back to where the unconscious bandit still hung upside down. She took a large bucket and a bundle of leafless branches from Peppercorn's saddlebags. She placed the bucket beneath the bandit's head, and cut the branches down until they fit inside the bucket. Then she sat down to wait.

While she waited, the bandit woke up.

"I'm...still alive...," he muttered.

"Can you feel your feet?" she asked him.

"No..." He looked blearily around, trying to focus his eyes. "What's going on?"

"You can't feel your feet at all?" she asked.

"No, I—"

"I guess it's time."

She leaned over and slit his throat carefully right at the artery. Then she stepped back and watched the warm, steaming blood pour neatly into the bucket. He began thrashing, and the blood started to fall outside the bucket, so she had to hold him still. The more blood that was caught in the bucket, the more it would satisfy the Lady Marzanna.

After a few moments, he grew still and the blood began to drain more slowly. She squeezed him a few times, but it didn't seem to make much difference, so she sat back down and waited.

Once all the blood had drained into the bucket, she drew her knife again and carefully, patiently skinned him. She tried to keep the skin as intact as possible, because she knew it would please the Lady. When she was finished, she placed the skin into the bucket with the blood and sticks. She dragged the bucket away from the corpse to the center of the room and knelt before it. Then she spoke in Old Izmorozian, begging that the Lady Marzanna grant her an audience.

"Lady Marzanna, *ochen' proshu*! *Pogovori so mnoy!*"

She repeated this several times while pressing her forehead to the dirt floor, then waited. Finally, she heard the cooling blood begin to stir in the bucket, and she lifted her head.

The bloody skin wrapped around the sticks and stretched upward until a thin, vaguely human shape stood in the bucket. She had no nose, and her eyes were a pulsing black. She smiled at Sonya, showing neat rows of black teeth that glittered in the firelight.

"It is nice to see you still alive, my precious *Lisitsa*." Her voice scraped across Sonya's face like windburn.

"My Lady, I am honored by your visit."

"Well, you did it just as *Tigr* instructed, so I thought I should reward you. Besides, I am curious to know what you seek."

"Do . . . you know Bàs, my Lady?"

She cocked her pointed, angular head to one side. "You ask of Bàs?"

"The Uaine worship a god of death with that name, and I wondered if you might know him, or even be related to him."

She laughed quietly, and it sounded like the wind shaking bare, dead branches. "Of course I know him. Because he is *me*."

"But...he is male, my Lady."

"Does Winter have a gender?" she asked. "Does Death?"

"No, my Lady."

"Neither do I. When we have met on the banks of the Eventide River, the reflection you saw was shaped by your expectation. The mortal mind cannot comprehend my true form."

"Of course not, my Lady. My apologies."

"Have you sought me out to ask such a simple thing?"

"No, my Lady. I was merely curious. I have sought you out because I wish to ask for a boon."

"Oh?" She leaned forward, her black eyes unblinking.

"I seek to defeat my brother, Sebastian Turgenev."

"Ah." Lady Marzanna nodded. "He is a powerful wizard, your brother."

"Yes, my Lady."

"But he is mortal, like any man. And he can only cast his magic on what he can see. Wait until night, when your blessed eyes see farther than his. Then a single arrow will solve the problem of your brother."

"I know I ask much, my Lady, but...I was wondering if there is a way I might defeat him without killing him."

The Lady Marzanna's stick-thin figure leaned back. "Ah. I see. You must get close to him in order to subdue him, but then he might freeze the very blood in your veins before you ever touch him. So you seek a way to nullify his magic."

"If such a possibility exists, then yes."

"It is no small thing you seek, but your work thus far has pleased me greatly."

"I'm happy to hear you are satisfied, my Lady."

"I also see the potential for even more pleasing efforts from you, armed with such a boon. Still, there will be a significant cost in granting you this gift, my *Lisitsa*. Are you prepared to pay it?"

"I am, my Lady."

She held out her sharp, spindly arms. "Then come and embrace me."

Sonya did not allow herself to hesitate. She immediately stepped into the cold, hard embrace of the Lady Marzanna. The Lady's thin arms wrapped around her like vines, pinning her own arms to her sides, and pulling her off her feet.

The icy, flesh-covered vines continued to coil around her until she was entirely covered except her face. She could not move or even turn her head. Panic hovered at the edge of her mind, but she forced it back. This was what she wanted. It was what she had asked for. The choice had been hers, and if it would mean allowing her brother to live and still fulfill her goals, then she would accept the cost.

The vines pulled down on her jaw until her mouth was forced open.

"One by one, these will pay the price," the Lady whispered into her ear like the gentle slash of a razor. "Then surely victory will be yours."

The Lady reached into Sonya's mouth and slowly, carefully wrenched out the first tooth. The sharp crack was accompanied by a bolt of pain and the bitter taste of her own blood. She unconsciously strained against the flesh-covered vines that bound her, and tears rolled down her cheeks, but she forced herself to remain silent, swallowing the groan that boiled in her belly.

"One by one...," the Lady Marzanna whispered again.

Then she reached for the second tooth.

PART FIVE

THE BATTLE OF SESTRA RIVER

"I pity those who live in peace;
For they will never know
The heady thrill of wrath's release,
Or the beauty of blood-stained snow."

—Orlov Gorvinovski, "To Taste Death But Once"

60

Sonya knew the mind was incapable of recalling pain. That was a blessing. But she did sometimes wonder if the body might have its own memory, one in which suffering could be deeply etched. The world seemed different to her now, though it was difficult to say in what way exactly. Not darker, because her fox eyes allowed her to see more than her human eyes ever could. Not quieter, because nothing escaped her fox ears. Perhaps...harder? Heavier? Neither of those were right, but for now they were the closest she could get.

The Uaine had set up camp a day's ride west of Gogoleth. As she led Peppercorn between tents, many of the warriors waved to her. She waved back energetically, greeting them by name if she recalled it, although her cheerful attitude was not entirely authentic. Her recent experience with the Lady seemed to drag down at her soul, and ever defiant, she insisted on fighting its weight. She would not let trauma change her.

Mordha's tent was the largest, and therefore easy to spot. She made her way there and found him deep in discussion with Angelo. They were speaking in the Uaine language, so she didn't know what it was about, but they sat on the ground, looking at a rough, hand-drawn map of the area, so she suspected they were considering the strategy for their assault on Gogoleth.

"There ye be, Sonya," said Mordha. "Blaine told us about yer brother. Ye find a way to fight his magic?"

401

"I have," she said.

He smiled at her, showing yellow teeth in his thick beard. "Good. Let us make our final plans for the battle, then."

Mordha sent one of his men to gather the others. A short while later, Blaine and his father arrived, followed by the other clan chiefs and their captains. Soon after, Jorge and Rowena arrived, along with the other necromancers. Mathilde crept in nervously, no doubt intimidated by the crowd of large, boisterous Uaine who filled the tent. Sonya was delighted to see that there was another familiar face with her.

"Olin!" She rushed over to the old man who had helped set her broken arm all those months ago.

"You remember my name?" The old man looked pleased.

"Of course! I gave you one of my claws," she said.

He patted a small pouch at his waist. "I carry it with me always, *Strannik*."

"Olin was the one who told us to go looking for you in the first place," said Mathilde. "I didn't even believe it was possible a true Ranger was among us until he showed me that claw."

Sonya grinned. "That makes me so happy."

Their eyes widened when they saw her open smile.

"Praise the Lady!" said Mathilde. "Another blessing!"

"Heh." Sonya ran her tongue across her sharp new fox teeth. Had she been given the option, it was not the blessing she would have chosen. She couldn't think of any practical use for fox teeth, and she'd had to practice talking to herself quite a bit during the ride from the salt mine just to make sure she was intelligible. Plus, she kept nipping her tongue, and that really hurt. "Yeah, I guess so."

"Oh, they suit you very well, *Strannik*," said Olin.

"Really?" asked Sonya.

"My heart soars with courage just seeing 'em," assured Mathilde. "Anyone who follows the old ways will feel the same."

Olin nodded vehemently in agreement. "Seeing you now reminds me of all the old stories. I reckon there's no way we can lose."

"Well, okay!" Sonya felt her heart begin to lighten for the first time since leaving the mine. Just a little, but it was enough for now. "I like the sound of that."

Then she heard Jorge's voice. "Sonya!"

He and Blaine hurried over, looking worried.

"Did ye find a way to stop your brother?" asked Blaine.

"I did." Sonya smiled less self-consciously now.

"Woo la!" said Blaine, looking impressed. "Can ye still kiss with those?"

"That's your first question?" demanded Jorge.

Blaine shrugged.

"I don't know..." Sonya's eyes glinted mischievously. "Might not be completely safe."

Blaine grinned back at her. "You were never safe."

"But, Sonya," said Jorge. "How are...your teeth going to stop your brother?"

"Oh, they're not," she said. "That was just the price."

"Ah." Jorge's forehead creased with concern. "Did...did it hurt?"

Sonya squeezed his shoulder. "It's nothing you need to worry about."

He nodded, but didn't seem convinced.

Mordha raised his voice, speaking in the Uaine language, and the clan chiefs and captains quieted down. Then he turned to Angelo.

Angelo nodded. "Thank you, Tighearna." He turned to Sonya. "We've developed a plan while we were awaiting you. Hopefully you like it as much as we do."

"Let's hear it," she said.

"We have two forces. The Uaine, and the peasant resistance inside Gogoleth. I suspect that putting those two groups together might prove...fraught?"

"Regular folk would be more likely to run screaming from undead than fight beside them," Sonya agreed.

Angelo nodded. "Since we can't put them together, I propose that we use their separation to our advantage. We will take the Uaine warriors and sluagh gorta north and circle around the city to the river. Then we will travel swiftly downriver by raft and assault the imperial garrison directly."

"Bold," said Sonya.

"It must be, because in part, it will be a diversion," said Angelo. "Before we launch the assault, you will infiltrate the city. I believe your two friends here have already worked out a way to get you inside. Once the imperial forces have assembled at the garrison to repel our attack, you will rally your people and take the city from the inside, hopefully encountering minimal resistance. If we are able to take the city and hem them in on both sides, I think it likely the enemy will retreat south. Depending on how many casualties they've sustained, perhaps even all the way to Aureum."

"What about the brother?" asked Blaine.

"Yes," said Angelo. "We were hoping Sonya can fill in that part of the plan."

"His magic doesn't work on me anymore," said Sonya. "I'll deal with him, and everyone else should just avoid him."

"Ye think he'll come for ye?" asked Mordha.

"Absolutely," said Sonya. "We just have to make sure he knows where I am."

Angelo nodded. "Then once you've begun to take the city, you'll need to make sure whatever light resistance you encounter can get word to the garrison that you've been spotted in the city. That will make things a bit more complicated. Perhaps an extra pair of hands would be helpful? Someone who wouldn't be a hindrance in battle?"

"Obviously, that would be me," said Blaine.

His father, Chief Albion, asked him something in the Uaine language, and Blaine gave a terse reply. Whatever he said clearly did not please the chief, and he began to object. But it was cut off by Mordha. Albion glared at Mordha for a moment, then nodded, still looking displeased.

"What just happened?" Sonya murmured to Blaine.

He shook his head. "Nothing to worry about. Me dad is just a wee...protective."

"He thinks what we're doing is going to be more dangerous than a frontal assault on the garrison?" she asked.

"Not exactly," he said. "It's...complicated. I'll explain it to you some other time."

Angelo cleared his throat. "If we may proceed? So it's agreed that Blaine will accompany Sonya into the city. What about you, Señor Elhuyar?"

Jorge winced. "Please don't. That sounds like my father. And I'm not certain I would be much help in a pitched battle. In fact, I might be a liability."

"You would be of great use to us," said Rowena. "The Bhuidseach will not be involved directly in battle, either. You could accompany us north to the riverbank, and assist us with preparing the sluagh gorta for battle."

"Oh, well, if you think I'd be of help, then I'd be happy to." He looked at Sonya. "Is that all right with you?"

Sonya didn't know why, but she felt a slight pang of jealousy. It was ridiculous, of course. Jorge was definitely not cut out for battle, so it made sense for him to offer the necromancers support. But it seemed like Rowena in particular had been occupying a lot of Jorge's attention. Was she trying to seduce him? The Uaine in general were a lusty bunch, but the necromancers seemed somewhat apart from all that. And even if she was, why should it trouble Sonya? Was she just being clingy? Jorge wanted to marry someone and Sonya couldn't give him that. She supposed it would be better if he found a person who could. Even if that person was a creepy, bone-white, glass-eyed necromancer.

"Of course," she said in a cheerful tone that she hoped didn't sound too forced. "Sounds perfect."

"I think that's everything, then," said Angelo.

Mordha spoke to the Uaine, most of whom probably hadn't understood the previous conversation. They all listened attentively, their eyes eager and their smiles fierce. Mordha's speech rose in volume and intensity and then he lifted his fist in the air and barked out a final phrase. The response was so loud it shook the tent.

"Good." Mordha nodded. "We are ready. Let us prepare for battle."

61

Sebastian had thought the garrison active before, but that had been nothing compared to what he observed now. Yet with everything going on, it somehow did not fall into chaos. The yard looked almost like an ant colony, with soldiers moving in all directions yet never crashing into each other. Perhaps it was a testament to the training and discipline of the imperial army.

Zaniolo's scouts had learned that the Uaine had positioned themselves to the north of Gogoleth on the banks of the Sestra River and seemed to be preparing for a frontal assault on the garrison. It was a daring, even reckless choice, but intelligence suggested that the Uaine were little better than nomad savages, so perhaps it was the best strategy they could devise. One advantage to their plan, Sebastian realized, was if they came by river, he wouldn't be able to simply open up the earth to swallow them whole. It was his fault they knew to avoid such a danger.

Battle was now not only inevitable but no more than a day or so away. Sebastian could feel the intoxicating mixture of tension and eagerness that permeated the garrison. It was impossible not to be swept up in it. Even the commander seemed to have settled back down. "We've done what we can. Nothing left but to fight," he had told Sebastian that morning.

That was not entirely true for Sebastian. There was one thing he wanted to do—perhaps needed to do, in order to face the coming conflict with a clear mind and steady will. He must speak with Galina Odoyevtseva.

When he knocked on the door of Roskosh Manor, he braced himself for the possibility that he would be turned away. He still remembered how upset she had been when he'd unintentionally suggested that Galina was more concerned with appearances than the heart and mind. The fact that he had done something so boorish was more than enough justification for her to deny him the pleasure of her company for as long as she deemed appropriate. Ideally, he would have liked to wait a little longer before asking Galina's forgiveness. But his damned sister and her army of the undead were on their doorstep and the idea of not being allowed to see his beloved Galechka one last time before the battle was more than he could bear.

Masha opened the door and looked at Sebastian for a moment in that cool, inscrutable way some servants had.

"Good evening, Captain Portinari. How may I help you?"

"I have come to beg Galina Odoyevtseva's forgiveness. Will you tell her I am here?"

Another tense moment as Masha looked upon him with an indecipherable expression.

"Please come in out of the cold, Captain. I will see if she is available."

Sebastian heaved an audible sigh of relief, only then realizing he'd been holding his breath. "Thank you, Masha. You are most kind."

He stepped into the foyer and closed the door behind him as Masha went to find Galina. He stamped his feet a few times on the thick rug to warm them and looked around at this place, which had once seemed so strange and opulent to him, but now was more familiar to him than his own home. It was, he realized, the seat of all his happiness. Certainly, it was more welcoming than the garrison. While Vittorio seemed to have settled down somewhat, Sebastian still felt he could not let his guard down around the commander. And while he appreciated Zaniolo's continued support and advice, he couldn't help feeling that the sly general had his own agenda, of which Sebastian was only a small part. No, this place, Roskosh Manor, was the only place he still felt he could truly be himself.

"Sebastian."

Galina's voice was quiet, but he felt his heart would have heard her say his name even if it had been a whisper on the other side of the manor.

He turned and saw her standing at the foot of the stairs looking as radiant as the dawn.

"Galina, my love." He hurried over and dropped to his knees in front of her. "I am so sorry. Will you forgive me?"

Her eyes were wide as she looked down at him. "*I* should forgive you?"

"I know I don't deserve your clemency after suggesting that your love might waver because of something so banal as appearances."

"Oh. That."

She leaned forward, took his hands, then drew him up so that he stood once again.

"You do not need *my* forgiveness, Sebastian, for in that regard, there is nothing to forgive. Yes, your concern was shortsighted and inadvertently insulting, but it clearly sprang from a place of love, and I should not have treated you as harshly as I did."

"Oh, my Galechka, you have no idea how happy I am to hear you say that." He felt tears of relief sting his eyes, and he didn't try to deny them. "If I had gone into battle thinking that you no longer loved me, I'm not sure what I would have done."

"Is the battle nearly upon us, then?" she asked.

"Yes, my beloved. We had thought the Uaine and their terrible army of the undead would attempt to breach the western wall of the city, but instead they have veered north. We now believe they intend to attack the garrison directly by way of the Sestra River."

"And there you will meet them in battle?" she asked solemnly.

He kissed her ink-stained hands, finding her knuckles at once sharp and soft on his lips.

"Don't worry, my Galechka. The filthy Uaine will never see the inside of Gogoleth. I will defeat them at the Sestra River so that at last the empire will be able to bring peace to our fair land. I swear to you we will marry in a time when there will be no more need of battles and magic, and we will be free to fill our days with poetry and words of affection."

Her smile was sad. Perhaps she worried for him, despite his assurance, but didn't want him to think she didn't have full confidence in his abilities. She leaned forward and kissed his forehead.

" 'Our hearts beg us hold fast to love with a grip that never ceases,' " Galina quoted from Konstantin Zhukov's *Hopeless, Victorious*. " 'But if we do, we may shatter our dreams. When we fall, it is in pieces.' "

He looked at her a moment, unsure why she had chosen that particular couplet. But it didn't seem as though she planned to elaborate, so he only kissed her hands again.

"I must return to the garrison, my beloved, and prepare."

"Good luck, my sweet *volshebnik*," she told him. "May we find this peace you dream of."

"It will be here before you know it!" he told her. "I swear!"

Her smile remained sad as she nodded. She stood in the foyer, her hands clasped in front of her as she watched him bow and leave.

He understood her sorrow, of course. Who would not feel bittersweet pride when seeing a loved one off to battle? But now, with her love restored to him, he was certain that nothing could prevent his victory.

62

Well, if I had any remaining doubts, they've been quashed," said Galina as she and Masha hurried through the streets of Gogoleth toward the Sturdy Sturgeon Tavern.

"Yes, miss," said Masha.

"How could I possibly marry a man who is more preoccupied with inadvertently offending me than he is with inadvertently *murdering an entire town*?"

"Not the *whole* town, miss," said Masha. "Ranger Sonya saved some of them at least."

Galina chose not to reply to that. Even Masha spoke of the Ranger in an almost reverent voice, as if she was some sort of holy woman.

"Miss..." Masha gave her a concerned look. "You don't still blame yourself, do you?"

"Well, I can't help wondering," admitted Galina. "If I hadn't had my little fit of temper, would he have been so emotional when he arrived at Les? Would he have completely lost control like he did?"

"You can't blame yourself for being a human being, miss," said Masha.

And there it was. Galina was neither a terrifyingly powerful wizard nor a bizarrely revered beast woman. In the end, despite her wealth, her intellect, and her noble blood, she was still just a regular person.

Word had already gone through town regarding the impending conflict, so there was hardly anyone on the streets, and the markets were all closed up. Galina and Masha soon reached the Sturgeon and went around to the back entrance as they usually did. But when they entered, the atmosphere inside was anything but usual. Instead of a small group of grim countenances huddled around a single table, there was barely enough room to fit all the bright-eyed, eager patriots ready to take back their homeland from the imperials.

The change was no doubt thanks to Sonya, whom Galina had arranged to smuggle into Gogoleth a few nights before, along with Blaine, the slightly shorter and more pleasant-looking of the two Uaine barbarians she had met in Kamen. Now the Ranger stood in the center of the room, grinning widely, probably to show off her latest "blessing" from the Lady Marzanna: a full set of sharp little carnivore teeth.

"Hey, there she is," Sonya called over the din in that aggressively "folksy" voice of hers. It was absurd for her to speak in such a lazy, slurring fashion, since Galina was confident that Lady Portinari had raised her to speak with proper elocution. "What's the latest?"

"Your brother stopped by," said Galina. "They plan to hold the garrison against the Uaine's river assault."

Sonya nodded. "All according to plan, then. I tell you, I still don't know if I like Angelo, but that Aureumian knows his stuff. I just hope the Uaine don't lose too many in the assault."

Galina surveyed the crowded room. "The Uaine aren't the ones I'm worried about."

"Would you relax, Galechka?" Sonya squeezed Galina's shoulders in an unpleasantly rough manner that was no doubt meant to communicate camaraderie. "What's a delicate *kukla* like you have to worry about, anyway? It's not like you're going to be doing any of the fighting."

Galina glared at her. If anyone else had spoken to her with such familiarity or called her a *doll*, it would have been unacceptable. But since it came from their beloved Ranger, not even Masha objected. In fact, she smiled obsequiously along with the rest, as if it was all quite charming.

"I just wish we could have gathered a few more to our cause before

411

the fighting starts," Galina said evenly, determined not to show her ire.

Sonya shook her head. "Angelo was adamant on this. We can't chance it. Some of them might be imperial informants, and then Vittorio would know the full scope of our plan."

"But that means we'll just have to *hope* the townspeople rally around you quickly once the fighting begins."

"Come on, Galechka. Don't you have faith that I can bring everybody together?"

"I suppose."

Galina was loath to admit it, but based on the reactions she'd seen so far, the townspeople would fall all over themselves to answer the call of a true Ranger of Marzanna. More and more, she understood what Lord Semyon Golovin meant when he wrote that "peasants are like dogs who would rather chew on the tired old bone they already have than reach for a new one with meat."

"So, uh..." Sonya suddenly looked a little unsure of herself. "I was hoping you could do me a favor."

Galina certainly liked this shift in demeanor. "What can I do for you, Sonya?"

"Well, since you won't be marching with us—"

"Oh," said Galina, who had assumed she would be. In fact, she'd envisioned marching side by side with Sonya, a mass of shouting townspeople at their backs.

"I mean, no offense," said Sonya. "But once the fighting begins, you'd just be a hindrance. Blaine and I wouldn't be able to focus completely on what we'd be doing because we'd always have to make sure you were okay."

"Yes, I suppose that...makes sense."

"But here's what I want to ask, and it's something I think only you can do."

"What is it?"

"From the way you talk about her, it sounds like you get along pretty well with my mom. If people know she's been associating with Vittorio and my brother, they might...misunderstand, you know?

Think she's with the imperials. So I was hoping that you could convince her to stay safe at Roskosh Manor with you until things settle back down."

Galina was surprised by Sonya's concern for her mother, whom she had not even attempted to contact since her arrival. Perhaps beneath her ludicrous swagger and beastly deformities, there was a young woman who, not unlike herself, loved her mother deeply, yet struggled to relate to her in any meaningful way.

Galina smiled and pressed her hand to Sonya's cheek. "Sofyushka, it will be my distinct honor to look after your mother during this conflict."

Sonya gave her a big toothy smile, which Galina found unnerving, and embraced her.

"Maybe once I beat some sense into that brother of mine, he can still marry you," Sonya whispered into her ear. "I like giving you a hard time, but you seem all right for a noble. I guess I wouldn't mind having a sister like you around."

Galina did not know how to respond to the sudden expression of candid affection. When Sonya released her from the excessively strong embrace, Galina stood there dumbly for a moment before summoning a warm smile.

"The feeling is mutual," she lied.

63

Ｎow and then Jorge felt he was able to step back and truly appreciate a particularly evocative moment in his life. This, he decided, was one to remember. A quiet beauty before the storm.

He sat on a stump beside a crackling campfire, surrounded by a vast field that was starting to show patches of grass through the snow. In the distance rose the austere Cherny Mountains, still completely covered in white. The Otchayaniye Falls spilled down the side of the mountains in a long, elegant waterfall, kicking up a fine mist that glittered like a curtain of gems in the sunlight. The falls fed into the Sestra River, which then wound through the field as it made its way south toward Gogoleth.

That natural perfection was somewhat marred by the large rafts on the riverbank that were already packed with slough gorta. The undead stood patient and motionless, their yellow milky eyes gazing at nothing.

The living members of the Uaine army were gathered nearby, kneeling on the cold, wet ground with their hands clasped before them as if in supplication. The necromancers walked slowly from one to the next, offering a bleeding wrist to each. If an Uaine warrior still had the blood of a necromancer in their stomach when they died, they would immediately rise as a sluagh gorta and continue fighting. The necromancers performed this blood ritual before every battle, ensuring that even as the ranks of the living shrank, those of the sluagh gorta grew.

This contrast of natural beauty and unnerving blood ritual seemed so striking and surreal to Jorge, he wanted to capture the moment so that he would never forget it. He thought, not for the first time, that he should begin a journal to chronicle his strange adventures with Sonya. Maybe once they had liberated Izmoroz and things settled down, he would.

At last, every warrior had partaken of necromancer blood. Bhuidseach Rowena trudged over to the fire almost as if she were sleepwalking. He quickly stood and offered his stump. She smiled wanly and sank down onto it. It would have been impossible for her to look any paler, but the toll of losing so much blood was evident in her sluggish movements and unfocused gaze.

He held out a small glass vial filled with a restorative liquid. "This should help," he said.

"Thank ye." She took the vial and drank the bitter draught down in one go, then let her bloody arm drop.

"Perhaps you shouldn't...". He took a bandage from his pack and knelt down next to her, then carefully wrapped the self-inflicted cut on her wrist. He still found the thin, raised scars left behind from previous rituals that peppered her slender white arm unnerving, even after he had grown accustomed to the undead. "You'll want to keep that clean, I should think."

"Thank you again," she said.

"This is why you asked me to come along, after all," said Jorge. "I better see to the others."

Jorge took his kit of bandages and restoratives and attended to each of the necromancers in turn. The others had never been as friendly or welcoming as Rowena, but they were far too weary from blood loss to turn down aid.

The Uaine warriors, meanwhile, were making their final preparations for battle. Now that they'd taken the blood, they only had about eight hours before it lost its efficacy. They were already climbing aboard the remaining rafts behind the sluagh gorta.

"Jorge!" bellowed Tighearna Elgin Mordha from the final raft. "Time ye sent yer signal!"

415

"Yes, Tighearna!" He returned to his pack and carefully removed the small firework. He was no artist, and certainly no Viajero, so it was clumsily made. But he hoped it would work properly and not merely blow his hand off.

He planted the small stake into the ground a little ways from the campfire, then took a smoldering twig from the fire to light the fuse. Once the fuse flashed and began to crackle, he backed quickly away, just to be safe. He watched tensely as the fuse worked its way up, doing his best to ignore the expectant looks of the Uaine. They had apparently never seen fireworks before and were very curious about the whole thing. Of course, if it failed, he was certain they'd never let him live it down.

At last the fuse reached the black powder and the firework shot into the air with a hiss. It rose over fifty feet before bursting into a ball of glittering yellow and white. The Uaine warriors cheered and clanged their swords together.

"Hopefully Sonya saw that in Gogoleth," Jorge said as he returned to where Bhuidseach Rowena still sat by the fire.

Mordha shouted something in Uaine. Jorge turned to Bhuidseach Rowena and asked what it meant.

"It means...eh...*Ride the river!*" She gave him a somewhat stern expression and weakly shook her fist in a half-hearted attempt to imitate Mordha's passionate tone.

"Ah," said Jorge.

The necromancers were in no shape for battle, so they stayed behind with the camp, guarded by the elite Dìonadairean Bàs warriors, which was an honor guard dedicated to protecting them. Now the Dìonadairean Bàs waded into the river and took hold of the rafts. When Mordha gave the signal, they shoved the rafts toward the center of the river, where they were swiftly caught up in the strong current. Somewhat haphazardly, the train of rafts, bristling with warriors and sluagh gorta, began the journey downriver toward Gogoleth and the garrison.

Jorge watched the rafts grow farther and farther away until they were no longer visible, then he sighed and looked back at the fire.

"Do ye wish to join yer friends in battle, rather than nurse the Bhuidseach?" asked Rowena.

Jorge shook his head. "I'm no warrior. I know our cause is just, but I see no glory in battle, and take no joy in death."

"'Tis a luxury to have such views," said Rowena. "One which the Uaine canna' afford. Battle is all we know and all we treasure. Everything else is but a means to carry it further."

"Will it ever be enough?" asked Jorge. "Will you ever rest?"

"Does Death ever rest?" she asked.

64

Sebastian stood on the garrison's observation platform with the three generals and watched the ball of yellow-and-white fire explode in the air roughly a mile north of Gogoleth.

"What in God's name was that?" General Bonucci took off his tall hat, allowing his bald head to gleam brightly in the late-winter sunshine.

"A signal of some sort, I expect," said General Zaniolo. "These Uaine certainly don't appear to be very subtle."

"So much the better." General Marchisio leaned over the platform and shouted to the adjunct who waited below. "Inform the commander that the enemy has commenced their attack."

"Yes, sir!" The young officer saluted sharply, then hurried away.

"It doesn't make sense, though," said Zaniolo. "Now that they are aware of our...tactical advantage"—he gave Sebastian a significant look—"their best chance would be to sail swiftly down the river hoping to catch us unprepared and attack before Captain Portinari can muster a magic assault large enough to wipe them all out."

"It does seem foolhardy," said Marchisio. "Now that they've signaled their advance, we'll be watching them come down the river toward us."

"And how far is your range, Captain?" asked Zaniolo.

"As soon as I can see them clearly, sir," said Sebastian.

"Perhaps they merely underestimate him," suggested Bonucci.

"Possibly," conceded Zaniolo. "But it's never a good idea to base one's strategy on the hope that the enemy is ill-informed."

"Quite right, General," said Vittorio as he climbed up onto the platform.

"Commander, sir!" The generals and Sebastian saluted.

"As you were, gentlemen," said Vittorio. "Now, what is the status?"

"The Uaine have used some sort of…explosive signal, sir," said Marchisio.

"Explosive signal?"

"A clustered ball of white and yellow lights that quickly dispersed," said Zaniolo.

Vittorio's bushy eyebrows rose. "Fireworks?"

"You know of these things, sir?" asked Sebastian.

"A Raízian invention, primarily used during celebratory festivals. I've never heard of them used in warfare."

"Sir," said Zaniolo. "There have been several secondary source reports of a young Raízian man seen accompanying the Ranger."

"I see," said Vittorio.

The Ranger was how they all referred to Sebastian's sister. He preferred it that way. If he only thought of her as *the Ranger*, perhaps it would give him the emotional distance required to fulfill his duty. At least, he hoped so.

"Permission to ring the call to arms, sir?" asked Marchisio.

"Granted," said Vittorio.

Marchisio rang the large copper bell bolted to the observation platform, and the garrison sprang to life. Soldiers spilled out of the barracks, mess, and armory. At first it looked to Sebastian like a disorderly mob, but the many hours of drills paid off. Without any additional commands from the generals, the soldiers quickly coalesced into orderly lines, a row of shield bearers, followed by a row of spear bearers, then two staggered rows of archers, all standing at attention. To either side of the infantry were the cavalry units, all except Sebastian's 404th, which Vittorio had decided to hold back in reserve, with Rykov commanding in Sebastian's stead.

"Lovely," murmured Vittorio. "Order out of chaos. They look splendid, gentlemen."

"Thank you, sir," said Bonucci.

"Returning to your earlier concern, Zaniolo," said Vittorio. "Is it possible the signal is meant to mislead us into thinking they will attack from upriver, when in fact they plan to attack from another direction?"

Zaniolo shook his head. "Unlikely, sir. Our scouts reported visual confirmation of the entire Uaine army, including their undead, camped on the western banks of the Sestra last night. The undead move quite slowly, so there is no way they could have circled back to assault the west gate in time. And even if they were to somehow accomplish that feat, the west gate is sufficiently manned that once they sent word to us, they would be able to hold out until we sent reinforcements."

Vittorio nodded gravely. "Then either they are foolish, as General Bonucci suggests, or they have some other scheme afoot. Let us focus on the battle before us, but also remain alert for possible subterfuge."

Sebastian was relieved to see the commander in such an equanimous mood after the temperamental outbursts he'd witnessed during the past few weeks. He only hoped that Vittorio kept his composure during the coming battle.

They waited in silence for some time, taking turns watching the river with the telescoping spyglass. Below, the soldiers remained unspeaking, but exchanged anxious looks. Sebastian imagined they felt the same conflict of emotions that he did. Everything that had happened to him throughout this winter led to this day. All his hard work, his struggle, his sacrifice, and his suffering had been in preparation for defending Gogoleth from the army of undead that would soon be upon them. Often it had seemed like the day would never arrive. Now that it had come, he wondered if he was truly ready.

At last Zaniolo grunted quietly. "There they are."

He handed the glass to Vittorio, who looked through it and nodded.

Sebastian couldn't make out many details yet, but he could at least see the shape of what appeared to be a fleet of rafts moving swiftly toward them, every one of them crowded with enemies.

"I'm surprised they'd bother putting their undead on the rafts," said Zaniolo. "If they don't need to breathe, it would have made more sense to have them walk along the river bottom in an attempt to take us by surprise."

"Had they done so," said Vittorio, "Captain Portinari would have simply frozen their monsters in place within the river, and they would have lost their most formidable force." The commander glanced at Sebastian, and for a moment there was that flash of rage in his eyes. Then he looked back toward the enemy. "But *unfortunately*, they knew to avoid such a tactic."

"Yes, well..." Zaniolo cleared his throat. "It could still be useful to freeze the river, since it would slow them down significantly, making them easier long-range targets."

"Agreed," said Vittorio. "Captain, once General Marchisio has decided the enemy is within arrow range, freeze the river."

"The *entire* river, sir?" asked Sebastian. "I'm not sure I could—"

"A mile in either direction, then," Vittorio snapped impatiently.

"Y-yes, sir." He wasn't certain he could do that, either, but only because he had never tried. The commander expected him to push himself to his limits during this battle, and that was exactly what he intended to do.

They watched the rafts draw closer. Below, the soldiers were motionless, no longer even shifting their weight. The garrison was so quiet, Sebastian could hear the quiet clank of arms and armor.

"Archers at the ready!" Marchisio roared.

The sudden shout startled Sebastian, but the phalanx of archers at the back of the assembled army did not hesitate. As one, they smoothly loosened their bows, then took arrows from quivers and nocked them.

In a quieter voice, Marchisio said, "You may now freeze the river, Captain."

"Yes, sir."

The enemy was still too far away for Sebastian to see them clearly, but he could see the river just fine. He gripped his gem and focused on the flowing water, summoning all the cold hard dread that lurked within his heart. Fear of failing the commander again, fear

421

of confronting his sister again, and fear of what would happen to his beloved Galechka if he faltered. Such feelings had weighed heavily in his gut these past few days, at times so intense he could hardly move. Now he used those feelings to define an intense cold unlike any that had ever assaulted the river before.

The section of river in front of them froze in place so abruptly, the curves and dapples of its surface appeared as if sculpted. The gleaming white ice then traveled rapidly in either direction, expanding so forcefully that small cracks appeared along the rocky bank as the river expanded.

"By God, it worked!" said Bonucci.

Zaniolo chuckled quietly. "Look at them flounder on the ice."

Even from this distance, Sebastian could see figures stumbling off the rafts and onto the ice, many of them slipping and falling repeatedly in an almost comical display.

"Archers draw!" shouted Marchisio.

As one, the archers pulled their bowstrings taut.

"Release!"

The sky was dark with arrows that arced upward, then rained down upon the enemy.

"Hmm," Marchisio said after a moment.

The arrows had struck many in the front lines, but none of them fell, or even seemed to notice they'd been pierced through. Instead, their full focus now seemed to be on walking slowly and carefully toward the garrison across the perilous surface of the frozen river.

"Perhaps fire arrows?" suggested Bonucci.

"Let's hope," said Marchisio. Then in a louder voice, "Archers! Arrows alight!"

The archers stuck the tips of their arrows into the torches that had been set for that purpose.

"Archers draw!"

The line of flickering arrows were pulled back.

"Release!"

The fire arrows were even more fearsome in flight, raining down on the enemy like the coming of Hell itself. Yet it seemed to make little difference once they struck the undead. The flames were doused immediately upon impact.

"It seems they've been coated with some sort of fire-resistant salve," said Zaniolo.

"Captain, can you make the arrows explode on contact?" asked Marchisio. "Like you did with those torches?"

"Or could you make them burst like you did with those miners?" asked Bonucci.

"Er, yes, but only one at a time." Sebastian hadn't realized his exploits were so familiar to the generals, and wasn't sure how he felt about it.

"We need a more sweeping attack to thin their numbers," said Vittorio.

"What if Captain Portinari thawed the river now?" asked Bonucci.

"What?" Marchisio scoffed. "He just *froze* it."

"No, no, it makes sense, actually," said Zaniolo. "They've abandoned their rafts, you see. Even the living ones, who are weighed down with those horrid barbaric chain mail shirts of theirs. Potentially we could drown every living warrior in their army. Would the undead even know what to do without their guidance?"

"Even if their undead warriors are autonomous," said Vittorio, "we could cut the total number of the enemy by as much as a third."

"Sh-should I do it now, then, sir?" asked Sebastian.

"Yes, of course!" snapped Vittorio, his face flushing. "If you hadn't noticed, Captain, a battle has commenced!"

"Y-yes, sir."

Sebastian knew the commander had every right to be so harsh with him. Even so, the frustration he felt at the treatment kindled a deep, sullen anger within him. As inappropriate as he knew such a feeling to be, he realized he could utilize its heat.

He focused his will on his gem and released that anger at the river. It not only thawed immediately, but began to steam and roil, spreading outward in either direction in a seething wave.

"Wonderful idea, Captain!" Zaniolo clapped Sebastian on the back. "Why stop at drowning the enemy when you can boil them alive!"

"Eh, yes." Sebastian had not meant to take it quite that far, but he was glad of the praise.

Marchisio laughed as he gazed at them through the spyglass. "Thrashing about like panicked animals!"

The undead soldiers sank beneath the surface immediately without struggle, but as the scalding water reached the living Uaine warriors, they flailed about in anguish. Sebastian could hear their screams even from such a distance. Only the back half of the army managed to regain the rafts or reach the shore before being overtaken by the surge of boiling water.

"These are much more manageable numbers," Vittorio said approvingly. "Well done, gentlemen."

"Mordha managed to survive, however," muttered Zaniolo as he squinted through the spyglass.

"Mordha?" asked Bonucci.

"The tall one who just reached the shore. According to our informants, he is their 'warlord.' And next to him..." Zaniolo continued to gaze through the glass. "Well God damn him to Hell." He handed the glass to Vittorio. "Sir, do you recognize the man currently talking to Mordha on the riverbank?"

Vittorio took the glass and observed for a moment, then a string of curses flew from his mouth so forcefully, they were accompanied by a stream of spittle.

"Who is it, Savitri?" demanded Marchisio.

"Angelo Lorecchio." Zaniolo spat. "Traitor to the empire, now doubly so."

"I've never met him in person," admitted Bonucci. "Is he as wily as people say?"

"I'm afraid so," said Zaniolo. "And he doesn't look overly perturbed by this setback, which worries me a great deal." He glanced at Vittorio, but the commander was still cursing and glaring at the distant traitorous Lorecchio. "General Bonucci, ready the infantry."

"For what?" asked Bonucci uneasily.

"Anything," replied Zaniolo.

Then Sebastian heard a strange, high-pitched wail that chilled his blood.

He turned toward the riverbank where he had spent so many hours practicing, and saw a gray head emerging. It was sparsely covered by clumps of long wet white hair, and it wore a thin brown tunic. Its eyes were glassy, and its lipless grin showed yellow, broken teeth. As it continued to emerge from the river, Sebastian saw that its grayish skin was puffy and almost spongelike from absorbing so much water, and it sloughed off in places to reveal the hard muscle and sinew beneath.

The undead creature let out another eerie wail, and this time, it was joined by several other creatures who were emerging behind it. Ten, twenty, Sebastian gave up counting as more continued to rise from the river and make their slow, unhurried way toward the garrison. The soldiers shifted uneasily, and some whispered quietly, perhaps praying.

"Dear God in Heaven...," whispered Bonucci, his face twisted in loathing at the sight of the undead rising from the river.

"Quickly, Sebastian." Zaniolo's voice was tense. "Can you freeze the river?"

"It...will take a while, since I've just made it boil," said Sebastian.

Marchisio grabbed his arm so hard it hurt. "Can you split open the earth to swallow them up?"

"Not without risking our own forces."

Zaniolo cursed under his breath, then turned to Bonucci. "*Well*, General?"

Bonucci flinched, his eyes looking a little wild.

"What in hell are you waiting for?" demanded Zaniolo.

"Y-yes, of course." Bonucci took a deep breath, and his expression hardened. Then he turned and looked down at the daunted soldiers below. "To arms, men! We will not allow these abominations to shake our resolve!"

The infantrymen readied their spears, and the cavalry drew their swords, but the look of fear was unmistakable on many faces as they gazed at the monstrous creatures that trudged slowly up the bank toward them in growing numbers. The undead wailed again, and the sound, now a chorus of hundreds with still no end in sight, made horses shy and rear.

"Steady!" shouted Bonucci, his face pale. "Damn your eyes, I say *steady*, men! And steady those horses!"

425

The army of undead continued to march out of the river. Sebastian noticed that the ones in the back were not dressed in brown tunics, but in the mail vests of Uaine warriors. Furthermore, their skin was not gray, but a rosy red, as if recently boiled.

"They've already turned...," he said quietly. "All the ones we killed..."

"What do you mean?" demanded Marchisio.

"God damn them," said Zaniolo. "It appears as soon as we strike down a regular Uaine warrior, they join the ranks of the undead army. We haven't diminished their numbers in the slightest."

They all glanced at Vittorio, but he was still cursing and fuming at Lorecchio and did not seem aware of or interested in anything else. The generals looked back at each other, faces grim and pale, but unsurprised. Had they expected the commander to falter just when his leadership was needed most? Was Commander Vittorio really just talk after all? And if so, how could they knowingly serve under such a man?

Marchisio's voice was resolute. "We must engage regardless."

Bonucci nodded. Then he lifted his voice and bellowed, "Charge!"

A roar of men's voices rose up to match the screech of the undead. The archers let fly with a volley of arrows to cover the infantrymen as they charged forward, while the cavalry fanned out to the sides.

Again the arrows did little to slow the oncoming force, and only served to remind everyone how impervious the enemy was to pain and injury. The cavalry had better luck harrying their flanks. If a mounted soldier got close enough to lop off the head with his saber, the undead fell to the ground and did not rise again. But the horses continued to shy away from the unnatural creatures, and only the best horsemen could force their mounts to ride within striking distance more than once or twice.

Then the line of shield bearers crashed into the front of the undead army as the infantrymen closed the gap. The spear bearers thrust their points between the cracks, skewering the creatures easily. But the creatures only grasped the spears that protruded from their chests and pulled themselves closer. Soon a mass of undead were pressing down on the shields such that the bearers were in danger of collapse.

Bonucci yanked Sebastian toward him, panic starting to show on his face. "Surely there's *something* you can do, Captain!"

Sebastian gripped his gem tightly and began to probe the insides of the creatures. He could feel no blood to boil, but there was plenty of river water absorbed in their skin. He found one creature that had nearly broken through the wall of shields. With a desperate will, he heated the creature's waterlogged flesh. The creature stopped pressing forward and began to convulse, which gave the shield bearer a moment of relief. But the creature's skin continued to swell until finally it burst, flinging gray flesh, now searingly hot, in all directions, scalding both the shield and spear bearers.

"Damn you! You're just making things worse!" Bonucci shoved Sebastian roughly aside.

"General Bonucci, calm yourself!" Zaniolo's voice was as cold and hard as winter steel. "We are officers of the imperial army and we do not give in to *hysteria*."

Bonucci looked as though he were about to retort, but then glanced over at the still raving Vittorio and winced. He took a deep breath, then looked back at Zaniolo.

"You're right, of course, General. What need have we of magic or trickery? As always, we will claim victory with our discipline and ingenuity."

The generals began shouting down to their adjuncts below, giving them messages to relay to the captains on the field as they tried to find a formation that would work against their slow but implacable foe. Sebastian didn't know what to do. He felt urgency all around him, and his heart twisted with empathy as he watched the brave soldiers of the imperial army fight desperately against their merciless and unfeeling foes. He longed to aid them, but feared that his attempts to help would once again make things worse.

"Sebastian!"

Commander Vittorio spun Sebastian around to face him. The

commander's face was bright red with rage, and his eyes bulged so that he truly did seem mad. He pointed at the distant Lorecchio.

"Kill that man immediately! Boil his blood so that it bursts from his eyes!"

"Y-yes, sir!" Sebastian had never tried such a thing from this distance, but perhaps if he could see the man a little more clearly. "Can I use the glass, sir?"

"Fine, fine!" The commander shoved the spyglass at Sebastian. "Just do it!"

When Sebastian trained his glass on the man they called Angelo Lorecchio, his heart nearly leapt out of his chest. For a split second, he could have sworn he was looking at his father. They were the same age, the same build, same hair, even the same stern, serious pinched gaze.

"Well?" demanded Vittorio.

"I-I'm trying, sir. It takes a few moments."

But just as Sebastian began to gather his focus on the gem, he heard a new voice shout from the base of the observation tower.

"Commander, sir! She's taken the city! The Ranger has taken the city!"

"*What?*" There were now flecks of white spittle on Vittorio's lips. "Explain yourself, soldier! Has the west wall been breached?"

The young soldier below looked ready to collapse. His military jacket was torn at the shoulder, his face was ashen, and he was clutching at an arrow still lodged in his arm. But the brave man spoke with a firm, clear voice.

"No, sir! The Ranger just appeared in the middle of the city! She's rallied a mob of peasants, and they're attacking anyone dressed in imperial uniforms!"

Vittorio ground his teeth together so hard, Sebastian could hear the squeak. He glared at the soldier, then at the distant Lorecchio, then at the battle that raged along the riverbank. With what appeared to be tremendous effort, he closed his eyes and took a slow, deep breath.

"Captain Portinari?" His voice was almost a groan.

"S-sir!"

"Belay the previous command. Eliminating the Ranger is our top priority. Take your men into the city. Kill your sister, then put down that mob by any means necessary before they are able to attack our army from the rear."

"Y-yes, sir!"

"Do not fail me again, Sebastian."

65

Sonya felt drunk on glory and freedom as she watched the good people of Izmoroz rise up against their Aureumian oppressors. They were armed only with knives or axes, hoes or rakes, but the soldiers they faced were those who had been left out of the battle, likely because of inexperience or incompetence. Furthermore, the soldiers were outnumbered and taken completely by surprise. The townsfolk swarmed over them with few losses. In fact, some of the soldiers, clean-shaven Izmorozian boys who perhaps felt guilty for joining the army in the first place, even tore off their uniforms and joined the crowds. Sonya urged the people to accept anyone who surrendered, and mostly they did. This was a revolution, after all, not a massacre.

Sonya wished she could have brought Peppercorn, but they'd been smuggled into the city inside a wagon full of salted pork, so that hadn't been possible. Instead she sauntered down the street with Blaine, pausing now and then to shoot an imperial soldier who had managed to outrun the townspeople.

"Don't forget we need a few of those warriors to get back to their Tighearna." Blaine walked beside her, the flat of his massive sword casually resting on his shoulder.

"To draw out my brother, I know," she said. "I've already let several go. I'm sure at least one of them made it."

His expression grew solemn. "You sure this es gonna work? Against your brother, I mean?"

"The Lady said his magic won't work on me directly anymore. So you just hang back and make sure nobody else gets close. I'll take care of the rest."

He nodded, though it was clear he was still concerned. He'd been at Les, so he knew what Sebastian could do. She considered telling him that *her* Lady Marzanna and *his* Bàs were the same entity. That might ease his worry. But that was a complicated topic best suited for a less chaotic time. As thrilling and intoxicating as the present moment was, she had to make sure things didn't get too out of control. With all this pent-up righteous fury being released, it could slip into utter havoc and indiscriminate killing at any moment. And then there were those who were selfishly taking advantage of the situation. She'd already caught a few looters. She hadn't killed them, of course, but they were now lying unconscious in the street. They might now become victim of a little looting themselves, but that seemed appropriate.

The townsfolk were gravitating toward the Imperial Church. The idea of a single location where holiness resided was a distinctly non-Izmorozian concept, and clearly one that rankled many of the townsfolk. By the time Sonya and Blaine reached the church, a large and angry group had gathered around it. People wielding torches shouted and spat as four sturdy young men dragged the wailing priest out through the front door. It was the same one who had harangued her during her last visit to the city, and she suspected that perhaps the people's angst was also somewhat directed at him personally.

"That a holy man?" asked Blaine.

"Something like that," she said.

"Please! Spare me!" begged the priest. "I've never done anything to you! I've only ever tried to *help*."

Sonya walked casually through the mob to the priest. As soon as people saw her amber eyes and fanged grin, they quickly stepped aside, some even bowing their heads.

"Hey, Holy Father, remember me?" she asked as she drew near.

The priest stopped struggling against the men who held him and stared at her. "You . . . you're the one leading these people?"

"Nah, I just got them started."

"But…" His eyes darted around. "But these people *respect* you. They'll listen to you! Please! Tell them to let me go!"

"Respect *me*?" she affected surprised. "Even though I'm an *ignorant savage with the stink of the wild about me*?"

His eyes widened. "You…you were that girl with the Raízian!"

"Aww, you *do* remember me! How sweet. Well, turns out, Holy Father, I wasn't the one who needed protection, huh?"

"Yes! You're right! I was foolish! It is *I* who need protection! Please! Help me!"

She shrugged. "I mean, we only met the once. These people know you way better than me, so I trust they know what's best for you."

She turned and walked back to where Blaine stood watching a short distance from the crowds.

"Having a bit o' fun, eh?" he asked.

"Couldn't resist," she said. "Nobody's perfect."

"Do ye think they're going to kill him?"

"It's possible," she admitted. "But it's more likely they'll just mess with him awhile, then send him on his way."

They watched as the crowd's animosity toward the priest continued to build. People began waving torches in his face, and each time he shrieked like a little girl, it drew mocking laughter from the crowd. Sonya had to concede that their wrath was escalating, making murder of an unarmed old man look increasingly likely. Should she step in? But she understood their anger. And did she have the right to tell these people what to do when they were just beginning to taste freedom, some of them for the first time?

"Disperse at once!"

A tight formation of mounted imperial soldiers charged toward the crowd holding the priest. Their sabers were drawn and it was clear from their bearing they were not the panicked, undertrained raw recruits that had been left to keep order in the town. They were seasoned warriors, likely just deployed from the battle at the garrison. That meant that word of the revolution had reached their commander. Hopefully it meant Sebastian would be here soon as well.

"Time for us to step in," she told Blaine.

He nodded and gripped his sword with both hands.

Sonya shot one soldier out of the saddle as Blaine sprinted toward them. Had she been on Peppercorn, she could have closed the gap while still shooting, but now she had to choose whether to keep firing arrows, or run after Blaine to engage in close combat. She took down one more soldier, but then they crashed into the crowd of panicking townsfolk, and things became too chaotic for her to get a clear shot, so she shouldered her bow, drew her knife, and charged into the fray, grinning with eagerness.

The soldiers laid about them with their sabers indiscriminately, cutting down anyone within reach, young or old, even if they were merely trying to flee. Blaine had a head start on Sonya and reached them first. Unfortunately, he went for the horse. It was the obvious thing to do when a person on foot confronted a mounted opponent, but it still tore at Sonya's heart to hear the poor animal's shriek of pain as he fell, pinning his rider to the ground.

While Blaine finished off the trapped soldier, Sonya vaulted off the thrashing horse and slammed into another soldier, pulling him off his horse. The moment they hit the ground, she cut his throat, then moved on to the next. She leapfrogged from rider to rider, swift and brutal as a winter wind, cutting ribbons of flesh as she went.

All around her there were flickering sabers, flailing bodies, wails of fear, screams of pain, and the heavy smell of blood. She was dimly aware that she was not merely smiling now, but drooling. Somewhere deep inside, she knew it wasn't right to enjoy it. This wanton slaughter on both sides was unfortunate at best. Yet the pleasure that surged through her limbs with each slash of her knife was unmistakable. She loved it.

The last soldier managed to cut her cheek with the tip of his saber. She fixed her eyes on him, still smiling as she licked the blood that trickled down to her chin. Something about her expression made him recoil in fear, and perhaps revulsion, but she didn't pay it any mind. The roar of bloodlust in her head had become as deafening as a waterfall. Her thoughts were little more than a jumble of impressions and instinct that vibrated with primal glee. She leapt upon the bold soldier who had cut her and disarmed him by hacking off his thumb. With her free hand she grabbed a fistful of his hair and bent his head back. Then she opened her mouth and finally found a use for her new teeth.

It was her brother's scent that brought her back to her senses. She lifted her head, her face now smeared with blood, and let out a long, shuddering breath. She found herself astride the horse. Her legs were wrapped around the dead soldier's waist, and she held him in her arms like a lover. His throat had been torn out, as if by a wild beast. Had she done this? Had she swallowed a man's flesh?

She jumped down from the frightened horse, and forced her way through the crowds of townspeople who were still panicking in the aftermath of the assault. She needed air. She needed to clear her head. She needed to think like a human. The beast instinct had taken over in a way it had never done before. Each of the Lady's gifts brought her closer to the wild. Had she already reached her limit? If she lost any more of her humanity, would she be lost as well?

Then she caught her brother's scent again, and remembered. Not just what had pulled her back to sanity, but why she had sacrificed so much of her humanity in the first place.

"Blaine!" she shouted over the crowds.

He looked up from where he was bandaging a survivor. His eyes went wide when he saw her. She realized her face was still smeared with blood, so she spit in her hand and wiped it off as best she could.

"My brother," she called. "He's here!"

Blaine lurched to his feet and took up his sword.

"Everyone!" she shouted. "Get back! Run!"

But most of them were wounded, or in shock, and didn't move.

"Where es he?" yelled Blaine.

Sonya's sharp fox eyes scanned the square and the neighboring streets.

"There."

Her brother was riding resolutely down the center of the street wearing an immaculate green imperial officer's uniform, complete with funny little cap. He was alone except for a hulking, young red-haired Izmorozian man who seemed barely able to fit into his own jacket.

When the two entered the square, they didn't see Sonya immediately. Instead their eyes fixed on the remaining crowd of townspeople, and particularly on the dead soldiers that lay among them.

Sebastian's face twisted into an almost unrecognizable mask of fury. "My men!"

He gripped the massive diamond that Galina said magnified his power and lifted his other hand toward the crowd.

"Sebastian! No!" shouted Sonya.

But he seemed not to hear her. He made a sweeping gesture with his hand and the crowd of people were blown right off their feet, as if by a sudden intense blast of wind, and thrown in all directions.

"Sebastian!" Sonya tried again. "Let them alone! It's me you want!"

He turned and locked eyes.

She held up her hands. "Please, Sebastian. Can we just talk? I don't think either of us want to repeat what happened last time."

His gaze wavered a moment at that reminder. She knew it. He *did* feel guilty about what he'd done in Les. He wasn't totally irredeemable.

But then his expression hardened, and he firmed his grip on his diamond.

"We won't repeat it," he said. "Because this time, I won't let you goad me. I won't give you the chance."

His eyes blazed with a desperate anger as he gestured toward her. The air rippled directly in front of her, but she felt nothing. A moment later, Sebastian was knocked backward off his horse as if he'd been struck, and the diamond flew out of his hand.

Sonya grinned tensely at Blaine. "See? No problem."

The smile Blaine returned was more one of relief, but she didn't blame him for that.

Blood streamed from Sebastian's nose, but he staggered to his feet and reached for the diamond that now lay on the cobblestones.

"Sorry, little brother."

In a single, fluid movement, she unslung her bow, drew an arrow, and fired.

Sebastian gave an anguished yelp as the arrow pierced through his hand. He stumbled back and drew his wounded hand to his chest, where it stained the front of his once pristine jacket a dark red.

"We have to keep that diamond away from him," she told Blaine.

"Aye." He charged forward, his sword held crosswise in front of him.

"Preferably without killing or maiming him further," she called.

She didn't know if he heard, but it didn't matter because the absurdly large Izmorozian soldier who had been looming behind her brother drew his own sword and charged forward to meet Blaine. Their swords clashed so hard they drew sparks. For a moment, Sonya felt that old pang of envy at seeing impeccable swordsmanship, and wished her father had taught her some of it. But she had her own methods, which were far more effective in situations like this.

She drew an arrow and aimed at the big redhead. But Blaine caught sight of what she was doing out of the corner of his eye.

"Don't ye dare!" he shouted. "You focus on your brother. If this is all I can do for ye, then I will do et!"

She sighed. He was right. That would have been rather rude of her. She let the two large men continue to bang their swords together and returned to her brother. He still seemed to be reeling from the backlash of his failed magical attack and wounded hand, but despite being a weak little spoiled baby, he had managed to summon up the determination to retrieve his diamond. He now grasped it in his uninjured hand and bared his teeth at her.

"You think you can beat me?" he screamed. "You...you're not even a person anymore. Look at you! More animal than human."

She stiffened for a moment, then took a calming breath. "I'm still your big sister. Don't you see? I could have killed you several times by now, but I don't want to."

"Well, I *do* want to kill you!"

His lip curled into a snarl as he gestured at her. She felt a brief chill run through her body. Then her brother gasped and doubled over, a splash of blood leaping from his mouth.

"I mean it, Sebastian! You can't hurt me, so why don't you give up before I have to come over there and beat you senseless."

A new voice, deep and loud, shouted, "I think not, odious savage!"

A mounted soldier charged between her and her brother, sweeping his saber down at her. She easily dodged to the side as she nocked an arrow. But when she fired the arrow at him, it spun away as if knocked aside by an unseen force. She glanced over at her brother and saw him smirking. He might not be able to use magic on her directly, but he could still use it against her.

"Commander!" Sebastian shouted to the man. "She's somehow immune to my magic!"

"I see." The man dismounted his horse, looking grim as he leveled his sword at her. "If I accomplish nothing else today, it will be your death."

"You must be this Vittorio I've been hearing so much about," said Sonya. "Your mustache looks dumb."

"I care not for the opinion of a savage beastling."

Her brother had rendered her bow useless, so she put it aside and drew her knife. "I wonder if my brother will stop acting like an ass once I kill you."

"Come try your luck then."

"The only luck was you showing up just now."

She rushed forward, her knife extended as if preparing to thrust. He moved to parry, no doubt planning on following that with a counter, but instead of following through with her thrust, she rolled to the side instead, sliding across the snowy cobblestones and turning to slash at his ankle. But he was quicker than she'd given him credit for, stabbing his sword into the stone beside his foot at the last moment to block her strike. Then he pivoted around to kick her. She knocked his kick aside with her own foot, and allowed her momentum to take her sliding out of striking distance before regaining her footing.

"Interesting." She tossed her knife from one hand to the other. "You posture like a lion, but you fight like a viper. I guess I better stop underestimating you."

She lunged forward again, feinting first left, then right until she was close enough to slam her fist down on the forearm of his sword hand, then bring her elbow up under his chin. He staggered away from her, but managed to keep hold of his sword, mostly because at the last moment, he'd rotated his arm to keep her from breaking the thinner bone in his forearm.

"You fight like an honorless savage, just as I knew you would," he told her, rubbing his forearm.

She feigned another lunge and when he didn't take the bait, she released her knife in mid-thrust. The blade buried itself in the shoulder of his sword arm. He grasped the handle with his free hand to pull it out, but she delivered a roundhouse kick to that arm, which made him jam the blade in deeper instead.

Vittorio left the blade where it was and, gritting his teeth, went on the offensive. He began to drive her backward with impressive speed and strength, considering the knife still buried in his shoulder. But as he pushed her across the cobblestones, he left a trail of blood behind him. He was running out of time and he knew it. His attacks became more vicious and desperate, while she merely continued to dodge and wait for an opening.

At last she saw it. A thrust that went a little too far to pull back quickly. She ducked under it and came up on the inside, right against his chest so that she could feel the heat coming off him. She grabbed her knife with both hands and twisted, causing him to howl with pain and at last drop his sword.

He threw himself backward hard, and since her hands still gripped her knife, the blade was ripped free of his shoulder. But his momentum was so great, and he had already lost so much blood, that he kept stumbling backward until he lost his footing and fell onto the hard cobblestones. She had him now.

"Sir!"

Another imperial on horseback appeared, blocking her path to the commander.

"They've broken through!" this new imperial shouted to Vittorio. "Bonucci and Marchisio have been killed, the army has been routed, and the undead are storming the city! We must flee!"

Vittorio cursed and spat as he struggled to his feet, his face creased with fury.

"Oh no, you are not getting away," Sonya muttered as she rushed forward.

But she was broadsided by a pair of screaming townspeople and knocked to the ground. As she struggled to untangle herself from them, she saw her brother smirk at her over his shoulder as he regained his horse. By then, Vittorio had recovered his own mount. The large redheaded soldier had apparently survived his fight with Blaine and climbed up behind Sebastian.

"No, no, no!" she seethed as she pushed the people off her and staggered to her feet.

"Sonya!" shouted Blaine. "I need ye!"

He stood over by a large group of townspeople who were now wailing with newfound terror as they watched an army of undead march down the street toward them. They were pushing each other aside and climbing over those who had fallen in their panicked attempts to flee.

"Please! Calm down! They are not the enemy!" he shouted to them, but they either didn't believe him or were too frightened to understand. Either way, it was clear he needed help before things got worse.

She bared her fanged teeth in frustration as she looked from the hysterical people to the fleeing Vittorio.

She pointed her knife at the commander's back. "Next time," she whispered.

Then she ran over to the crowds and grabbed Blaine. She had to shout into his ear to be heard over the clamor.

"I'll calm the people! You tell the sluagh gorta to stay where they are!"

It took Sonya a while to bring sanity back to the square, and by then Sebastian and his imperial comrades were nowhere to be seen. She had won the battle, but she had lost her brother. Perhaps forever.

66

But, sir, I can't leave without Galina!" Sebastian said as the three horses forced their way through the chaos and riots of a city gone mad.

"God damn you, boy!" Vittorio yanked his horse closer, his uninjured arm raised in a fist. "I'll knock that—"

"Commander!" barked Zaniolo. "Are you certain that's what you want to do? After everything you've lost today, you want to further damage the empress's prize as well?"

Vittorio's lips curled up in a way that was unnervingly like Sonya's animal snarl, and his breath hissed through his clenched teeth. But after a moment, he lowered his fist.

"Fine. We will get her. But then we are *abandoning* this whole God-forsaken territory."

They rode as swiftly as they could through the thronged streets to Roskosh Manor, running down anyone not fast enough to get out of the way. At last the large, stately manor came into view. Sebastian leapt from his horse before it had even come to a stop and ran up the steps to the front door.

He banged on the door fiercely with his uninjured hand.

"Galina, my love! Open up quickly!"

After a maddeningly long time, the door opened, but it was Masha who answered.

"Captain Portinari, may I help you?"

Her tone was cold, bordering on rude. It was so unexpected that Sebastian paused for a moment before shaking off his surprise.

"I—I need to speak with Galina! Immediately! The city's been overrun by a fanatic mob of traitors! We must escape!"

"They are not a fanatic mob of traitors." He heard Galina's voice behind Masha. "They are true patriots of Izmoroz who have finally cast aside imperial oppression."

Masha stepped aside to reveal Galina standing in the foyer beyond. Instead of her habitual gentle smile and melancholy eyes, he found her expression so cold and hard that he almost didn't recognize her.

"What are you talking about, my—"

"I am not yours, Sebastian, and I have not been for some time," she said curtly.

"I—I don't understand."

"I confess that the honorable thing to do would have been to break off the engagement then. But I realized it was shortsighted to cast aside such a valuable source of intelligence simply because I found your cruelty toward your fellow countrymen loathsome."

"You…*used* me?" He stared at her. Even her voice sounded different. Who was this person who spoke to him so cruelly? Could this really be the woman he loved?

"It was necessary for the freedom of Izmoroz," she said. "Because of the affection I once held for you, I will refrain from calling upon the Izmorozian warriors who wait nearby so that you may have a chance to flee with your…" She cast a withering glance behind him at the still mounted Vittorio, Zaniolo, and Rykov outside. "Your comrades. I pray I do not live to regret this kindness."

Then she turned her back on him.

"You…"

His hurt and grief mingled with the throbbing pain of his injured hand and the hollow shame of defeat to become a wild, desperate rage unlike anything he'd ever known.

"You think you can get away with this? You think you can do this to me?"

He clenched his gem and thought how nice it would be to see her delicate frame inflate and burst from internal air pressure.

"You...traitorous *bitch*! I will—"

"That is quite enough of that, Sebastian."

His mother's voice, so unexpected yet so familiar, took all the fight out of him. He watched in astonishment as she strode calmly across the foyer toward him. She placed her hands on his shoulders and looked with a regal sadness into his eyes.

"Let us depart, my child."

He stared up at her for a moment, then said, "Y-yes, Mother."

His mother glanced back at Galina over her shoulder.

"Galina Odoyevtseva, I thank you for sheltering me during this conflict, but Sebastian is right. You *are* a traitorous bitch."

Then Sebastian and his mother descended the steps to where Zaniolo, Vittorio, and Rykov waited. Vittorio's expression seemed to have settled into a grim calm that bordered on despair, though his back was still straight and his head still held high.

He offered his hand to Sebastian's mother. "My lady."

She nodded and allowed him to help her up behind him, while Sebastian climbed back onto his own horse.

"We must make haste," Vittorio said as he kicked his mount. "It's only a matter of time before this rabble goes searching for people to burn at the stake, or flay alive, or whatever it is they do here."

They rode as quickly as they could to the western gate, which they found completely abandoned.

"Many of our troops were Izmorozian," Zaniolo said to Sebastian. "Most likely they joined with their brethren when they saw which way the tide was turning."

Sebastian nodded, but he didn't understand how it had come to this. He had thought most of the people embraced the empire as a means of safety and order just as he did. Had a few fanatics infected the rest of the populace? But Galina was not the sort to be influenced by such populism. Or was she? He couldn't be sure he knew her at all now...

The imperial refugees left Gogoleth and began the long journey south to Aureum on the Advent Road.

"Damn shame about Bonucci and Marchisio," said Vittorio. "They were good, loyal men."

"Yes," said Zaniolo. "Those undead monsters swarmed the tower and tore it down. I was lucky to be thrown clear, but they were not. I tried to save them, of course, but they insisted it was more important that I report the outcome of the battle to you."

Sebastian's mother fixed Zaniolo with an oddly expressionless gaze. "How noble of them."

"Quite," he agreed.

Once they had left the chaos of Gogoleth far behind, they stopped along the side of the road so that Sebastian and Vittorio could dress their wounds.

"There you are." Zaniolo tied off the bandage on Sebastian's hand. "That should hold until we can find an actual medic to look you over. I suspect you will need sutures for it to properly heal."

Sebastian stared down at his wounded hand, swollen and throbbing with pain. It was not the greatest pain he felt in that moment, however. The wound his sister had inflicted was not nearly as cruel as the one Galina had inflicted on his heart.

"Thank you, General," he said dully.

"Listen, Sebastian," Zaniolo said quietly. "Things will be . . . very different once we reach Magna Alto."

Sebastian could not imagine anything in his life being the same after that day, so he had no idea what specific "thing" the general might mean.

"How so?" he asked.

Zaniolo glanced over at Vittorio. The commander stood bare-chested in the cold, his expression unreadable as Rykov carefully dressed the knife wound in his shoulder.

"This was the commander's last chance to make amends to the empress." Zaniolo shook his head. "I can only imagine her wrath when she learns of his failure. I fear that when we reach the capital, his punishment will be severe."

"Why is he going, then?" asked Sebastian.

Zaniolo smiled sadly. "Because he loves Empress Morante, and has for most of his life. Perhaps you know something of ill-fated love."

Sebastian looked down at his hand. "I do."

Even then, after learning of her betrayal, and despite nearly killing her, he knew he still loved Galina Odoyevtseva Prozorova. What a terrible thing was love. What a dreadful weapon it could become.

67

Everywhere Sonya looked, there was celebration. The Sturdy Sturgeon Tavern was packed with drunken men and women singing old victory songs of Izmoroz. What their voices lacked in pitch, they made up for in passion, and it was beautiful.

It also hurt Sonya's sensitive ears, and after an hour or so, she decided to step outside. She made sure to bring her bottle of vodka with her, of course. She didn't want to think about her brother, or about the moment she had completely lost herself to instinct and torn out a man's throat with her teeth. She found vodka very helpful when she didn't want to think about things.

She sat down on the cold front stoop and gazed out at the dark, moonlit streets of a newly liberated Gogoleth. Her sharp fox eyes could see the motionless, unblinking ranks of sluagh gorta that stood a few blocks away. Among them she saw not only the ones who had been raised back in Uaine, but also those who had died earlier that day in battle.

Blaine came out from the tavern and sat down beside her without saying a word.

She handed him the bottle and said, "It doesn't seem right somehow. Us celebrating while our dead allies look on."

"Why not?" Blaine took a swallow from the bottle. "They don't care 'bout that anymore. We need nights like this to keep us going, but they don't."

"It still feels strange to me. I suppose it's one of those cultural differences." She looked over at him. "The Uaine sustained heavy losses during this battle."

"Aye." He took another swig and stared up at the evening sky as the stars began to come out. Then he grinned at her. "We'll have to get to work repopulatin' immediately."

"I can think of worse things to do," she said.

He leaned in closer. "I was hoping, maybe I could plant a babe in *yer* womb. Me and you would make a fine warrior, aye?"

"Oh, I don't have one."

"Eh?"

"A womb. I don't have one anymore. It was the first thing Lady Marzanna took from me."

"Ah."

She retrieved the bottle from him and took a long, burning swallow. The memory of having her womb ripped out was something else she did not want to think about.

After a few more moments of silence and another swig of vodka, however, she decided there was something else she *did* want to think about. She hooked her arm around Blaine's neck and drew him in close so that her lips grazed the lobe of his ear.

"I've had enough of the singing. Let's go have some fun, you and me."

"You want t' invite Jorge along?"

She laughed. "I love that idea!" Then she sighed. "But he'll say no."

"Oh, aye." Blaine nodded. "Wanna ask 'im anyway?"

She grinned. "You mean just to watch him turn red and stutter out his apology?"

"Aye."

"Perfect. That's when he's cutest."

68

Rowena sat among the drunken Izmorozian singers in the tavern, wondering why she was there. Well, she knew why *she* was there. Because Jorge was there. The question was why *he* was there. He didn't seem to be particularly enjoying himself. He sat across the table from her, sipping his Izmorozian liquor, watching the celebration around him as if he was not a part of it. She supposed that he might have felt more kinship with them all if he'd fought alongside them. But as he'd said, he was no warrior. She understood that strange distance, perhaps better than most. She was Uaine, and yet she was also Death Touched, which was something apart from merely being Uaine. She was respected, perhaps even revered, but she was always apart.

"Hey, Jorge!"

Sonya and Blaine lurched over, arm in arm, both grinning from ear to ear, their faces flush with drink.

"Enjoying yourselves?" Jorge asked.

"Thought we'd go enjoy ourselves somewhere a bit more private, y'know?" Blaine leered.

"Oh, um, yes…" Jorge seemed uncomfortable, and most likely jealous. Rowena wasn't sure which he fancied more, Sonya or Blaine, but in this case, it didn't matter.

"Wanna join us?" asked Sonya.

Rowena thought that seemed a sensible suggestion which would satisfy all three of them, but Jorge's eyes widened in alarm, and his face became quite red.

"I...that's...a very generous offer. It's just...it violates at least three laws of my religion that I can think of right off the top of my head."

Blaine sighed and nodded.

"Told ya," said Sonya.

"Ye did," agreed Blaine.

"Sorry, to, um, disappoint you both." Jorge forced a smile that looked like it cost a great deal of effort.

"Well, if yer sure," said Blaine.

"I am. Have fun, though."

"Good night, Jorge," said Sonya.

"Good night, Sonya."

Jorge watched as they walked awkwardly arm in arm up the steps to the rooms above, and Rowena watched him. When he turned back, he saw her inquiring expression.

"What?" he asked.

"What does yer religion have against fucking?"

"Why is that the one word every Uaine knows?"

"It's a good word."

"I suppose...," he admitted. "Regardless, I can assure you that my religion is not against...er, intercourse."

A suspicion began to form in Rowena's mind. "Have you never done it?"

"No, I must wait until marriage."

"But isn't marriage a life commitment?"

"Correct."

"What if the fucking is bad? You won't know until et's too late?"

"Er, I suppose that is a danger..." He sighed, and glanced back to the staircase where Blaine and Sonya had disappeared. "Sorry, if you don't mind, I...I think I'll go check on Master Velikhov at the college. Make sure he weathered the conflict okay. Although knowing him, he might not have even noticed."

She nodded. "Good night, Jorge."

She watched him leave the tavern, not looking at all like he had been instrumental in a glorious victory. She pitied anyone whose god was so cruel as to deny them the simple pleasures in this terrible world. No wonder he was so unhappy.

She sat alone for a little while, sipping her clear, fiery drink and watching the Izmorozians cavort around her, acting like children who had never tasted alcohol before. There was a strange sort of desperation beneath it that she had never seen in her own people. She wondered what fueled it.

Mordha sat down at her table with a fresh bottle.

"Well?" he asked in the Uaine language as he refilled her cup.

"Things are progressing," she said. "Although I still have grave doubts about whether we can count on Jorge when the time comes. He's too attached to the beast witch."

Mordha nodded, not looking particularly surprised. "Do you at least have the formula for the preservative?"

"And the fireworks."

Mordha's thick eyebrows raised. "Well done."

"They're more than just recipes, Tighearna. I will need him to teach me the preparation techniques."

"There is time. Spring thaw has only just begun. I estimate at least a month before the bulk of our forces reach Izmoroz."

"What of the beast witch? Now that she's served her purpose, she could be a serious hindrance."

"She'll be gone by then," said Mordha. "Angelo is putting that plan into motion as we speak."

69

Galina did not really know why she was at the Sturdy Sturgeon that night watching rowdy peasants guzzle an astonishing amount of cheap vodka. Masha had suggested it would mean a lot to the people if she was there, and so she'd come.

But even Masha had given in to the boisterous celebration and was now giggling like a schoolgirl as some leering, unwashed peasant flattered her outrageously. It was so demeaning, it made Galina feel ill just watching her.

If Galina was being honest with herself, perhaps some of her unpleasant mood lingered from earlier in the day. She had not expected it to be so hard to turn Sebastian away. The look of hurt in his eyes when he'd learned the truth had stabbed her as deeply as any blade. Then the scathing words Lady Portinari had delivered as she left had driven the hurt even deeper.

Galina had cared for Sebastian in the beginning. That much she was certain of. She had been duplicitous, it was true, but he had betrayed her first by becoming a pandering, imperial sycophant who relied upon everyone around him for his moral compass. Or perhaps it had been a doomed match from the start. Whenever she considered the picture as a whole, that was the conclusion she reached time and again.

Then why did it hurt so very much?

"Excuse me, Galina Odoyevtseva. May I join you?"

Galina glanced up to see the Aureumian deserter, Angelo Lorecchio.

"If you wish." She couldn't decide if his company was more or less preferable to solitude.

"I suppose this isn't really your sort of party," Angelo suggested dryly. "Nor your people."

"Not really, no."

He nodded. "Well, it was very generous of you to aid them, then."

"I did it for *all* Izmoroz, Mr. Lorecchio, not just these peasants. The nobility were suffering under the empire as well. We had become mere figureheads, without any real power of our own. The sheer hopelessness of it all was crushing my father's soul. I certainly couldn't just stand by and watch."

Angelo nodded thoughtfully. "Political transitions are always difficult and unpredictable. I should know, I've seen a few. Have you considered what should happen next?"

"The nobility will form a new council and rule Izmoroz jointly, just as they did before the empire came."

"Oh dear." Angelo gave her a pained expression.

"You have some concerns?"

"Well, it's ... not really any of my business ..."

Galina sighed. "It's been a long day, Mr. Lorecchio. Please don't vex me further. If you have something to say, then say it."

"I fear that Sonya has altogether different plans for the future government of Izmoroz."

"Oh?"

"Just before you arrived at the tavern in Kamen, she told us, and I quote, 'After we get rid of the empire, getting rid of the nobility is next on my list.'"

Galina did not react outwardly, but deep in her stomach, she felt something drop into place. She looked over at Sonya Turgenev, who despite her noble blood was lurching drunkenly up the stairs with her Uaine barbarian in tow, most certainly about to indulge in some premarital intercourse. The commoners around them not only knew this, but were cheering as the two climbed the steps. Once they reached the top, she even had the brazenness to blow them all a kiss, which sent them into a renewed frenzy of cheers and drinking. Yes, Galina could not say she was entirely surprised by this revelation.

"I see," she said at last. "Well, I thank you for this information, Mr. Lorecchio. I hope you will continue to keep me apprised of the situation. And rest assured, if there's anything I can do for you in return, I will be only too glad to help."

Angelo smiled. "I understand perfectly, Galina Odoyevtseva."

EPILOGUE

The two beings met in a part of the forest where no human had ever tread. They did not so much appear, as reveal that they had always been there.

An animal observed them as they sat together on an old log. The animal could not easily distinguish one human from another, but these were clearly not humans. They were, in fact, something the animal had never seen before, and yet they felt familiar somehow.

"You've been quite busy of late, sibling," said the one who had hair as red as blood and smelled like iron.

"Certainly," said the one who had hair as black as midnight and smelled of lilies. "You didn't think I'd let you get your own way forever, did you?"

"Well, I *hoped* not. That would be terribly dull. But was this all you have in store?"

"Fear not, my dear sibling. This was but the opening sally of a much larger effort."

"I am always so entertained by your jests. But do so many mortals have to die every time?"

"Just as the fate of all snow is to melt," said the black-haired one, "the fate of all mortals is to die."

"I suppose. But must they also suffer so?"

"That is their own doing," said the black-haired one. "Mortals

453

insist upon suffering. We must grant them as much pain, misery, and hardship as we can, or they will not be satisfied. It's in their nature."

Then the black-haired one turned to the animal who had been watching them and smiled, showing black teeth that gleamed sharply in the moonlight.

"Isn't that right, my precious *Lisitsa*?"

—————

Sonya woke with a feeling of deep and nameless dread. She sat up, trying to chase down the details of her dream. But the harder she strained, the more it slipped out of mind until she was left with nothing but the lingering smell of lilies and iron.

The tavern below was silent, and the room was dark. She gazed at Blaine's scarred, muscular back. The moonlight spilled in through the window to rest upon his long blond hair, giving it an almost otherworldly glow. But his beauty did little to soothe her disquiet.

She looked down at her hands and found they were shaking. It was as if her body remembered something that her mind did not.

The story continues in...

THE QUEEN OF IZMOROZ

Book Two of the Goddess War

Acknowledgments

This book began as research into my ancestral Poland. This shouldn't surprise anyone familiar with the Drowning of Marzanna, an annual ritual still practiced to this day in parts of the country. On the first day of spring, an effigy of Marzanna, goddess of winter, is thrown into a river to symbolize the change of season. I wish I'd had the forethought to ask my grandmother more about our heritage, but she passed away in 2009. To fill in the gaps, I found the book *Poland: A History* by Adam Zamoyski immensely helpful.

I also used this book to indulge in my love of Russian literature, which began while studying acting at Carnegie Mellon under the guidance of several instructors then on loan from the Moscow Art Theater. The influence of Chekov, Tolstoy, Lermontov, Gogol, and others should be fairly obvious. I also found *Catherine the Great: Portrait of a Woman* by Robert K. Massie and *Natasha's Dance: A Cultural History of Russia* by Orlando Figes quite illuminating. I am also indebted to Natalie Staniford and Maude Meisel for help with Russian translations and usage.

I'm grateful for the enthusiasm and hard work from my editor, Brit Hvide; my publisher, Tim Holman; and the rest of the team at Orbit books. And as always, I would be lost without the support of my agent, Jill Grinberg, and the amazing crew at JGLM.

extras

orbit

www.orbitbooks.net

about the author

Jon Skovron is the author of the Empire of Storms trilogy from Orbit books, as well as several young adult novels, including *Misfit* and *Man Made Boy*. He lives just outside Washington, DC, with his two sons and two cats.

Find out more about Jon Skovron and other Orbit authors by registering for the free monthly newsletter at www.orbitbooks.net.

if you enjoyed
THE RANGER OF MARZANNA

look out for

WE RIDE THE STORM
The Reborn Empire: Book One

by

Devin Madson

*War built the Kisian Empire and war will tear it down.
Fifteen years after rebels stormed the streets, Kisia is still
divided. Only the firm hand of the god-emperor holds the
kingdom together. But when a shocking betrayal destroys a
tense alliance with neighbouring Chiltae, all that has been
won comes crashing down.*

*In Kisia, Princess Miko T'sai is a prisoner in her own castle.
She dreams of claiming her empire, but the path to power could
rip it, and her family, asunder.*

*In Chiltae, assassin Cassandra Marius is plagued by the voices
of the dead. Desperate, she accepts a contract that promises to
reward her with a cure if she helps an empire fall.
And on the border between nations, Captain Rah e'Torin and
his warriors are exiles forced to fight in a foreign war or die.*

1. MIKO

They tried to kill me four times before I could walk. Seven before I held any memory of the world. Every time thereafter I knew fear, but it was anger that chipped sharp edges into my soul.

I had done nothing but exist. Nothing but own the wrong face and the wrong eyes, the wrong ancestors and the wrong name. Nothing but be Princess Miko Ts'ai. Yet it was enough, and not a day passed in which I did not wonder whether today would be the day they finally succeeded.

Every night I slept with a blade beneath my pillow, and every morning I tucked it into the intricate folds of my sash, its presence a constant upon which I dared build dreams. And now those dreams felt close enough to touch. We were travelling north with the imperial court. Emperor Kin was about to name his heir.

As was my custom on the road, I rose while the inn was still silent, only the imperial guards awake about their duties. In the palace they tended to colonise doorways, but here, without great gates and walls to protect the emperor, they filled every corner. They were in the main house and in the courtyard, outside the stables and the kitchens and servants' hall—two nodded in silent acknowledgement as I made my way toward the bathhouse, my dagger heavy in the folds of my dressing robe.

Back home in the palace, baths had to be taken in wooden

tubs, but many northern inns had begun building Chiltaen-style bathhouses—deep stone pools in which one could sink one's whole body. I looked forward to them every year, and as I stepped into the empty building, a little of my tension left me. A trio of lacquered dressing screens provided the only places someone could hide, so I walked a slow lap through the steam to check them all.

Once I was sure I was alone, I abandoned my dressing robe and slid into the bath. Despite the steam rising from the damp stones, the water was merely tepid, though the clatter of someone shovelling coals beneath the floor promised more warmth to come. I shivered and glanced back at my robe, the bulk of my knife beneath its folds, reassuring.

I closed my eyes only for quick steps to disturb my peace. No assassin would make so much noise, but my hand was still partway to the knife before Lady Sichi Manshin walked in. "Oh, Your Highness, I'm sorry. I didn't realise you were here. Shall I—"

"No, don't go on my account, Sichi," I said, relaxing back into the water. "The bath is big enough for both of us, though I warn you, it's not as warm as it looks."

She screwed up her nose. "Big enough for the whole court, really."

"Yes, but I hope the whole court won't be joining us."

"Gods no. I do not wish to know what Lord Rasten looks like without his robe."

Sichi untied hers as she spoke, owning none of the embarrassment I would have felt had our positions been reversed. She took her time about it, seemingly in no hurry to get in the water and hide her fine curves, but eventually she slid in beside me with a dramatic shiver. "Oh, you weren't kidding about the temperature."

Letting out a sigh, she settled back against the stones with only her shoulders above the waterline. Damp threads of hair trailed down her long neck like dribbles of ink, the rest caught in a loose bun pinned atop her head with a golden comb. Lady Sichi was four years older than my twin and I, but her lifelong engagement to Tanaka had seen her trapped at court since our birth. If I was the caged dragon he laughingly called me, then she was a caged song-bird, her beauty less in her features than in her habits, in the way she moved and laughed and spoke, in the turn of her head and the set of her hands, in the graceful way she danced through the world.

I envied her almost as much as I pitied her.

Her thoughts seemed to have followed mine, for heaving another sigh, Lady Sichi slid through the water toward me. "Koko." Her breath was warm against my skin as she drew close. "Prince Tanaka never talks to me about anything, but you—"

"My brother—"

Sichi's fingers closed on my shoulder. "I know, hush, listen to me, please. I just...I just need to know what you know before I leave today. Will His Majesty name him heir at the ceremony? Is he finally going to give his blessing to our marriage?"

I turned to find her gaze raking my face. Her grip on my shoul-der tightened, a desperate intensity in her digging fingers that jolted fear through my heart.

"Well?" she said, drawing closer still. "Please, Koko, tell me if you know. It's...it's important."

"Have you heard something?" My question was hardly above a breath, though I was sure we were alone, the only sound of life the continued scraping of the coal shoveller beneath our feet.

"No, oh no, just the talk. That His Majesty is seeking a treaty with Chiltae, and they want the succession confirmed before they talk terms."

It was more than I had heard, but I nodded rather than let her know it.

"I leave for my yearly visit to my family today," she went on when I didn't answer. "I want—I *need* to know if there's been any hint, anything at all."

"Nothing," I said, that single word encompassing so many years of uncertainty and frustration, so many years of fear, of knowing Tana and I were watched everywhere we went, that the power our mother held at court was all that kept us safe. "Nothing at all."

Sichi sank back, letting the water rise above her shoulders as though it could shield her from her own uncertain position. "Nothing?" Her sigh rippled the surface of the water. "I thought maybe you'd heard something, but that he just wasn't telling me because he..." The words trailed off. She knew that I knew, that it wasn't only this caged life we shared but also the feeling we were both invisible.

I shook my head and forced a smile. "Say all that is proper to your family from us, won't you?" I said, heartache impelling me to change the subject. "It must be hard on your mother having both you and your father always at court."

Her lips parted and for a moment I thought she would ask more questions, but after a long silence, she just nodded and forced her own smile. "Yes," she said. "Mama says she lives for my letters because father's are always full of military movements and notes to himself about new orders and pay calculations."

Her father was minister of the left, in command of the empire's military, and I'd often wondered if Sichi lived at court as much to ensure the loyalty of the emperor's most powerful minister as because she was to be my brother's wife.

Lady Sichi chattered on as though a stream of inconsequential talk could make me forget her first whispered entreaty. I could have reassured her that we had plans, that we were close, so close, to ensuring Tanaka got the throne, but I could not trust even Sichi. She was the closest I had ever come to a female friend, though if all went to plan, she would never be my sister.

Fearing to be drawn into saying more than was safe, I hurriedly washed and excused myself, climbing out of the water with none of Sichi's assurance. A lifetime of being told I was too tall and too shapeless, that my wrists were too thick and my shoulders too square had me grab the towel with more speed than grace and wrap it around as much of my body as it would cover. Sichi watched me, something of a sad smile pressed between her lips.

Out in the courtyard the inn showed signs of waking. The clang of pots and pans spilled from the kitchens, and a gaggle of servants hung around the central well, holding a variety of bowls and jugs. They all stopped to bow as I passed, watched as ever by the imperial guards dotted around the compound. Normally I would not have lowered my caution even in their presence, but the farther I walked from the bathhouse, the more my thoughts slipped back to what Sichi had said. She had not just wanted to know, she had *needed* to know, and the ghost of her desperate grip still clung to my shoulder.

Back in my room, I found that Yin had laid out a travelling robe and was waiting for me with a comb and a stern reproof that I had gone to the bathhouse without her.

"I am quite capable of bathing without assistance," I said, kneeling on the matting before her.

"Yes, Your Highness, but your dignity and honour require attendance." She began to ply her comb to my wet hair and immediately tugged on tangles. "And I could have done a better job washing your hair."

A scuff sounded outside the door and I tensed. Yin did not seem to notice anything amiss and went on combing, but my attention had been caught, and while she imparted gossip gleaned from the inn's servants, I listened for the shuffle of another step or the rustle of cloth.

No further sounds disturbed us until other members of the court began to wake, filling the inn with footsteps. His Majesty never liked to linger in the mornings, so there was only a short time during which everyone had to eat and dress and prepare for another long day on the road.

While I picked at my breakfast, a shout for carriers rang through the courtyard, and I moved to the window in time to see Lady Sichi emerge from the inn's main doors. She had donned a fine robe for the occasion, its silk a shimmering weave that defied being labelled a single colour in the morning light. Within a few moments, she had climbed into the waiting palanquin with easy grace, leaving me prey to ever more niggling doubts. Now I would have to wait until the end of the summer to discover what had troubled her so much.

Before I could do more than consider running down into the yard to ask, her carriers moved off, making space for more palanquins and the emperor's horse, which meant it wouldn't be long until we were called to step into our carriage for another interminable day travelling. Tanaka would grumble. Edo would try to entertain him. And I would get so bored of them both I counted every mile.

Tanaka had not yet left his room, so when the gong sounded, I went to tap on his door. No answer came through the taut paper panes and I leant in closer. "Tana?"

My heart sped at the silence.

"Tana?"

I slid the door. In the centre of the shadowy room, Tanaka and Edo lay sprawled upon their mats, their covers twisted and their hands reaching across the channel toward one another. But they were not alone. A grey-clad figure crouched at my brother's head. A blade hovered. Small. Sharp. Easy to conceal. Air punched from my lungs in a silent cry as I realised I had come too late. I could have been carrying fifty daggers and it would have made no difference.

But the blade did not move. Didn't even tremble. The assassin looked right at me and from the hoarse depths of my first fear my cry rose to an audible scream. Yet still he just sat there, as all along the passage doors slid and footsteps came running. Tanaka woke with a start, and only then did the assassin lunge for the window. I darted forward, but my foot caught on Tanaka's legs as he tried to rise. Shutters clattered. Sunlight streamed in. Voices followed; every servant in the building suddenly seemed to be crammed into the doorway, along with half a dozen imperial guards shoving their way through.

"Your Highnesses, is everything all right?" the first demanded.

Sharp eyes hunted the room. One sneered as he looked me up and down. Another rolled his eyes. None of them had seen the man, or none of them had wanted to. Edo pushed himself into a sitting position with his arms wrapped around his legs, while Tanaka was still blinking blearily.

"Yes, we're fine," I said, drawing myself up and trying for disdain. "I stepped on a sharp reed in the matting is all. Go back about your work. We cannot leave His Majesty waiting."

"I hate being cooped up in this carriage; another day on the road will kill me more surely than any assassin," Tanaka said, stretching his foot onto the unoccupied seat beside me. "I hope His Majesty pushes through to Koi today. It's all right for him, getting to ride the whole way in the open air."

"Well, when you are emperor you can choose to ride wherever you go," I said. "You can be sure I will."

Tanaka folded his arms. "When? I wish I shared your confidence. This morning proves that His Majesty still wants me dead, and an emperor who wants me dead isn't likely to name me his heir."

It had been almost two years since the last attempt on either of our lives, and this morning's assassin had shaken me more than I dared admit. The way forward had seemed clear, the plan simple— the Chiltaens were even pressing for an announcement. I had been so sure we had found a way to force His Majesty's hand, and yet...

Across from me, the look Edo gifted Tanaka could have melted ice, but when it was returned, they were my cheeks that reddened. Such a look of complete understanding and acceptance, of true affection. Another day on the road might kill me too, if it was really possible to die of a broken heart like the ladies in the poems.

Edo caught me looking and smiled, only half the smile he kept for Tanaka. Edo had the classical Kisian features of the finest sculpture, but it was not his nose or his cheekbones or his long-lashed eyes that made the maids fight over who would bring his washing water, it was the kind way he thanked them for every service as though he were not the eldest son of Kisia's most powerful duke.

I looked out the window rather than risk inspiring his apologetic smile, for however blind Tanaka could be, Edo was not.

"His Majesty will name Grace Bachita his heir at the ceremony," Tanaka went on, scowling at his own sandal. "And make Sichi marry him instead. Not that Manshin will approve. He and Cousin Bachi have hated each other ever since Emperor Kin gave Manshin command of the army."

Edo hushed him, his expressive grimace the closest he ever came to treasonous words. He knew too well the danger. Like Sichi, he had come to court as a child and was called a guest, a member of the imperial household, to be envied such was the honour. The word *hostage* never passed any smiling courtier's lips.

Outside, four imperial guards rode alongside our carriage as they always did, rotating shifts at every stop. Sweat shone on the face of the closest, yet he maintained the faint smile I had rarely seen him without. "Captain Lassel is out there," I said, the words ending all conversation more surely than Edo's silent warning ever could.

In a moment, Tanaka was at my shoulder, peering out through the latticework. Captain Lassel could not know we were watching him, yet his ever-present little smirk made him appear conscious of it and I hated him all the more. The same smile had adorned his lips when he apologised for having let an assassin make it into my rooms on his watch. Three years had done nothing to lessen my distrust.

Tanaka shifted to the other window and, looking over Edo's shoulder, said, "Kia and Torono are on this side."

The newest and youngest members of the Imperial Guard, only sworn in the season before. "Small comfort," I said.

"I think Kia is loyal to Mama. Not sure about Torono."

Again Edo hushed him, and I went on staring at the proud figure of Captain Lassel upon his horse. He had found me standing over the assassin's body, one arm covered in blood from a wound slashed into my elbow. At fourteen I had been fully grown, yet with all the awkwardness and ill-assurance of a child, it had been impossible to hold back my tears. He had sent for my maid and removed the body and I had thanked him with a sob. The anger had come later.

The carriage began to slow. The captain rose in his stirrups, but from the window I could see nothing but the advance procession of His Majesty's court. All horses and carriages and palanquins, flags and banners and silk.

"Why are we slowing?" Tanaka said, still peering out the opposite window. "Don't tell me we're stopping for the night, it's only mid-afternoon."

"We can't be," Edo said. "There are no inns within three miles of Shami Fields. He's probably stopping to give thanks to the gods."

Removed as we were from the front of His Majesty's cavalcade, I had not realised where we were until Edo spoke, but even as the words left his lips, the first kanashimi blossoms came into view, their pale petals spreading from the roadside like sprinkled snow. A flower for every soldier who had died fighting for the last Otako emperor. Though more than thirty years had passed since Emperor Tianto Otako had been captured here and executed for treason, it was still a fearful sight, a reminder of what Emperor Kin Ts'ai was capable of—an emperor whose name we carried, but whose blood we did not.

Mama had whispered the truth into my ear as a child, and with new eyes I had seen the locked gates and the guards, the crowd of servants and tutors, and the lack of companions for what they were. Pretty prison bars.

The assassins hadn't been coming for Miko Ts'ai at all. They had been coming for Miko Otako.

"Shit, Miko, look," Tanaka said from the other side of the carriage. "Who is that? There are people in the fields. They're carrying white flags."

"There's one over here too," I said, pressing my cheek against the sun-warmed lattice. "No, two. Three! With prayer boards. And is that...?"

The carriage slowed still more and Captain Lassel manoeuvred his horse up the line and out of view. When the carriage at last drew to a halt, I pushed open the door, stepping out before any of our guards could object. Ignoring their advice that I remain inside, I wound my way through the halted cavalcade, between mounted guards and luggage carts, hovering servants and palanquins bearing ladies too busy fanning themselves and complaining of the oppressive heat to even note my passing.

"Your Highnesses!" someone called out behind me, and I turned to see Tanaka had followed, the gold threads of his robe glinting beneath the high sun. "Your Highnesses, I must beseech you to—"

"Some of those men are carrying the Otako flag," Tanaka said, jogging to draw level with me, all good humour leeched from his expression.

"I know."

"Slow," he whispered as we drew near the front, and catching my hand, he squeezed it, gifting an instant of reassurance before he let go. I slowed my pace. Everywhere courtiers and councillors craned their necks to get a better view.

Some of the men blocking the road were dressed in the simple uniform of common soldiers, others the short woollen robes and pants of farmers and village folk. A few wore bright colours and finer weaves, but for the most part it was a sea of brown and blue and dirt. Their white flags fluttered from the ends of long work poles, and many of them carried prayer boards, some small, others large and covered in long lines of painted script.

Upon his dark horse, His Imperial Majesty Emperor Kin Ts'ai sat watching the scene from some twenty paces away, letting a black-robed servant talk to the apparent leader of the blockade. The emperor was conversing with one of his councillors and Father Okomi, the court priest. They might have stopped to rest their horses, so little interest did they show in the proceedings, but behind His Majesty, his personal guards sat tense and watchful in their saddles.

In the middle of the road, Mama's palanquin sat like a jewelled box, her carriers having set it down to wipe their sweaty faces and rest their arms. As we drew close, her hand appeared between the curtains, its gesture a silent order to go no farther.

"But what is—?"

I pressed my foot upon Tanaka's and his mouth snapped shut. Too many watching eyes. Too many listening ears. Perhaps it had been foolish to leave the carriage, and yet to sit there and do nothing, to go unseen when His Majesty was mere days from announcing his heir... It was easy to get rid of people the empire had forgotten.

Only the snap and flutter of banners split the tense silence. A few guards shifted their feet. Servants set down their loads. And upon his horse, General Ryoji of the Imperial Guard made his way toward us, grim and tense.

"Your Highnesses," he said, disapproval in every line of his aging face. "Might I suggest you return to your carriage for safety. We do not yet know what these people want."

"For that very reason I will remain with my mother, General," Tanaka said, earning a reluctant nod. "Who are these people?"

"Soldiers. Farmers. Small landholders. A few very brave Otako loyalists who feel they have nothing to fear expressing such ideas here. Nothing you need worry about, my prince."

My prince. It wasn't a common turn of phrase, but we had long ago learnt to listen for such things, to hear the messages hidden in everyday words. Tanaka nodded his understanding but stayed his ground, tall and lean and confident and drawing every eye.

"General?" A guard ran toward us. "General Ryoji, His Majesty demands you order these delinquent soldiers and their company out of his way immediately."

Ryoji did not stay to utter further warning but turned his horse about, and as he trotted toward the head of the cavalcade, I followed. "Miko," Tanaka hissed. "We should stay here with—"

"Walk with me," I said, returning to grip his hand and pull him along. "Let's be seen like heirs to the Crimson Throne would be seen at such a time."

His weight dragged as Mother called a warning from behind her curtains, but I refused to be afraid and pulled him along with me.

At the front of our cavalcade, General Ryoji dismounted to stand before the protestors on equal ground. "As the commander of the Imperial Guard, I must request that you remove yourselves from our path and make your grievances known through the proper channels," he said. "As peaceful as your protest is, continued obstruction of the emperor's roads will be seen as an act of treason."

"Proper channels? You mean complain to the southern bastards who have been given all our commands about the southern bastards who have been given all our commands?" shouted a soldier near the front to a chorus of muttered agreement. "Or the southern administrators who have taken all the government positions?" More muttering, louder now as the rest of the blockade raised an angry cheer. "Or the Chiltaen raiders who charge into our towns and villages and burn our fields and our houses and murder our children while the border battalions do nothing?"

No sense of self-preservation could have stopped a man so consumed by anger, and he stepped forward, pointing a gnarled finger at his emperor. Emperor Kin broke off his conversation with Father Okomi and stared at the man as he railed on. "You would let the north be destroyed, you would see us all trampled into the dust because we once stood behind the Otako banner. You would—"

"General," His Majesty said, not raising his voice, and yet no one could mistake his words. "I would continue on my way now. Remove them."

I stared at him sitting there so calmly upon his grand horse, and the anger at his attempt on Tanaka's life flared hot. He would as easily do away with these protestors because they inconvenienced him with their truth.

Slipping free from Tanaka, I advanced into the open space between the travelling court and the angry blockade to stand at General Ryoji's side.

"No blood need be shed," I said, lifting my voice. "His Majesty has come north to renew his oath and hear your grievances, and if they are all indeed as you say, then by the dictates of duty something will be done to fix them. As a representative of both the Otako family through my mother's blood and the Ts'ai through my father's, I thank you for your loyalty and service to Kisia but must ask you to step aside now that your emperor may pass. The gods' representative cannot make wise decisions from the side of a road."

Tense laughter rattled through the watchers. They had lowered their prayer boards and stood shoulder to shoulder, commoners and soldiers together watching me with hungry eyes. Their leader licked his lips, looking to General Ryoji and then to Tanaka as my twin joined me. "You ask us this as a representative of your two families," the man said, speaking now to my brother rather than to me. "You would promise us fairness as a representative of your two families. But do you speak as His Majesty's heir?"

General Ryoji hissed. Someone behind me gasped. The man in the road stood stiff and proud in the wake of his bold question, but his gaze darted about, assessing risks in the manner of an old soldier.

"Your faith in me does me great honour," Tanaka said. "I hope one day to be able to stand before you as your heir, and as your emperor, but that is the gods' decision to make, not mine." He spread his arms. "If you want your voices heard, then raise your prayer boards and beseech them. I would walk with you in your troubles. I would fight your battles. I would love and care for all. If the gods, in their infinite wisdom, deem me worthy, I would be humbled to serve you all to the best of my ability."

His name rose upon a cheer, and I tried not to resent the ease with which he won their love as the crowd pressed forward, reaching out to touch him as though he were already a god. He looked like one, his tall figure garbed in gold as the people crowded in around him, some bowing to touch his feet and to thank him while others lifted their prayer boards to the sky.

We had been careful, had spoken no treason, yet the more the gathered crowd cried their love for their prince the more dangerous the scene became, and I lifted shaking hands. "Your love for my brother is overwhelming," I said to the noise of their prayers and their cheers. "But you must now disperse. Ask them to step aside, Tana, please."

"Isn't this what you wanted?" he whispered. "To let His Majesty see what he ought to do?"

"He has already seen enough. Please, ask them to disperse. Now."

"For you, dear sister."

"Listen now." He, too, lifted his arms, and where the crowd had ignored me, they descended into awed silence for him. "It is time to step aside now and make way for His Imperial Majesty, representative of the gods and the great shoulders upon which Kisia—"

While Tanaka spoke, I looked around to see the emperor's reaction, but a dark spot in the blue sky caught my eye. An arrow arced toward us, slicing through the air like a diving hawk.

"Watch out!"

Someone screamed. The crowd pushed and shoved in panic and Tanaka and I were trapped in the press of bodies. No guards. No shields. And my hands were empty. There was nothing I could—

Refusing the call of death, I snatched the first thing that came to hand—a prayer board from a screaming protestor—and thrust it up over our heads. The arrowhead splintered the wood. My arms buckled, but still vibrating, the arrow stuck. For a few long seconds, my ragged breath was all the sound left in the sultry afternoon.

"They attacked our prince under a flag of peace!"

The shout came from behind us, and the leader of the blockade lifted his arms as though in surrender. "We didn't! We wouldn't! We only ask that His Majesty name his heir and—"

An arrow pierced his throat, throwing him back into the men behind him, men who lifted their prayer boards and their white flags, begging to be heard, but imperial guards advanced, swords drawn. One slashed the throat of a kneeling man, another cut down someone trying to run. A few of the protesting soldiers had swords and knives, but most were common folk who had come unarmed.

"Stop. Stop!" Tanaka shouted as blood sprayed from the neck of the closest man. "If I do not—"

"Back to your carriage!" General Ryoji gripped Tanaka's arm. "Get out of here, now."

"But they did not—"

"No, but you did."

I followed as he dragged Tanaka away from the chaos and back to the cavalcade to be met with silent stares. Mama's hand had retreated back inside her curtained palanquin, but His Majesty watched us pass. Our eyes met. He said not a word and made no gesture, but for an instant before doubt set in, I was sure he had smiled, a grim little smile of respect. Wishful thinking. No more.

Edo stood waiting at the door of the carriage and slid out of sight as Ryoji marched Tanaka up to it and thrust him inside. He held the door open for me to follow, and I took my seat, trembling from head to foot.

Still holding the door, the general leant in. "Do you have a death wish, boy?"

"I was the one trying to stop anyone getting killed, General, if you didn't notice."

"And painting a great big target on your back while you did it."

"They loved me!"

General Ryoji snarled an animal's anger. "You think it was you they were cheering for? They weren't even seeing you. That was Katashi Otako standing before them once more."

"And I'm proud to look—"

"Your father was a traitor. A monster. He killed thousands of people. You—"

Words seemed to fail him and he slammed the door. A shout to the driver and the carriage lurched into motion. Tanaka scowled, ignoring Edo's concerned questions, while outside, more people willing to die for the Otako name bled their last upon the Shami Fields.

 ## 2. RAH

It's harder to sever a head than people think. Perhaps if one were skilled with an axe, it could be done in a single blow—so long as the body was not trying to run away at the time—but out in the grasslands, decapitation is done with a knife. The first incision is easy. Then you drag your serrated blade through the flesh and think you'll soon be done. I thought so my first time. I thought it would be quick and simple and not involve such thick globs of blood.

But it is our way. The Levanti way. So though we grumble, we saw through still-warm flesh and long-dead flesh alike to free the soul within. Even when we are far from home.

"Why not just leave them?" Eska said, pacing behind me, every step a thud upon the track as though it had insulted his mother. "It will be night soon."

Blood darkened one man's face like the ragged remains of a mask. It had burst from his eye and poured from his throat—a slash there having done half my job already.

"Come on, Rah, let's go. They were not worthy enemies."

"All spirits are equal," I said. "You should have remembered that before you gave the order to kill them."

"Don't give me that whisperer shit. They attacked us."

I stood, a sigh deflating my chest as I looked upon the poor dead bastards. "We leave no soul behind," I said. "Lok, Amun, Juta, cut 'em."

Obligatory grumbling followed as the two men stepped forward, the boy between them.

"Juta is a not yet shorn, he—"

"Must learn." I returned Eska's scowl. "And opportunities to practice may be scarce." I nodded to Juta, his long hair caught back in an untidy ponytail. "You know what to do."

"Yes, Captain."

"I'll work beside you."

Laughter filled the evening as the rest of our hunting party moved away from the slaughter, only Eska remaining to loom his disapproval over me. "We don't know this land well enough to travel by night," he said as I knelt in the dirt with the fallen. "Not without the aid of the Goddess Moon."

"Our eyes will soon adjust to having only one moon in the sky."

Eska grunted. "That makes it no less wrong. How can they stand so much darkness?"

I lifted a dead man's head onto my knees and, using the slash in his throat as a place to start, began cutting. Blood dripped through the incision to stain the ground. Another thing you learnt early was to keep your knees apart.

Farther along the track, Amun was making quick work of his man, while Lok worked as slow and steady as ever. Juta's face had screwed up in concentration.

"Kishava says it's more than an hour's walk back."

I lodged my blade between vertebrae and regarded my second. His dark skin glowed in the last of the summer sunlight, but there was nothing bright about his expression. "If you think you can do this faster, then by all means take over."

"I don't think you should be bothering at all," he said, the hushed words for me alone. "These are not our people."

"No, but a soul is a soul, and that is why I am the captain and you are not. If you're so concerned about our pace, then fetch a sack for the heads. Maybe two."

Eying the others, he knelt at my side. "The sacks are all full," he said, his lips almost to my ear. "Full of the meat we came out here to hunt."

"I know. Move it around or leave some behind."

"We need the food, Captain."

"You think I don't know that?" I said, twitching my knife free to slice the last cords of flesh in the dead man's neck. "But what sort of Levanti would we be if we abandoned our honour the moment we stepped from our homeland?"

Leaning closer, Eska snarled, "This is the sort of thinking that got us here in the first place."

"If you want to lead the Second Swords, then challenge me," I said, locking my gaze to his—this man I had called friend long before either of us had sworn our lives to protect the herd.

In silence he chewed at nothing, drawing attention to a scar tracing the line of his jaw. A lucky escape from a stray axe blow the day we had lost Herd Master Sassanji to a Korune raid.

"No?" I shoved him away when he did not answer. "Then get a sack. You'll carry it back to camp and the heads will be your responsibility until we find a temple."

He got to his feet, all long-limbed grace. "Yes, Captain." He pressed his fists together in salute, however brief, and walked away. His barked orders soon cut through the incessant buzz of insects and the complaints of a dozen Swords with nothing to do.

Beside me, Juta's hands dripped blood, making the task twice as hard, while Amun had already finished and owned the look of someone who had been trying not to listen.

I rushed the rest of the job, making such a mess of the spine it looked like I had torn the damn head off. Watched by dead eyes, I spoke a prayer to Nassus under my breath. He might have preferred the One True God all the missionaries spoke of, but the Levanti god of death would have to do.

Wordlessly, Eska brought a bloodstained sack and I dropped the head in. Light was fading fast, darkening the forest in which we'd been hunting when the men attacked. The fools. I had tried to tell them we meant no harm, but they had understood our language as little as we understood theirs. The fight had lasted mere seconds yet had left me shaken. No Levanti returning from exile had ever described the locals as aggressive.

With the dregs in my water skin, I rinsed my hands and wiped them on the dead man's sleeve. "All right, let's go," I said. "Before someone else comes looking for trouble. Kishava?"

The tracker swung a sack of deer flesh onto her shoulder. "We'll have to move fast," she said as the rest of the group gathered their share. "Night is coming."

"Then we move fast."

With a sack of heads slung over each shoulder, Eska strode into the trees in Kishava's wake and I signalled for the rest to follow, Juta the last before I brought up the rear. Though he was not yet a Sword, he carried as much as the others. His scowl of concentration had not dissipated.

"Arm sore, boy?"

"Like I've been strung up all day," he said, pushing back a blood-ied clump of hair that kept falling into his face. "Damn flies." Juta swatted them away from his bloody burden, but they came right back.

With both my hands occupied, I could only shake off the swarm-ing insects that leapt from my sweaty arm to my sweaty brow and onto the sodden back of my tunic.

"Did we really have to do that, Captain?" he asked as we

followed the trail of Swords cutting a dark vein through the trees. "They weren't warriors."

"Was Matriarch Petra a warrior?"

"No."

We walked on through the lengthening shadows. "Was her soul freed?"

"Yes."

"Then you've answered your own question. In the eyes of Nassus, all souls are equal. To leave one trapped in its flesh would do great injury to the Creator."

He nodded, lowering his gaze to the dry undergrowth. He had listened to the lesson, but it ought not have been mine to teach. I had learnt at the herd master's feet as did all young Levanti of the Torin herd. Or had done before Herd Master Reez let the missionaries come. Had let them help. Let them stay. Let them talk.

Bitter heartache pierced my soul, and just for a moment, I wished it all undone, wished we were home beneath the baking sun taking kills back to the herd. But it could not be undone. And allowed the choice again, I would have given the same orders.